James Swallow is the *New York Times*, *Sunday Times* and Amazon bestselling author of the Marc Dane novels *Nomad*, *Exile*, *Ghost*, *Shadow* and *Rogue*. He is a BAFTA-nominated scriptwriter, a former journalist and the award-winning writer of over fifty books and numerous scripts for radio, television and interactive media.

He lives in London, and is currently working on his next novel; find him online (along with more about the Marc Dane series and free downloadable fiction) at www.jswallow.com.

Also by James Swallow

Nomad
Exile
Ghost
Shadow
Rogue

JAMES SWALLOW
OUTLAW

ZAFFRE

First published in the UK in 2021 by
ZAFFRE
An imprint of Bonnier Books UK
4th Floor, Victoria House, Bloomsbury Square,
London WC1B 4DA
Owned by Bonnier Books
Sveavägen 56, Stockholm, Sweden

A CIP catalogue record for this book is
available from the British Library.

Hardback ISBN: 978-1-83877-461-5
Trade paperback ISBN: 978-1-83877-462-2

Also available as an ebook

1 3 5 7 9 10 8 6 4 2

Typeset by IDSUK (Data Connection) Ltd
Printed and bound in Great Britain by Clays Ltd, Elcograf S.p.A.

Zaffre is an imprint of Bonnier Books UK
www.bonnierbooks.co.uk

For everyone who fights for truth

ONE

The house in the photograph was little different from the others facing the ocean, along the breezy stretch of Cape Cod's coastline.

Each home they passed resembled something constructed out of the same kit of parts – uniformly two storeys tall, sporting shingled roofs turned brown-grey in the dying daylight. Spotless white close-board fences hemmed in unimaginative lawns and the occasional topiary ball of greenery. Trees, where they were, stood spindly and low to the ground, forced down by the constant wind off the sea. Vehicle headlights illuminated them in brief, skeletal flashes as the bulky black Cadillac SUV negotiated turns on the unmarked road.

Hiroshi Saito studied the picture of the house on his smart-phone, the device strapped to the inside of his forearm in a pouch. He flicked the screen with a gloved finger and the image swiped away, replacing it with the face of the target.

The new photo was something from an official document, per-haps a passport or a security ID, and it made Sean Harlow look washed-out and old. Saito's briefing said the man was in his late forties, but the image aged him another decade. He had deep-set eyes and a long gaze with no focus.

Did Harlow know someone wanted him dead? Saito tried to put himself behind that face and see things from his perspective, to understand what sort of man he was. It would help when the moment came to kill him.

Saito darkened the smartphone's screen, covering it with the cuff of his windbreaker, and concentrated on letting his vision adapt to the evening gloom. Inside the SUV, the only light came from the dashboard dials set to night-mode red. The splashes of crimson over the assassin and the other men riding with him gave their faces a faintly demonic cast. The Japanese man was the smallest of them, a spare but solid figure of below average build, with a round and inexpressive face.

In the seat next to Saito, the driver, who hadn't uttered a word since the team had gathered in Fairhaven two hours earlier, now broke his silence.

'Next turning. One minute out.'

He pointed with a finger over the steering wheel. He had a low New England drawl and a face that was all hard angles. The driver's manner suggested to Saito that he had been police at one point in his life, before circumstances drew him into a darker profession. They shared a similar origin.

In the back of the Cadillac, the other two members of the kill team zipped up their jackets and checked their pistols. Both were broad and muscular; one man sported a dull white scar on his narrow chin, and the other man had a heavy, Neanderthal brow. They had an air of boredom, as if participating in this was somehow beneath them. It made Saito frown.

He'd expected the usual protocol on arrival in Massachusetts, but it was not to be. Typically, Saito would lead a unit of private contractors sourced from the Moscow-based mercenary group his paymasters favoured. Admittedly, he disliked the Russians for their coarse demeanour, but he respected their skills.

These men worked directly for one of the committee, for the American, and they were coloured by his arrogance. Their employer had insisted on having his own people be part of any sanction taking place on United States soil, and none of the other members of the committee had seen fit to question that.

The American didn't trust Saito. He didn't trust foreigners as a matter of policy, and he made that clear through his business transactions and the politicians he backed. And yet he was happily part of a cabal of men from across the globe who enriched one another through their clandestine dealings, nationality be damned.

The American, like the rest of the committee, put ideology aside where money was concerned. Still, this was his territory, so Saito was beholden to his wishes.

He followed along with the pre-mission rituals, making sure that the sound suppressor was fully set to the muzzle of the Glock 17 semi-automatic on his lap. Satisfied, Saito slipped the gun into a deep inner pocket of his windbreaker and waited. He pulled an elasticated half-mask of black cloth up over the lower half of his face, and the others did the same.

The SUV slowed to a crawl, rolling quietly down the side road, finally coming to a halt a hundred metres short of the driveway leading to the target's house. Saito exited silently, the other armed men following. As they moved in, the vehicle reversed, easing back into the thickening darkness. It would wait at the turning, out of sight of the main road, ready to whisk them away once the objective was complete.

They advanced, sure-footed and careful to stick to the shadows. Ahead, the house from the photograph was a charcoal sketch with soft, homely glows burning in the windows. A spotlight embedded in the lawn threw brightness up a flagpole, atop which the Stars and Stripes snapped and crackled in the stiffening wind.

'Movement,' said the man with the scar, indicating a direction with a terse nod of the head. Saito saw a figure inside the house walk past one of the windows, out towards the eastern corner where the study was located.

He'd committed the floor plan of Harlow's home to memory on the flight into Boston, and he knew that there was a side door closer to the study. A blink of hazy, distant white flickered in the corner of Saito's vision, and he saw the stroke of the beam from Chatham Light far down the shoreline as it crossed the trees and vanished out to sea. He waited for it to pass again, and in the moments between the lighthouse's sweeps, he moved across the lawn to the house. The other men came up in formation, moving to their designated positions with their weapons out and ready. The long-nose shapes of their silenced pistols stayed down, close across their chests.

Saito didn't anticipate needing their talents tonight. They were there to cover the front and rear of the building, in case the target got past him and tried to flee. But that wasn't a likely scenario. Harlow was an analyst, a desk jockey, and unlikely to put up a fight.

At the side door, Saito pulled a pump tube the size of a lipstick from a sleeve pocket and sprayed the handle and hinges with a fine mist of liquid lubricant. He let the lighthouse sweep past twice more, and then put his free hand on the handle, applying slow, steady pressure. It turned gently and soundlessly, the door coming open.

Saito opened it enough so he could slip through the gap, conscious that the wind would push a draught of cold air in with him. He pulled the door shut and drew his pistol.

He was in a corridor that ran the length of the house. At the far end, flickering light from a television in the lounge threw odd shadows on the wall, and Saito heard muffled voices from whatever programme was playing.

The door to Harlow's study was five metres away, slightly ajar. As he watched, the man moved past the gap, lost in thought, tapping a pencil to his lips. He appeared to be looking for something.

Three steps brought Saito to the study door. He put the flat of his hand on the unpainted wood, raised the gun to chest height, and pushed forward.

Harlow sat in a mesh-back office chair at a side-on angle, leafing through a stack of papers. The small room was built around a desk and workspace, and every square metre of the walls groaned with heavily laden bookshelves, pictures and other ephemera. The man caught the motion from the corner of his eye and jolted back in shock, into the narrow depths of the study.

'Wait!' Harlow's hands came up in a warding gesture, as if that could stop the bullet that would end him.

Saito had no intention of waiting, and his finger tightened on the trigger. He had no interest in who Harlow was, past any data relevant to the task of efficiently ending his life. He managed a communications office for one of the American security services, he had previously served in the US Navy on board nuclear submarines, he was a divorced father of two sons, and he owned a decrepit boat and three firearms, the closest of which was in a gun safe two rooms away.

Sean Harlow's life was surplus to requirements. Someone wanted him removed from the world, perhaps because he was an impediment to the ambitions of others or because he knew something he was not meant to know. It didn't matter.

Saito was the instrument of that cold and uncompromising truth, and if the assassin held any disquiet about that, for now he repressed it. Until Harlow spoke again.

'Please don't kill them.' He whispered the plea, turning it into something intimate between gunman and victim. Into Saito's hesitation, he added more. 'You've come for me. Okay. But they're not part of it. Please.' His eyes welled with shimmering tears and he swallowed a sob. 'Please don't.'

Harlow's gaze flicked to a framed photograph on the wall. Two teenage boys with big smiles, unlucky enough to have been born with their father's pudgy nose but blessed with laughing eyes. For a fleeting moment, Saito saw a memory of his own family reflected in those happy faces, and he didn't like what it stirred in him.

From down the hall, he heard the television switch channels abruptly, and the cries of delight from two young voices.

Harlow's sons were supposed to be with their mother in Hartford this weekend, as the details of their separation agreement stipulated. The data provided by the American's people had stated categorically that the target would be alone here for the next forty-eight hours. The expected outcome was that he would be found dead some time early next week, after being reported missing by his employers or discovered by a curious neighbour.

The plan did not account for two more targets, both young men whose social media usage was considerable, whose silence would be noted by their friends within hours, not days, whose eliminations would greatly complicate this operation.

And even as part of Saito's mind calculated these new variables, another part dredged up the old memory that he could only ever half-bury, half-ignore.

'Please don't hurt my boys,' Harlow implored him. 'I won't resist you. I won't cry out or try to run. But give me your word, I'm begging you. They're all I have.'

'You have my word,' said Saito. The voice came from him, but it was as if someone else spoke. A version of Hiroshi Saito that didn't exist anymore. 'They will live.' Saito had broken protocol, but now it was done, he felt compelled to add something else, like a confession. 'I have a child of my own. A girl.'

'What's her name?'

Saito shot Harlow through the forehead and he fell back, the frangible bullet from the Glock tearing into his brain matter, killing him instantly.

'Rumiko,' said the assassin, uttering her name for the first time in a very long while. 'My daughter's name is Rumiko.'

Saito slipped carefully out of the study and moved back towards the side door. The plan had been to terminate Harlow and then turn over the house to make it appear as a robbery-murder. Harlow was a man of good means, and he was known to possess a collection of military challenge coins of some moderate value. Saito's post-kill actions would be to set the scene for the local police, take the coins and leave enough false clues to fog what had really happened.

He removed a sealed plastic bag from a pocket and scattered the contents, a collection of hairs and fibres painstakingly gathered from the furniture of a homeless shelter a few miles away in New Bedford. Perhaps he could still salvage something of the plan.

Then a suffocated yell from the lounge told him that would not be possible.

Saito drew himself up and walked to the end of the corridor. He found the man with the thick brow standing over two cowering youths on their knees before him. The older of the boys was already injured, bleeding badly from a cut on his cheek where the other man had pistol-whipped him.

'The fuck is this?' said the gunman, gesturing at the youths with his pistol. 'They ain't supposed to be here.'

'Your orders were to wait outside,' Saito insisted.

'This messes shit up,' said the other man. 'You gonna deal with it?'

Saito nodded at the door. 'Go. Leave them. They are not important.'

'What?' The other man's jaw worked beneath his half-mask. 'That's not gonna work. You got a problem doin' kids? I'll handle it.'

'I said *we leave them*,' insisted Saito, as an old fury stirred in him.

'What you say means dick to me,' the gunman replied, and fired two shots into the younger boy. The first went in the belly, the second through his neck. The older brother let out a howl and grabbed at his dying sibling, and a third bullet went through the back of the other youth's skull.

Harlow's sons slumped against each other and bled out there on the wooden flooring, while the gunman moved to the coin collection displayed on the wall and tore down the racks.

Saito watched the two boys die. The old fury in him ossified, becoming thick and sluggish, as if the blood in his veins had turned solid.

Finally, he found his voice again. 'There ... was no need for that.'

'Seriously?' The gunman hesitated, sizing him up. 'Next time you come to America, bring your goddamn balls.'

Saito still had his pistol in his hand, and for a fleeting moment he thought about putting a round in the middle of that thick brow. But the fire and the fuel he needed to complete that action were absent.

He couldn't muster the rage. It had passed through him like liquid mercury, impossible to grasp. Instead, Saito felt hollow inside, sickened at himself.

At length, he spoke.

'Finish up, then. Make it look convincing.'

Saito left through the front door, summoning the scarred man with a low whistle. After a few minutes, the other gunman followed him outside, carrying the coin collection under one arm. As the door clicked shut, Saito saw that he had made a mess of the lounge to sell the lie they wanted the police to accept.

The attenuated beam from the lighthouse at the Coast Guard base washed over them as they pulled away in the vehicle, heading back towards the Mid-Cape Highway. The coin collection went into a lake in the nearby state park, and once they were heading west, Saito made the call.

He checked the time as the encrypted Blackphone connected. It would be before midnight in Paris, where the man who held his leash waited.

Pytor Glovkonin answered on the second ring.

'*Report*,' he demanded.

Anyone else might have delegated the job of taking the call to a subordinate, and, given the man's great wealth, Glovkonin could certainly have afforded to do so. But the Russian oligarch did not trust anything that was done at arm's length, so he micromanaged and interfered with every element of his operations.

Glovkonin liked to say that he 'kept the chain short' but in reality, his deep-seated suspicious nature was one of the core forces that drove him. Saito had come to understand this after he had been indentured to the Russian as his personal hit man and troubleshooter.

'It is done,' said Saito. 'Do you have further orders for me?'

There was a pause, and Saito could picture the Russian considering that question.

'*You've been difficult to locate recently. Off the grid, as it were. Why is that?*'

Saito worked hard to keep the sudden tension he felt from his voice.

'I have been dealing with other tasks. Preparatory work. Prevention of blowback.'

The last phrase would hopefully be enough to put off Glovkonin from pressing the point. A large part of Saito's job was ensuring his primary was isolated from any connection to the illegal actions committed at the Russian's behest.

'*Good.*' Saito waited for Glovkonin to end the conversation, but the line stayed open. '*I take it you played well with my American colleague's men? There were no complications?*'

'Nothing that need concern you.'

Saito knew that Glovkonin would want a better explanation than that, but this wasn't the time.

'*Good,*' repeated the Russian. '*I look forward to telling him. I think he wanted it to be a mess, in point of fact. He's quite out of his depth over here with us. Having something to complain about would mollify him.*'

As often happened, Saito felt as if Glovkonin was talking to himself, performing out loud for some invisible audience, rather than to his assassin. When he didn't reply, the Russian became bored.

'*I will require your presence in a few days. Make sure you are ready to move when I make contact.*'

'Understood.'

Saito was about to cut the call, but Glovkonin – as always – wanted the last word.

'*Whatever you are doing on your own time,*' he said coldly, '*if it interferes with my requirements, I will have no further use for you.*'

The line went dead, leaving the threat hanging in the air.

If the day came when Glovkonin no longer considered Saito a useful asset, the assassin would be crossed off as easily as Harlow had been. If he was considered disloyal, he would be ended.

Saito glanced at the other men in the car. Perhaps people like them would be sent to do it. The committee had many resources to call upon, as well as more insidious ways to hurt him.

He reached for those buried memories again, glimpsing them in his thoughts like part of a rocky shoal breaking the surface of black waters.

His daughter's face. The last thing she said to him. The years that had passed since he breathed the same air as her.

Saito's lost anger rekindled. *I am already disloyal,* he told himself. *I have already defied my masters.*

The question now was, how far would he take it?

The driver eyed him. 'Boss cracking the whip on you, huh?'

Saito turned away, ignoring the comment.

'Get me to the airport.'

Three hours later, Saito was on the red-eye overnight to Cairo, and he dwelled on his unanswered question every step of the way.

TWO

If money had a stench, then the elegant town house in Saint-Germain-des-Prés should have reeked of it.

Built in the late 1700s for a wealthy Parisian aristocrat who didn't hear the winds of change coming, the gaudy apartments had once been burned to their shell by the city's disenfranchised poor. Those radicals, who led its occupants to the steps of Madame Guillotine during the bloody days of the French Revolution, would have been sickened to see the place now, and to know the history that surrounded it.

Having the benefit of being located in one of the most desirable parts of the 6th Arrondissement, and despite the turmoil of the revolution, the building had passed up and up through the hands of moneyed men over the centuries that followed. They banked its worth again and again, until now its asking price was in the region of indecent. The value of a single brick could have fed a family on the poverty line for months. It was, if one considered it honestly, an obscenity of sorts.

The men who owned it didn't see it that way. Those long-dead, decapitated aristos whose blood had stained the boulevards might have recognised the current owners as kindred spirits because, like them, they saw their money as something to insulate them from the common world.

They had never lived in the reality that most people experienced. Never once known an empty belly or the particular dread that came from having nothing to your name.

It would not have occurred to Pytor Glovkonin to think of himself as like them. An outside observer wouldn't see the difference in the tall and imposing Russian, viewing the petro-chemical magnate as exactly the same kind of middle-aged white male oligarch as the three billionaires with whom he shared the room – but to Glovkonin there was one vital difference. He had been poor.

The legacy of it showed in the gaunt, defined lines of his face, in the scars hidden behind an impeccably trimmed beard and beneath the sleeves of his Savile Row suit. He had grubbed in the mud as a boy, caught in the gears of the decaying Soviet system. He had lived with nothing, lying about his age to join the Red Army in a vain attempt to flee destitution, only to find he had submitted himself to the same decrepitude by a different name.

But by his bootstraps, as the Americans liked to say, Glovkonin had fought and lied and bribed and murdered his way out of that. After decades, he was rich beyond the wildest dreams of that dirt-smeared child. He was the definition of a self-made man.

This, he believed, earned him the right to hate the others in the room with a particular kind of loathing. None of them had worked to get what they had. Each had been born into an impenetrable bubble of wealth and privilege, like some untouchable scion of ancient monarchy. They had been *given* everything, whereas he had *earned* it.

And they'd never known true fear, not like the Russian had. He looked forward to introducing them to it, in due course.

'How long has it been since we were all in the same room?' The Italian laughed at his own question, but his dark eyes were cold where his smile did not reach them. Cutting an urbane and dashing figure, he liked to hold the attention of the room as much as he could.

A predator, that one. They had crossed swords in the past, and Glovkonin had the man's measure. *A raptor, hiding behind the colours of a peacock.*

'Two years,' the Swiss replied, his age-lined face creasing, his bland tone retaining the same robotic, shallow affect he always displayed.

The banker with the calculator in his head. The eldest of the group, Glovkonin considered him the dullest, the man's only concession to personality expressed in the garish silk shirts he wore. *Bloodless and without any passion.*

'Don't like it,' grumbled the American. 'No need for it.' Thickset and so red-cheeked he seemed permanently wind-burned, he nursed a glass of whiskey and glared out of the window, absently running a hand over his balding pate.

The braggart. Glovkonin saw this one's greed more clearly than in any of the others, driving him forward in everything he did. *The biggest pig with his snout in the trough, in all the ways that could be true.*

For a moment, he wondered what they saw when they looked at him, and the thought made the Russian's lips compress into a firm line. *Unworthy*, he told himself. *Unfit to be among them.*

The Swiss plucked a speck of lint from the cuff of his tailored jacket.

'Some matters must be discussed face to face. Even the best communications security can be defeated.'

He would know, of course. His billions came from stock market manipulations and information banking, from a business empire made of computers that played games with numbers, and changed the course of nations with a mouse-click.

The American gave a grunt that was neither agreement nor complaint. He was much more the 'meat and potatoes' type, or so he liked to have people believe. His deep investments in agriculture allowed him to play the part of a Middle-American son of the soil, the farmer who had made good through sweat and hard work. All lies, of course. The closest he came to the country was riding around the manicured lawns of stud farms and golf courses.

'It's important we mark this occasion,' noted the Italian, his voice carrying.

There was a singular enmity in Glovkonin's heart for this man, above and beyond his more general antipathy towards the others, perhaps because they were so alike in age and manner. While the Russian had become rich on oil and gas contracts seized during the fall of the Communist state, the Italian's inherited aerospace and engineering holdings had cemented his position in the top percentile of the world's most wealthy. Glovkonin especially detested the Italian's studied, indolent manner, the way he acted the caricature of the moneyed playboy breezing through life, as if everyone else were bit-part actors in a movie where he was the star.

The Italian most of all, but each of them lacked the focus the Russian had been born with. He believed, in the fibre of his being, that none of them *deserved* what they had. So it would be right for him to take it from them.

'Perhaps a toast, then?' Glovkonin turned and signalled the Italian's assistant, an austerely beautiful young woman in a grey trouser suit with a Germanic, unsmiling aspect.

The woman looked to her master for confirmation, and at length the Italian granted it.

'Excellent suggestion,' he allowed. 'Willa, if you would?'

She nodded, moved to the bar at the far side of the room and poured for them. When the woman handed Glovkonin the glass, he raised it in salute.

'To the Combine.'

The other men winced when he said the name of their gathering out loud. Glovkonin could not understand why they reacted in such a fashion – as if to utter the word would somehow bring them to ruin. They thought it gauche, the act of someone tactless and ill-mannered.

At length, they echoed him, and he couldn't resist a chuckle.

'And what an august collective it is. I am proud to be a part of it.'

'It's better if we are only whispered of, not spoken of full-throated and openly.' The Swiss looked at him coldly over the rim of his glass, without taking a sip. 'I have seen what happens when our exposure is too great. It puts us at risk.'

'Of course,' noted Glovkonin. 'As the most senior member of this committee, we respect your experience.' He cocked his head, drawing up information that his own spies had worked hard to find for him. 'You took your father's place in this group after his passing, yes? He did so much for the Combine before Berlin fell to the Red Army.'

The Swiss banker's blank face grew a scowl. 'Yes.'

The group's origin story was shrouded in lies and obfuscation, deliberately cultivated to give such details the whiff of an outlandish conspiracy theory, and indeed when Glovkonin had first heard of the Combine, that was what he'd believed. But certain facts were too solid to be anything other than real.

The Combine's birth arose from the avarice of men like the banker's forefather – men who understood that war was an inevitable consequence of the human condition, and sought to profit from it. This cabal, its membership untroubled by conscience and petty morality, had slowly evolved as the decades passed. From their first dealings as quartermasters to every battle they could monetise, they grew to stoking and ultimately *inventing* conflicts, maintaining a cycle of struggle that never ended. All was permitted, as long as it made them prosper.

Sometimes Glovkonin wondered how rich one would have to be in order to declare victory. The money was the only way to keep score.

'How each of us came to be here isn't relevant,' the Italian was saying, 'or by whatever means we employed to assure our rise.' He gave Glovkonin a warning look. 'All that matters is that we work together to maintain our dominance.'

Does he know that I murdered the woman whose place I usurped? Glovkonin met the look in full and waited, testing the other man's resolve. *Would he dare to say so openly?*

He doubted it. Ultimately, these men didn't care about whose blood was shed, as long as the cut of the knife served to enrich them.

Before, the Russian had suffered the ignominy of working outside the Combine's controlling committee as one of their 'associates', like a damned supplicant petitioning for entry to a king's castle. It didn't take long for his patience with that to grow thin, and he had followed the more expedient path of assassinating the bitter French media heiress who had stood in his way.

The last time he had visited these apartments, the others had done everything they could to remind him he was an outsider. It had taken years to prove himself to the Combine's inner circle, but now that threshold was in the past, and he stood on an equal footing.

Whether they like it or not.

'What matters is the goddamn work,' snapped the American, turning towards them. 'We're here, so let's do what we came for.' He gestured at the Swiss. 'Say what you have to say.'

'We appreciate you taking the lead on this.' The Italian tried to appease the other man. 'The preparation work you've done has been exemplary.'

'My people know their jobs,' said the American, taking the compliment with a brusque sniff. He threw a nod at Glovkonin. 'Your boy, the Jap . . . We didn't need him there to watchdog.'

'If you say so.'

Glovkonin let the comment go. In point of fact, the primary reason for deploying Saito was to observe the American's operations at first hand.

How else will I be able to destroy him when the opportunity presents itself?

The others constantly talked about their ideal of a 'stable instability', a state of fear in which they could hold the nations of the world and farm them for profit. Glovkonin saw that, too, but with he alone at the reins. It was the next logical move: from outsider to inner circle, and from there to total control.

He smiled. *Don't get ahead of yourself, Pytor. One step at a time.*

The American read the smile as Glovkonin's acquiescence, and carried on with more confidence, his tone taking on its typical bellicosity.

'Look-see, the God's honest truth is that we paid a lot to get where we are. Nothing's gone to plan, you can't deny. Failures and half-successes . . .' He shook his head. 'Too many setbacks.'

'No one denies that,' said the Swiss. 'But we can spend time apportioning blame and complaining about the Fates, or we can move forward. Adapt. *Progress.*'

The Italian chuckled. 'To think of the money we poured into widening the cracks between nations and classes . . . And then Mother Nature comes along and moves that needle for us!' His amusement became a full-throated laugh, and he raised his glass in a mocking salute. 'Gentlemen, I give you coronavirus! We couldn't have done better if we'd cooked up that unpleasantness ourselves!'

Glovkonin considered the Italian's glib tone as he blithely dismissed the deaths of hundreds of thousands to the viral outbreak that had gripped the world for months on end.

The American gave a sage nod. The man's biomedical holdings had turned a pretty penny from their sales of the viral vaccines across North America and beyond, cashing in on the catastrophe at the right moment.

'We optimised this crisis for our benefit,' said the Swiss. 'In a sense, the pandemic served as an unexpected force multiplier for our project. It exacerbated societal tensions already present, and we are in the ideal position to use that to our advantage. With our opposition effectively nullified, thanks to our newest member's work –' he gestured to Glovkonin, who accepted the faint praise – 'we are poised to execute the larger objective.'

For a moment, Glovkonin considered the fate of Rubicon, the corporate parent entity to the private security group that had been such a thorn in the Combine's side over the last few years. Once a Fortune 500 company, it barely existed now, gutted by a brutal hostile takeover that Glovkonin had carefully engineered, its name tainted by accusations of terrorist links, thanks to a clever disinformation campaign. Some fragments of Rubicon still remained at large – he frowned at the thought of these loose ends – but they were of little importance.

The Combine had many enemies, but astute political manoeuvring, blackmail, bribery and extortion had placed their group firmly in the ascendant. Rubicon had been the last major obstacle to the Combine's greater goals. Now the path was clear.

'By the time I get back to the States, we'll be good to go,' said the American. 'We just need the equipment you promised.'

He kept his distance from them, fingering his collar nervously. Glovkonin knew much of his reticence at being in Europe came from the inherent view of many of his countrymen, of the rest of the world as 'the other', the outside from which all threats to them came. The experience of the pandemic had only strengthened that divisive belief.

'As soon as we have it in place, we can flip the switch,' he concluded, making the gesture. 'And I, for one, am going to be happy to sit back and watch those assholes runnin' around like their hair is on fire.'

'One thing continues to concern me,' said the Russian. 'Given the ... volatility of your government in recent years, can we be certain it will fall in line after the event? You are closely connected to the Senate. You know their minds.'

The other man waved the question away. 'Sure, they'll stamp their feet and squawk about it in public . . . But they'll come around once they see the new situation benefits them.' He nodded at his own answer. 'Politics breeds pragmatists, don't you know?'

Glovkonin smiled again. 'I will take your word for it.'

'I want to go over the logistics once again,' insisted the Swiss.

The Italian rolled his eyes and signalled his aide to refresh his drink. 'If we must.'

'We have people to do that,' the American said testily.

Glovkonin's lip curled. 'Do you really want to swing the axe without being certain the blade is sharp?'

On the far side of the Rue Bonaparte, a few doors down from the apartments, a cargo truck sporting the jolly logo of a defunct food service company was parked awkwardly in front of a shuttered clothing store. The building was empty, its previous tenants priced out by extortionate rents, which meant no one was around to question the vehicle's presence.

Despite the fact it was early for lunch, the handwritten note on the windscreen reading *Au Déjeuner* sold the lie to anyone passing by. The truck had been there long enough for the security team in the expensive apartments across the way to consider it inert.

It was impossible to tell from the outside that part of the truck's rear cargo box had been replaced, the panel refitted with an adaptive plastic screen opaque from outside, and transparent from within. Like a one-way mirror, the panel allowed anyone inside the truck to conduct surveillance on the apartments and remain unseen.

That was the plan, at any rate. But it wasn't working out that way.

'Why do we keep losing it?'

Lucy Keyes ran a hand through the tight weave of braids over her head, and leaned in close to the rack of electronic equipment bolted haphazardly to the inside of the truck. Ochre-dark, with an athlete's build and a boyish face, the ex-soldier chafed at the inaction. So close to the targets they had been seeking for so long, it was hard for her to resist the impulse to go kick in the door and start shooting. She kept her voice low. The tones of her New York accent

were like those of an ex-smoker, roughened by damage she had
suffered from a lethal bioagent that had nearly killed her.

'You told me this hardware would do the job for us.'

Sat in front of the gear on an upturned beer crate, Marc Dane
held up a hand to ward her off.

'I can't focus with you hovering. Give me some breathing room.'

Whipcord-thin and hawkish, he had never quite lost the pale
cast brought on by an urbanite upbringing, and a career that had
mostly been spent behind computer screens. His watchful gaze was
framed by the dirty blond hair and unkempt stubble he'd let grow
too long. Marc had a South London growl that came out sharper
than he meant it to, his attention on the flexing forms of sound
waves that washed up and down on the screen of his laptop.

Lucy kissed her teeth, but she did as he asked, backing off to sit
gently atop a heavy shape shrouded by old painter's cloths. They
had to stay sure-footed inside the truck, careful not to move too
fast in case they made the vehicle rock on its shocks.

It was imperative not to draw any attention to their presence
here. After everything it had cost them to get this close to the Combine's inner circle, they couldn't risk blowing the opportunity.

Marc reached up to one of the electronic modules and adjusted
the gain on a dial by a minute amount. The waveforms stabilised,
and the crackly hiss of static whispering around the truck morphed
back into a human voice.

'*The equipment is being assembled, and everything will be in place
for zero hour.*'

The tinny echo the monitoring software put into the speech
didn't mask the distinctive Russian accent, nor did it damp down
the obvious confidence in the man's tone.

'There he is,' said Lucy, sneering at the sound of Pytor Glovkonin's
voice. 'Hello again, asshole.'

'*You need to be right on your mark with this!*' The reply was terse
and irritable, the Midwestern drawl turning acidic. '*I'm the one at
the sharp end when it goes down, don't forget that!*'

'*We have our cut-outs in place,*' said another voice, in a smooth, self-amused tone. '*My friend, we've been preparing this for a long time. And we've learned from our past mistakes.*'

'*No more cat's paws,*' said another, with a soft Germanic lilt. '*Our error was in using others as proxies. Now we will act directly.*'

Marc shook his head. He wasn't happy with the take from the listening gear, but now the meeting across the street was well under way, he didn't dare mess around with it for fear of losing the pick-up completely.

Mounted on a cheap camera tripod, a device that resembled a military-specification torch was aimed at an angle through the one-way panel, directly at the window of the meeting room. It projected an ultraviolet argon ion laser invisible to the human eye, beaming it directly on to the glass. Next to the emitter, a dish-shaped photoreceptor hungrily gathered up the beam elements reflected back from the window and ran that pattern through processor software in the laptop.

'*If even a whiff of this gets traced back to us,*' continued the man with the American accent, '*it is game over and I for one do not—*' The man's voice stuttered and disintegrated into static once again.

'Shit.'

Marc went to the dial. He had operated laser microphones many times as a field technician with the British intelligence services, using them to detect the minute vibrations in the window glass caused by the sound generated inside the room. But the audio take continued to drop out, and he constantly adjusted the laser power, fighting to keep it in the audible range.

Lucy raised an eyebrow. 'We have a problem?'

'They have passive countermeasures in the room up there,' said Marc, frowning. 'Vibrational interrupts putting out random bursts of subsonic noise to mess with any listening gear.'

'You didn't plan for that?'

'Of course I bloody did,' he shot back. 'But I've got to make do with what we have to hand. I can't exactly order this kit from

Amazon.' He blew out a breath. 'Sod this. There's a reason I quit being the bloke in the van. It's always a pain in the arse ...'

What felt like a lifetime ago, Marc's work with MI6's covert OpTeam programme had largely centred on seeing exotic locations and danger zones from the inside of a dingy vehicle much like this one. Back then, that had been all he wanted – staying out of harm's way and serving Queen and country while others ventured forth to take down Great Britain's enemies.

But that life had been torn away by traitors inside his agency, collaborators working with the Combine to suborn MI6 from within. It ended with the destruction of Marc's team. He went on the run, putting him on a new path that led straight to a man called Ekko Solomon, the enigmatic owner of the Rubicon Corporation.

Reflecting on that traumatic experience, Marc could see how it had been a state-change for him. Ripped out of his comfort zone and forced to face danger head-on, he had been tempered in the fire. Now here he was, a different man in a different place.

The bloke in the van wouldn't even recognise me now.

Solomon had given Marc something he hadn't been able to find anywhere else: *purpose.* He became a part of Rubicon's most secret asset, the Special Conditions Division, a privately funded security and intelligence unit with no allegiance to any government, no remit other than to work against threats to freedom and global safety. *No nation but justice,* as Solomon had once said.

Marc remembered the earnest rumble of the African's voice. Few men in Marc's life had impressed him as much as Solomon, with his quiet charisma and his ability to see, clear-eyed, into the hearts of the people he gathered around him.

But the man was dead now, murdered on the orders of the cabal of rich men who sat sipping their drinks up there in those expensive apartments, as they plotted to make the world dance to their tune.

That thought hardened Marc's resolve and he concentrated on the dial again, adjusting it by increments until the audio cut back in.

The careful Germanic voice rose out of the clatter of the interference, returning in mid-sentence.

'. . . to be considered. Let us be clear, by many measures what we are doing will be considered a military attack on a First World state. An act of war.'

'There's no need to be so grandiose.' The reply came from the Russian. 'Wars are for smaller players. Games of tanks and soldiers. Our objective is very different.' The microphone buzzed through his pause. 'I consider it as a much-needed rebalancing of the global power dynamic.'

'Well, that sounds fucking terrifying,' muttered Lucy. 'Whatever these pricks have planned, it's not going to be rainbows and unicorns.'

For some time, Marc and Lucy and the handful of survivors who had escaped the collapse of Rubicon had been gathering scraps of intelligence, building their way toward a single objective – an all-or-nothing revenge strike on the Combine. But the closer they came, the more they suspected that Glovkonin and his wealthy co-conspirators were gathering momentum for their most audacious play yet.

And now Marc was hearing them say it out loud. He grimaced, suppressing a shudder, as the thought that had been dogging him for the past months rose once again: nothing will stop them unless we do.

For her part, Lucy had advocated taking a more kinetic approach to the situation. Marc had argued her out of destroying the building with all of the Combine committee members in it, not just because blowing a hole in an upmarket Parisian neighbourhood would have been nigh-impossible to do without serious collateral damage.

Solomon's death had been hard on her. The man had been as much a mentor to the ex-Special Forces operator as he had been to Marc, and she wanted bloody revenge. But to take the full measure of payback, they had to be smart. What they were doing was guerrilla espionage, high speed and low drag, applying force only when they could strike at their enemy's weakest point. In a stand-up fight against a group with the resources and the reach of the Combine, they would not prevail.

Lucy knew that as well as Marc did, but that didn't mean she had to like it.

'Signal's dropped again,' he told her, as the static came roaring back. 'Keep the recorders going, I'll try to get it again.'

Marc did the only thing he could – turning up the UV laser's power in the vain hope that the backscatter from the window would come in clearer.

The static rumbled and faded, and they heard a few seconds of clear, dead air. The conference room in the apartments was silent.

'Did they leave?' Lucy shot him a look. 'Is the mike still working?'

'It's working.' Marc's skin prickled with a sudden rush of fear, the unexpected silence echoing louder than a screaming siren. He bolted to his feet. 'They detected the laser ... They know we're here!'

He shot a look through the misty plastic of the one-way panel and confirmed his assumption. Four men in dark suits, wearing amber shooter's glasses and sporting radio earpieces, had emerged from the entrance of the apartment building. Hands dipped to grab the holstered weapons beneath their jackets; one of them looked in the direction of the truck and started towards it.

ALEPH trained its operatives well, drawing hardened men and women from the ranks of military forces across Eastern Europe. Everyone in the employ of the Moscow-based mercenary contractor had a common profile that included proficiency with weapons of multiple kinds and zero qualms about using them. ALEPH were the people you hired when you wanted the application of lethal violence with no questions asked. Their skill set dovetailed perfectly with the ruthless intentions of the Combine.

Moving quickly, two men formed up at the front of the cargo truck, pointing their guns into the vacant cab, scanning for any motion inside. The second pair came around the rear, communicating by hand signals.

One took aim at the rear doors, and the second reached for the release bar, positioning himself to wrench it open in a rush.

From inside the truck came a harsh noise, a guttural sound like a circular saw blade spinning against metal. The noise became a stuttering growl, then a roar, and the truck rocked as the weight inside shifted.

The man with his hand on the bar reacted, yanking it down, but halfway through the action the door exploded open and struck him in the face. A silver and black shape howled out of the truck's interior, crashing down onto the street in a skirl of tyres on asphalt.

The second gunman spun away, dodging the mass of a sleek Aprilia racing scooter as it blew past, trailing a dust cloth behind it. He barely had time to register the rider bent forward over the handlebars and the woman riding pillion before the vehicle bit into the road and fled, towards the intersection at the end of the road.

Inside the truck, a sparking, fizzing ball of white fire burned through the surveillance gear mounted on the inner wall, the sun-hot flare of a thermite charge disgorging plumes of grey smoke as it melted the equipment to slag.

The gunman sprinted after the Aprilia, casting around as he ran. The scooter was nimble and fast. If it hit the flow of Paris's mid-morning traffic, it would vanish and the pair spying on his principals would be lost. That could not be allowed to happen.

A few metres away, a youth with a crash helmet perched atop his head sauntered back towards another moped, having just dropped off a delivery of hot food from the bulky thermal box on the back. He gawped at the sight of the ALEPH mercenaries. The gunman shoved him out of the way and mounted his ride, gunning the battered Vespa's engine. The delivery rider started in on a torrent of angry invective, but swallowed it when the gunman waved a pistol in his face. Hands raised, the rider made the smarter choice to back away and let the ALEPH operative steal his wheels.

Marc guided the scooter around the slower-moving vehicles without losing speed, ignoring the chorus of French swear-words and blaring horns. He felt Lucy shift behind him, one hand snaking around his belly to hold on, the other gripping a compact Sig Sauer P320 pistol. The Sig was tucked low, the gun's barrel resting unpleasantly close to his crotch, and he squirmed.

'Watch where you point that!' he yelled over the rumble of the traffic.

Lucy didn't register his discomfort, her head turned to look back the way they had come.

'We've got company!' she called. 'Tell me you pulled the memory card before we bolted.'

'Give me some credit.'

Marc would have patted the pocket where the solid-state drive rested, but he didn't dare take his hands off the controls for even an instant.

He risked flicking a glance into the scooter's wing mirror and caught sight of a figure in a black suit on a moped behind them – a man who was very definitely *not* a delivery rider. Beyond him, a grey 5-series BMW came up fast, and by the way it wallowed into a chicane, Marc knew it was an ALEPH-issue security special, heavy with armour plates and bulletproof glass.

'Lose them,' added Lucy, as if that wasn't already the only thought on Marc's mind.

Up ahead, the Rue Bonaparte opened out into an intersection crossing over the Boulevard Saint-Germain, and traffic lights showing red had halted the vehicles in front of the scooter. Marc used his body mass to steer, guiding the nimble racer with his shoulders and his knees, briefly mounting the kerb and threading the needle between two iron posts. Pedestrians bolted out of his way as he veered back on to the road, closing on the crossroads.

The BMW momentarily stalled, but the gunman on the stolen Vespa mirrored each move they made, the delivery bike spitting out black exhaust, the empty thermal box on the back flapping open in the wind.

Lucy leaned forward and spoke into his ear. 'I see a gun!'

He won't start shooting in the middle of rush hour . . .

Marc's thought was still taking shape when something buzzed hornet-loud past his right ear, and proved him wrong.

'Shit!'

Ignoring the crimson stop signals, Marc threw the scooter out into the stream of traffic crossing in front of him, and put more power to the Aprilia's screaming engine. Cars swerved to avoid the scooter, colliding with one another, but Marc concentrated on finding the sweet path between all that fast-moving metal, veering around and into the flow of the vehicles.

'Still on us!' Lucy shouted a warning. 'Lights changing!'

Behind them, the mass of waiting cars started to move, and the armoured BMW bulldozed its way through to the front of the pack.

Ahead, on the far side of the intersection, where the road continued on past the local Benedictine abbey towards the river, the street was clear of traffic. No traffic meant no cover, and Marc had a horrible mental image of the Beemer roaring up to slam them off the scooter and into the pavement.

A shape caught his eye, an ornate sign rising over a narrow stairway descending into the ground: the entrance to the nearest Métro station.

'Hold on.'

At the last possible second, Marc jerked the scooter's handlebars and veered toward the entrance. Shouting, screaming people threw themselves out of the riders' path as Marc took the Aprilia over the lip of the steep line of stairs, and juddered down into the subway.

Behind them, the BMW skidded to a screeching halt, but the gunman on the stolen Vespa was still on them, coming down in their wake.

Rush-hour travellers flattened themselves against the tiled walls as Marc rose up in the saddle and let the racing scooter buck like a bronco as it hammered over the stairs. They skidded into the mid-level where the ticket hall opened out to escalators leading to the platforms, and the Aprilia's revving rear wheel drew a comma of black on the floor as Marc hauled it around.

Automatic ticket barriers closed off entry to the station's lower levels, but one was locked open with a makeshift *Hors D'usage* sign strung across it. Marc twisted the handlebar to gun the engine, hearing the nasal snarl of the other moped echoing behind him. Once again, he threaded the needle and aimed the scooter through the narrow gap, ripping away the sign, scraping his knees and elbows against the barrier's frame as he pushed them through it.

A square of white tile near Marc's shoulder exploded as another bullet narrowly missed, and the ticket hall was suddenly filled with new cries of panic as the shocked commuters saw the gun.

The ALEPH man followed Marc's lead, but the other bike didn't fit quite as easily through the skinny opening. The thermal box on the moped, usually filled with bags of hot takeaway food, snagged on the panels of the barrier and, for a moment, the bike stalled. Then, with a tearing sound, the box ripped away and the pursuer was on the move again.

Marc made use of the precious extra seconds, dragging the handlebars around to put the scooter's front wheel on the descending escalator. Lucy moved with him, and together they brute-forced the Aprilia through a knot of people. The scooter juddered down the metal steps, forcing the passengers riding the moving stairway to vault onto the median divide to avoid them.

Marc didn't let himself think about the danger, all too aware that weighing this up with rational thought would stop him dead. He pressed on, trusting instinct and luck.

They shot off the end of the escalator and hit the platform at a bad angle, enough that the scooter slipped into a wicked shimmy that forced Marc to overcorrect, risking a skid that would have thrown them into the curved wall. Colourful posters flashed past as they thundered along the length of the subway platform, and another bullet pitted the floor beneath the scooter as their pursuer emerged behind them.

'He's persistent,' spat Lucy, before nodding ahead. 'And we're running out of road.'

At the far end of the platform, more temporary out-of-order panels walled off the opposite exit, trapping them in the Métro station with no means of escape other than the route they had taken down.

'Okay.'

Marc acknowledged Lucy's warning as they zipped beneath an illuminated sign, indicating the imminent arrival of the next train. Instead of slowing, he accelerated as the platform's end came up to meet them.

At the last possible moment, Marc jerked the steering and the scooter fell, dropping to the gravel-covered sleepers down on the railbed. A wave of white light from the front of the arriving train coming up behind blazed around them. Marc didn't dare to look back, leaning into the wind and over the handlebars, as if that might give the Aprilia an extra boost of speed.

A shadow flickered behind them and Marc knew that the ALEPH gunman had followed their lead.

Lucy shouted again. 'Still on us!'

Darkness swallowed them as they entered the tunnel, and Marc fought to keep the scooter steady over the rough, bumpy path beneath the wheels. Horribly aware of the live rail threading close to the front wheel, Marc feared what the thousands of volts coursing through it could do if he or Lucy accidentally made contact with it.

With no civilians to get in the way and his target clear ahead of him, the gunman on the moped opened up, hoping to put a pistol shot into his fleeing targets.

Marc felt Lucy's weight shift and he instinctively leaned the opposite way to counterbalance her. She twisted at the waist and fired back with her Sig, aiming more by luck than judgement.

They blew through the bright lights of Odéon station, the next stop on the Number 4 line, and Marc registered flash-frame impressions of startled Parisians ducking back from the edge of the platform as the two bikes thundered by.

Then they were back in the dark again, only this time Marc could see the crimson glow of indicators over the walls of the tunnel up ahead. In a few moments, they would catch up to the train in front of them, which would already be slowing to halt at the next stop at St-Michel.

'I'm out!' shouted Lucy, the slide locked back in her gun.

'Forget it!' Marc yelled back. 'Just hold tight and hope!'

'What . . .?'

Marc pitched up the front wheel and sent the Aprilia into a bouncing side-slip, going through an opening between two support beams that took them from the northbound track to the southbound side. The move put them directly in the path of an oncoming train, the brilliant white glare of its lights dazzling them both. In less than sixty seconds, it would strike them head-on.

He gambled on the ALEPH gunman coming after them, and the bet paid off. The mercenary was so fixated on running down Marc and Lucy, he put his own safety a distant second.

Marc pumped the brakes and veered back the way they had come, bouncing across to the other side of the tracks. Blinded by the oncoming train, their pursuer reacted too slowly, and the southbound train clipped him, smashing man and moped into the tunnel wall with an ugly, grinding crunch of metal.

'Oh, damn,' said Lucy, around a shallow cough. 'He won't walk away from that.'

'Speaking of walking . . .' Ahead of them, the other train had stopped in St-Michel, blocking their route. The Aprilia came to a halt in a crunch of gravel. 'We need to ditch this.'

'Copy that.'

She helped him dump the scooter into a maintenance arch. They both stripped off the dark, nondescript jackets they had been wearing, revealing brighter, louder clothing below, more suited to tourists. Marc pulled a khaki baseball cap from his pocket and put it on backwards, while Lucy threw a thin denim shirt over her shoulders.

It wasn't much of a change, but it modified their look enough that anyone with their descriptions would need to take a second glance to be sure. As passengers moved off and onto the waiting train, it was easy for the two of them to walk up the access ramp to the platform and get lost in their movement.

Staying close to each other, but not enough to seem as if they were a couple, Marc and Lucy followed the other passengers towards the exit. Every instinct screamed at Marc to get out of there as fast as possible, but a hurried step or a furtive manner would make them stand out a mile to any watchers observing the platforms via closed-circuit television.

Then everyone stopped moving. A voice came over the station's public address system and told them that there had been 'an incident'. The station was being evacuated, and the voice asked for everyone to be patient and remain calm.

A ripple of sullen, city-dweller irritation washed over the crowd, and Marc kept his expression neutral as a group of police officers appeared at the exit. The cops scanned the faces of the passengers as they threaded by them, and his pulse quickened again, the momentary adrenaline drop after ditching the scooter fading.

There was nowhere else to go. The train in the station had stalled, its doors open wide, and the platform exits were thick with cops. Their window of opportunity to escape was closing by the second.

Do they have our faces?

It was likely, Marc decided, both of them caught on traffic cameras or monitors inside the Métro. But not much time had passed, and it was doubtful that any pictures of them had yet been sent for a facial recognition pass through the Paris police's databases.

When that did happen, the *flics* would see the Interpol alerts next to their names and the warnings that tagged Marc and Lucy on counter-terror watch lists. All hell would break loose.

A hand grabbed Marc's arm as two of the policemen came closer, another snaking up and around the back of his neck. He had no time to react before Lucy pressed herself into him and pulled Marc into a hungry, open-mouthed kiss. A shock flashed through him. For a second their connection was electric, it was fire. He gave into it.

Then just as fast, Lucy disengaged and slapped Marc hard across the cheek.

'*Comment osez-vous?*' she snapped, with an arch sniff, plucking a pair of large sunglasses from her pocket and turning away to put them on.

Marc coloured, suddenly aware of the two cops laughing at his expense. Then they were moving away, with Marc on the escalator, rising towards daylight.

Outside, he blinked in the sun's glare and turned around the peak of his cap to shade his eyes. He found Lucy a few metres away, at the kerbside by the river, waiting with a taxi already attracted by her summons. She gave him a look and beckoned.

'C'mon.'

'What was that about?' he said, as they climbed into the vehicle.

'Distraction,' she replied. 'Those cops will remember you getting slapped, but not what we looked like.'

'Yeah.' Marc rubbed his cheek. 'Give me some warning next time?'

She smiled as the taxi pulled away.

'Don't pretend you didn't enjoy it.'

THREE

Lucy rode the bus a stop past the Parc de Noisiel, then walked back as if she'd planned to do that all along. It was the last in a line of three stages, changing from a taxi to public transport, varying her path to put off any potential followers.

Washing her route was old school spycraft. It had become practically second nature to her, since she'd moved from the straightforward work of being a sniper for Uncle Sam to the more clandestine gig of a covert security operative. But on some level, this spook shit grated on her.

Lucy Keyes had found her rhythm in the world as a soldier, in the green machine where targets were designated and rules of engagement were clear. A million miles from the backstreets of Queens in New York where she'd grown up, in the army she found the thing that her life had lacked up to that point – *focus*. She liked the precision, the way it echoed her work with her weapon. Find the target, lock in the range, put the cross hairs in the right place and then – *send it*. Mission accomplished. Move on to the next one.

Spy work was something else entirely, hard on you in a way that regular soldiering never was. Being a covert meant never coming home from the fight. It meant you were carrying your battlefield around with you wherever you went, because every person giving you a cautious glance could be the enemy, no matter what they looked like or how they dressed. Lucy had been conditioned to the idea combat was *there* and safety was *here*, and a line existed between the two.

She'd learned a different reality coming to work for Ekko Solomon and the Rubicon Group. Some days, she wished that the enigmatic African had left her to mark time in the cell at the military stockade where he first found her.

That thought made Lucy's lip curl in a sneer.

Are you crazy?

She asked herself the question. She would have still been there now, prowling the bounds of the prison, getting softer, growing more bitter by the day.

Lucy crossed the road in front of the low cluster of vacant office buildings, jogging up to the side entrance that appeared, to all intents and purposes, bolted shut. The windows of the bottom floor were boarded up with sheets of thick, rain-stained plywood, and the levels above were dark, the blank glass layered with sheets of opaque blue plastic. It was a careful disguise designed to give off the impression that no one was in residence.

The offices had belonged to a company that had crashed and burned during the long months of the coronavirus lockdown, and ownership of the place had been lost in the cracks of the system. In the suburbs of Torcy, in Seine-et-Marne out to the east of the French capital, it was close enough to the Combine's holdings for the team to react quickly, and hopefully far enough out that their targets wouldn't find it if they looked.

With few entrance and exit routes and good lines of fire that Lucy herself had validated, it was perfect for a staging area, the kind of blandly ordinary building that slipped past the eye and didn't lodge in the memory.

She paused at the side entrance, checking to be sure no one saw her slip inside. A keypad got her access, and she waited for the door's magnetic lock to snap closed before she moved on. Above her, concealed out of sight, a compact thermal camera kept watch on the doorway and the street outside. Had Lucy been a stranger, she would not have got this far.

She took the stairs to the third floor in quick, loping steps, taking pains to avoid the tripwires set up with nine-banger stun grenades attached, there to catch any intruder who made it past the first line of security.

The upper floor of the building had formerly been a field of office cubicles but now it was a wide open space, split up by a few round pillars. One corner of the floor was a couple of makeshift dorms, curtained off from one another with more of that blue plastic sheeting, and in the centre there was something approximating an operations deck.

Most of the tables and chairs were cheap, off-the-shelf camping kit and plastic garden furniture, along with a threadbare old sofa they'd found in a storeroom.

At one end of the set-up, a thin East Asian woman in a blood-red hoodie sat in a semicircle of computer monitors and laptops, nesting over a black snarl of cables emerging from a military specification gear case. Kara Wei's expressionless features were lit by the cold glow from her screens, her large eyes dancing as she lost herself in infinite lines of computer code. She didn't look up as Lucy approached.

'What went wrong?' she demanded.

'The situation was fluid.' Lucy's reply was equally terse. 'We had to bug out early.'

She left it at that, irked at the hacker's monotone accusation.

Over the past six months, Lucy and Kara had barely had a conversation longer than a couple of sentences. It was a long way from the relationship they used to have – a friendship after a fashion, a mutual respect for each other's skill set between sniper and hacker. But that was before Kara had used Rubicon's assets for her own personal agenda and put the team in harm's way. Ultimately, a lot of secrets had come to light about Kara – *hell, that wasn't even her real name*, Lucy reflected – and a lot of trust had burned up.

Lucy was still salty about that. The woman she had thought was her friend was a mask the real Kara wore, a persona to pretend with, for someone ill-at-ease with human contact. The individual underneath was someone more calculating, and Lucy hated that she had been fooled.

But the hacker was one of the best in the game, and when the SCD team were scattered and lost following the collapse of the Rubicon Group, she had shown up to help them. Perhaps that counted for something.

Months later, Kara was still here, still helping them. But it was hard to let go of the resentment.

The hacker raised her head.

'I lost the remote feed from the laser mike so I have next to nothing. If you've come back empty-handed, that's going to make things even more difficult.'

'I'm fine, thanks for asking,' Lucy snapped, and she poked a finger through the bullet hole in the baggy arm of her blouse.

Kara gave a shrug, as if she didn't understand the statement.

'Where's Marc?'

'On his way.' Her exasperation from the blown surveillance operation suddenly boiled up to the surface. 'I'm sure he's looking forward to your heart-warming welcome.'

'Let's take a breath.' A broad-shouldered man with short hair and kind eyes appeared in the opposite doorway, drawn by the rise in Lucy's tone. 'We're on the same side here.' He had his hands out in front of him, in a conciliatory gesture, as if physically pushing air into the space between the two women.

Benjamin Harun was on the opposite end of the spectrum from Kara in every conceivable manner. French, welcoming, and the dictionary definition of the word 'burly', Marc had once described the ex-Foreign Legion paratrooper as *built like a brick shithouse*, and it was accurate. Lucy preferred to think of him like those cartoon caricatures of an old-time circus strongman, lifting black iron barbells with one thick arm and twirling his well-cared-for moustache with his free hand.

Like Lucy, he had been a soldier, but Benjamin had given that up after losing too much in dusty, desolate war zones. She knew for a fact he hadn't touched a gun in years, and he'd come into

Rubicon's orbit to work as the resident therapist and counsellor for the company team. Right now, he was the stabilising influence the survivors needed.

'Sure,' said Lucy, to no one in particular, as she moved to the part of the room set up as a basic kitchen. She helped herself to a bottle of water from a humming mini-fridge and microwaved a packet of instant rice. The comedown from the operation had two side-effects: first, it made her ravenously hungry; and second, it killed the giddy rush of excitement she felt in the moment. In the action, she could almost be having fun, but afterwards the cold, hard reality seeped back in.

'Where *is* Marc?' Benjamin trailed after her, raising an eyebrow.

'We separated,' she noted. 'After everything went to hell, figured it was the smart play to avoid any potential tails.'

'Were you tracked?' Kara called out the question and Lucy ignored it.

'He'll be here,' Lucy continued.

'We can collapse this site and fall back to our alternate in thirty minutes,' said the Frenchman. 'If you believe we are compromised.'

Lucy's gaze drifted to another of the black plastic gear cases. Inside were their meagre stocks of weapons and ammunition. She visualised a potential attack scenario, with ALEPH gun-hands swarming the abandoned building.

They could shoot their way out if they needed to. She'd picked this place precisely because of that.

She shook her head. 'We'll stay on station. Marc will be coming here, and so will Malte when his plane gets in.'

Benjamin gave her a nod. 'Malte checked in an hour ago. He's leaving Hong Kong in the morning.'

'And?' Lucy couldn't hide the hope in her voice. After the fuck-up earlier, she was desperate to get some good news.

'*Successful,*' said Benjamin, in a passable imitation of the other man's voice.

She released a breath. 'Good. That's real good.'

Malte Riis, the team's taciturn Finnish wheelman, had taken on a solo sortie to connect with an old Rubicon source in the Chinese Ministry of State Security, and after months of foreplay the contact had finally given up the intelligence they needed.

No one wanted to talk about how much the data had cost them. The war chest the team had started with months ago had been depleted far quicker than anyone expected, and it wouldn't be much longer before they were running on fumes.

Lucy sat in one of the lawn chairs, placing her Sig Sauer on a folding table beside her, and set in on the pack of hot rice, spooning it into her mouth and chewing mechanically.

'We have other options,' Benjamin said, at length.

'We really *don't*,' she said, her mouth full. 'We all committed to the job. You were there. We knew there would come a moment like this. The *go* or *no-go*.'

'We passed that point weeks ago.' Kara threw in the comment from across the room, making no attempt to pretend she wasn't listening to their conversation.

Lucy's lip curled.

She's right, damn it.

Benjamin could have agreed, but that wasn't his way. The Frenchman preferred to let people come to the truth on their own.

Lucy's sense memory snapped her back to that morning at a desolate airstrip on the coast of Mozambique, where the survivors of the Rubicon cull had gathered in the wake of their defeat. Still reeling from the shock of losing everything they had, still burning with the sorrow and rage from the deaths of three of their own, it came down to the choice they had made on that day.

With pretty much nothing but the clothes on their backs, a few guns and a bag of encrypted hard drives, the last remnants of the Special Conditions Division had traded their futures for a shot at something that seemed impossible. *Vengeance.*

All of them, in one way or another, owed Ekko Solomon their lives. The African had brought them back from the brinks of their personal abysses, given them purpose and agency. There was a bill to come due.

Lucy wanted to believe that their goal was in reach, but she couldn't lie to herself. It had cost half a million euros in digital currency and gigabytes of data in trade to place Marc and Lucy across the street from the Combine's meeting today, in the right city on the right day at the right time.

And what do we have to show for it?

'Door,' Kara said abruptly.

'What?' Lucy's head snapped up, and she reached for the Sig.

'Someone at the door,' Kara repeated, as if she were explaining herself to a slow child. She indicated one of her monitors. 'Marc's back.'

Lucy put down the gun and sighed. A few moments later, the Brit emerged from the stairwell looking worn-out and wary. His eyes flicked around the room, instinctively checking the exit routes and the corners where hidden threats might lurk.

She wondered if Marc realised the changes in himself. The first time Lucy had seen him, through the scope of a PSG-1 sniper rifle, Marc had been all raw energy and instinct, running on smarts and luck and not much else. Surviving had tempered him, knocked off the rough corners, turned him into something different. He still had that reckless streak, though, and a tendency to overthink things.

He pulled out a sliver of black plastic – the memory stick from the surveillance gear – and tossed it to Kara. The hacker snatched it from the air like a cat snagging a bird, and made a face.

'This is all you brought back? What about the equipment? The truck?' She inserted the data stick into her laptop and ran a scan on it. 'You know it took me two weeks to source it.'

'Had to leave everything behind.' Marc shot Lucy a look, intuiting what discussion had already taken place. 'ALEPH didn't give us much choice, yeah?'

'Do you want to know how much money you've burned today?' Kara said flatly.

Marc's jaw hardened. 'Is that going to help our mission?'

Kara swallowed any comment she was going to make and returned to checking the content of the memory stick. Audio files from the laser mike stuttered from a concealed speaker as she ran the data through filtering subroutines.

Marc sat heavily, falling into a chair across from Lucy, and he gratefully accepted a bottle of water from Benjamin.

The Frenchman jutted his chin towards Kara.

'She's trying to help. Keeping us informed as to the resource situation.'

'We know the situation, mate,' Marc noted. 'We're aware.' Lucy watched him take a long pull on the bottle. 'Before, we could have leaned on our support structure, called in specialised help, dialled up the right hardware or whatever . . . But now we're using scraps.' He gave a thin, humourless smile. 'We're travelling economy class.'

'More like steerage.'

Lucy couldn't stop herself from casting a look over at a particular gear pack by the door, among their go-bags set there ready to grab if they had to bolt. Inside the pack were the remaining hard drives salvaged from a Rubicon off-site server, the only backups of an intelligence database called the Grey Record.

Rubicon's operatives had gathered that intelligence over many years, storing material on threat forces, terror groups, criminals and other international non-state actors. Lucy and the others had acted upon what they uncovered, quietly neutralising hazards by fair means and foul, following Ekko Solomon's crusade to make the world a little safer. *Small actions with large consequences*, he had always said.

But when the Combine plundered Rubicon, the Grey Record was the prize that glittered in the ashes – a trove of data and untraceable funds that men without conscience and ethics could have exploited for their own ends. Lucy, Marc and the others had ultimately destroyed all copies of the files except those in that pack. Some of what they had salvaged they traded for what they needed; some of it they used to get them to where they were now. Illegal hardware, smuggled guns and fake passports, the bribes and everything else – it cost money. Working without the deep pockets of a global megacorporation to back them up required a whole new way of operating.

It hadn't escaped anyone's notice that the SCD team were now using the same tactics as the terror cells and criminal groups they'd once hunted. Lucy reflected on the irony of that.

Part of the Combine's gambit to obliterate Rubicon had first been to destroy any credibility the company's private military contractors might have, by falsifying evidence of the SCD's involvement in a bloody attack on a military base in Cyprus. The team had always operated on the margins, frequently over the limits of what was considered legal, but always within the bounds of a strict moral code. None of that changed the fact that the world at large now believed they were terrorists.

Kara turned away from her keyboard and hesitated. Lucy knew what she was going to say next before she spoke. The hacker had a solution to their ills, if only they were willing to take it.

'I can get us eight million dollars by sun-up,' she told them.

Lucy scowled. 'You said six million last time.'

'The offer has increased,' she replied.

Marc stood up, shaking his head. 'We've had this conversation, Kara.'

The hacker pressed on, ignoring the warning tone in his words.

'There are Grey Record files we haven't even touched. Actionable material that we could trade for serious money.'

'*Actionable* material,' echoed Benjamin. 'You mean *blackmail* material.'

'I know people willing to take it off our hands,' Kara went on.

In her former life as a mercenary hacker for the notorious Ghost5 collective, she had moved through the darkest parts of the dark web. Lucy had no doubt Kara could reach out to any of the unsavoury bottom-feeders lurking on the edges of the net.

'And what do you think they'll do with it?' Lucy glared at the other woman. 'Everything we've taken from Solomon's files, we have managed. We know how it was handled, who it went to. We know what side of the line we stand on, Kara. Can you say the same thing for these people you're talking about?'

'Why does that matter?' Kara didn't wait for her to answer. 'It's a straightforward equation. We need resources. Those cost money. We have a tradable commodity and potential buyers—'

'That commodity we're talking about is people's lives.' Marc cut through her words. 'Rubicon created the Grey Record to find bad actors out in the world and deal with them. It contains the names and details of whistle-blowers, covert sources and confidential informants. I'm not willing to give that to someone who might use it to ruin the lives of innocents. No matter what the cash value. I've said it before, and I meant it, I'll chuck the lot in the sea before allowing it into the wrong hands.'

Kara was quiet for a long moment. Dealing with real people as opposed to digital avatars wasn't her best suit, and she took the time to frame her reply.

'Marc, I understand your point. I understood it when Solomon said it. But he's dead, and we're running out of money. There is going to come a moment where we will need to decide where we draw the line.' She looked briefly in Lucy's direction, then away. 'If we want to get back at the Combine, we may have to give up the luxury of the moral high ground.'

'Give it up?' Marc's voice dropped. 'Haven't we've given up enough already?' When the hacker didn't reply, he shook his head again. 'No. We are not doing this. End of.' He looked around, taking in Benjamin's and Lucy's gazes. 'Right?'

They returned a nod, and Lucy lingered on him, wondering exactly when it was that the Brit had grown from being one of the team, to the man who called the shots.

At the airstrip, she remembered. *The day after we lost Solomon.*

They'd come out of that experience changed, but Marc more than anyone.

Marc gestured at Kara's monitor. 'We got something back there, even if it's fragments. So let's get to work on what's at hand, worry about the rest later.'

'Okay,' said Kara.

With the subject closed, she set to bringing up the audio recording they had captured from the Combine assembly.

Saito kept low in the back seat of the battered Lada, the collar of his coat turned up and most of his face hidden behind the dark material of a shemagh around his throat. In the gloom of the hot, close night, he was invisible in the shadows.

He felt the joins in the roadbed vibrate up through the car's creaking suspension at they sped west along the Port Said highway, past the lines of warehouses near the river. He was still unsettled from his reception at Cairo International Airport, the Egyptian customs officers having decided to arbitrarily put him through an unnecessary secondary processing after his long flight from America.

For a brief moment, he feared that this might be the work of Glovkonin, reaching out through a proxy. His greatest anxiety was that the Russian would uncover what Saito had been hiding here in Cairo, and take revenge for it.

But it soon became clear that the officers were more interested in making sport of the weary foreigner, and Saito changed their minds by offering to pay an on-the-spot 'fee' to smooth his entry into the country. An hour later, he was here, minutes away from his destination.

They left the highway and veered off through the El-Mazallat district, passing beneath the towering minarets of the Al-Rahman al-Rahim Mosque, reaching into the night sky like giant segmented fingers. The Lada navigated a maze of backstreets, and the temple seemed to move with them, turning in place, dominating the darkness from every angle no matter where they were.

Saito looked blankly into the facades of the buildings they passed. He was trying to wall off his anxieties, but it was getting harder and harder to build the bricks high enough. The mental compartments in which the assassin stored the various parts of himself were breaking up.

In the past, it would have been impossible for Hiroshi Saito to conceive of duplicity towards his masters in the Combine. He kept one mental silo for his duty and his mission, holding in there the soldier-assassin who could kill without hesitation. In another, there was the man bound by an oath to blood that could not be broken. And in the last, there was the truth of who he had once been, the dismal reflection of an old self he didn't dare look at.

That wasn't working anymore. The barriers were crumbling. He closed his eyes and saw his daughter's face. The memory hit him like a shock of cold water and he blinked it away. *No.* He could not dwell on her. He had to maintain focus. Stay in the present.

If I allow myself to look inwards, I will see only the weakness. I must maintain the mask. Nothing else can be shown.

Saito could not stop ruminating on what happened in the house in Cape Cod. The admission he had made to the man Harlow felt cathartic, inevitable.

Why am I here, if not because of this? I have already committed myself!

His daughter's name ghosted on his lips, as he silently formed the shapes of the characters. He wanted to say it aloud again, to hear it out in the world.

Deep inside himself, a distant scream echoed from the man he had once been.

What have you done, Hiroshi? What have you let yourself become?

The Lada jerked to a sudden stop, snapping Saito out of his reverie. The aging, grey-faced man in the driving seat glared at him in the rear-view mirror. They had arrived.

Saito paid with a fold of notes and dragged his bag on to the street, the driver barely waiting for the door to close before the vehicle rumbled away. Along with the heavy fumes from the Lada's exhaust, the night air smelled of marine diesel and stale river water.

Wary of drawing attention from the clusters of men idling in nearby doorways, Saito walked stiffly towards a building that backed on to the Nile, a run-down three-storey thing of concrete slabs behind a courtyard and sheet-metal gates. Unlike the other constructions around it, a wall five metres high surrounded this place, and a sign atop the gate said the workshop within specialised in maritime engine repairs. So did a dozen other places within a stone's throw; it was a cover, and everyone within a four-block radius knew. But they also knew enough not to say any more about it.

A swarthy youth in the baggy shirt of a French football team opened an inset door in the gates at Saito's approach, and he did little to conceal the Russian Bizon sub-machine gun hanging from a strap over his shoulder. Saito didn't recognise him, but the youth beckoned him inside.

They passed underneath makeshift covers that by day would cut the sun and by night, conceal activity in the courtyard from overhead drone flights or satellite cameras.

The walk across the enclosure seemed to take an age. With each step Saito took, he drew closer to the point of no return. Up ahead, the youth in the football shirt held open the door into the building, and light flooded out. It was a daunting sight, for such a humble threshold, but it came to Saito that the doorway represented his last chance to step back from this.

He could give the youth and his comrades the right word and they would deal with the captives inside the building, erasing

Saito's problems and dumping their remains in the river. He could turn around and leave, go back to the life he had surrendered himself to. No one would know. Glovkonin and the Combine would remain ignorant.

Nothing would change. Except that the rot inside Hiroshi Saito's soul would keep growing, and he would hate himself more and more each day.

Saito took a breath and stepped inside.

The building held the heat in its thick, unmoving air, and there was a dampness from the river that he could taste at the back of his throat. The youth led Saito past another guard, this one a surly older man who might have been the younger one's father. The other man gave Saito a grim nod, then returned to the pages of a leather-bound book in his hands. He had another of the Bizon SMGs resting against his leg as an afterthought.

Saito was taken to the woman first. She was, predictably, in the cell with the heaviest door. Saito heard her singing to herself, quietly mimicking the cadence of a famous American pop star and drumming her fingers on the walls.

She had tried to kill a guard only two weeks earlier, by forcing a jagged fragment of brick into his throat. It was her fifth escape attempt, and the third man she had left with a permanent reminder not to underestimate her.

Saito nodded to the youth, who unlocked the door and then took a step back, bringing up his gun to a ready position. The singing stopped with a flourish as Saito entered the cell.

The small chamber had a high barred window that didn't let in much of the night air, and an enclosed light behind a shatter-proof dome spilling yellow illumination over the peeling walls. The woman crouched on the low cot that took up one side of the room, facing a stainless steel toilet and sink combination like those found in any supermax solitary. She gave Saito a wan smile and ran a hand through her hair, glancing at the youth.

'He's scared of me,' she said. Her accent was bland and hard to place.

She had dark hair and a fair complexion, and the kind of features that didn't lend themselves to easy categorisation. Average but not unattractive, perhaps of Greek or Italian extraction. She could have been American, French, perhaps Eastern European at a push. Saito remembered how she had looked when he first met her, in a dingy taverna in Athens, and tried to find that woman in the face of this one.

'I've heard him talking to his old man,' she went on, enjoying the youth's obvious discomfort. 'He thinks I'm a monster. A *Si'lat*.' She turned the last words into a long, silky snake-hiss, showing her teeth and playing into the role. 'You know what those are?'

Saito was aware of the young man at the corner of his vision, moving uncomfortably from foot to foot, gripping his gun tightly.

'A demon from Arabic mythology. A shape-changing woman who steals the life from unwary men.'

'He's right.' Her tone switched in an instant to demure and soft. Although she hadn't actually physically altered in any way, the woman changed her posture, her expression and her mannerisms in the span of just two words. She gave off the impression of being someone totally different. Someone vulnerable and afraid. 'Have you come to let me out? I'm ever so sorry. I'll be a good little girl from now on.'

Saito shook his head. 'Stop with the games, Grace. It is tiresome.'

Her persona switched again, and she mimicked Saito's level diction and posture.

'Stop with the games,' she echoed. 'And if we are speaking of what is tiresome, how about months locked up in this place?'

He beckoned her to stand. 'Come with me.'

Saito's information about the woman was thin. He knew only that she had once been a covert operative run by the American Central Intelligence Agency as a high-level infiltrator, trained to subsume herself into deep-cover identities and adopt other personas with a pathological level of dedication. By her own admission, Grace had become bored with that life and broken away to become a freelance chameleon-for-hire.

The Combine had used her as a stalking horse against their enemies in the Rubicon group and the British intelligence services, having Grace double as the missing-presumed-dead lover of the Englishman, Marc Dane. She was eventually unmasked, and with her usefulness at an end, Glovkonin ordered her termination.

Saito should have followed those orders. He was still uncertain as to why he had ultimately let her live.

A monster has its uses, the assassin told himself, *even one as amoral as her.*

'We're going to see him?' Grace followed as Saito walked up the stairs to the upper floors, with the youth trailing cautiously behind them. 'They haven't had the two of us in the same place for months, not since they dragged us up here from Mozambique.' Her tone made it clear she was fishing for information, her manner shifting as she tried to find the right way to charm him into a reply. 'I reckon they thought we'd collaborate on an escape plan.'

'Believe me when I tell you that this confinement has been for your protection as much as mine,' said Saito.

'Bullshit,' she snapped back. 'You could've turned your back and let me walk away. Do it now. I'll vanish. You know I can.'

'Yes, I know,' he admitted. 'But I do not trust you to remain silent.' Saito stopped and looked at her. 'You are a transactional creature, Grace. Guided by only one thing. A single question.'

'And what's that?'

'*What will benefit me?*'

She paused, and then chuckled, her guard falling for a moment. 'Damn. You got my number, don't you?'

Saito looked towards the youth.

'Where is he?'

The young man gestured at the ceiling with the Bizon, and the trio ascended the last flight of stairs to the top of the building.

Up there, more sheets of white sailcloth-like material crackled in the breeze off the river, forming a canopy over the whole of the rooftop. Light spilling from the nearby Rod El Farag Axis Bridge boosted the weak amber illumination from a couple of battery lanterns.

They came across two men on either side of a chessboard, care-worn wooden pieces laid out in a complex late-game pattern. One of the men was rough-hewn and wiry, and he had the look of an ex-soldier about him. Like the youth and his father, this one also had a Russian sub-machine gun, but he kept it to hand on a leather strap over his shoulder. He scrutinised the board over a glass of dark tea cupped in his hands, lost in the plotting of poten-tial stratagems.

Saito saw immediately that the guard was wasting his time. His opponent had framed any future moves with the king and the pawn, building a trap that could snap shut no matter what course he took.

The other player was the broken mirror of the man he had once been, splintered pieces reassembled in hopes of recovering what he had lost. Carved from weathered teak and tall, even as he sat, the African's patrician face was marred by burn scarring and the eye he had lost on the right side. One of his arms, lying awkwardly across his lap, would never work properly again, and the dam-age to his leg was suggested by the wooden walking stick resting against his chair. Like Grace, he wore shabby clothes in the local style, but even in those he kept an air of composure at odds with his circumstances.

Ekko Solomon looked up and his one good eye found Saito, his brow furrowing.

'You've arrived too late for this evening's match.' He caught sight of Grace and his frown deepened.

'The Réti endgame,' said Saito, indicating the board. 'You've already won.'

The ex-soldier saw it, too, and admitted defeat, conceding with a gruff nod. He rose, finishing his tea in a gulp, and stepped back. Without hesitating, Grace slipped between the men and dropped into the vacated chair, peering at the chess pieces. She picked up a crimson-coloured queen and toyed with it.

'I have had plenty of time to improve my game.' Solomon gripped the handle of his walking stick and leaned forward. 'What do you want, Saito?'

'Already asked that,' noted Grace.

At length, Saito gestured for the guards to give them some privacy, and he found a third chair, bringing it closer. He looked over the river towards the Giza side, putting his thoughts in order.

'I regret the circumstances that have brought you here,' he began. 'It was necessary.'

'We are both alive because of you,' rumbled Solomon. 'When those soldiers dug me out of the rubble in Mozambique, you were the one who concealed my survival from the Combine.' He nodded at the woman. 'Her capture should have ended in her execution. Instead, you had me cared for and Grace confined. Then you sent us north, to this safe house. You have never said why.'

'I've got some ideas,' said the woman. 'Keeping us as bargaining chips. As trade for something he wants.'

'That is not his way,' noted Solomon. 'Is it?'

Saito did not reply.

Grace made a show of looking around.

'This isn't a Combine enclave, though. Far too déclassé for them.' She pulled a face. 'I'm guessing ... GRU Fourth Directorate?' The Russian intelligence agency's Mid-East and African division had numerous covert stations throughout the Arab nations, and Saito admired the woman's perception. She saw she was right, and smirked. 'Which means either you're running this yourself as a side deal, or that rat-bastard Glovkonin is pulling the strings.'

'It is not Glovkonin,' said Solomon, dismissing the notion. 'He would not have let us live this long.'

Saito gave a curt nod. 'An exiled Russian general whose life I once spared repaid that favour, by providing this place and these men.'

'So, what's changed?' Grace eyed him, her tone light but the question sharp. 'I mean, me and handsome here are still breathing, and you show up out of the blue . . .'

'We are alive because we have value to Mr Saito.' Solomon sipped his own tea. The motion was slow and steady. He was still learning to deal with his new limitations. 'I await his answer to my previous question.'

'I want . . .' Saito hesitated. Saying the words aloud would make it real, and he would not be able to turn away from that truth any more. He pressed on. 'I want an end to it. I want to get *out*.'

'Don't we all, honey.'

Grace poured herself some of the tea and spooned a large amount of raw cane sugar into it.

'I have an offer,' Saito continued. 'If you help me with my goals, then you will have your lives and your freedom.'

Grace gave a bitter chuckle. 'I'm eager to hear the details, really, and this may be dumb of me to say the quiet part out loud, but why the hell would you ever trust me? Or him, for that matter?' She made a to-and-fro gesture. 'What's our *transaction*?'

Saito glanced at Solomon, then away.

'As long as the Combine exists, neither of you will be safe.' He nodded towards the African. 'You are a living embodiment of their failures – a man of similar means to them but uncorrupted by wealth's power. They cannot allow you to exist.' Then he turned to Grace. 'And you . . . You are a tool, a weapon they bought and then discarded when it became inconsequential. If you are not dealt with, they look weak. And believe me, these men have murdered indiscriminately in order to appear strong.'

Grace scowled at his description of her, but she did not reply. Saito saw two real, authentic emotions flicker in her eyes: *hate* and *fear*.

For his part, Solomon said nothing, but his silence spoke volumes. Saito had their full attention now.

He continued. 'First, as you are both no doubt considering how you might collaborate to kill me and escape, let me make it clear that if I do not make a call to a certain telephone number in the next hour, a data packet revealing the facts of your survival and your location will be transmitted to Pytor Glovkonin and the active measures group at the CIA. If that were to happen, I imagine neither of you would live to see the dawn. If you agree to comply with my requests, that packet will be held back, only to be released if you deviate from the task.'

'There's the stick,' muttered Grace. 'Got a carrot, too?'

'You both have good cause to seek the Combine's destruction. I am within the bounds of their cabal.' Saito placed a hand on his chest. 'Imagine what access I have. Think of how you could use that against them.'

Solomon and Grace sat silently as Saito told them the story of a man – a good man in a bad place, who had been forced into making terrible choices. His code and his decency were cut away from him piece by piece, until the day came when he was nothing but a killer in the employ of the venal and the vicious.

That man could never walk back from those choices. He had shaken hands with the Devil. But he still had a chance to make one thing right.

Saito felt his daughter's name on his lips again.

'I've sold my soul,' he said, at length. 'This act of defiance is the only thing left to me.'

'You think you can buy it back? Your soul?' Solomon gave him a level look. 'Believe me when I tell you that redemption is not a thing of scales and balances. It is a road that never ends.'

Saito stood up, and the two guards reacted, fingering their weapons. He waved them off with a raised hand.

'Do you accept?'

The two of them gave a wary nod.

'What the hell else am I going to say?' sniffed Grace.

Saito considered her for a moment. 'I will continue to monitor your movements. If either of you attempt to betray me, there will be consequences.'

'Understood,' said Solomon. 'Where are my people?'

Saito shook his head. 'I do not know. There have been sporadic sightings, but nothing confirmed. Both the Combine and Interpol have operatives watching for any appearance of agents from the Rubicon team.'

'Could be dead,' offered Grace.

'Like us?' Solomon eyed her. 'No. If that were so, it would be apparent. The Combine would not keep it quiet.' He looked back at Saito. 'To do what you ask, I'll need to find them.'

Grace's lip curled in a smirk.

'Well, there is *one* of them who'll be easy to track down. I mean, unless things have changed more than I expect in the last few months, I imagine he'll still be right where you left him.'

FOUR

The gold tower on the Avenue de Grande Bretagne became obsidian as night fell, the sheer face of the building shot through with streaks of light where certain floors remained illuminated, even though the working day was done.

The city-state of Monaco never really rested. Down in the streets spreading out towards the dark waters of the ocean, the energy of the place was constant, an invisible background hum of money and power.

Once, Henri Delancort had considered being here the summit of his achievements, living amid the glamour and glitz of the megarich, a far cry from the Montreal suburbs of Pointe-Claire where he had grown up. Delancort had worked hard to achieve all he had, and for a while it had been worth it. As the personal assistant and confidential aide to the founder of the Rubicon Group, he had made something of himself. He was proud of what he was.

Strange to think I ever felt that way.

Delancort exited the elevator on the fourth floor and began his march through the ruins of that life, his footsteps echoing as he threaded his way towards his office space.

Rubicon's presence in the tower was a pale shadow of what it had once been. A year ago, every level of the building had been given over to the operations of the corporation, with hundreds of staff administering Rubicon's holdings in aerospace, medicine, engineering, telecommunications and private security. Most of them were gone now, their workspaces relocated, their contracts forcibly terminated in the wake of the hostile takeover that had sounded Rubicon's death knell.

The tower was a honeycomb of ghost floors, atriums and rooms that had previously buzzed with activity now vacant, silent. Like the assets that had been under the Rubicon aegis, the building was being sold off for parts. A large Ukrainian banking and shipping concern had bought much of the complex, and they were already in the process of moving their people in. What remained of the Rubicon Group was little more than a shell, reduced to paying for tenancy in the tower that the company had built.

Delancort stalked past darkened offices, his angular reflection a captured phantom in their glass partitions. He felt numb, going through the motions, doing what was expected of him and nothing more. The man he saw in the windows, with the fox-like face and the prim manner, was a facade. As hollow as the building, Delancort had more than enough space to hold his regrets.

Someone was waiting for him in the office, and when Delancort saw who, he smothered his worried reaction with a blank look.

'Finally here,' said Andre, getting up from behind Delancort's desk. He made no attempt to explain what he had been doing there or why he was invading the other man's privacy, vacating the chair with an idle shrug. 'I was starting to wonder where you were.'

'I was told to come in, so I came,' Delancort replied flatly, refusing to rise to the bait.

He put down his briefcase and slid around the side of his desk, bumping into a filing cabinet as he moved. When he was Ekko Solomon's number two, Delancort had a workspace three times this size, a corner office with an excellent view of the hills. Here, they were in the armpit of the tower, in a spot constantly in shade during the day and darkened during the evening. He firmly believed that the current owner of the dregs of the company had put him there deliberately.

As if the thought of that man conjured his name, Andre invoked it.

'Mr Glovkonin asked me to bring these new directives here personally.' He waved a USB drive in the air.

'Doesn't he know how to use email?'

'He has me to handle that.'

Untidy piles of storage boxes filled the corners of the office, giving it a claustrophobic feel. Andre wandered around them, picking at their lids.

The other man had a slender frame, dressed in a suit that hung so badly on him, it was clear he had no idea how to wear it. Andre had a coarse French accent but he chose to speak English to Delancort, who wondered if that were some sideways insult towards his Québecois origins.

'What's wrong, Henri? Don't you like my company?' Andre finally sat in the room's only other chair, flicking the drive stick around in his fingers.

'You're really not my type.'

'I'm not,' he agreed. 'Not like the guys at that club . . .' He feigned confusion. 'What's it called? La Bleue? You go there a lot on your downtime, don't you?'

The rumours about Andre – *no last name, just always Andre* – said that the man had been a criminal hacker before he worked for Pytor Glovkonin, and Delancort saw no reason to doubt it. Andre liked to drop broad hints suggesting he knew intimate details of everyone's lives, using that to intimidate whoever wasn't automatically cowed by his connections to the Russian oligarch.

Tonight, Delancort was too tired and too irritated to let it go, and his mask of weary compliance slipped. He glared at the other man.

'Do you think for one moment I give a shit about your opinions of my lifestyle? I have been threatened by more impressive specimens than you.' He made a dismissive gesture. 'Deliver your message and then go away.'

Andre hesitated. He clearly had not expected Delancort to push back, and now that Henri had, the ex-hacker did not have a response.

'Here.' Scowling, Andre tossed the memory stick on the desk. 'Read it.'

Delancort woke his computer and inserted the drive. He found the files it contained and set to work decrypting them.

Andre stood up again, reminding Delancort of his superior position by looming over the desk.

'It must be hard for you to watch this happen, eh?' He gestured vaguely at the walls. 'Seeing the other board members pull away one by one. Keller, Cruz, McFarlane, cashing out. You can't blame them. Leaving the sinking ship, right?' He shook his head, blowing through his teeth. 'Your boss Solomon pretty much dragged this place down to the grave with him.'

Delancort's fingers froze over the keyboard and he closed his eyes. Every day he was forced to come back to this place was a reminder of Ekko Solomon, of the mentor who had given him a second chance.

The man I turned my back on.

He tried – and failed – to push the poisonous thought away. When Glovkonin and his allies in the Combine had launched their attack on Rubicon, Solomon had fled and asked Delancort to join him. But he had refused, believing that to carry on the fight would only result in more destruction.

For years, Delancort had tried to talk Solomon out of his private crusade, using the Special Conditions Division and Rubicon's resources to fight the Combine's machinations. It wasn't a battle they could win – Delancort had truly believed that. And in the end, he had been correct. But Solomon would not accept his counsel. His mentor was dead because he'd refused to give up that battle, and Delancort was sentenced to remain here in the ashes of that defeat.

Andre was right as well, in his own insulting fashion. Delancort had borne witness to the slow degradation and dissolution of everything Solomon had built. Trapped here, mired in the legal bindings of the contracts he had signed with Rubicon, sleepwalking towards his own end, with only his mistakes to keep him company.

'I hope you're not thinking of making a run for it yourself,' Andre went on, insincerity oozing from his words. 'That'd be a bad idea. I mean, technically you're still under investigation by Interpol because of that whole corporate-sponsored act of terrorism.' He gave a shrug. 'I mean, maybe it was some big mistake, maybe it was a false flag thing, a fake? But until that's decided, you take any kind of walk you're not supposed to and you are a fugitive.' Andre warmed to his subject, finding his feet again as he pushed home the point. 'No nights out at the club for guys on the run, huh?'

Delancort barely listened to him. The contents of the memory stick had his attention – the directives from G-Kor's head office in Moscow. The man controlling Rubicon's fate had ordered the transfer of hundreds of thousands of euros, from the company accounts in Monaco to a small technology provider in Istanbul.

Altin Elma.

The name of the Turkish company rang a distant bell in Delancort's mind, but he couldn't place it. He had the vague recollection of it being one of Rubicon's former satellite companies, but nothing more than that.

Usually, Glovkonin's orders wouldn't have passed through Delancort's hands at all, but a quirk of Rubicon's corporate structure meant that the ranking company man in the Monaco office had to sign off on a payment of this kind. And with Ekko Solomon dead, that man was Henri Delancort.

He scrutinised the paperwork. Altin Elma had been tasked to work on a priority project but there were no details, only a payment due for its completion. He weighed up what he saw. This was not the first time that such unexplained movements of money and materiel had occurred since the hostile takeover. It was Glovkonin's company G-Kor stripping assets and plundering resources, attempting to keep the details hidden from legal oversight.

'So?' Andre snapped his fingers in front of Delancort's face. 'What are you waiting for? Approve it and move on to the next one.'

'This does not seem correct,' he noted. 'I need more details.'

'You don't need anything!' Andre's tone hardened. 'You think I came here to argue with you? Shut up and do what you are told.'

Delancort's mouth thinned to a hard line, and he put aside the transfer authorisation for a moment, looking at what else Glovkonin demanded. There was a second and a third directive on the memory stick, and as Delancort read on, his stomach twisted into knots.

The second directive was another transfer. This one specified the complete movement of all operating capital in Rubicon's salary holdings. Effectively, it would see every last euro set aside to pay the company's remaining caretaker staff siphoned off to Russia. It would leave them with nothing.

He knew what the third directive would say before he read a word of it. It was a contractual termination order, the tool to fire the last few people who worked for what remained of the Rubicon Group. Delancort sat back in his chair, staring at the death warrant for the company he had dedicated his life to.

Glovkonin had known this was how things would play out. Delancort always suspected the Russian had forced him to remain at his post out of spite, perhaps because he had not been able to take out his ire on Solomon.

He wants me to personally sign off on these directives. He wants to make me pull the trigger.

'Do I have to tell you again?' said Andre.

Delancort looked up at him, and for the first time he realised that there were shadows moving in the adjacent office. With the light of day gone, he could make out two men in the other room, the forms of figures in military-style jackets, prowling about and waiting for the call to violence.

ALEPH. It has to be them.

The Combine's pet thugs were always hanging around the tower, menacing presences meant to keep Delancort and the others in line.

Early on, in the first days after the G-Kor takeover, some people who were obstructive or overly vocal suddenly failed to report to work. There was talk of 'accidents' and after that, everyone toed the line.

If I do this, will I be the next to be discarded?

His hand hesitated over the computer's fingerprint scanner, which would read his imprint and digitally authorise the directives to progress forward.

Once he signed off, Delancort would have no more value. But what other choice did he have? He couldn't look away from the shadows in the other room. There was nowhere else he could go.

He pressed his thumb to the scanner, and the computer gave an answering beep.

Grinning, Andre reached over and pulled the memory stick from its reader.

'That's more like it.' He flicked a cocky salute. 'Enjoy the rest of your evening, Henri.'

Delancort watched Andre walk away into the gloom, back towards the elevators. After a moment, the shadows in the other office detached and followed, leaving him to clasp his trembling hands together and listen to the hammering of his heartbeat.

The night air was unseasonably warm, so Marc shrugged off his black TEC hoodie and lay back on the rickety sun lounger. He closed his eyes and listened to the river-rush sound of traffic on the motorway a few kilometres distant.

Atop the empty office in Torcy, someone had left behind a makeshift smokers' den when they abandoned the place. A pair of patched and broken loungers and an unsteady table of rain-swollen wood sat near a coffee can overflowing with stale cigarette butts and the caps from beer bottles, hidden out of sight by air conditioning units and the roof access shed.

It was bad op-sec to be up here. Although the office wasn't overlooked by any other buildings, there was no concealment, nothing to stop Marc from being spotted by a drone passing overhead. With the right kit, a watcher would be able to pick out his face.

He cracked open one eye. The sky above was a thick layer of grey cloud, under-lit by street lights and so low he could almost reach up and touch it. Anything coming down to look at him would have to be close enough to swat with his bare hands.

Been there, he thought, *done that.*

The access shed door clanked and swung open. Marc turned his head to see Lucy emerge, a plastic carrier bag dangling from one hand.

'Hey,' she said.

She wore the same sort of fleece as Marc's, with the hood pulled up and her braids pooling around her neck.

'Hey yourself.'

Lucy automatically looked up into the sky, and Marc smirked.

Same impulse, he told himself, *same training.*

'Shouldn't be up here—' she began, but he waved her off.

'I know, I know. But honestly, I'm willing to risk it for some peace and quiet.'

She halted. 'Oh. Okay. You want a little *me* time, I get it.' Lucy turned to go.

'Don't.' Marc shook his head. A moment ago, he'd wanted the chance to be alone for a while, but now she was here, that seemed selfish.

Lucy understood, and she wandered over.

'So what are you at?'

He nudged the coffee can ashtray with the tip of his trainer.

'Having a crafty ciggy.'

'You don't smoke.'

'Thinking about starting. Need something to de-stress.'

He closed his eyes again, and listened to the other lounger creak as Lucy sat. She was close enough for him to sense her there, just within reach.

'Filthy habit,' she noted. 'I got something better.'

He heard the rustle of plastic and then the low pop of a stopper. Fluid gurgled and the rich aroma of liquor reached his nostrils.

He opened his eyes and found her offering him a disposable plastic cup containing a generous measure of brown liquid. In the other hand she had produced a bottle of Rémy Martin XO.

'Cognac? Where'd you get that?'

She gave him an *isn't it obvious* shrug.

'We're in France, duh. They practically wean their kids on this.'

He took a sip and savoured the smooth burn. The little indulgence helped. It gave Marc something else to think about instead of the day's disappointment.

Lucy read his thoughts as if they were being projected out in front of him.

'The scrub of the surveillance data is almost done. But I gotta level with you, it doesn't look good. With that and the other partial leads . . .' She paused and took a drink. 'Well, like they say, that dog won't hunt.'

Marc nodded. 'We've still got Malte's take to look at when he gets in. That could make the difference.'

'It better.' Lucy topped up her cup and Marc's, then paused, staring into the liquid. 'You know what today is?' He shook his head and she continued. 'It's Ari Silber's birthday.'

'Oh.'

A slow jab of regret pushed into him. They all missed the veteran pilot, with his easy smile and his endless catalogue of war stories. Ari had flown them into and out of dozens of bad situations, but the life had finally caught up with him in the skies over East Africa. He'd got them down safe, but Ari hadn't escaped the burning fuselage of their crashed aircraft. Marc felt a breeze on his face and for a moment, the sense-memory of smoke and burning aviation fuel was right there. He scowled, rejecting it.

Ari wasn't the only one they had lost. Their flight from the Combine had taken Assim Kader along with him, when the young Saudi hacker was gunned down. And then there was Solomon.

Marc raised the cup. 'To absent friends.'

Lucy nodded. 'Absent friends.'

She downed the contents of her cup in one go, and refilled it. Marc looked away and pretended that he didn't see the shimmer of tears in her eyes.

'This one time, when we were on Solomon's Airbus over the Atlantic, middle of the night, he told me something.' Marc let the story come up as he nursed his drink. 'Started off as two pilots bullshitting each other, yeah? Me the chopper guy, him the jet jockey. Comparing notes on the worst things we'd ever had to deal with in the air.' He made a winding motion with his free hand. 'When I served in the navy, the helo crash I survived when my Lynx went down . . . That was because of a storm. Lightning struck the rotors and we lost power. He told me the same thing happened to him once.'

'Ari flew F-15s for the Israeli Air Force, right?' said Lucy.

Marc nodded. 'He's on this moonless night flight, skirting a storm over the ocean, and he drifts off course. Lightning strike hits his bird, *zap*, fries the avionics, everything goes dark.' He made a flat, winged shape with his hand, drifting it through the air. 'So now he has no radio and it's black as pitch outside, he can't tell how high he is or what direction he's heading. If he's going the wrong way, he'll keep flying out over the sea until his tanks are dry and . . .' Marc dipped the wing in a steep dive. 'So what does he do?'

'He turned in to the storm.'

Marc paused. 'You've heard this one?'

She shook her head and showed a sad smile. 'No. But I know Ari.'

Marc went on. 'He turned in to the storm, because he figured it was moving towards the coastline. He flew that bent jet right through the wind and the rain, got it back to dry land, and lived to tell the tale.'

Lucy leaned closer. 'And the moral of the story?'

'When you're in the storm . . . you have to keep going.'

She gave a low chuckle. 'I see what you did there.'

'We have to keep going, Lucy,' he told her. 'Whatever the setbacks, however long it takes to burn down the Combine. Otherwise, what's all this for?'

'I just . . .' She covered her pause with another sip of cognac. 'For every two steps forward, we get pushed back one.' She met his gaze. 'And they're close, Marc. Glovkonin's people, ALEPH . . . they almost had us in Tangiers.'

He nodded, remembering their fraught escape the previous month.

'Yeah. If Kara hadn't worked her magic, we'd be dead and gone.'

Mentioning Kara Wei's name made Lucy's manner harden. She wasn't going to let go of her baggage over her former friend's betrayal any time soon, even though the hacker was doing all she could to mend that trust.

'We're not going down that road.' Lucy's eyes hardened, before Marc could say more. 'I don't wanna get into it.'

'We need to be a team,' Marc told her, holding her gaze. 'You need to put aside your problems with her.'

'That an order?' She cocked her head. 'I mean, you're leading now, right? It's your mission, you set this running.'

'It's everyone's mission,' he shot back. 'Don't act like that's what you're sore about.'

'Oh, you know what I'm sore about?'

She rocked back, her ire building. The flash of vulnerability she'd shown a moment before vanished.

'Yeah, I think I do.' Marc matched her tone. 'None of us have any illusions here. We're working without a net. We screw up and there's no one to bail us out. This . . .' He made a circling motion. 'This is all we have. We have to pull together.'

Lucy opened her mouth, and he knew she was about to throw back a retort – but then her annoyance waned.

'Okay,' she began, 'all right. Because you ask me. I'll back it off. But don't expect me to be best buds with her again. Kara's not the woman I thought I knew.'

'You're right, she isn't,' he admitted. 'So work with who she *is*.'

Lucy made a show of studying him. 'She's not the only one that's different.'

He looked away, shaking his head. 'Don't start in on me. I'm winging this. I'm not . . .' Marc stumbled over the name before he could say it.

'Not Solomon?' Lucy said gently.

He felt the tension crawling back into him.

'I don't know how he ever managed to stay so cool about it. It's like the weight of the fucking world. Benjamin, Kara, Malte, even you . . . Looking to me to steer this.'

'You took the lead, so you take the burden,' she told him, moving closer again.

'I hope I can carry it.' He sighed. 'That's why I need my team. It's why I . . . need you.'

Lucy looked back at him, and Marc felt as if he was losing himself in those striking amber eyes.

'Ari always told me to live in the moment,' she said, her tone shifting, deepening. 'Never really got that until he was gone.' She rolled back the hood and leaned in towards Marc. 'I don't wanna think about what we don't have. Let's stick to what we got.'

Marc gave in to the impulse and closed the distance, meeting her. She kissed him deeply, gently, the slow fire of the cognac on their lips.

He dropped the cup and reached for her, but she held him away, placing one hand on his face. Her fingers were cool on his cheek. She didn't speak, a question in her eyes.

He hesitated. Marc and Lucy had been to the precipice of this before, more than once, but never gone beyond it. In fire and danger, in adversity that had taken them to the edge of death, a bond between them had been forged, something that defied simple description. It was more than *trust*. That word wasn't strong enough, powerful enough to encompass it.

And suddenly he saw how foolish it was to believe there might be a moment that was right, that was perfect, when things would be clear and uncluttered between them. There was only what they had, right here and right now.

Marc drew her closer, and he felt her push against his body as they kissed again. Heat charged through him and his blood raced. He drew back the zip of her fleece, unbuttoned the top beneath, and ran his hand over the smooth skin of her belly. Her fingers came up under his T-shirt, spreading, exploring him.

He broke off to take a husky breath. 'You're not going to smack me in the face again, are you?'

'That depends,' she whispered.

The Gulfstream rumbled through a pocket of turbulence that set the glassware rattling in the executive jet's cabin. Glovkonin gave an irritated grunt of disapproval as the tumbler of Stolichnaya Elit before him migrated across the table of its own accord. He snatched up the vodka and drained it, grimacing.

The clean sting from the alcohol had barely abated when the pilot came over the intercom to apologise for the disturbance. There was a storm cell over the Kerch Strait, he explained, forcing them to take a longer route from the Crimean peninsula and down the Russian coast on their approach to Sochi.

Glovkonin glared out of the window, unable to shake the sullen mood that had taken root in him before departing Paris. He looked down through broken cloud illuminated in strobing blinks of light from the jet's running lights. Slices of shimmering water were visible here and there, sections of the Black Sea glittering like shards of onyx.

Unable to settle, he shifted in the soft leather of his chair, uncomfortable wherever he rested. It was uncommon behaviour for the Russian, and he recognised that in himself. It was his frustration, working its way to the surface.

The transfer of the equipment for the Combine's new project was the Italian's responsibility, and that had been made very clear to him before the meeting in the apartments had been disrupted and cut short. But Glovkonin's plan to push the other man aside and have the committee grant *him* that obligation had not come to pass. He had never had the chance to make his move, and now he was a step behind.

Glovkonin loathed any suggestion of him being out of pace. The best he could do would be to make up the loss on the fly.

It was a matter of faith. He had little confidence in the other man's abilities beyond his skills at bedding pliant women, gambling and separating his many gullible investors from their money. There was too much at stake with this project to put it in the hands of a man so profoundly flippant. Glovkonin leveraged his own contacts in the Russian Federation to ensure that he would also be a key participant in this transfer.

And if I can further my own personal goals at the same time, so much the better.

The Italian was too much in love with his own legend, cutting back and forth across Europe acting the playboy while others in the Combine worked in the shadows. They were impediments to Glovkonin's advancement, of course, the American farmer and the Swiss banker as well, but he disliked the Italian the most.

Making an attempt to shake off his bad mood, he cheered himself with the thought that the self-aggrandising peacock would be dealt with soon enough. Glovkonin had already killed his way into the Combine's inner circle, and he had no intention of stopping there.

The others have to suspect that, he thought. *They're not fools. They know I have ambition and the will to back it.* But he knew the answer. *They don't believe they can be threatened. That will be the arrogance that brings them down, in the end.*

He sensed a presence behind him and turned to find Misha, one of his bodyguards.

'A call for you, sir,' he said, in his rolling Georgian accent. 'It's the Frenchman.'

The ex-Spetsnaz operative waited patiently, cradling a wireless telephone in the beefy paw of one hand. Glovkonin took the handset and dismissed Misha without a word.

'Report,' he demanded.

Andre's voice had an odd echo, a sure sign that the call was being scrambled.

'*The directives have been delivered and enacted.*'

'Any resistance?'

'*No. They're like whipped dogs. I think some are actually relieved it is over.*' He paused, and Glovkonin could hear him smirk. '*By tomorrow night, the last pieces of the Rubicon Group will be dissolved. You won, sir.*'

'Not yet. I don't want any more loose ends,' he noted. 'We are at an important juncture.'

'*Of course.*' Andre paused, taking his time over the next issue they were to discuss. '*And the fugitives?*'

Glovkonin took the opportunity to dress him down.

'Your performance in that arena has been lacking, to say the least. While you have been wasting time chasing blind leads on the dark net, the targets came to me. They were within *striking distance*, do you understand what that means?'

'*I can only apologise again, sir,*' Andre said quickly. '*They're difficult targets – experienced, hard to track. I know their digital systems expert, and she's very skilled . . .*' He drifted off, falling silent, sensing Glovkonin's irritation at his excuses.

The Russian reached for a data tablet in the pocket of his seat, activating it by pressing his thumbprint to an embedded reader. The screen lit up with a gallery of image captures, some taken from cameras outside the apartments in Paris, others co-opted from police body cameras and CCTV feeds. With terse flicks of his hand, Glovkonin paged through photos of the duo who had attempted to surveil the Combine committee's gathering.

The images didn't show them clearly but he knew their names. *Marc Dane* and *Lucy Keyes*. Still not dead, despite a good many attempts to end their lives.

'Have the other members of the committee seen this material?'

'*No, sir. I secured it immediately after the . . . ah . . . incident.*'

'Keep it under wraps. I want any new information brought to me first, am I clear?'

Andre paused again. His loyalty belonged to the Combine as a whole, who had taken him on after the hacker collective he worked with had been torn apart by law enforcement in a dozen countries. But the Frenchman had a base cunning about him, and he was intelligent enough to understand where the power lay in this relationship. He was smart enough to back the right horse.

'*Very clear, sir.*'

Glovkonin studied a blurry shot of Dane and Keyes, the pair of them caught ascending a staircase up from a Métro platform. For months now, he had been personally directing the hunt for them, drawing on the Combine's resources to track down and terminate them. They had resolutely remained unfound, fleeing from ALEPH's investigator teams whenever they got close.

But rather than running and working to stay one step ahead of the Combine's pursuit, Dane and Keyes had flipped the dynamic. *They* were tracking *him*.

A bold move, he had to admit. But so very reckless. And perfectly in line with what he knew of the Englishman's character.

'I should have anticipated this,' he said, almost to himself. 'Perhaps we can make it work for us.'

Andre answered the next question before he asked it.

'*We don't know what they know,*' he admitted, '*but it can't be much. Look at the risk they took to bug that meeting. It's a gamble . . . And they botched it, you know?*'

'They still escaped,' Glovkonin snapped, as the hacker's tone become overly familiar. 'What about Solomon's former aide there in Monaco? Have they made any contact with him?'

'*Delancort?*' Andre sneered the man's name. '*We would know if he had any unusual communications. He's being monitored.*' There was another pause. '*If Delancort is considered a loose end, I can have it tied off.*'

Glovkonin turned that thought over in his mind.

'I will let you know. For now, continue with your assignment. And *do better.*'

He cut the call and handed the phone back to Misha.

The jet shuddered again and banked into a shallow turn. Within the hour they would start their descent towards Sochi, angling in towards the coastal resort, across the beaches and the complex left over from the 2014 Winter Olympics.

Glovkonin paid little attention to that, his thoughts orbiting the problem at hand. He would have to move carefully, planning each gambit like the exchanges in a championship chess match. Tracking Dane and the other Rubicon survivors risked splitting his focus, when his first priority was removing the Italian from the board. Would it be possible to use one against the other? It was an enticing idea, and he let himself consider the shape and weight of it.

Dangerous, he admitted to himself, *but compelling.*

And at the rare heights through which Pytor Glovkonin moved, there were so few games worth the effort.

FIVE

'Malte's here.'

Lucy was making coffee in the corner of their covert workspace when Kara sing-songed the warning, and she gave a sideways nod, still busy with her morning eye-opener. Time in the military, and then working for Rubicon's Special Conditions Division, had weaned her off what she'd grown up with thinking of as coffee. She was now a full-on hallelujah convert to the dark and powerful nectar that her European team-mates drank. She brewed it strong and savoured the aroma, making sure she had an additional full mug to offer the Finn as he emerged from the stairwell.

'Welcome back,' she told him.

Malte Riis nodded and gratefully accepted the mug, slipping his pack off his shoulder. He looked tired from the long flight. Pale, clean-shaven and average in build, he was the kind of guy your gaze would slip right off if you saw him in the street – something that had been a benefit in his early career as an undercover officer for the Finnish *rikospoliisi*. In his work with Rubicon, Malte's speciality was behind the wheel, serving as the team's primary driver, but since the collapse of the SCD he'd drifted back to his original skill set. Everyone had adapted to the new circumstances, and his had sent him on a months-long assignment to Hong Kong, chasing up vital intelligence from sources across the border in mainland China.

He glanced around the room, taking everything in with those hard cop eyes of his, without uttering a word. Malte's gaze lingered on Marc, busy hooking up a video projector, and then he pointedly glanced back at Lucy. The Finn's expression didn't alter, not one iota, but he was still asking a question.

'What?' she said, more defensively than she meant to.

How could he know?

Neither Marc nor Lucy had said anything to anyone about what had happened on the roof the night before, but Malte was giving her a look that made her feel like they were both wearing T-shirts that read *Yeah, We Had Sex.*

'Nothing,' said the Finn, without weight.

He grabbed his pack and carried it over to the table, exchanging nods with Kara and Benjamin.

'No pressure,' began Kara, without preamble, 'but things here were a bust, so everyone's counting on you to bring us a game-changer.'

'Huh.' Malte considered that for a second. 'Lucky.'

From a concealed compartment in his pack, he drew out a USB drive and tossed it to the hacker. Kara cupped the thing in her hands and blew on it, giving the device a blessing.

The room fell silent as the rest of them let Kara do what she did best, waiting as she sifted valuable nuggets of information from the files Malte had couriered to them. How his contact had come across them was not a thread that Lucy wanted to pull on, but she suspected there were elements inside the Chinese Ministry for State Security who were playing both sides against the middle. Messing with a Combine strategy was win-win to them; the nationless group of elites were as much a problem to the People's Republic as they were to the free world.

Enemy of my enemy and all that shit, Lucy told herself.

None of them wanted to think about what had been done to get this vital data. It had to be worth it.

Eventually, the hacker emerged from her labours and looked up at them with a start. She hadn't been aware of them watching her.

'So, good result. Merging the take from Paris with this puts us in a slightly better position,' noted Kara. 'We now have a partial picture of the Combine's current plans.'

Marc picked up a tablet computer and read the files mirrored there.

'Intercepted communications from cellphone networks in Eastern Europe,' he noted. 'We have Combine assets discussing a transfer that will take place in the next forty-eight hours.'

'A transfer of what?' said Benjamin, worrying at his moustache. 'People? Money? Weapons?'

'Unclear.' Kara gave a brisk shake of the head. 'When they discuss the payload in question, the phrase that keeps turning up is *the equipment*. No more detail than that.'

Lucy shot Marc a look. 'I heard that. When we had the laser mike on them in that fancy-ass apartment, one of them said—'

'*The equipment is being assembled, and everything will be in place for zero hour.*' Pytor Glovkonin's studied tones issued out of a speaker atop Kara's computer stack, the waveforms from the playback writhing on the screen.

'That sounds ominous,' said Marc. 'All right, whatever this is they're on about, based on their past form we can be sure it's going to be a show-stopper. The Combine don't put this much grunt into anything small-scale, it's not their style.'

'Synchronous suicide bombings. Portable nuclear devices. Biological weapons.' Kara ticked them off on her fingers.

'Cyberwarfare,' added Malte, giving the hacker a pointed look.

'Yes, that too,' she admitted. 'And those are the gigs we know about. As Marc says, the Combine like to go big. Each attempt they've made in the past five years to move the needle to their advantage has been through manipulation of a terrorist atrocity with a high body count.'

'Rubicon interfered with their operations so they took us out of play,' mused Benjamin. 'Or so they think. Without us around to put a drag on their ambitions, I fear that the Combine might want to make up for lost time. Do something truly unpleasant, on a grander scale.'

'Worse than nukes or viral warfare?' Lucy scowled, and unconsciously reached for her throat. She had taken a dose of a Combine-sponsored bioweapon the year before in Belgium.

'It is the nature of the unrepentant bully, when thwarted, to hit back twice as hard,' said the big man. 'And you have thwarted them quite a bit, *oui*?'

'We have to know more about what they're planning so we can put a stop to it.' Marc put down the tablet and drew himself up. He took in the rest of the team with an earnest look. 'We've been searching for a way to take them out, once and for all. This could be it.' He came closer, his hands moving in the air. 'They've cut our legs out from under us, scattered us to the winds. The Combine reckon we are *finished*.'

'Are they wrong?' muttered Malte, around his coffee. He cast a meaningful look at the shabby surroundings of the abandoned office.

'That's up to us.' Marc threw a nod in the Finn's direction. 'Glovkonin and his mates swan around like they're unopposed, yeah? We'll use that to our advantage. Their weak point is their arrogance.' He gave a dry chuckle. 'Blokes like them, it always is.'

'So the chatter about this transfer comes from Eastern Europe.' Lucy paced her thoughts out loud. 'We got an idea of where, exactly?'

'Russian Federation,' said Malte. 'Voronezh. Saratov.'

'And a lot of pings on the Caspian Sea coast,' added Kara. 'Those locations correlate with known criminal hubs, Russian military assets . . . and G-Kor corporate holdings.'

G-Kor was Pytor Glovkonin's rapacious energy and construction conglomerate, and the front for much of the oligarch's illegal enterprises. In the New Russia, the company was essentially a state-within-the-state, allowed to operate above the law as long as the government remained well compensated for looking the other way, and the wider interests of the Kremlin were not threatened.

'So smart money says *the equipment* is military hardware.' Lucy mused on that. 'Another bomb? We know they were after a suitcase nuke at one time.'

Marc shook his head. 'Possible, but I don't think so. Jurgen would have heard something, he would have sent up a flare.' Marc's contact Jurgen Goss worked with the International Atomic Energy Agency's Office of Nuclear Security, the group responsible for gathering intelligence on the illegal proliferation of atomic weapons and radioactive material. 'They learned their lesson after the Exile device got loose. It must be something else.'

'There's more than one flavour of WMD,' said Kara, with a cat-like smile that didn't reach her eyes.

Benjamin cleared his throat. 'I do not want to talk out of turn . . . I am the new addition here, so to speak. I haven't been in the field on these other operations like the rest of you . . .' He ran a hand over his head, frowning. 'But I would be remiss if I did not ask the question. We have actionable intelligence in our hands, but the resources at our disposal lessen by the day. We could get this information into the hands of any one of a dozen national security agencies – the CIA, MI6, DGSE, Mossad. We could let them take the lead. The list of those who have suffered at the hands of the Combine is lengthy.'

'Fair point,' said Marc. 'But don't forget, there's people in those organisations who have prospered from the Combine's actions as well. And if we turn over what we know, we risk showing our hand to Glovkonin and his mates.' He paused. 'I'm willing to trust the people in this room and not many more.'

'There's also the whole thing about being wanted fugitives,' said Kara, snapping the words briskly. 'Her Majesty's Government threw Rubicon under the bus to protect their own when that fake attack video surfaced. They did everything they could to distance MI6 from the Special Conditions Division.'

Lucy grimaced, recalling the so-called 'deepfake' footage that had superimposed her face and Marc's over those of killers who had assaulted a UN military installation in Cyprus's Green Zone. The vision of seeing herself cast as a cold-blooded terrorist stuck with her, embedded in her mind's eye. She glanced at Marc and saw the same distance in his expression, and she knew he was remembering it, too.

'The Central Intelligence Agency would not be receptive, either.' Kara was still speaking. 'They've had Rubicon on their watch lists for quite a while, thanks to Lucy's antics in their backyard.'

'Bottom line – we do this ourselves or not at all.' Marc summed it up with a terse nod.

But Lucy was still dwelling on those chilling images, turning them over and over in her thoughts. The world had seen the doctored videos and accepted them at face value, branding the team as murderers. And while the men and women directly responsible for those acts had been crossed off, the lie was out there with a life of its own. As much as she wanted to burn down the Combine, Lucy still held out the hope of one day clearing their names. But she had no idea how to achieve both goals.

'How do we proceed?' said Benjamin.

'We need an entry vector,' noted Marc. 'A way to get close to the Combine's operations and crack it open. A weak point.'

Kara gave a slow nod. 'I have a primo option for that.'

Malte raised a quizzical eyebrow.

'Show him what we have,' said Lucy, jutting her chin towards Kara.

With the Finn busy halfway around the world, the rest of the team had worked on cracking one of the toughest challenges they'd ever faced – learning the true identities of the men who made up the Combine's ruling cadre.

To kill a demon, first you have to be able to name it.

As it turned out, the advice Lucy had gleaned from old horror movies worked just as well as it did with one-percenter shit-heels who thought they were untouchable.

As Kara brought up new files on to her screen, Marc activated the projector and threw a mirror of that display on to the cracked plaster of the nearest wall.

'This has cost us a big, big wedge of what we had in black budget money,' he explained to Malte, who took it in. 'Months of bribes and blind alleys and intelligence gathering, all for some names and faces. Now we're going to find out if it was worth the price.'

The first face up on the wall was a familiar one – the angular features of Pytor Glovkonin, caught in a long-lens shot stepping down the gangway of a business jet.

'We all know this prick,' offered Lucy, her anger turning cold. 'And we all know who he took from us.'

'He's smart, but he's arrogant as fuck,' said Marc, with the certainty that only first-hand experience could bring. 'Greedy with it. He knows us, knows our faces. Chances of getting close to Glovkonin without him being aware of it are very low. We can't risk it.'

'Next candidate,' said Kara. The image switched to a blurry picture of a portly older man, who looked to Lucy like her stuffy high school principal. 'Swiss banker. Rolling in cash, mostly other people's, wired into the global monetary grid like he's Neo in *The Matrix*. This is their money guy.'

'Rutger Bremmens.' Marc gestured at the picture. 'Top of the heap at KantonBank Basel Zeta, one of the largest financial institutions in Europe, in the big six globally. That picture is five years old, and it's the most recent we could find. Bremmens is the oldest member of the Combine's inner circle, and he's the most reclusive. Rarely leaves Switzerland other than for meetings with the rest of the cabal, and *never* sets foot outside Europe. He's got an estate in the Jungfrau region where he lives alone, heavily protected by the top echelon of mercs hired from ALEPH. He's single-handedly responsible for ruining the economies of at least four Third World nations, and he makes millions profiting off insider trading and illegal currency manipulation. As far as we can find, he has no family, no lovers, no nothing.'

'Sits up there counting his francs and jerkin' off to the stock market,' muttered Lucy.

'Next.' Kara tapped her keyboard again, and the old man was replaced by a middle-aged guy with a ruddy face, wearing a shiny grey suit with a loud tie. The ensemble was incongruously topped with a brightly coloured baseball cap that sat off kilter on his head. 'The farm boy.'

Marc carried on with his briefing. 'Connaught Cassidy III, American agriculture and construction magnate. Odds are, if you eat something anywhere inside the continental US, it's gone through one of Cassidy's companies at some point. He owns farms, food processing plants, warehouses, trucking concerns. His hands are in tobacco and biomedicine. Fingers in a lot of pies, this one, and he likes his politics.'

'Publicly, the redder the state the better,' noted Lucy, 'but privately he doesn't care as long as it gets him the green. This guy splits his time between his holdings in Iowa, Kentucky and Washington DC. Currently on his sixth wife. Same as Bremmens, he likes his home turf better than anywhere else. Plays up the whole shit-kicker-made-good angle, and I believe he has "America First" tattooed on his cock.'

'Really?' said Benjamin.

Lucy shrugged. 'He's the type.'

Marc gave a crooked smile. 'She's not wrong. Cassidy is your textbook profiteer. If he can screw money out of something or someone, he'll do it without hesitation. What he doesn't use to fund his expensive habits, he invests in buying political influence, and covertly bankrolling domestic extremist groups, like the America Alone Alliance and the Soldier-Saints.'

Malte gave a sullen grunt at the mention of the Soldier-Saints. He and Lucy had faced off against that radical militia group during an attempted bombing in San Francisco, and barely lived to tell the tale.

Kara moved on to the final image. 'And here's our guy.'

Where the other pictures had been fuzzy and off kilter, as if shot quickly and surreptitiously by some clandestine observer, this one was crisp, clean and square on. It looked more like something that would have been posted on the account of a high-rolling social media influencer than a surveillance photo. In it, a swarthy man in a sand-coloured suit stood in conversation with a managerial type, next to a crimson Ferrari Enzo on the forecourt of some opulent hotel. He carried himself with obvious confidence, grinning, caught in the middle of gesturing. Heavy gold rings were visible on his hands, along with a large, diamond-studded Jacob & Co. wristwatch.

'I can see this one is a subtle sort of fellow,' deadpanned Benjamin.

'Giovanni Da Silvio,' said Kara, 'of the Da Silvio Ingegneria fortune. Born in Turin, parents died early, leaving him at the head of an engineering and transportation empire with global reach and deep, deep pockets. The other Combine committee members tend to keep themselves off the radar, even Glovkonin, but this one likes to hide in plain sight. Outwardly, he's your stereotypical idle-rich billionaire – but that's his protective coloration. He's in deep with organised crime networks in Russia, Europe, America and Asia, and his speciality is trafficking.'

'In what?' Malte cocked his head.

'Anything and everything.' Marc picked up the thread again. 'Drugs, weapons, people . . . if it's illegal, he'll ship it – after he takes his own bit off the top first, of course. Da Silvio is the Combine's transportation and logistics guy, so if there's something going on, he's the one moving the hardware for it. This *equipment* they're talking about.'

Lucy stood up and walked towards the projection on the wall, studying the Italian's face.

'We're targeting him. He doesn't know any of us by sight, and he's always moving around, following the party circuit. We can get near to this one.'

Malte nodded. 'How?'

Kara put up a new display, this one a video file showing stream-lined shapes like manta rays flashing across the surface of an emerald lake, leaving bright white wakes behind them. On the shoreline, crowds were lined up to watch.

'Da Silvio Ingegneria co-sponsors an international powerboat championship, taking place at a dozen venues around the Med and elsewhere. The race's investors are a who's who of Bratva and Mafia types, and they use it to launder cash. Motorsport is one of the most expensive pastimes in the world, after all . . .'

The video switched to shots of the exclusive owners' boxes, the camera panning past Da Silvio and a group of hard-eyed men who were cheering on the racers.

'The fourth meet in the race series happens this week,' said Marc. 'In Sochi, on the Russian Black Sea coast. And that's where we're going to work this bloke, use him to pry open the Combine and reach inside.'

'It sounds simple when you say it like that,' said Benjamin.

Marc didn't reply, but he caught Lucy's eye and his expression was firm and unreadable.

'Start packing up the kit,' he ordered. 'We need to be on the way by sunset.'

The fear that prickled along the back of Delancort's neck became a claw, digging its talons deeper into his skin the further he walked between the buildings.

In the Beausoleil backstreets, across the open border with France where many of Monaco's working population resided, the fading haze of the sun grazed the tops of the skinny residential blocks. In the narrow canyons between them, the air was still and heavy, steeped in gloom.

Delancort made his way towards the security door that would give him entrance to the apartments where he lived, too anxious to throw a look over his shoulder in case he saw what he feared. From the corner of his eye, he glimpsed movement in the shade, reflected in the window of a parked car. Perhaps a figure watching from a doorway . . . perhaps nothing.

He believed that ALEPH's thugs were following his movements outside the office, to intimidate him. To let him know that he lived only as long as he had value to the men who'd broken Rubicon. Delancort was afraid that time had come to an end, however.

How much longer could this go on, until he vanished like the others who had outlived their usefulness? Would it be quick? Would they make it look like an accident?

Delancort had taken to being extremely careful when crossing the street, for fear that some unseen hand might suddenly shove him into the path of an oncoming vehicle.

He was ten metres from the door.

The muscles in his thighs bunched, and he had to fight down the urge to break into a sprint. He pulled the electronic key fob from his pocket and made ready with it, holding the thing in a white-knuckle grip. His heart hammered in his chest.

Why was this even necessary? Why follow him home when they knew exactly where he lived?

Why not wait inside for me, unseen and unexpected . . .?

Delancort's blood ran cold as the terrifying thought suddenly occurred to him. It would be simple for one of ALEPH's operatives to gain access to his home. He pictured it now – seeing himself open the door to his apartment, only to find a killer within.

He blinked sweat from his eyes. His mind raced. What if he kept walking? He could find somewhere safe, somewhere public. Surely they would not try to hurt him in front of witnesses?

Was he willing to take that risk?

He was five metres from the door.

A metal barrier with a glass insert, the door was an unlovely retrofit that sat awkwardly over the shabby-chic 1950s build beneath. The apartments had once been three residences, a row of tall town houses in the Victorian style, before a developer had knocked them together into a single building. Juliet balconies of white-painted iron looked out over the street, and Delancort picked out his own, momentarily afraid he might see someone up there staring down at him.

'*Merde.*'

He swore under his breath and made a desperate attempt to take back control of his racing pulse.

This is what they want, Henri. He tried to talk himself down. *They need you to live in fear. It is how they keep control of you!*

At the door, he reached out with the fob to press it against the locking pad, and it slipped from his fingers, clattering to the floor. Cursing again, he grabbed at it, scrambling to seize the key before it skittered away over the ground and out of his reach.

He felt the talons in his neck, digging deep. With shaking hands, Delancort snatched back the fob and lurched into the door, hearing the buzz of the electronic lock as it finally opened.

Only then did he look back. The street was empty.

He slammed the door shut, hearing the bolts click back into place, and then Delancort sprinted the five flights of stairs up to the floor where his apartment lay. He didn't dare take the elevator. The notion of being trapped inside the steel box made him physically sick.

At his apartment door, he spent a full minute examining the surround and the fibrous *bienvenu* mat that lay before it, making sure nothing seemed out of place. He tried to remember if anything was different from when he had left that morning.

At length, he took a deep breath, opened the door and cautiously stepped inside.

Nothing.

Locking the door behind him, Delancort swept quickly from room to room in the low-ceilinged, airy apartment, making certain that he was alone.

The interior of his residence reflected his personality. For the most part, it was minimalist, with a fastidious precision to the sparse décor. The few touches of character were confined to a couple of vintage theatre posters and a bookcase of hardcover art albums. Delancort sat heavily on his sofa, dropping his briefcase on the floor, and he poured himself a stiff drink.

'I can't keep living like this,' he said aloud, but the words choked off before he could build on the thought.

Are they listening to me? If they're following me, then they've bugged my home!

Delancort looked around, wondering where any listening device could be placed. The answer, of course, was *anywhere*. He had seen enough of the SCD's operations in the past to know what kind of technology was available, and how easy it was to secrete it.

I'm not safe here. I'm not safe anywhere.

He walked to the window, and looked down as he drew the blinds.

Down on the street stood a woman with short dark hair and mirrored sunglasses, and she looked directly at him. She wore khaki cargo trousers and a military-style jacket unsuitable for the warm weather. Without breaking eye contact, she reached up and touched the black comma of a headset coiled around her right ear.

The woman nodded in response to a voice only she could hear, and started towards the security door.

Delancort dropped the half-full glass and ran to the laundry cupboard, tearing out the bed sheets and towels inside. Hidden beneath was a black nylon daypack stuffed with *in-case-of-emergency* items – including a bundle of euros, false identity papers, a change of clothes and a stun gun he had never learned how to use.

Lucy Keyes had shown Henri how to put together this 'go-bag' in the event of a critical need. He remembered mocking her gently about her concern for him, insisting that he would never make use of it.

He pulled the pack on over his jacket and dashed back towards the door. On the threshold he hesitated, listening to the thudding of his heartbeat in his ears.

Am I really going to do this?

With the door half-open, Delancort turned around, staring into his apartment. How could anyone conceive of doing such a thing – of dropping everything in their life in a heartbeat and fleeing into the unknown? It was impossible!

It is insane!

The low buzzing as the security door opened echoed up the stairwell and the sound hit Delancort like an electric shock. He ran the opposite way from the stairwell, to the fire exit at the end of the landing, shouldering open the push bar.

Sunlight flooded in, briefly blinding him as he staggered out onto a metal balcony up over the service alley behind the apartments. Down past the grey boxes of air conditioning units, a zigzag of steel steps led to ground level. Delancort took the steps three at a time, the metal clanking against the outside wall of the building with each shaky footfall.

On the lowest level, he kicked open a wire-mesh gate and spilled out into the alley. Lines of parked scooters and a pair of Smart Four-Twos blocked his path back to the front of the building, but he had no intention of going that way. A side passage led to steps downhill, and he could follow it all the way to Avenue de Villaine, and into the city beyond.

'Stop,' said a voice behind him.

Delancort's panic spiked and he hauled the pack off his shoulder, desperately digging inside as he half-turned, half-staggered towards the passageway. The woman in the sunglasses leaned on one of the Smart cars, watching him patiently.

How had she got around him or anticipated his escape route?

His hand closed on the pistol grip of the stun gun and he tore it out of the bag, brandishing it at the ALEPH agent.

'Back away!'

She reacted by raising her hands.

'Do not do anything foolish.' Her words were brisk and Russian-accented.

A flash of recognition came to him. Did he *know* her? One of the many skills Delancort possessed that had made him an excellent aide-de-camp to Ekko Solomon was his memory for faces. The more he studied her, the more he was convinced this woman was not a stranger.

Then it came to him. She had been there when Glovkonin had set off his clever little coup against Rubicon's board of directors, working with his cat's paw, the man called Lau.

She advanced towards him.

'I just want to talk.'

'No!' he snapped, and squeezed the stun gun's trigger.

Nothing happened. The plastic pistol was supposed to spit out a pair of wired metal darts that would conduct a paralysing charge into whomever they hit. But the device remained resolutely inert, and belatedly Delancort remembered that he had not read the instruction leaflet that came with it. He mashed the trigger again, fumbling at it.

'The safety's on,' said the woman, before she rushed him.

She punched him in the chest with one hand, winding him as she wrenched the stun gun out of his grip with the other.

Delancort coughed and backed into a moped, almost falling over it.

'See?' The woman held up the hornet-striped gun, making a show of flicking off the safety slide on the side. 'Like this.'

The next thing Delancort knew was the snap-click of the darts firing, and then his muscles on fire as the voltage surged through him. He hit the asphalt, quaking violently. He couldn't speak, he couldn't cry out, unable to do anything but hold on until the agony ceased.

'Warned you,' she said.

At length, the woman dragged him back to his feet and shoved him in the direction of the apartments. Delancort moved, one leaden footstep after another, dimly aware of her guiding him back into the building, then into the elevator, to the top floor. The stun gun vanished into one of her pockets, but he was so shaken he could barely conceive of the idea of resisting. It was all he could do to prevent himself from throwing up.

Delancort remembered that the apartments above his were vacant. There had been a water leak up there and the landlord had closed them off for refurbishment. The woman propelled him towards one of the doors, pushing him hard in the small of the back.

He staggered in through a hall stripped down to bare plaster, and then into a denuded space that mirrored his own living room. Floorboards creaked under his hesitant steps as he moved towards the only item of furniture, a metal chair. Without being ordered to, Delancort collapsed into it, working hard to normalise his breathing. Around him, the room was still and the corners were thick with shadows.

'Who . . .?' He tried to frame a question. 'Why . . .?'

'Did you injure him?' A voice came out of the gloom and Delancort looked up to see an East Asian man with a serious expression and searching eyes. He addressed the woman. 'That was not necessary.'

'I don't tell you how to do your job.' Her voice lost its Russian edge, becoming harder to place. 'He pulled a weapon on me. I had to show him that was a mistake.'

The man approached and offered Delancort a bottle of water.

'My apologies. She has an unfortunate tendency towards violence.'

'Yes.' Delancort tried to recover some of his dignity. 'Quite.' He took the bottle and managed a mouthful. The shakes retreated, and so did the fog in his memory. He mustered the closest thing to a defiant glare he could manage, staring up at the woman. 'I remember you now. You were there on the day Interpol came to the office.' Delancort sneered, because they all knew that the 'Interpol' team had been a cover story for the Combine's machinations. 'You're with ALEPH. Your name is Milost.'

She shrugged. 'Call me Grace.'

Delancort looked away, back to the room's other occupant. He searched his recall and found what he was looking for.

'And you. Well, we have never met, but the Special Conditions Division had a file on you, Mr Saito. You tried to kill my colleagues.'

'From time to time, we are called upon to do distasteful things, Mr Delancort,' said Saito. 'It is an unfortunate truth.' He looked away, towards a half-open door across the room. 'I know you of all people understand that.'

Delancort blinked. 'I don't know what you mean.' He straightened up. 'Whatever you want from me, ask it. Stop playing games!'

'Why did you betray Ekko Solomon?'

Saito's question hit him like a gut-punch.

'No . . . No, I did not. I tried to make him understand . . . Those terrible acts we were accused of – we had to stand up and decry them. If we fled, we looked like criminals! But he would not hear me.'

Saito gave Grace a cold look as Delancort spoke of the accusations against the Rubicon team, but she didn't seem to notice.

At length, Saito's attention returned to him.

'So you stayed behind and you surrendered. To save your own neck from the executioner's block.'

'Yes.' Delancort looked at the floor, his reply weighing him down. 'I thought, if I stayed inside the circle, I could do something. *Resist*. But I could only stand by and watch. Everything we had built, taken apart. Demolished.' A hot, bright ember of resentment kindled in his chest, and he crushed the plastic bottle in his grip. 'Is that what you want to hear? Does that give you the excuse Glovkonin needs? I made the worst choice of my life and people are dead because of it!'

His voice rose to a shout as the regret and anger came boiling out of him. 'I did what I thought was right, and I have paid for it!' He pushed off, out of the chair, certain that every word he spoke now was one step closer to his death. 'I pay for it every single day!'

'Henri.'

He felt a firm hand on his shoulder. The voice was roughened and damaged but impossible to mistake.

Delancort turned towards it and his hand flew to his mouth in astonishment. Shock hit him at the sight of the man who had entered the room through the shadowy doorway. It was unmistakably Ekko Solomon, but in a state Delancort had never seen before.

He had always known Solomon to cut an elegant and suave figure, to be ready for anything. The change wrought on the man was unprecedented. His face was scarred around one ruined eye. He supported himself on a wooden cane. Like Saito and Grace, he wore unremarkable clothes of a military cut and there was a new stiffness in his gait that spoke to a bone-deep pain and injuries that were still healing.

'*Tabarnak . . .!*' The first cogent thought that formed in Delancort's mind became a curse, a denial. 'No! This is a trick. Solomon is dead. Dane told me so, and he would not have lied about that—'

'Marc and Lucy, and the others, they do not know. Only a handful of people are aware I survived.' He nodded towards Saito. 'I am here because this one chose to keep this secret from his Combine masters.'

'I do not believe it!' Delancort took a step back, shaking his head. 'I refuse!'

'He makes a good point,' Grace said, in an idle tone. 'I mean, you could be a double for all Henri here knows.'

'I am Ekko Solomon.' His dark eye glittered. 'I am guilty of every crime they said I committed. I am guilty of putting my people at such risk. I will show you.'

He pulled open his jacket and the shirt beneath it, then grabbed Delancort's wrist, pressing his hand to the burn-scarred flesh of his chest.

Delancort felt something distinctive there. It took him a moment to realise it was an odd, crescent-shaped scar seared into the skin. Like the mark of a branding iron.

Delancort's fingers touched the imprint where the keepsake Ekko Solomon had always worn around his neck had been burned into him. Lost in the explosion that the world believed had killed him, but now permanently etched into his chest, was the outline of the trigger from a Kalashnikov assault rifle. The gun Solomon had carried in another life as a child soldier.

Delancort found his voice.

'It is you.' Then he shook his head, a tide of sorrow and remorse filling him. 'I let you down. I am so sorry, sir.'

'Never.' Solomon drew him into an embrace. 'You have always been my most trusted friend, Henri. You have always done what you believed to be right.'

For the first time in what seemed like an eternity, Delancort felt a flash of hope. He withdrew and sat back in the metal chair, his mind reeling.

'If you are here, if you are with them –' he nodded towards Saito and Grace – 'what does that mean? Rubicon is in ruins. The Combine gutted it.' He shook his head and a sudden, wry bark of laughter escaped him. 'We are what remains . . . *les fantômes.*'

'There are other survivors from Rubicon's Special Conditions Division,' noted Saito. 'Dane and Keyes, perhaps two or three others. Glovkonin has invested significant resources in the search for them, but to no avail. They have proven remarkably proficient at concealing themselves.'

'We need to find them,' said Solomon.

Delancort studied his former employer, measuring him for anything that could have been a lie or a misdirection.

JAMES SWALLOW | 91

'How do you know that these two are not manipulating you?' He gestured towards Saito and Grace. 'These are the soldiers of our enemies. How can you ask me to trust them?'

'Another good point,' said Grace, with a smirk. 'I wouldn't trust me.'

'I do not,' said Solomon, and he placed a scarred hand on Delancort's shoulder again. 'Henri, you are the conscience that kept me in check. I have always had faith in you. I ask you now, give me a measure of that in return.' He nodded to himself. 'I came here to get you out of this mire, to repay you.'

'Where can we go?' Delancort shook his head. It was hard to push back the bleak tide that had overwhelmed him. 'What can we do?'

'We will do what we have always done.' Solomon showed a smile. 'Seek justice.'

SIX

Sochi was the last point on the map before Russia hit the water, a busy resort town on the northern shores of the Black Sea that extended up and down the coast. Encompassing hotels, cafes and bars along the warm reaches of the seafront, the town seemed slightly displaced, as if it were a decade out of sync with resorts of similar character down on the Mediterranean.

Dating back to the age of the Tsars, Sochi's charms and temperate weather had always been a draw for those with the money to enjoy it. Post-Revolution, in the Soviet era it became the holiday home for the elite of the Communist Party, before transitioning after the 1990s into a place where the oligarchs and the people who wanted to be them came to summer. Then the 2014 Winter Olympics had opened Sochi up in new ways, and not all of them for the better. Endeavours both political and criminal flourished there, even after the athletes had gone home with their medals. The remains of the sports complex built for the games – the ice dome, the skating palace, the stadium and the rest – still stood along the line of the stony beach. They were monuments to Russian enterprise, but exactly *what kind* of enterprise was open to debate.

Marc glanced up at the open-roofed shape of the Fisht Olympic Stadium as he walked by, adjusting his sunglasses to hide the fact that he was checking his whereabouts for any potential tails. Seeing nothing untoward, he kept moving, idly drumming his fingers on his thigh as he walked towards the nexus of the complex.

The area was busy with people, tourists and locals rubbing shoulders with the travelling army of sports fans that had come to temporarily colonise the town for the race. Sochi was alive with activity, as the clock ticked down to the start of the latest heat in the Veloce Cup Championship, an international challenge series where high-performance single-seater powerboats raced against one another along shoreline circuits.

Out on the water, Marc could see lines of drum-shaped inflatable marker buoys and the tall flags of the starting line bobbing in the gentle swell. Overhead, a big Bo 105 helicopter in international orange made lazy sweeps back and forth, as the camera crew on board captured footage for internet live-streams and the giant repeater screens erected along the waterfront. The gathering crowds waved at the helicopter as it buzzed above them like a gigantic bee, and Marc automatically turned his head as the camera's eye swept over him, pulling down the peak of his cap to hide his face.

A handful of the craft were already on the water, going through qualifying time trials to fix their starting positions for the race proper. Low-slung and aerodynamic in form, the racers looked more like segments of aircraft wings than boats, and they left stark white wakes behind them as they shrieked past the crowd-line. Each brightly coloured powerboat – neon green, flame red, electric blue – was adorned with a patchwork of sponsorship decals.

The crowd gasped around him and Marc saw one of the racers lift a pontoon out of the waves as it made a turn too steeply. For a second, the boat looked as if it might flip over, but then the craft's velocity bled off and it settled again. A scattering of applause congratulated the driver on their skill, but it was half-hearted. Marc had the impression that the crowd hoped to see some fire along with the thunder.

He threaded through the attendees towards the race village. It was a sprawling campus of temporary pergolas, pop-up buildings and maintenance tents erected in a cluster around the dockside and the wedding-cake form of the modernist Hotel Marine Luxe. The new hotel faced directly on to the water on a plaque of reclaimed land, built in the brief post-Olympic boom. Its contemporary, curved lines enclosed hundreds of high-end suites, a casino and a conference centre, the latter of which had been temporarily taken over by the race event. The Marine Luxe was an obvious attempt to outdo the Zhemchuzhina, Sochi's famous Soviet-style landmark hotel, and from what Marc had learned, much of the cash to make that happen had come from sources close to Giovanni Da Silvio. Small wonder, then, that the Italian had made the Marine Luxe the hub for this heat of the race he sponsored.

Marc approached a gateway that divided the public spaces from the race operations area, and pulled a slim plastic pass from inside his shirt, letting it dangle freely on the end of a lanyard. The pass identified him as a member of the press and it granted limited access beyond the first layer of security. A bored-looking young woman in a deliberately revealing dress waved him through with a fake smile, and he made his way past temporary boathouses set up along the line of the docks.

'Through the first gate, no problems,' he said quietly, almost swallowing the words.

A wireless radio bead in his ear picked up the comment through bone induction and a moment later Kara's voice buzzed back at him.

'*Understood, Active. Overwatch, do you have eyes yet?*'

Lucy responded immediately, and Marc resisted the urge to look up.

'*Negative, no angle on Active at this time.*'

The smell of engines lingered in the air. Marc glanced into the team enclosures as he passed them. Most were empty, with their craft already out on the waves for the qualifying runs, but a few of the dart-shaped racers were up on supports, their technical crews busy making last-minute adjustments before they hit the water. He watched a swarm of mechanics fitting hatches back to a boat painted with the stars and stripes of the American flag, getting it ready to go. They showed the same kind of controlled chaotic energy as the pit crews of a Formula 1 Grand Prix, except that instead of changing tyres, these people were fitting custom propellers to massive outboard motors.

Banners crackled in the stiff breeze off the sea, the lines of the pennants stretching for the length of the docks. Marc noticed the colours of sponsors from all over the globe, from European concerns like Koastwell GmbH and Hawkeshead, to Riverine Tech from the USA and Australia's Horizon Integral.

Zack Ridgeway – the garrulous motorsport journalist whose stolen pass now dangled around Marc's neck – had been more than happy to talk at length about the behind-the-scenes happenings at the Veloce Cup. The night before in a seafront bar, oiled by plentiful vodka and Marc's winning smile, Ridgeway's explanations provided a more detailed briefing than Marc could have hoped to get from hours of remote study.

According to the journalist, Da Silvio's event drew strong interest from the offshore racing community, but the Veloce Cup had to work hard to compete with rival championships based in China and Abu Dhabi. There was talk of corruption, of course. In an arena of professional sport worth millions of dollars, it came as no surprise that there were accusations of dirty tricks and actual inter-team sabotage at previous Veloce meets. In addition, safety did not appear to be a primary concern for the race management, despite their insistence to the contrary. The year before, two drivers had been killed in a collision that still had not been adequately investigated.

'They like the prospect of some bumps and shunts, a bit of smoke on the water,' Ridgeway had noted, somewhere around his eighth or ninth shot. 'The organisers think it makes them look edgy and cool.'

Marc imagined the journalist still sleeping off the alcohol in his hotel room, unaware that his affable drinking companion, who had been so generous with his expense account, had lifted his press pass as they shook hands and went their separate ways. Marc peered at the careworn Cabot dive watch on his wrist. It wouldn't do to outstay his welcome here. The purpose of this little sortie was to scout the location and confirm what security precautions were in place throughout the Marine Luxe, where Da Silvio currently occupied the Presidential Suite.

He passed another security checkpoint entering the hotel's conference complex, near the open expanse of an exclusive swimming pool. Marc counted two guards, both craggy-faced no-nonsense types wearing Bluetooth earpieces and wide-cut sports jackets capable of concealing firearms. After signing in under Ridgeway's name, he pocketed his sunglasses, took a drink from one of the servers orbiting the entrance atrium and pretended to look at his smartphone. In reality, he used the device to pinpoint the locations of the discreet security cameras mounted in the chandeliers and ceiling corners. He logged the data and transmitted it to Kara before moving on.

The conference centre was broken into two sections, half of it given over to administration and race operations, the other a wide, airy lounge that looked towards Sochi proper and up the coastline through floor-to-ceiling windows. Screens showed the feed from cameras on the shore, from drones and the helicopter, but most of the people in the lounge weren't watching.

The owners and their entourages hung out here, where they could mingle, neck flutes of Cristal and graze off an expensive buffet. The people in the lounge were here to be seen, which made Marc's job a lot easier. He walked the room, mentally dividing it into sections for each group or clique.

He spotted a cluster of quiet, sullen men with Bratva tattoos visible at the collars of their tailored shirts. Directly opposite them, and as far away as they could be and still be in the same room, he noted the presence of a group of Sicilians in dark Armani suits of similar cut, who were carelessly loud and expressive, as if daring someone to take issue with their boisterous behaviour. The Bratva men stared daggers across the room at them, but the other group pretended not to notice.

Marc walked up to the windows, and looked out over the marina.

'*Smile*,' said Lucy's voice. '*This is Overwatch, I have eyes on Active.*'

Marc scanned the horizon, looking towards Sochi's taller buildings framed by the white-capped mountains beyond them, and found the tower block Lucy was using as her perch, about half a kilometre distant. Marc reached up and tapped the peak of his cap in salute. Somewhere up there, the sniper peered back at him through the scope of a high-powered rifle.

'Safety on, if you don't mind,' he muttered.

'*Not my first rodeo, slick*,' she retorted.

Marc nodded to himself. If circumstances evolved to the point where Lucy actually had to pull a trigger, they were beyond any hope of recovery.

'*I have the data packet*,' said Kara. '*Good take, more please.*'

'Active is moving.'

Marc finished his drink and wandered back towards the restrooms, slowing his pace as he passed near the doors leading into the main operations centre. The nearest security guard had his attention on one of the screens, and the moment Marc knew he was not being observed, he extended his path to the doors and carried on through.

Inside, the ops centre was busy with race technicians and staff talking into headsets, monitoring the second-by-second progression of the powerboats around the track markers. Everyone's attention was on the front runner, the Koastwell boat with its lightning-flash paint scheme carving sharp turns around the markers.

Marc stood near an idle computer monitor and pretended to watch. Out of sight, he held his smartphone close to the machine's tower and tapped a tab on the device's screen. A rectangle of black glass and anodised metal, the phone could have been this year's latest model, but it was a custom piece of tech carried only by the former members of Rubicon's Special Conditions Division. The 'spyPhone', as Kara had once christened it, was loaded with state-of-the-art intrusion software and near-field systems that could wirelessly interface with most modern computer hardware. Controlled remotely by the hacker, it gave her access to the race control network, injecting a Trojan Horse subroutine into the computers that would let her set a back door for any digital infiltration.

'*Okay, we own it,*' said Kara, after a moment. '*Active is clear to move on.*'

'Copy.'

Marc noted that some of the technicians had become aware of him, so he exited the ops centre before anyone decided to challenge his presence. Outside, the guard was still engrossed in the qualifying runs, so Marc gave him a wide berth. He found his way into the conference centre's administration area, which operated with a skeleton staff. Finding another unoccupied workstation, he repeated his trick with the phone.

The second time, Kara's Trojan program entered the network belonging to the hotel itself, snaking its way into the operating system. In a few hours, the hacker would be able to map the entirety of the Marine Luxe's digital infrastructure, and with luck, find what the Rubicon team were looking for.

'Second payload delivered,' whispered Marc. 'I'll do one more sweep and then extract. Mobile, you copy?'

'*Understood.*' Malte spoke up for the first time.

The Finn waited a block away behind the wheel of a blocky UAZ Hunter 4 × 4, ready to pick him up outside the hotel.

Marc made his way back into the conference centre, but two steps into the room he felt a heavy hand on his shoulder.

'Sir,' said a thick-accented voice.

Marc turned to find the guard he had previously avoided now towering over him. The man was as broad as he was tall, and radiated a hard, canine energy, his eyes narrow and flinty.

'You are not allowed in there,' said the guard. 'You explain why.'

'Sorry, chap.' Marc mimicked Ridgeway's posh accent and gave a weak smile. 'Looking for the pisser, you know?'

He could tell immediately that the guard wasn't buying it. Undercover ops had never really been Marc's strong suit, and it took all he had not to look nervous. Behind the big man, across the atrium the other members of the security team were reacting to the arrival of a VIP, as a figure in a striking suit came striding into the room.

'I will need to check pass,' said the guard, and he lifted his arm to speak into a microphone at his cuff.

The man in the suit swept past, in mid-conversation with a severe-looking Germanic woman holding a bulky digital tablet, and Marc was momentarily startled to make eye contact with none other than Giovanni Da Silvio himself. The Italian barely registered him, but Marc saw an opportunity and he went for it.

'Signor Da Silvio!' He called out the Italian's name and gave him a jaunty wave. The big guard, momentarily wrong-footed by Marc's action, didn't stop him as he stepped around and offered his hand. 'Hello! Zack Ridgeway, from *Power Sports Online.*'

The Italian automatically accepted the handshake, and that was enough of a signifier to make the guard back off.

'Indeed. Have we met?'

Marc saw no glint of recognition in Da Silvio's eyes, and inwardly breathed a sigh of relief.

'*Active, what are you doing in there?*'

Kara's voice crackled in his ear, but Marc ignored it and feigned a smile, putting more distance between himself and the guard.

'No, no. I believe my editor contacted you about scheduling an interview?'

Marc had no idea if the real Ridgeway's editor had done anything of the sort, but he had to extract himself from the guard's attentions and this was the most expedient way to do it. But he had traded one risk for another.

Da Silvio was still walking, and Marc fell in step with him – or at least, he tried to. The Italian's severe-looking assistant moved to put herself between the two of them the moment the perfunctory handshake finished.

'Willa?'

The Italian gave the woman a questioning look and Marc saw her fingers dance over the tablet's touch-sensitive screen.

She pulled up Da Silvio's itinerary, and he glimpsed flashes of other data panels on the device. Marc recognised the tech – an encrypted digital 'book' used by the billionaire's aide-de-camp to manage his affairs.

Willa looked at Marc and gave a curt shake of the head.

'We have nothing on our calendar.'

'Oh.' Marc looked disappointed. 'That's a pity. Perhaps we could find a moment? My readers would be fascinated to hear from the man who has put so much into the Veloce Cup . . .' He opted for flattery, gambling on Da Silvio's vanity to keep him from becoming suspicious. 'We'd love to do a feature on you.'

'*Active, you need to disengage. If he makes you, we're blown.*' Lucy's tone was even, but he could tell she was annoyed with him. '*Back off.*'

They were at the red velvet rope of the lounge's private section now, and Marc had little option but to follow them inside and continue to spin out the lie, or risk discovery. If he didn't follow through, it would raise suspicion. Da Silvio didn't seem to notice, however, and the guards let Marc pass. He'd been right to assume that moving in the Italian's orbit was as good as an access-all-areas badge.

'That sounds delightful,' Da Silvio replied, 'but I'm afraid I can't speak with you right *now*, Mr Ridgeway.' The Italian gave him an indulgent nod and a practised smile. 'I have an important lunch meeting with one of my colleagues. My assistant will take your details and we'll see if we can arrange something. *Ciao!*'

He walked away, ushered to a table by the window by a smiling waiter.

The brush-off was polite and polished, so smooth that Marc was barely aware he'd been totally dismissed until the woman called Willa glared at him and pulled up his press pass to study it closely. Thankfully, the badge didn't have a photo image on it.

'Please do not approach Signor Da Silvio again without discussing it with my office first, is that clear?' Her tone was so icy the words had frost on them. 'If it happens again, your pass will be revoked and you will be barred from the event.'

'My mistake. I apologise for being a little too eager.' Marc made his reply suitably contrite, using it to cover himself as he drew out his phone and palmed it.

There's an opportunity here, he told himself, *if I can push my luck a little more.*

Marc's spyPhone was still operating in intrusion mode, and he shifted slightly so that the device's wireless connection could auto-seek the tablet in Willa's hands. He and the woman were close enough to touch, close enough for Kara's hacker programs to work their magic between the two devices.

Willa continued to tap at the tablet's screen.

'Signor Da Silvio will not be available for any additional press interviews. I have your contact information. If the situation changes, you will be alerted . . .'

She trailed off, raising an eyebrow. The device gave a low chirp and Marc saw a warning panel pop up on the screen, quickly followed by another and another. It was reacting to the spyPhone's attempt to infiltrate its system.

'*Active, this is Overwatch, abort intrusion!*' Kara snapped out the words. '*Whatever tech you're messing with, it's pushing back!*'

'Ah.'

Marc felt his colour rise and he thumbed the disconnect key, slipping the phone back into his pocket. Willa's digital book was far better protected than the computer networks used by the hotels and the race, by an order of magnitude. He covered his dismay with a cough and stepped aside.

'Okay then. Thank you for your time. I'll wait to hear from you . . .'

But the woman had already moved on, forgetting him the instant she turned away. Marc sensed someone behind him as Willa moved to greet them with a cool, professional smile.

Looking up from under the peak of his cap, Marc saw the face of the man who had arrived for lunch with Da Silvio, a carved-granite aspect reflected in the mirrored glass behind the lounge's bar. His blood ran cold.

'Mr Glovkonin,' Willa said to the new arrival, her voice as clear as a bell. 'Welcome to Sochi. Signor Da Silvio is waiting for you. Right this way.'

Pytor Glovkonin – undeniably, the guiding hand behind every shade of hell that Marc and his team had gone through over the last five years. The man who held ultimate responsibility for the deaths of Marc's friends and colleagues, who had threatened the lives of his family, schemed to tear down Rubicon and launch ploy after murderous ploy against thousands of innocent people . . . All so he could make himself that bit richer.

Here he was, unaware that the object of his enmity stood in the same room.

His back to the Russian, Marc turned to stone, unable to move, unable to look away. He watched Glovkonin's reflection as he passed by – no more than five metres from Marc – and marched into the dining room where the Italian sat at his table.

The seconds stretched into an eternity. Marc kept remembering the feeling of the security guard's hand on his shoulder, the moment replaying, but this time it was Glovkonin, with his hard, penetrating gaze boring into Marc's back. He felt as if there was a screaming chorus echoing around him, as if everyone in the lounge was ready to turn and point the finger towards him.

The brief surge of panic made him light-headed, and Marc shut it off before it could take hold. He turned and moved away, hyper-conscious of trying to appear perfectly normal as he avoided the roving gaze of Glovkonin's personal security detail. The two bodyguards hovered near the VIP area's entrance, grimacing at everything.

'*Active, report status.*' Lucy's tone had altered, growing concerned. '*What's going on?*'

'Active is heading to exfil,' said Marc under his breath. 'Mobile, come and get me.'

He exited the conference centre and moved quickly across the airy marble lobby of the adjoining hotel, towards the main doors. He pulled at his collar. Marc couldn't get away fast enough.

Malte gave a grunt of acknowledgement. '*Mobile on site in sixty seconds.*'

Lucy heard the tightness in Marc's words. '*Do we have a problem down there?*'

'Things have just got more complicated,' he replied, feeling the sick twist in his gut from the ebb of adrenaline.

'I took the liberty of ordering for you, I hope you don't mind.' The Italian gave Glovkonin his usual indolent smile as he took his seat. 'The *kambala* here isn't as impressive as they claim, but it bears indulging.'

'I have sampled it before.'

The local delicacy of Black Sea flounder was an acquired taste, and in truth Glovkonin much preferred the amber trout from the nearby farms in Adler. He let the waiter fill his glass with an indifferent white wine and took a drink.

'Of course, of course,' smiled the other man. 'You must know Sochi quite well. I sometimes forget this is your home country, it's so temperate! It is so little like the Russia I expect.' The smile became a grin. 'Palm trees and blue water! Hardly what one thinks of when your country is mentioned.'

'You have made yourself quite at home,' Glovkonin countered.

He was going to add more to the thought, but movement by the entrance to the VIP area caught his eye. He saw a bearded man in a baseball cap and jacket hurriedly walking away, and something about his gait was familiar to the Russian. Glovkonin watched, waiting for the man to turn his head so he could see his face, but he never did, disappearing into the hotel.

'That's true,' said the Italian, unaware of the other man's distraction. 'Places like this, on the borders between nations, on the edges of oceans, I love them. There's something special in the air. A little danger . . . A lot of opportunity, yes?'

'If you insist.'

Glovkonin put down the wineglass. He was caught between two impulses. On the one hand, he didn't want to spend more time than he needed to in the Italian's self-aggrandising presence, but on the other, he didn't trust what the other man would do if he wasn't there keeping an eye on him.

A group at the back of the VIP area had finished their meal and were on their way out. The Italian spotted them and stood up, opening his hands.

'Ah, my friends! Are you enjoying your day?'

Glovkonin studied the group and immediately wanted to sneer. These men were cohorts from one of the larger Bratva gangs, the upper echelon of Russian organised crime – uncultured, thickset thugs in ill-tailored suits who wore too much gold and swaggered their way through life. He remained in his seat as the Italian greeted the men warmly, treating them like the equals they most certainly were not.

Most of them were interchangeable brutes who would have been better suited to the inside of a bare-knuckle boxing ring than this expensive restaurant. They all seemed out of their depth except one – a pit bull of a man with a flash of cunning in his gaze.

Glovkonin recognised him. Prior to arriving in Sochi, he had directed the hacker Andre to gather information on the Italian's criminal contacts, and this man showed the most promising, most serviceable character traits.

The underworld called Pavlo Chumak 'the Salt Seller', and the man's prolific dealing in hard drugs and sex trafficking were purported to be worth billions of roubles. Chumak's criminal empire extended through the Ukraine and along much of the Black Sea coast, and his reputation warned of a hair-trigger temper and an inventive talent for violence.

'Pytor Glovkonin.' Chumak looked him up and down, appraising him like one of his women. 'I know you.'

'But of course . . .' said the Italian. 'Such great men, no doubt you know one another.'

'Never met before today,' Chumak rumbled, his voice the rough snarl of a lifelong smoker. 'But who could mistake Moscow's blessed son, here to take the waters in our relaxing climate?'

On cue, Chumak's men chuckled at their leader's jibe.

Glovkonin ignored the open sarcasm in the criminal's tone and finally rose to his feet. He offered his hand and Chumak took it. The man had a dry, heavy grip.

'I have heard much about you,' Glovkonin said neutrally.

Chumak's grip tightened and Glovkonin saw a narrowing around his eyes, a twist of suspicion on his lips.

'That so? Who has talked about me? This one?'

He jerked his head in the Italian's direction, and Glovkonin saw how his men tensed at the veiled accusation.

The Salt Seller has a healthy dose of paranoia, Glovkonin noted. *Useful to know.*

'All of it respectful, of course,' said Glovkonin, and that appeased the criminal. He released his grasp.

Chumak made his excuses and left with his entourage, and Glovkonin returned to his seat. Across the table, the Italian gave a theatrical sigh.

'I have to keep a lot of people happy,' he explained. 'You know how it is.'

'Perhaps you should try making them afraid of you instead,' Glovkonin said coldly. 'More efficient in the long run.'

The Italian chuckled and waggled his finger at Glovkonin.

'Ha, you do like to tell me how to do my work, don't you, Pytor? It's almost as if you believe you could do better.' His smile did not reach his eyes.

'You have your approach, I have mine.'

'And yours has not been without its missteps, let us be honest. While my approach, as you put it, has worked well enough.' The Italian talked around the salad course, eating like a starving man. 'You really don't need to be here, looking over my shoulder.'

'Is that what you think this is?' Glovkonin feigned innocence. 'Perhaps I am here to watch you work and to learn from you.' He inclined his head. 'I am the newest recruit to the Combine's committee, after all.'

'And you do have much to learn.'

The Italian winced at the mention of the group's name, his casual mask slipping for a moment.

'You hate it when I say the word.' Glovkonin chuckled. 'You act as if I utter a curse.'

'I understand the value of subtlety,' retorted the other man. 'Secrecy.'

It was all Glovkonin could do not to laugh out loud at that.

'So says the playboy. Parading in front of the world's media with his speedboats, supermodels and fast cars. Glad-handing and back-slapping with criminals. This is a use of subtlety beyond a simple peasant like me. Please, elucidate.'

The Italian's smirk returned. 'Hiding in plain sight is the perfect camouflage.'

He tried constantly to charm Glovkonin, but the attitude that allowed him to manipulate so many others rebounded harmlessly off the Russian's contempt.

'I know you do not want me in Sochi. But the transfer of the equipment is too essential to be left to one person.' Glovkonin shifted in his seat, confident of the conversation going in the direction he wanted. He leaned closer, his voice dropping. 'Chumak and men like him – you have them so close at hand. Why? Why take the risk?'

'Because they are useful. Those contacts ensure that our operation will move forward without hindrance.'

'I wonder, is it because you like the thrill of mixing with killers?' Glovkonin shook his head. 'They are dangerous.'

'Not to me.' The Italian's smile turned cold. 'You think I'm a pampered fool, don't you, Pytor?'

'I would not judge.' It took effort to utter the lie and maintain his disinterested expression.

The Italian looked out of the windows, as the crowd on the shoreline gave a whoop of excitement. Glovkonin followed his gaze and saw two powerboats thundering towards the finish line, one in a green livery and one in orange.

The green boat gave the other vessel a well-timed shunt as it passed, and the orange craft spun out of control, skidding across the wave-tops and into a spray of white water. The move was vague enough that the driver in the green boat would be able to pass it off as an accidental contact, but Glovkonin didn't doubt it had been deliberate. The crowd knew it, too, and they roared their approval.

The rumours the Russian had heard about the fierce competition between the Veloce Cup's race teams, of violence and intimidation, seemed quite believable. This was a hazardous sport, after all.

'People have spent so many months cooped up, and now they want some excitement!' The Italian laughed and clapped his hands, enjoying the spectacle as a rescue dinghy raced out to the stricken vessel. 'I like the taste of blood, my friend,' he said, showing teeth. 'Perhaps it is the legacy of Imperial Rome in my spirit!' He held up his thumb, and then tilted it downwards, imitating some ancient emperor sealing the fate of a luckless gladiator. He was amused with himself. 'I am not afraid of it, and I am not afraid of those poorly educated thugs.'

'Men like Chumak can kill every day and show no remorse,' insisted Glovkonin. 'They must be treated with respect. Unless . . .' He trailed off, and drew a thumb across his throat in a cutting motion.

'I can deal with Chumak.' Irritation flared in the Italian's words, as he grew annoyed at Glovkonin's hectoring manner. 'There is a contingency plan. It's not something you need concern yourself with.'

'Of course.' Glovkonin inclined his head, as if admitting defeat, and changed the subject. 'I've had my people secure the relevant documentation for the transit.'

'Good.' The Italian nodded to himself. 'The transport will arrive on race day. We'll make the transfer then, and by the time the victors are standing on the podium, the equipment will be halfway to its destination.' His smile returned. 'Well, if you must insist on remaining, Pytor, at least try to enjoy yourself. Anything you want is available.' He sipped his wine and sat back in his chair. 'This is the winner's circle.'

When the meal was at an end, they parted ways.

After his bodyguards Misha and Gregor had cleared it for him, Glovkonin entered one of the Marine Luxe's opulent washrooms.

He found a quiet corner, and from an inner pocket in his jacket, he recovered an ultra-slim custom satellite smartphone, pulling with it a hair-thin wire that connected the device to a tiny solid-state microphone and camera concealed behind one of his jacket's black buttons.

The smartphone had recorded the conversation in the lounge, capturing the sound clearly and securing a good angle of the Italian's face as he ate and talked. Glovkonin wound carefully through the playback until he found the right moment.

The Italian's words crackled in the hush. *'There is a contingency plan. It's not something you need concern yourself with.'*

He nodded to himself.

'Perfekt.'

His rival had handed him everything he needed.

Glovkonin activated the phone's encoding software and made a call. Andre answered immediately.

'I'm here, sir.'

'I am sending you something,' he explained, appending the audio-video file to an upload. 'Clean it up.'

'Does it need any . . . embellishment?'

'No.' Glovkonin's smile returned. 'Alterations could be discovered and our time is limited. I want it to be as untouched as possible. Build on it. You will know what to do.'

'Understood,' said the hacker.

The elevator deposited them on the fifth floor of the Rubicon tower, and Delancort squeezed out, past a cluster of hatchet-faced bankers belonging to the building's new owners.

'This way,' he said, beckoning the woman with the long blonde hair following in his wake.

She walked with the pinpoint pace of a fashion model on a catwalk, scanning the corridor through a pair of oversized glasses.

'Didn't think I'd come back here again,' said Grace.

'I remember.' Delancort shot her a venomous look. 'Do not assume I have forgotten what you did. Solomon might be willing to work with you, but I have no trust in you.'

'Smart boy,' she retorted. 'The feeling's mutual. But right now our interests align. So try to act professional.'

He swore under his breath. The woman's presence made him anxious. She was sly and calculating, and he could not get a read on her. As someone who prided himself on being a shrewd judge of character, Delancort felt ill at ease around someone whose persona changed from moment to moment.

Grace had been operating under a different alias and a different face on the day Rubicon's enemies had come to destroy it. She had been part of the team working with Lau, a former comrade of Ekko Solomon's from the old days. Lau had led the way towards Rubicon's dissolution, supported by the Combine, but ultimately he had lost his life when his usefulness came to an end. Delancort had been there at that moment, in a conference room a few floors above, and he shuddered at the memory.

Although she would hate to admit it, Grace was as much a tool of the Combine's agenda as Lau had been, and she, too, would have been dead now if not for Solomon's intervention. But Delancort found it hard to believe that Grace would feel any kind of obligation. She was the epitome of self-serving. Delancort knew that ugly trait, because he recognised it in himself.

He paused at the door to a server room, and tapped in the six-digit skeleton key code Solomon had given him. The magnetic locks on the door clicked open.

'In here,' he said, slipping inside.

Grace took off her glasses and gave a low whistle.

'What happened to this place?'

'You did,' Delancort retorted. 'When you helped bring Rubicon to its knees.'

Half the size of a hockey field, in the past the server room space had been lined with rows of air-cooled computer towers. Now it was almost empty, with a cluster of units arranged in one corner, near an operations desk.

Grace made a face. 'Awkward.'

Delancort crossed to the desk and woke the monitor there.

'This will take a few moments.'

He sat and pulled up a control interface, arriving at what was essentially the front gate of the Rubicon Group's core mainframe.

Like everything else, it was a shadow of its former self. Orders had been signed to decommission it, and Delancort could see that some of the work had already begun. Thick coils of cabling and server blades had been removed and placed on trolleys, ready to be wheeled away for scrap.

Normally, it would take a three-layer password and identification matrix to get Delancort into the mainframe, but Solomon was the architect of this system and he had a back door in place, a secret short-cut code that only Rubicon's former CEO was aware of.

Delancort held up his phone and played an audio file into the monitor's sound pick up.

'When we are born, we cry that we are come to this great stage of fools.' Solomon's bass tones filled the room.

'Alack, alack the day,' said Grace, her accent briefly becoming cut-glass English. 'A Shakespeare quote? How clichéd.'

He ignored her, following up the voiceprint identifier with another alphanumeric string that Solomon had made him memorise.

Good Day, Mr Solomon. The text appeared in a dialog box next to a menu of options. How do you wish to proceed?

'We shall begin by undoing,' Delancort said, half to himself.

With untrammelled access to the bare-bones network, there was still enough agency in the system to initiate a series of high-level executive actions. Once committed, these could not be reversed. Delancort started by shunting the company's last remaining cash reserves into a program that split the money evenly, sending an untraceable payment out to the thousands of employees who had lost their jobs in Rubicon's collapse. It wouldn't change their lives, but it was better than leaving them with nothing.

An alert window pinged into being in the corner of the screen.

'What's that?' demanded Grace, pointing at it with a long nail lacquered in crimson.

'A warning prompt,' said Delancort. 'The system signals any change in high-level operational directives. So we can assume that someone will come to investigate.'

'You could have told me that first,' she sniffed. 'Shit.'

Grace hiked up her skirt and pulled a compact quad-barrel derringer pistol from a holster strapped to her thigh. She walked away with the gun at the ready, her footsteps fading.

Delancort continued his work. The order Andre had given him – the payment from Rubicon's coffers that had gone to the Turkish company Altin Elma – preyed on his mind.

That instinct had never failed him. Delancort always trusted his suspicions, so he very much *did not* trust the Altin Elma transfer. Sweeping the mainframe, he copied everything on the network relating to the subsidiary and downloaded the files to a flash drive. He pocketed the plastic stick and then set to the last part of the task.

One by one, he typed a series of file codes into the system and erased all trace of whatever was attached to them. Each file related to an asset, to a resource, to something that Ekko Solomon had been keeping on the fringes of the Rubicon mainframe.

Lost in the display, Delancort watched the data delete and over-write itself, a blur of virtual pages dissolving before his eyes: ship's logs for the *Themis*, Solomon's private yacht; unfiled technology patents; records of ownership for something called Draccios; blue-prints for an A26 submersible; personnel files on every member of the SCD, living or dead; and more, flashing past too quickly for him to read.

A faint smile pulled at his lips. For the first time in a long while, Henri Delancort felt good about himself. Finally, he was doing something right, something that didn't leave him feeling soiled. A spark of defiance he believed had been snuffed out was rekindled. He glared at the screen, imagining Pytor Glovkonin's face.

'Fuck. You.'

As a rule, he abhorred foul language, but on this occasion, it seemed warranted. Necessary, even.

'What are you doing?'

The voice was loud, gruff and terrifyingly close. Delancort jerked in shock and turned in his chair.

One of ALEPH's security team stood behind him. Delancort had been so engrossed in his work, he hadn't heard the man enter. He looked around nervously. Grace had abandoned him.

'I asked you a question!' The guard opened his jacket and pulled out a stun baton, a short black rod of dense plastic that ended in two metal tines. 'Take your hands off that keyboard!'

'I . . .' Delancort had not planned for this. He had assumed – wrongly, it appeared – that Grace would deal with this kind of thing while he concentrated on the digital part of their little enterprise. 'It is not a problem!'

'We will see.' The man advanced on him, brandishing the baton with one hand, reaching up to a radio handset clipped to his collar. 'Get me Andre,' he said into the mike.

'Hey.' Grace appeared from behind one of the isolated servers, her pistol dangling at the end of her arm. 'You know, as much fun as it might be to watch you make him dance with that thing –' she nodded towards the stun baton – 'I can't let you do it.' Grace looked at Delancort, raising an eyebrow. 'You done?'

'I suppose so. Yes.'

He returned to the keyboard and logged out.

'Wait.' The ALEPH operative's face twisted in confusion. He took a step towards Grace. 'I know you.' And then he grinned. 'Milost! It's me. Gera! From before? What is going on?' He indicated her hair. 'You changed it.'

Milost had been the woman's cover name during the hostile takeover. Delancort saw the expression on her face change from smug amusement to cold purpose.

'Ah, well.' She shook her head. 'You recognised me. That's a pity.'

Her derringer came up and she shot Gera in the chest. The report of the weapon echoed like a thunderclap.

Delancort flinched, momentarily afraid that she would turn the gun on him next. But Grace walked slowly up to the man, who lay shaking and choking on the ground, and with care, she put a second bullet through his forehead.

She looked up and found Delancort staring at her.

'What? Thank me later.' Grace beckoned him towards her. 'Come on. It's time to go.'

SEVEN

Grace had stashed a car across the road from the Rubicon tower's secondary entrance on Avenue de Citronniers, and Delancort followed her across to it. He couldn't stop himself from throwing nervous glances over his shoulder. Every instinct in him screamed that he should run, but in the elevator Grace waved her quad-barrelled derringer in his face and warned him that if he did, she would put a bullet in his knee and leave him for ALEPH. He believed her.

The first inkling that the alarm had been raised came as the telephone on the reception desk started ringing, but by then they were already past it, going through the revolving doors and out into the bright, hot day.

Delancort could see men in black jackets appearing inside the entrance atrium. He turned away, afraid that he might make eye contact.

'Get in the back and don't touch anything,' ordered Grace. The grubby white Peugeot hatchback was an older model, with a compact shape suited to Monaco's narrow streets and a decidedly dilapidated look to its frame.

Delancort had barely closed the rear passenger door before Grace crunched the gears and the car shot away from the kerb with a screech. The abrupt motion threw him against the shapes of two large blue duffel bags stuffed into the back seat and footwell.

ALEPH black-jackets were swarming out into the daylight as the Peugeot rocketed past them, and one man foolishly tried to grab at the door handle as it sped by. Delancort saw him take a tumble, while his compatriots sprinted towards a silver BMW X5 parked nearby.

'They're giving chase,' he said, still pinned to the duffels by the inertia of Grace's wild, slaloming course.

'I'm counting on it,' she shot back, working the Peugeot up through the gear changes.

'How exactly do you expect to get away from them?' Delancort eyed her, yanking on a seat belt that kept sticking, the tab refusing to click home. 'They will get the police on our trail . . . And they are much more likely to listen to ALEPH than anyone connected to Rubicon!'

In the wake of the accusations that had decried the Rubicon Group and Ekko Solomon's team as renegades and terrorists, the government of Monaco had formally stated that the principality no longer welcomed the company, giving them a few months to close up their affairs and vacate the city-state. Rubicon had no friends here anymore – not after videos had surfaced showing their operatives gunning down UN soldiers in cold blood.

It didn't matter that the footage was faked; the damage had been done, and Monaco had a reputation to maintain. Delancort had no doubt that the local police would relish an excuse to kick them out early.

'Don't fret about the cops,' she told him, wrenching the wheel over as she made another sharp turn. 'Gera's buddies back there will wanna double-tap you before you ever see the inside of a cell.'

He swallowed hard, looking back through the rear window. In the near distance, he saw a flash of silver hood as the BMW pursued them.

The road dipped sharply, the route cutting past the lush greenery of Kleiner Park as they followed the route that would take them towards the seafront. Tourists and well-dressed locals alike vaulted backwards from the kerb's edge as they sped past the entrance to the Fairmont Hotel, and the hatchback briefly caught air as it juddered over a speed bump.

Delancort bounced off the bags again, and this time he grabbed on for dear life. There was a heavy, ice-cold mass inside each of them, wrapped in a sheath of plastic.

He pulled at the neck of one of the bags and saw what looked like a handful of yellowing straw inside.

'Don't mess with those,' warned Grace. 'You have any idea how hard it was to get them on short notice?'

Delancort had not been involved with the woman's preparations for today's sortie, and he knew little more than his assumptions that she had sourced a weapon and a car. He knew that Solomon was playing his part, too, as was Saito, but where they were he had no idea.

They kept the larger part of their plans from Delancort to protect him, so Solomon insisted, but he glumly acknowledged that it was more to protect *them*. If captured, he had no illusions about being able to resist an interrogation, so the less he knew, the better for everyone else.

The Peugeot swerved around the tight descending turn on to Avenue Princesse Grace and raced downwards, towards the du Portier roundabout. Grace threaded them around the other road users without losing pace, gunning the motor as she tried to coax more power from it. Up ahead, Delancort could see a dusty flatbed truck chugging along at an unhurried pace, the driver apparently unaware of the unfolding chase.

Behind them, hard sunlight came off the silver BMW in a dazzling blink as the other car roared up and shunted them.

'Asshole!'

Grace pumped the brakes and gave back another hit that threw Delancort around in the back. She changed gears and accelerated away, just as a bullet hole cracked the rear windscreen.

The ALEPH operative in the BMW's passenger seat had a pistol with a long length of silencer attached, resting it on the wing mirror as he took his time over his shots.

As they took the next corner at speed, another bullet over-penetrated through the Peugeot's trunk and Delancort could have sworn he felt it rattle around by his knees. Then the BMW put on a burst of acceleration, trying to come level with them. He shrank down, trying to make himself less of a target, his face pressing into the rough material of the duffel bags. That was when Delancort realised the yellow straw wasn't anything of the sort. It was a clump of long blonde hair.

Delancort recoiled as the Peugeot veered over and sideswiped the BMW. The black-jacket driver over-controlled and bounced across a cluster of low concrete planters, ripping into the silver car's bodywork and stripping its paint. As the Peugeot extended its lead, the BMW swerved and lost ground, jerking to a stop. The men in the vehicle shouted at the driver as he struggled to restart the engine.

Passing under an elevated roadway, they skidded into a left-hand turn and the hatchback almost didn't make it, briefly mounting the kerb and clipping a metal barrier. Delancort's heart leapt into his mouth, as for one terrifying second he envisioned the car crashing through the fencing and plunging down the three-metre drop beyond, and straight into the sea.

They were coming up on the Boulevard Louis II tunnel now, and he saw the old truck passing into the dimness beneath. An image flashed in his mind as the tunnel mouth yawned open to swallow them, remembering low-slung Formula 1 racing cars shrieking into this same black void during the Monaco Grand Prix.

But that faded against Delancort's grotesque fascination with the two dead people he had discovered inside the duffels. Both of them were fully dressed, one of them a blonde woman, the other an emaciated man around Delancort's height. With a start, he realised the corpse wore one of his better suits.

'Hold on,' said Grace, as the car dived into the shadows of the tunnel.

She deliberately wrenched over the steering wheel and slammed their vehicle into the tiled wall, flipping it around in a nerve-shredding spin.

Delancort blacked out for a moment, and when he came to again, strong hands were half-dragging, half-carrying him across the asphalt. He lifted his head and saw the ruined Peugeot slewed across the roadway, with a puddle of petrol widening beneath it. Grace shoved the dead woman into the driver's seat, and when she was done, she lit a road flare with the flick of her wrist.

'No ...'

Delancort raised his hands.

Can't she see the fuel spill?

'It is all right, Henri.'

The person carrying him spoke, and Delancort realised he was being supported on the shoulder of a scarred, dark-skinned man with a walking stick.

Dressed in oil-stained jeans, a grubby T-shirt and a leather vest, Ekko Solomon's face was lost beneath a flat cap. He looked so ordinary.

But that appeared to be the point. Solomon directed Delancort into the back of the dusty flatbed idling a few metres away up the tunnel. In his present garb, he was completely believable as the driver of the weather-beaten truck.

The Peugeot went up in flames with a sudden *whoosh* of combustion. Solomon clambered into the cab and Delancort held out a hand to Grace as she ran to the truck. She ignored it and scrambled aboard, banging twice on the back of the cab with her foot.

The truck lurched into gear and snarled away down the tunnel, chased by thick black coils of smoke that rolled off the low ceiling and snaked down after them.

By the time the BMW arrived at the scene, the Peugeot was already an inferno, and the bodies inside it would be burned beyond recognition before the flames could be doused. Suddenly the pieces of the plan Delancort had not been told about were crystal-clear. His last mission of rebellion back at the Rubicon tower would end here, with two corpses in a fatal crash in the Louis II tunnel.

Grace gave him a look as she pulled the blonde wig off her head. 'Congratulations. You're dead.'

He slumped low in the back of the flatbed, his heart hammering against his ribcage as he tried to grasp that notion. His hands were shaking so much he could barely clasp them together.

Grace produced a packet of Gitanes and a lighter, but paused as she became aware of Delancort staring fixedly at her. She gestured irritably with the unlit cigarette.

'What?'

The staging area Kara had secured for them was north-west of Sochi's airport, on the far side from the Olympic Park and the zone of new builds where the Marine Luxe Hotel was situated.

The hacker dug up the forgotten shell of an old state-run kindergarten for their temporary bolt-hole, a derelict quadrangle of low prefabricated buildings in a 1960s Soviet style. Piles of rubbish shoved around by the wind had collected in corners, and judging by the vintage of the debris, Marc guessed the place had been shut down and abandoned some time before the end of the Cold War. A torn map hanging lifelessly from one wall still showed the red expanse of the Union of Soviet Socialist Republics and the split between East and West Germany. Water-bloated textbooks exposed pages showing pictures of men and women in snow-white spacesuits with the letters *CCCP* etched in crimson across their helmets, and here and there, cheap blown-plastic toys lay in piles, green with algal growth. It was a decaying time capsule from a different era, and looking at the decrepitude of the place, it was hard to imagine that it was less than a kilometre from a state-of-the-art sporting complex. This tiny pocket of Russia was lost to another world, forgotten by its indifferent neighbours.

All of which made it an ideal location to lie low. In one of the classrooms, Kara had set up what she nicknamed 'the den' – a bunch of folding tables, a portable solar generator, comms gear and her computer rig. It could be broken down and packed into a couple of kitbags in less than two minutes. Other rooms across the corridor were serving as bivouacs, one for the men and one for the women.

As for the room where Marc and Lucy now stood, it appeared to have been a music class in another life, with walls painted in a bright shade of yellow now cracked and peeling. She stared through a broken sash window, out on to the overgrown jungle that once was a playground. She'd hauled him in for a grilling, out of earshot of the others, the moment he had returned with Malte.

'What the fuck was that?' Her voice was tight and angry. 'You had a job to do, you did it. Why did you stick around?'

'I took a risk,' he replied. 'I saw a – what is it you lot call it? – a *target of opportunity*, yeah?'

'My lot?' She rounded on him. 'You mean the quiet professional black ops specialists?' Lucy shook her head. 'Why can't you stay in your goddamn lane? You could have blown the whole mission!'

'I didn't,' he shot back. 'I can handle myself. I learned from watching you.'

Her annoyance blew its bounds. 'That fucking asshole Glovkonin was *in the room*, Marc! If he saw you—'

'He didn't,' Marc insisted, and he came forward, reaching out to put a hand on her shoulder, softening his tone. 'Lucy, listen . . .'

She batted the hand away and gave him a fierce look.

'Don't you dare give me that *don't worry your pretty little head* routine, I mean it.'

Her retort stung him more than he'd expected.

'That's what you think I was going to say? *Really?* Have I ever once, in all the time we've known each other, patronised you?' She didn't reply and he felt his colour rise. He realised her response wasn't just about what had happened in the VIP lounge, and he backed away. 'See, this second-guessing? This is what happens when two people cross the line with each other. Ever since Paris, ever since we . . .' He faltered over the words.

Lucy raised an eyebrow. 'Ever since we knocked boots?'

Marc scowled. 'It's different between us.' He shook his head. 'I knew it was a mistake. Less bloody complicated before.'

'Well, I got flash traffic for you.' She prodded him in the chest, her eyes bright. 'Things don't stay the way they are forever. Have you been asleep for the past year? *Everything* has changed! You, me, them . . .' Lucy gestured in the direction of the others. 'Rubicon doesn't exist anymore, it's just a name, it's just us! We have to move with that. A second ago you were saying you're not the guy you used to be, but now you're going back in the other direction? It doesn't work both ways, Marc!' She took a long breath, cooling her temper. 'You really think it was a mistake?'

'No, of course not. I didn't mean that.' He couldn't meet her eyes. 'I'm . . . afraid I'm going to ruin what we have, Lucy. I don't want that to change.'

'Too late.' She waved at the air. 'It's gone. Broken into a million pieces. But that's okay, because we can build something else. You just have to know what that is.'

He tried to find a reply, and he couldn't. There was a void in Marc. A place where he hadn't looked since his lover Samantha Green had died, on an operation that had taken the lives of his team and almost ended his as well. Deep in that hollow lay the question: *where is this leading?*

Marc Dane had a mission; he had a reason to move forward and a reason to fight. But what existed beyond that? Everything moved so fast, and he never settled down long enough to let that question catch up to him.

Lucy Keyes was right here, the first person who had ever made Marc feel like he could be someone better, that he could have something more. But looking that truth in the eye would give it a shape and a form, and if he did that it became *real*.

And if it was real, it could be taken from him.

'When we lost Solomon, you picked up the mantle,' she said. 'You didn't debate, you just did it. And the rest of us followed you because we believe in you. But you've gotta decide if you are that guy or the lone wolf. You can't be both.'

At length, Marc gave a rueful nod.

'I'm still getting to grips with this,' he admitted. 'The leadership thing . . . And the . . . uh . . . the other thing.'

'Figure it out,' she told him.

Saito looked up as Andre entered the reception of the Princess Grace Hospital, and the other man caught sight of him. Glovkonin's errand boy was startled to find him in the lobby of the clinic, and his jaw actually dropped open.

Which was exactly the response Saito wanted. The ex-mercenary hacker was getting in the way, with the Russian using him for work in the field. It was imperative that Saito made sure he remained inside the Combine's circle of trust, and the last thing he needed was Andre trying to sideline him and curry favour with Glovkonin.

Andre stalked across to him, frowning deeply, followed at a remove by a pair of grimacing ALEPH operatives who surveyed the room for potential threats.

Saito glanced at his watch. 'I was beginning to suspect you would not appear.'

'What are you doing in Monaco?' Andre's hands clenched. 'I wasn't told you were coming—'

'You are not told everything,' Saito informed him. 'I came to check on your progress. My arrival is timely.' He nodded slightly, in the direction of the offices deeper inside the building. 'Did you cause this?'

'Indirectly,' Andre said, then switched back to his previous questions. 'You should have informed me you were coming. I would have had the men meet you at the airport in Nice.'

'And give you time to prepare?' Saito shook his head. 'To conceal this mess?'

If he made his presence sound like a test, the Frenchman would be less likely to speak of it to Glovkonin or anyone else. Andre still had the hacker mentality from his old life before joining the Combine, where even the slightest questioning of his competence was taken as a grave challenge. It made him predictable. Now he would be concentrating on that imagined slight, and less likely to discover that Saito had actually been in Monaco for the last two days.

Andre's jaw stiffened. 'I wanted to make sure the facts were certain before I reported in.'

'I have the facts.'

Saito showed him a scan of a document – what appeared to be a preliminary report from the duty coroner. It was a decent fake, already inserted into the hospital's database, designed to reflect the false narrative that Solomon and his people had set up.

The fabricated paper trail would reflect that an unknown female and a male matching the description of Henri Delancort had perished in a fatal car accident. If the Monaco police were inclined to dig deeper, the cracks in the falsehood would eventually show, but it would be weeks before that happened.

'Delancort is dead, then.' Andre said it with a smirk, recovering his poise. 'It saved us the effort.'

Saito ignored the comment. 'You have a vehicle?'

'Outside—'

'We will make the call together.'

Saito felt a faint satisfaction as he watched the colour drain from Andre's face.

The ALEPH operatives flanked them from the Princess Grace's entrance to a parking structure where a silver BMW waited. Saito noted with a raised eyebrow the cosmetic damage the vehicle had suffered, then climbed in with Andre quick to follow. The two black-jackets took up places outside the car, standing sentinel while Saito dialled a number on his satellite phone.

'Wh-what are you going to tell him?' said Andre, shifting uncomfortably in the other seat.

Saito didn't answer, instead raising a single finger to silence the other man as he activated the speakerphone setting. The line connected, and the Russian spoke.

'*What is it?*'

'Henri Delancort died in Monaco this morning.'

There was a long pause as Glovkonin took that in.

'*You are there?*'

'Yes.'

'*Why?*'

The Russian had expected him in Sochi, and his irritation at being disobeyed was immediately clear.

'My job is to ensure that you and your colleagues in the committee remain untroubled by any unexpected or problematic events. I am acting in that capacity now.'

'*I suppose so.*' Glovkonin gave a sniff. '*Explain, then. Did that fool Andre exceed his remit?*'

The Frenchman stiffened at the mention of his own name and made to speak, but again Saito raised his finger.

'Andre is not to blame. He attempted to intervene, but the situation was beyond his control.' Saito gave a curt precis of the circumstances, describing the crash in the Louis II tunnel and the fire that followed. 'Delancort paid someone to get him out of the city, but they lacked the competence required. It cost him his life.'

Andre was eager to speak up, so Saito gave him permission with a nod.

'Sir, it appears that Delancort accessed the remaining elements of the Rubicon server and implemented a number of executive-level commands. I am in the process of determining what they were.'

'*How was that possible?*' Glovkonin's voice crackled harshly over the satellite link. '*You were told to monitor his every move!*'

'He used a back-door access protocol,' said Andre. 'A code we didn't even know existed!'

'*Solomon,*' Glovkonin growled. '*Even in death, he still interferes.*'

'Quite,' offered Saito.

'Find out exactly what Delancort did, and put a stop to it.'

'Yes, sir.' Andre nodded, clearly relieved to be off the hook. 'And I will make sure—'

'Go away,' said the Russian. *'I wish to speak privately to Mr Saito.'*

Andre blinked, then exited the car. Saito watched him loiter outside the BMW, his arms folded tightly across his chest.

'We can proceed,' he said.

'I want you here in Sochi by the day's end,' he snapped. *'I don't need you to act on your own initiative. I need you to obey me – is that understood?'*

'As you wish.'

'Measures are being taken and you are required. There will be – how did you describe them? – certain problematic events to deal with in the immediate future. The removal of impediments.'

Saito had no illusion as to what those impediments were. Glovkonin's ambitions to raise himself to the leadership of the Combine were his driving motive, and not for the first time, Saito wondered how the others on the committee could be ignorant of that fact. But then these were men of the most towering conceits that Saito had ever known. It was likely they knew full well of the Russian's desires, but believed themselves to be untouchable.

Saito wondered what might happen if he revealed what he suspected to the Italian, the Swiss and the American. What would they do? Would they be grateful?

Would they release him?

Across the distance between them, Glovkonin seemed to reach into Saito's silence and pull those thoughts from his mind.

'I want to remind you of something, Saito. I know the bargain you made with the Combine. The leverage you willingly gave them so that your daughter would live an untroubled life.'

Rumiko's face shimmered in Saito's mind, as if he were seeing her through a veil of water. His throat tightened as two intense, opposed emotions gripped him. Fear for the girl's life. And rage at the Russian's casual threat to hurt her.

'*We approach a critical juncture,*' continued the voice on the sat-link, the man's tone becoming silky, almost reasonable. '*And I need your complete focus. So I want you to remember what you have to lose.*'

'I know,' Saito said stiffly. His fingers tightened around the case of the phone. He felt powerless and furious, torn apart by the conflict, and desperate not to allow any of that to show in his voice. 'I am fully committed to your service.'

Glovkonin's silence extended, becoming unbearable. Then the Russian spoke again.

'*I hope that is true, for her sake. It is far, far too late for you to grow a conscience.*' He paused again, then gave his next orders. '*The transfer of the equipment is in three days. Everything must be in place by then.*'

'I am on my way,' said Saito, but the words came from a ghost that spoke with his voice.

The team gathered around an electric heater in the middle of a gutted classroom. The derelict school didn't have a single window that wasn't broken or missing, so the wind cut right through the place, and after sunset it turned stone-cold.

In a threadbare folding chair, Lucy leaned forward with her elbows on her knees, her attention fixed on Kara Wei. The hacker stood stiffly in front of a laptop screen as she conducted her briefing.

'I've completed my analysis based on the software implants we now have in the hotel and the race operations networks, the telemetry from Marc's spyPhone, and some additional data I gathered.'

Kara's diction became mechanical. One summer when they were kids, Lucy and her brother had made it to Disney World with their mom, and she remembered the Hall of Presidents there, the animatronics of old white guys moving stiffly as they uttered pre-recorded snippets of speech. Kara behaved like that, rooted to the spot, doling out chunks of information with all the warmth of a data download.

Marc weighed in from where he stood, leaning against the far wall.

'If we want to disrupt the Combine's current operation, we need solid, actionable intelligence on their plans. That means names, dates, places . . . We need to know who they are talking to and what they're using before we can throw a spanner in the works.'

Kara nodded. 'With that in mind, I've formulated an approach vector.' She tapped a keypad and the laptop screen flicked to a grainy image of a Germanic-looking blonde in a grey trouser suit, holding a large digital tablet in the crook of her arm. 'The device you see here is a hardened portable logistics and intelligence hub. Basically, it's a secure hand-held databank used by Giovanni Da Silvio's personal assistant to manage his day-to-day affairs. His whole life is on that thing.'

'Sounds like my mother with her smartphone,' offered Benjamin. The Frenchman scratched his chin with a thick finger. 'She'd be lost without it.'

'The top dogs running the OpTeams at MI6 use similar gear,' said Marc. 'Tough nut to crack.'

'They call it a SecuredBook, or just "the book" for short,' said Kara. 'I have the model number and details of what software it uses. If we can access it, we have the keys to the kingdom.'

'Steal it?' In another lawn chair beside Lucy, Malte asked his question around a steaming plastic mug of black tea in his hand.

'If the book goes missing, the Combine will know their operation is compromised, so that's a no straight off,' said Marc.

'We couldn't lift it even if we wanted to.' Kara enlarged the image, zooming in on a tiny diamond-shaped tattoo on the blonde's wrist. 'See that? Beneath her skin is a radio frequency ID chip that pings the book every three seconds. If the book is more than two metres from the operator, an alert sounds. More than five metres, an alarm goes to Da Silvio's security team. More than ten, and the book automatically frags its internal circuitry with an electrical charge. After that, its only use would be as a paperweight.'

'The Italian brands his staff like cattle?' Lucy scowled at the image on the screen. 'Classy.'

'There must be more than one person who has this RFID chip,' said Benjamin. 'Can't we find another?'

'We could,' Kara agreed. 'Da Silvio's assistant Ms Willa here has her own flunky, a guy called Drake, and Drake has the chip, too. We'd need to abduct him and dig it out of his arm.'

'Messy,' noted Malte. 'Noisy.'

Marc nodded. 'This has to be a zero-footprint operation. No traces, no unnecessary risks.' He pointedly did not look in Lucy's direction as he said the last.

'In active mode, the book is shielded from wireless intrusion, as Marc found out the hard way,' said Kara. 'But it gobbles up power and it needs to be recharged roughly every seven hours. In the charging cradle, the book uploads all the data it has to a stand-alone, air-gapped server.'

'So, the cradle is the weak link in the chain.' Marc peered at the laptop screen. 'We get to it when the book is offline, in charge mode. We mirror the download. Job done.'

'There is always one device in the cradle being recharged, and one in Willa's personal custody,' said Kara. 'My information suggests that the cradle is in the office of the penthouse suite at the Marine Luxe.'

'Break into the most secure floor of Da Silvio's hotel, copy the files, and extract without detection.' Lucy ticked off the actions on her fingers. 'I gotta admit, that kind of op isn't this crowd's specialty. We're usually a little more on the . . . ah . . . *kinetic* side.'

Malte let a breath out through his lips, making a soft explosion sound.

Benjamin sat back in his chair, the plastic creaking under his weight.

'Any other options?'

'Yes,' noted Kara, 'which have progressively lower degrees of success, or are beyond our means with the resources at our disposal.'

Marc pushed off the wall and crossed to stand before them.

'Okay. This is the way we're going. Prep your gear, then get some rest. We'll brief individually on mission-specific tasks.'

'We're doing it tonight?' Lucy cocked her head.

'No time like the present,' said Marc. 'If it goes well, we'll be back here by sunrise tomorrow with the take, and we can figure out our next move from there.' He paused. 'Any other questions?'

No one said anything, and he dismissed the others with a nod. Lucy followed Malte and Benjamin to the door, but she hesitated on the threshold. Marc gave Kara a searching look.

'What?' said the hacker.

'The telemetry you got from me bouncing an attack off the book, back at the hotel. There's no way that would get you all the intel you have on the device.'

He folded his arms, and Lucy waited, wanting to see how this played out.

'I told you, I gathered additional data.'

Kara turned away. She didn't want to have this conversation.

'You're going to have to do better than that,' he replied.

Kara gave a frustrated hiss, a noise like a pissed-off cat.

'It's better you don't know the full details. I acquired information from some of my trusted sources. It is genuine, if that's what you're worried about.'

'What sources?' Lucy demanded. 'Your nasty little troublemaker pals down on the dark side?'

'Yes, exactly.' Kara didn't hesitate. 'Cyber-criminals. Digital radicals. If you have a problem with that, then too bad. We don't have the luxury of dealing with the white hats anymore, Lucy – as if there even is such a thing.'

'What did you give them in return?' Marc said firmly.

'I made some things go away and I made some other things reappear.' The hacker nodded at her laptop. 'The ends justify the means. A few mid-level lowlifes get what they want and we get a way into the Combine's files. I call that a reasonable trade.' She shot Marc a look. 'Or would you rather we wing it, like you did today?'

Marc chewed on that for a moment. 'In future, I want you to square this kind of thing with the team first.'

'It would be easier to let me work the way I need to,' she insisted. 'Without outside interference.'

'Was I unclear?' Marc's tone turned steely.

'You want me to do as you say, not as you do?' Kara shrugged. 'All right. But it's a waste of time.'

'How's that?' said Lucy.

'I'm being a realist.' Kara glanced in her direction. 'We aren't Ekko Solomon's private vigilantes anymore. We're international fugitives. The world believes we're terrorists who gunned down innocent men. To them, we're no different to the black hats on the dark net.'

Marc stayed silent for a long moment before he spoke again.

'We're not doing this to change the way the world sees us, Kara. We're doing this to stop the Combine from rewriting the lives of anyone else.' He turned away. 'Both of you, get sorted for the off. We're green for go.'

EIGHT

Dawn was two hours beyond the horizon, but there were still people out on the yachts moored along the shore who were unwilling to let the party fade. Laughing and drinking, their slurred voices carried indistinctly across the calm water.

Nearby, in each of the boathouses lined up along the edge of the Marine Luxe Hotel, the racers bobbed in the swell or dangled on chains suspending them from maintenance racks. Soft lamps below the waterline lit each dock with a pale yellow glow, catching the shimmer of shoals of curious fish.

Larger, darker shapes moved beneath the surface as well. Two forms drifted towards a dock close to the main buildings, edging up to the side of the aluminium jetty. Presently, a pair of heads broke the water, cautious to remain in the shadows.

Breathing through the snorkel in his mouth, Marc folded back his dive mask onto his forehead and peered into the corner of the boathouse, letting his eyes adjust.

There.

He picked out a glowing red ember, the indicator light on the security camera keeping watch on the speedboat. With care, so as not to make any ripples, Marc slid a compact compound triangle bow from the sleeve on his back and nocked an arrow with a large, bell-shaped head.

Behind him, Malte silently laid a hand on his shoulder.

Someone is coming.

Marc dropped back down under the speedboat's hull as a security guard in a grey uniform shirt walked along the line of the dock, shining the beam of his torch into dark corners as he passed. The light passed over Marc and Malte without pausing, and they waited for the guard's footfalls to fade.

Marc rose again and aimed the bow in the direction of the camera, finding a spot a few degrees to the right of the device. He pulled the bowstring to him, pushing away with the frame, the cam wheels turning as the fibre went taut. The arrow loosed of its own accord, and Marc heard a *thwack* as it hit the wall and stuck there, beads of adhesive on the flat of the head forming an instant gluey gel to hold it in place.

The impact triggered a capacitor inside it, feeding a tiny electromagnetic discharger, and the camera's red light blinked out as the device's electronics were momentarily overwhelmed.

'Go!' snapped Marc, and Malte hauled himself out of the water like a seal beaching itself.

He grabbed Marc's free hand and pulled him up, and the two men sprinted across the boathouse towards the corner where the camera was mounted. They flattened themselves against the far wall, outside the device's cone of vision. Less than four seconds had elapsed.

Marc reached up and tore the arrow away from where it had landed, then tossed it into the water. A moment later, the camera's red indicator was alight again, and if anyone in the security centre noticed the outage, it would appear as a momentary glitch.

He put a hand to his throat, where a waterproof contact microphone pressed into his skin.

'Active One and Two on site, over.'

'*Overwatch copies.*'

Somewhere out in the darkness, Lucy was once more their lethal guardian angel, surveying the location down the night-scope of her PSG-1 sniper rifle.

'*Operations copies.*'

Kara was with Benjamin, out on the rigid inflatable boat they had deployed from, a short distance up along the headland. While he handled the boat, she worked systems intrusion, controlling a whisper-quiet quadrotor drone acting as their eye in the sky.

'Moving in,' said Marc, nocking another arrow as he pushed off from his concealment.

Staying to the shadows and out of the camera's sight lines, he threaded his way out of the boathouse and on to the greenery-lined path that led to the hotel's main building.

Malte kept close, moving silently over the wooden decking.

'There,' he said, nodding towards a clump of bushes out of the spill of light from the lamps lining the path.

'You first,' replied Marc.

As he kept watch, the Finn dropped into cover behind the bushes and peeled off his black outer layer, revealing a dark jump-suit beneath. He put his wet gear, snorkel and goggles in a collapsible sack and hid it in the undergrowth. They swapped places and Marc did the same. He carried two dry bags, one packed with kit for their sortie.

Malte made a low hissing sound and shrank into the shadows. Marc looked up and saw movement. The same security guard who had missed them in the boathouse was coming back their way.

'*Confirming a single male on foot, three hundred metres, closing,*' reported Kara.

Marc looked up. Somewhere overhead, Kara's drone surveyed their location with thermal imagers, picking out the body heat of the two intruders and the guard as bright blobs against a greyed-out landscape.

'*He's coming your way.*'

Malte gave Marc a sideways look, the unspoken question hanging between them. Had they done something to alert the guards? The mission had barely begun, and now it was in danger of falling at the first hurdle.

'*Overwatch has the target in sight,*' reported Lucy. '*I can take him. Your call.*'

Marc watched the man continue on towards them. The next pieces of cover were a series of pump units for the garden sprinkler system, but if he and Malte went for them, they would pass directly in front of the guard and certainly be spotted. The man was two hundred metres distant now and still coming.

He knew he only needed to utter two words – '*send it*' – and a heartbeat later a 7.62 mm NATO round would strike down the guard like a bolt from the blue. Even now, Lucy tracked her oblivious target, cross hairs leading him, ready to put a bullet through his skull.

One hundred and fifty metres and still approaching; this guy was only a rent-a-cop working for the hotel, not one of ALEPH's callous thugs. The thought of ending him just for working minimum wage didn't sit well with Marc.

'Negative,' he whispered. 'Zero footprint.'

From the coldly mercenary point of view, a sniper shot was the most expedient option, but it would leave them with a corpse to conceal and blood spatter on the decking. Marc shook off that thought, seeking a different approach.

'*Copy that,*' Lucy replied.

Without taking his eyes off the guard, Marc reached into the depths of his bow sleeve and his fingers found a cylinder the size of a cigar tube. He felt the pattern of ridges on the device and knew he had the right one. In a series of quick motions, he snapped the tube over the head of the nocked arrow on his bow, and drew on the string. He flicked out a sighting ring to aid with targeting, and pointed the weapon at the top of a nearby palm tree.

Marc let the arrow fly and it cut silently through the dark. The shaft hit the tree trunk with a dull thud – and then a moment later the tube at the arrow's tip began to emit a series of random chirps, like an angry cicada.

The guard halted, peering into the gloom, trying to ascertain the source of the sound. The distraction device continued to sing, drawing the guard towards it. At last, he turned his back on them and started towards the palm tree.

Malte didn't need any encouragement, and the moment the guard's attention was elsewhere, he broke from the bushes and bolted to the cover of the pump units. Marc went after him in a fast, loping run, staying as low as he dared.

The guard stood at the foot of the tree, shining his torch up into the crown of heavy leaves at the top, momentarily lost in trying to figure out where the noise was coming from.

'Active call signs, tracking no other hostiles in your area, you are clear all the way to the main building,' said Kara. *'Go now.'*

Marc patted Malte on the shoulder and once more the Finn broke into a full-tilt run, surging away from a standing start as quickly as an Olympic sprinter off the blocks. Marc shouldered his bow, weaving around the edges of the puddles of light from the lamps on the pathway.

They came up on the entrance that Marc had used the day before to enter the Marine Luxe's conference centre, but diverted away into the shadows, towards a concealed ramp that led down to the maintenance level. They followed the ramp's gentle curve until they were in a low-ceilinged concrete chamber that smelled of stale seawater and machine oil. Lit by a cloudy low-energy bulb, the space was dominated by a wide metal cabinet fitted to one wall, and according to the data Kara had skimmed from the hotel's network, it contained the cable ducting for the entire complex.

The cabinet was made of weathered steel plate, thick enough that it could have shrugged off a heavy calibre bullet at close range. There were no cameras down here, as clearly the invulnerable cabinet was thought to be deterrent enough. Marc smiled thinly at that thought.

We'll see about that.

Malte examined the two heavy-gauge locking mechanisms on the cabinet door.

'Key?'

Marc produced a twin-barrelled syringe from his dry bag.

'Sort of.' He uncapped the nozzle. 'Stand back, this is potent stuff.'

He injected a thick plug of gel into each of the locks, the gooey chemicals from the two barrels mixing as they flowed in.

Inert when separated, the chemicals formed a powerful binary compound when combined, creating a brief but intense exothermic reaction that could melt through steel. The gel fizzed and spat, burning out the locks from the inside, and within a minute, the mechanisms were ruined.

Malte produced a dive knife from an ankle sheath and used it to lever open the cabinet door. Inside, he found a mass of glowing fibre optics – hundreds of bundles of them bunched together in loops, as dense as the roots on a forest floor. The Finn pulled his spyPhone from his dry bag and handed it to Marc as he ran a gloved finger down the numeric tabs on the cables.

Marc found what he was looking for, and quickly connected the spyPhone to a non-conductive interrupt that clamped around the target bundle. Malte's phone booted up and he wedged it in among the cables, safely out of sight.

Malte tapped his throat mike.

'Connected. How copy?'

Kara's voice buzzed through their induction headsets. '*Operations has solid copy. Working, wait one . . .*'

Marc pictured the slight young woman down in the gunwale of the RIB as it bobbed out in the shallows, her hands skittering across the keyboard of her waterproof laptop. Kara's wireless connection to the spyPhone gave her a direct path into the hotel's network, quicker and cleaner than a brute-force hack from outside. She woke up the dormant software implants Marc had inserted the day before and set to work making the Marine Luxe's security net dance to her tune.

'Okay,' she said, after a brief silence. '*I've set up active loops on all camera feeds. Tremor alarms on windows and doors are ghosted. You're clear to proceed.*'

'Guards can still call it in, though,' noted Lucy. 'Can't hack people.'

'*I could,*' muttered Kara.

Marc and Malte backtracked up the ramp, catching sight of the patrolling guard in the distance. Evidently, he'd lost interest in the distraction device and resumed his beat, moving back along the line of the boathouses – better for them, as his attention was in the wrong direction.

Despite Kara's assurances, Marc still tensed when he opened the door leading into the conference centre atrium. No alarms sounded, and he slipped inside, casting around to find one of the security cameras he had spotted earlier. An unblinking digital eye was aimed at him, the red ember visible, but the device was sightless.

He moved on. The tables and low modernist sofas that had been busy with people the day before were empty, lit by the glow of Sochi's buildings coming in through the floor-to-ceiling windows. Off at the far end of the complex, the bar and VIP lounge were dark and silent.

'*Operations has no visual on active call signs,*' said Kara. '*I'm orbiting the drone around, but you're on your own in there.*'

'*Negative,*' corrected Lucy. '*I have line of sight on our boys, through the north-facing windows.*' She paused; her next words were urgent. '*Hold up. Two more guards moving your way from the main building.*'

Marc dropped behind a low planter and he heard Malte find his own cover. He saw shadows moving in the dimness, and not for the first time he found himself wishing for a pair of night-vision goggles. But they hadn't been able to source anything beyond a single set of bulky Cold War vintage scopes in time for the operation, and ultimately Marc had made the choice to leave the Red Army tank crew optics behind. Peering into the gloom, he regretted his decision.

The guards passed by them no more than three metres away, the two men engaged in a conversation about the poor result in the recent match between PFC Sochi and Spartak Moscow. Marc held his breath until they disappeared through a side door.

'*Clear?*' said Lucy.

'Clear.'

Marc broke into a sprint that took him across the atrium, up a staircase and on to the upper level, with Malte close behind.

'*Roof access in the east corner,*' noted Kara.

'Actives copy.'

Marc found the hatch in the grid of glass squares forming the top of the atrium and, with a hand up from Malte, he slid open the latch and climbed out. He pulled the Finn up to him and crawl-walked to the narrow gap between the edge of the conference centre roof and the hotel proper. The gap was less than two metres wide, but the drop beneath it was a black void, plunging down a good thirty metres to the hard marble path leading to the Marine Luxe's swimming pool.

Marc heard the low buzz of electric motors and saw a dark shape blur past overhead, as Kara brought the quad-drone back on station. He ignored it, finding his way to a narrow concrete beam that connected the two buildings.

'*All good,*' said Kara, but Marc hesitated. '*In your own time,*' she prodded.

'Yeah, yeah.'

Marc took a deep breath, tried not to think about the mess he would make if he fell, and then ran across the beam. His shoes slapped over the concrete and he skidded onto the hotel roof. Of course, Malte made it look effortless, making the gap in a couple of long-legged strides.

The hotel was a series of stepped tiers, rising up three more storeys over the conference centre, to the penthouse level where Da Silvio stayed for the duration of the Sochi heats. The man himself was up there in the master bedroom with the companion he'd chosen for the evening, the team's surveillance having put him there some time around two in the morning. Given the amount of alcohol the Italian had been observed imbibing, Marc hoped that he would be dead to the world by now.

Marc and Malte began the climb up the outside of the building, scaling the ornamental ledges and boxy outcroppings that adorned the exterior of the Marine Luxe. Normally, anyone attempting this would have been detected by security the moment they reached the roof level, but Kara's interception of the camera feeds and alarm triggers kept them hidden.

The intelligence that the hacker had bought from her dark web contacts included a copy of the penthouse's floor plan redacted from public records, and – most vitally – details of the sentinels who guarded Da Silvio while he slept.

For all his investment in the Combine and their machinations, it turned out that the Italian only employed men from the group's favoured private military contractor for issues outside his personal security. When it came to his own safety, the Italian had particular rules about who – and *what* – he considered trustworthy.

'We're here,' said Malte.

Marc followed him over the last ledge and onto the penthouse deck. Staggered glass panels coated with golden mirror-film caught the light from the city in warped reflections, and Marc took a second to centre himself.

Off along the coastline to the east, he could make out the first change in colour across the horizon, signalling the oncoming dawn. He rolled back his cuff to check the time on the Cabot dive watch around his wrist.

'Running a little behind,' he whispered. 'We need to step up the tempo if we want to be clear by sunrise.'

He heard the faint buzz of the drone circling around the building.

'*I'm seeing movement in the penthouse's sky lobby. Overwatch, you have it?*'

'*Ah, this angle sucks,*' Lucy replied tersely. '*I see a silhouette, but no clean image. I'm changing position.*'

'Understood, proceeding with caution,' said Marc, moving to a window with a set of concealed hinges. 'Making entry . . .'

He grabbed the twin-injector once again and applied generous blobs of the binary chemical to the joints. Mixed and exposed to air, the acidic gel dissolved the steel, turning it into oily slurry.

Malte levered the window up with the tip of his knife and popped the whole thing out of its frame, letting a mutter of sea breeze blow into the penthouse interior.

Inside the sky lobby, a metre-tall object in the shape of a bullet – which until now Marc had assumed to be an ornamental sculpture – suddenly began moving, sliding across the wooden flooring on hidden wheels in its base. A ring of sensor eyes around the upper quarter of the thing's 'head' rotated, and a fan of emerald laser light flicked on from a concealed emitter. The machine rolled steadily towards them, giving off a low, menacing hum.

'He's got a bloody Dalek,' said Marc, half to himself.

Kara's intel had mentioned the presence of automated security drones inside the penthouse, but still the sight of the machine came as a surprise to him. Pearl-white and sinister in its lines, the robot looked every inch the sci-fi monster.

'*Overwatch ready,*' Lucy said in his ear. '*I have movement but no joy. Light it up!*'

'Back off!' Marc hissed, pushing Malte away from the open window so the sniper would have an unimpeded line of fire right into the sky lobby. He snatched a tactical penlight from a D-ring on his belt and pointed it at the robot, as the thing pirouetted in the middle of the floor and rolled towards them.

He thumbed the switch and a disc of light hit the machine. It stopped with a jolt and made a quizzical clicking noise.

'Send it!' said Marc, and a split second later he heard the buzz of a bullet streaking past. He couldn't help but flinch at the sound. Too often, in his experience, that noise meant someone was trying to kill him.

Lucy's shot made a crater in the security robot's centre mass and it rocked on its rollers, but the thing remained functional. The clicking noise became strident, and the machine continued to approach.

'You pissed it off,' Marc said, into his throat mike. 'Go again!'

He illuminated the robot a second time, and Lucy obliged.

The follow-up shot did the trick, blasting splinters of plastic and circuitry out through the back of the machine. It stopped dead, electronics fizzing inside its casing.

Malte didn't wait, and swarmed through the open window, dropping cat-silent to the floor. Marc scrambled in after him, quickly and less elegantly than the Finn.

'*Did you get it?*' said Kara. '*I don't have eyes in the penthouse level, security up there is on a different server.*'

'I got it,' Lucy confirmed. '*Huh. Never killed a robot before. I'm like Sarah Connor up in here.*'

'Yeah, good job.' Marc looked around. 'About the other thing . . . I don't see any cameras.'

'Private,' noted Malte, with a raised eyebrow.

Marc nodded back at him. Given the reputation Giovanni Da Silvio had, he wasn't the kind of man who would want anyone recording what he did behind closed doors. It also explained the lack of human security guards. Robots couldn't be coerced or bribed into revealing what they were witness to.

'*Just be careful in there*,' said Kara. '*He has more than one of those machines.*' She paused for a second. '*I'm orbiting the drone around the outside of the building.*'

Marc nodded again. 'Active One copies. Sing out if you see anything.'

He hesitated by the windows, matching the geography of the penthouse level with the stolen floor plan he'd memorised. Across the sky lobby, a private elevator led down to the lower levels, with an emergency exit doorway next to it.

According to the architectural plans, that door opened on to a stairwell which ran to ground level, and also gave access to the security office on the floor below. There was a ready room down there, where a team of armed ALEPH operatives were stationed 24/7 while Da Silvio was in residence.

If things go pear-shaped, those men will be up here in less than a minute, Marc reflected. *All the more reason to go quiet-like.*

On the other side of the sky lobby was the penthouse proper, an L-shaped apartment taking up the rest of the top floor of the Marine Luxe. Between here and there were sculptures artfully positioned throughout, each lit from below by its own spotlight.

Malte rocked forward, preparing to take a step, but Marc put out a hand and shook his head.

'Motion sensors,' he whispered, waving his hand in the air.

There were tiny detectors built into the floor that could register the movement of a person and would activate the sky lobby's overhead lights accordingly.

He unlimbered the triangle bow and nocked another arrow with a jammer head. The sensor control pad was on the wall near the elevator controls, and Marc landed a shot right next to it. Once again the jammer did its work and the control pad darkened.

'Last one of those I have,' he noted.

Malte took a cautious step, then another, then slowly walked out into the middle of the room. The main lights stayed off, and his head bobbed.

'Good.'

Marc followed him towards the doors to the penthouse, mentally counting them off. The first led into the guest bedroom, closest to their objective, but they couldn't take the chance it might be occupied. The next door opened into a servants' entrance into the penthouse's galley-style kitchen, and through there, they would be able to access the dining room, living room space and the private office leading off it.

Malte crouched by the door and held out a gloved hand. Marc dropped the binary gel injector into his palm, and watched the other man squeeze a blob of acidic sludge into the electronic lock. Wisps of chemical smoke issued from it as the reaction began, but a familiar low hum pulled Marc's attention away.

At the far end of the sky lobby, another conical shape rolled out from around a corner and executed a mathematically perfect right-angle turn. Green laser light flickered as the second robot scanned the walls and doorways, and then rolled across the floor, closing the distance towards the middle of the lobby.

Waiting at the door, Marc and the Finn were completely exposed, and if they broke for cover the machine's sensors would detect them for certain. He pressed his hand to his throat mike.

'Kara,' he whispered urgently, forgetting radio protocol in the heat of the moment, 'the lift! Get the lift!'

She didn't understand what he meant. '*Active, say again?*'

'Shit!' The robot pivoted sharply in Marc's direction as he swore, clicking and whirring. The damn thing had heard him. 'Get the *elevator!*'

'*Oh.*' That seemed to register. '*Operations copies, wait one.*'

Marc jiggled the locked kitchen door in the vain hope that would help, but the acid gel could take anything up to a minute to eat through the mechanism, and couldn't be rushed. But it would only take ten seconds for the security robot to roll close enough to detect the two intruders, and then everything would go to hell.

He thought about calling on Lucy again, to notch up her second robo-kill, but the angle across the room was wrong and the risk too great that he or Malte might get hit by accident. He swore again, swallowing the curse.

Across the sky lobby, a two-tone chime sounded out of nowhere, and Marc's tension level was so high that the innocuous noise made him twitch. The elevator doors opened, a warm light spilling out from the empty car inside. The robot reacted instantly, twisting towards the new source of sound and movement, clicking intently as it rumbled towards it to investigate.

With a low crackle, the lock crumbled and came apart. Malte shouldered open the service door and Marc followed with haste, taking pains to shut it behind him as quietly as he could.

'Close one,' he breathed.

Malte jutted his chin at the door. 'Will it follow?'

'The robot? In here?' Marc didn't know for sure. 'Let's say no and hope I'm right.'

The Finn's expression made it clear that he didn't think much of that reply, and he moved away. Marc trailed him around an island worktop, the dim night-cycle lighting of the penthouse suite beyond glittering dully off the kitchen's stainless steel panels. The galley-like space was spotless and clinical, more like an operating theatre than a place to prepare food.

It opened on to a two-function area dominated by a round table in dark wood to one side and a broad conversation pit to the other. Marc froze, catching a whirring noise coming from the direction of the leather sofas in the pit. Then someone coughed and he realised he was listening to the raspy snores of a half-dressed, rugged-faced man lying on one of the couches.

He chanced a closer look. The man lay deep in a stupor from an evening of hard partying. The debris of a busy night lay on the glass table before him: an ice bucket full of meltwater and empty Cristal bottles, flutes of flat champagne and a mirror tile speckled with flecks of cocaine.

Marc recognised the sleeper as one of the speedboat racers from the team that the Italian sponsored, and glimpsed another figure at his feet. A younger guy, half-lost in shadows, propped up against the sofa. It took a moment before Marc realised with a jolt that the bluish tinge around his lips wasn't make-up. He did not appear to be breathing.

Marc's gut twisted. In the months that the survivors of the Special Conditions Division had been gathering intelligence on Da Silvio and preparing to move against the Combine, disturbing rumours about the man had cropped up more than once – unconfirmed reports of people joining his social circle only to disappear without trace, police investigations into drug overdoses and missing persons that went nowhere. And now Marc was looking at a victim of this casual abuse, a life discarded and forgotten with as little thought as one of the empty champagne bottles.

'Too late for him.' Malte spoke quietly into Marc's ear, his tone grave but firm.

'We can't just—'

Marc's jaw clamped shut, cutting off his own words. His gaze snapped up, looking across the penthouse towards a sliding door in a wall of frosted glass and matte black tiles.

He knew that beyond that was the master bedroom, and in there Giovanni Da Silvio would be sleeping off his overindulgence, untroubled by the wreckage left in its wake.

It wouldn't take much, Marc told himself. *We're close enough.*

His hands tightened into fists. He imagined silently crossing the room, sliding open the door, and ending Da Silvio in his sleep.

It's a better fate than he deserves.

Malte shared a mute look with him. The Finn still had his dive knife in his hand, and they both knew he could make the kill cleanly and in cold blood.

Ever since the collapse of Rubicon, the ruin of the men who controlled the Combine had been the shared goal of those who'd survived it. It was the justice that Marc, Malte, Lucy, Kara and Benjamin had devoted themselves to securing. It was the justice warranted by the victims of Da Silvio's callous disregard.

But killing him here and now would alert his ALEPH guardians and make it virtually certain that Marc and Malte's deaths would follow in quick succession. Glovkonin and the rest of the Combine's committee would carry on with their schemes regardless of the outcome.

At length, Marc reached up and pushed the blade away.

'Let's get what we came for,' he said softly. 'We'll add the rest to the butcher's bill.'

The office was a small affair – cabinets, a teak table and a couple of chairs, with a view out over the yachts towards the city. Malte shifted a chair and rolled back a rug, revealing a hidden panel in the floor and the safe beneath that, while Marc moved straight to the data cradle on the desk where 'the book' recharged.

He examined it closely. Anti-tamper switches would set off an alarm if the digital tablet was removed prematurely, and the same would happen if he made any attempt to directly interface with it. But the charging cradle itself was a different matter. It was the weak link in the chain.

As Malte used the last of the acid gel to burn his way into the floor safe, Marc found a micro-USB port in the cradle's casing and inserted a data cord into it. He connected the other end to his spyPhone, a twin to the one he'd left in the cable bus down in the basement.

'Moment of truth,' he muttered.

Marc ran the phone's code-cracker program, deluging the cradle's CPU with a torrent of commands, forcing the software into a reset cycle. If it worked, the cradle would be fooled into thinking the book had been inserted and obediently download its entire contents once again – only this time the data on the Italian's movements and plans would be diverted to Marc's smartphone.

With a clunk of retracting bolts, Malte opened the floor safe and gave an almost imperceptible whistle. Inside were shrink-wrapped bundles of euros, roubles and dollars, a dozen passports and what could only be a brick of uncut cocaine.

'Take the cash,' said Marc. 'Make it look like a robbery, yeah? And we could use a top-up for our operating budget . . .'

His spyPhone vibrated in his hand and drew his attention. The forced reset worked like a charm, and the operating lights on the cradle blinked as it came back on stream.

'*Operations.*' Kara's voice crackled in Marc's ear, and she sounded uncharacteristically edgy. '*Watch the clock. This is taking too long.*'

'It'll take what it takes.' Marc's phone showed the word READY and he grinned. 'Here we go.'

He tapped a tab on the touch-sensitive screen and waited for the download to begin.

And waited.

Malte sensed something was off, looking up from stuffing the bundles of money into his dry bag.

'Problem?'

'Oh, shit . . .'

Marc's belly filled with ice. The screen of the docked computer tablet blinked awake and a dialog box appeared. What Marc expected to see was the familiar shape of a loading bar indicating the transfer of files from the book to his phone, but instead the device demanded a security validation.

BIOMETRIC AUTHENTICATION REQUIRED, read the screen, with a countdown timer rolling beneath it. The clock was already at ten seconds and falling.

'The cradle has a biometric lock!' He hissed the words into his throat mike. 'Damn it, Kara, you never said anything about that!'

'*What?*' The hacker sounded dismissive. '*No, that's not right. There's nothing in the intel about biometrics. The reset should—*'

Marc cut her off. 'The reset isn't working!' He searched around the sides of the cradle and found something he hadn't noticed earlier. Mounted on the side of the frame was a tiny metal nozzle, resembling the tip of a spray gun. 'There's a breath print sensor on here. It must be keyed to Da Silvio's assistant . . .'

'*Oh, then we are screwed,*' Kara said flatly.

'*So those dark net assholes you roll with left out that important piece of information, huh?*' Lucy made a sneering noise. '*Nice job.*'

'*Not my fault,*' retorted the hacker.

'Take it and run?' grunted Malte, swinging his dry bag over his shoulder.

Marc shook his head. 'I pull the tablet from the cradle and it blanks the memory.'

He could hardly believe it. They were one step away from having the leverage they needed to tear down the Combine, and now everything was falling apart because of a single oversight.

Like the patterns of a fingerprint, a breath print was individual and unique, a combination of chemical markers in a human's exhalation that the sensor could pick up and analyse. But without Willa there to unlock the device, the data they wanted was untouchable.

The countdown on the screen hit zero and the tablet turned black.

'Abort,' said Marc, the word weighing heavily on him as he uttered it. 'It could have a time-out alarm programmed into it.'

'*Actives, confirm last,*' said Lucy, switching back to business in an instant.

'Active One confirms mission abort, repeat mission abort.' Marc swept his gear into his bag and jabbed a finger towards the door, getting a nod from Malte. 'We're on our way out.'

Malte dashed into the penthouse and Marc was on his heels, cursing their luck. They had left the office in enough of a mess to sell the lie of a theft gone wrong, and now the best result they could hope for was to get out in one piece.

The security robot waiting for them in the dining room had other ideas, however. Despite Marc's thoughts to the contrary, the thing had followed them into the penthouse, taking up station here while it scanned for possible intruders.

Lights on the front of the thing blinked on, and it spoke in gruff, synthesised Russian.

'*Stoy!*' In the quiet of the penthouse, the voice sounded as loud as gunfire. '*Do Not Move!*' It repeated the command in English.

Malte did not obey. He dived for the machine before it could react, stabbing his knife into the collection of lenses around its upper quarter. He managed to land two good hits before a panel in the front of the machine flicked open, and an electric stun prod telescoped out, clipping the Finn with its sparking tines.

Electricity shocked through him. Malte howled in pain and jerked back, stumbling over the dining table. Marc grabbed the first thing that looked like a possible weapon – a long piece of modernist sculpture in an alcove – and swung it like a baseball bat. He connected with the robot, and the machine backed off as a subroutine in its programming triggered a self-preservation protocol. But the luxury pile carpet in the penthouse wasn't the best surface for the robot's rollers and it skidded as it moved.

Marc saw the opportunity and gave it a hard kick with all his energy. It was heavier than it looked, but the blow overbalanced the machine, sending it crashing through a divider and into the conversation pit. The man who had been sleeping down there came to with a panicked yell, as Marc grabbed Malte's arm and pulled him back to his feet.

They barrelled back out through the kitchen and into the sky lobby as an alarm began to sound.

'*The security detail is on the way up*,' Kara said urgently. '*ETA twenty seconds!*'

'The window!'

Marc made for the open panel they had used to make their entry, but Malte struggled to keep up, still pale and shaky from the punishing voltage the robot had put into him.

Marc let the Finn go out first, shoving him ungently as the exit door across the sky lobby banged open to disgorge three ALEPH black-jackets. Marc vaulted after him and they scrambled across the roof, towards the stepped levels they had used to climb up.

'*Behind you!*' Lucy called, and Marc twisted, catching sight of an ALEPH operative emerging through the missing window.

In the pre-dawn light, he saw a PP-2000 sub-machine gun in the man's hand, the weapon's distinctive matte-black profile appearing in his mind's eye like a photo snapshot. Marc had a tech-nerd's memory for stats, and he knew exactly how many rounds of 9mm ammunition the weapon would be able to put into him in a single burst. He found himself wishing he'd brought something more formidable than a bow and arrow.

In the next second, he caught the hornet buzz at the top of his hearing, and the ALEPH gunman jerked as if reeled away on an invisible wire, tumbling back into the sky lobby.

'*You're welcome*,' said Lucy, as she racked another round into her rifle.

'*Active call signs!*' Kara's voice grew fuzzy as she shouted into her mike. '*I have men on the roof of the conference centre, they're moving to block your exit!*'

Marc craned his neck to get a better look down the stepped side of the Marine Luxe, and he saw the flicker of light off the spinning blades of Kara's quadrotor drone as it bobbed down over the lower levels. Shadows moved atop the lower atrium and indistinct voices came to him on the wind. Muzzle flare blinked like fireflies and the drone zigzagged away, struggling to stay airborne.

'*Ah, the quad took a hit,*' said the hacker. '*I've lost visual on you.*'

'Need another way,' grunted Malte. He made his way to the other side of the penthouse level and peered over the edge. 'Here.'

The Finn jumped over without waiting for the other man to agree with him. Marc dashed across, and found Malte on a balcony one floor below, already clambering over the edge, positioning himself to drop to another on the next level down. The balconies on the residential floors of the Marine Luxe were arranged in an offset pattern, staggered left to right.

They could follow them down towards the mezzanine, he realised. It was that, Marc reflected, or risk being gunned down in a hail of bullets.

'*You go over there, I can't cover you,*' said Lucy.

'Understood.'

He shifted his bag to centre the weight evenly and jumped down to the first level below. The impact smacked hard against the flat soles of his deck shoes, and he went over the concrete rail around the balcony, trying not to imagine what would happen if he slipped and missed his landing spot on the next floor. There was nothing but open air all the way down the ten-storey fall to the sun terrace.

Marc dropped again, this time landing on a balcony lit by the soft glow of lamps inside a huge suite. He saw the shocked faces of the residents as they bolted upright in bed, frightened out of their sleep by his arrival. He spared them a cheery wave and went over the rail again, dropping to the next floor. This time, he almost collided with a sun lounger and stumbled, momentarily losing his momentum.

From above came the metallic chatter of automatic fire and a burst of rounds smacked into the concrete, chipping divots out of the balustrade as the crimson threads of targeting lasers wavered in the air. Two of the ALEPH operatives were firing down the side of the hotel, evidently uninterested in any collateral damage they might incur to the building or its occupants.

Marc dismissed the idea of sending an arrow back up at them. He had no desire to expose himself to that withering fire. Instead, he grabbed the lounger and threw it over the rail as a distraction. The seat clattered against the side of the hotel as it fell, and it did the trick, drawing the attention of the gunmen as Marc dropped from balcony to balcony, hissing with effort with each landing and jump.

He made it to the roof of the mezzanine, still twenty metres off the ground and with no cover of any kind. Marc heard the men on the top of the hotel shouting, and saw the aiming lasers sweeping his way.

Malte stood at the edge of the roof, beckoning wildly.

'Run!'

Marc sprinted towards him, and the gunmen saw the movement. Shots slapped into the roofing felt around his feet, but as he moved, he suddenly realised what the Finn wanted to do.

A section of the roof extended out over the terrace to become the sun cover for a swim-up bar, and beyond that was the pool, shimmering in the moonlight. Malte threw himself off in a run-and-jump, hitting the water like a cannonball. Marc released a whoop of spent breath and hurled his body out into open air, twisting to land back-first.

He struck the surface with a smacking impact that stung like a bastard, and went under, bumping off the shallow bottom. Kicking away, Marc oriented himself towards the side of the pool and swam towards it, staying under as he crossed the distance. Bullets cut through the water in streams of bubbles as the shooters on the roof wasted ammo trying to tag him. At this distance, the best they could hope for was a lucky hit, but what was lucky for them would be fatal for Marc and Malte.

Waiting until the last possible moment, he burst out of the water and hauled himself up and out. Malte rose close by, coughing and wheezing. The gunfire had stopped and, looking up, Marc could see several hotel residents out on their balconies, awakened by the chaos.

On the floor directly above the pool, an angry man in a dressing gown shouted his fury at this disturbance, and belatedly the ALEPH gunmen had put up their weapons. Over the man's tirade of gutter Russian, Marc heard the peal of an alarm sounding through the building, and his heart sank. They had well and truly blown any semblance of stealth.

'This way,' called Malte, heading back through the hotel grounds.

Lights were coming on in quadrants as the security team came out to chase them down, dispelling the shadows that had previously given them sanctuary.

Marc tabbed his throat mike as he ran. 'Ops! Burn the phone in the cable bus, do it now!'

'*Operations copies,*' came the reply. '*We're on our way to pick-up.*'

From her station on the RIB, Kara sent a remote kill code to Malte's spyPhone where Marc had left it tucked in among the basement wiring. The signal destroyed the device by forcing a critical overload of its battery, setting it and the surrounding cables alight.

Marc heard the far-off sound of something combusting, and the hotel's exterior lights flickered as power faltered. Smoke emerged from the ramp leading down to the basement as the two men sprinted past it, running for the safety of the boathouses and the water beyond.

They halted by the bushes to recover their swimming gear. There was no time to change back into the wetsuits, but they couldn't risk leaving the kit behind, especially after the operation had fallen apart. The priorities now were escape and damage control. They could not afford to leave any clues behind for the Italian's men to find.

'Go, go!'

Marc urged Malte into the dark waters of the marina, spotting the low-slung shape of the RIB out on the water as Benjamin brought it around. He dived off the end of the jetty and pulled hard into the current, working against the drag of the bags looped over his shoulders.

The effort started to tell on him. Marc forced himself to push on, moving into the tide as the RIB grew from a black smudge on the water's surface.

He found a grab rope near the stern and pulled himself aboard, sloughing off the bags with a wheezy grunt. Malte was already down in the gunwale, panting hard.

Crouching low over the helm, Benjamin rammed the throttles forward to full and the RIB shot away, out into the Black Sea.

Marc crumpled against Kara, staring back past the churning outboard towards the hotel and the docks as they sped away. On the shore, beams from torches bobbed as the security team searched the grounds fruitlessly for the two intruders.

Lucy waited for them by the Hunter 4 × 4 when they came ashore out past the city limits, and Benjamin drove them back to the derelict school in silence, as the rising sun turned the sky purple-pink.

It was only when they stepped out into the shadows of the building that Kara finally broke the silence.

'The breath sensor must have been a recent security upgrade,' she said quietly. 'That's why it wasn't in the data.'

'Or maybe your black hat buddies left that out, because they knew it would screw us.' Lucy shot her a look. 'What is it they say? *For the lulz?*'

'Knock it off. Blame won't fix this,' Marc said, shutting down the argument before it could begin.

He felt tired down to his bones, and all he wanted was to sleep – which is why he didn't see the figure in the open doorway until she struck a match to light a cigarette.

Marc jolted back in shock, and from the corner of his eye, he saw Lucy tearing a pistol from her belt.

But he couldn't pull his gaze away from the face of the woman in the gloom, the flickering match giving her an infernal aspect.

'Aw, don't fight,' she said, with a smirk. 'It's so unprofessional.'

'*Grace*.' Marc said her name, the leaden sound of it falling from his lips.

The fraud who had impersonated a woman he loved, killed MI6 agents and almost murdered his friends. Here she was, coming out of the darkness to haunt him like a nightmare that would not fade.

'You should be a corpse,' spat Lucy, taking aim at her. 'Let me catch you up.'

Grace shook her head. 'Your boss wouldn't like that.'

She stepped aside, and behind her stood someone else – once a tall and elegant figure, now worn down by injury.

'My friends,' said Ekko Solomon. 'It is good to see you.'

NINE

'How did you find us?'

Marc sat forward on the edge of a folding chair, trying to grasp what he was seeing in front of him.

'That's the question you lead with?' Lucy shot him a hard look. She still held a gun in her hand, the muzzle of the Sig Sauer semi-automatic tapping against her thigh as the tension in her sought a release. 'How about starting with *what the fuck*?'

'I think that's implied,' noted Marc, casting about the motley group arranged around the decrepit classroom.

He didn't know where to look first. To one side stood Grace, leaning against a wall with a studied air of disinterest – the woman who had weaponised his past against him. Delancort, who had turned his back on them when the Rubicon team fled from their enemies, kept to the corner, eyeing his surroundings in the manner of a trapped animal. Solomon, the man he had come to consider as a mentor, and for the past few months, someone they had all believed to be dead, sat watching him intently from the corner of a broken school desk.

Solomon held himself up on a cane, and he looked as if he'd aged a decade since Marc last saw him. He was a broken reflection of the imposing, patrician figure Marc had come to know. Yet, despite that, it had not quite diminished him. Solomon looked at Marc with his good eye and nodded to him, that simple motion communicating volumes.

'We used the Grey Record to track you down,' said Delancort, venturing a reply to Marc's question, referring to the Rubicon Group's secret files. 'I followed the movement of money from those black budget accounts. With that to hand, finding you here in Russia was relatively simple.'

'I knew I should have scrubbed them.' Kara gave a low grunt. 'Makes sense. The only other person who knew about the existence of those accounts was Mr Solomon. He set them up, after all.'

'Indeed,' said Solomon. 'I hope you understand, it was too risky to attempt any contact before now. We had to come here, to see you face to face. So there would be no doubt.'

'I suppose so,' offered Benjamin, rubbing a hand over his bald pate. 'If someone purporting to be Ekko Solomon reached out to us, what would we have assumed?'

'That they were a fake,' agreed Marc. 'It's not like we haven't seen enough of those.' He pointedly glanced at Grace, who let the comment roll off her.

'Damn right.'

Lucy stalked across the room and took Solomon's chin in her hand, staring into his face. He didn't react, and she tilted his head left and right, examining the healed wounds on his cheek. Then at length, Lucy undid a few buttons on the man's shirt and stared at the livid scar on his chest.

Solomon remained still, waiting for Lucy to come to her own conclusions. Her hand dropped away and her mask of defiance slipped for a moment, her sorrow shining through.

'I'm sorry,' she said, her voice thickening. 'If we'd known you survived that explosion, we never would had left—'

Solomon held up a hand. 'I was buried under a collapsed building. I expected to perish. You have nothing to apologise for.'

Marc closed his eyes for a moment and he was back there in Mozambique, recalling a night of fire and death out in the burning wilderness. In a brutal showdown at a petrol station on a deserted highway, the Combine's killers had come to end the lives of the Rubicon survivors.

They had nearly succeeded. At the end of it, Solomon had held off the enemy attackers and paid with his life, caught in an explosive trap laid for the assassins.

Or so they had believed.

Malte stood up and walked to Solomon, offering him his hand.

'Welcome back, sir.' The Finn gestured at his face, indicating the other man's burn scars. 'Hurts?'

'I live with it.' Solomon smiled slightly and shook his hand. 'It is preferable to the alternative.'

Marc waited for the same reaction in himself – an expected flood of relief that his friend and mentor had returned to them. It did not come. Instead, there was something else – a hard, obdurate unwillingness to accept these new circumstances.

'Let's hold off on the reunion party,' he insisted, and the steel in his words was enough to make Lucy and Malte draw back. 'No one's happier than me that you're alive. But the company you're keeping raises a lot of questions.' He gestured at Grace and Delancort. 'And then there's the whole issue of why you're not rotting in some Combine black site.'

'You recall Mr Saito?' Solomon uttered the name of the Combine assassin, and Lucy stiffened. The man had stabbed her in the gut and left her to bleed out in their first encounter, and while she had later returned the favour, Lucy wasn't the kind of woman to let something like that be forgotten. 'He is responsible for my recovery. Saito had plentiful opportunity to turn Grace and me over to his masters. Yet he did not. In point of fact, he is the reason we are here.'

'Saito let you go?' Lucy's tone made it clear what she thought of that.

'Maybe he did it so you could lead him to the rest of us,' said Marc.

Solomon shook his head. 'No. If that were so, would we be having this conversation? Saito is a victim of the Combine, as we are. He was coerced into their service by threats against those most dear to him. I believe we can turn this man.'

It took an effort for Marc to put aside his personal feelings towards Saito and consider the possibility with a clear eye. Someone as highly placed in the Combine apparatus as the Japanese assassin would be a perfect tool to use against them, as Glovkonin had used insiders within Solomon's company to destroy Rubicon.

Delancort cleared his throat. 'Speaking for myself . . . The past few months have given me ample time to re-evaluate my choices.' He met Marc's gaze. 'What I told you that day on the roof in Monaco . . . I still believe I was right. But I understand now that you did what you thought was right.' He sighed. 'I thought we could weather the storm. But instead Pytor Glovkonin forced me to watch him systematically dismantle everything Rubicon stood for.' Delancort considered his next words. 'You and I have never seen eye to eye, Dane. But this goes beyond our personal differences.'

Marc accepted his explanation. There was no love lost between them, but he had to admit he respected Delancort's intelligence, even if he disliked the man's prissy personality.

'I'm willing to give Henri the benefit of the doubt – he's earned it.' Marc carried on, turning his attention to Grace. 'But you? That's a different story. I'm asking myself why you don't deserve a bullet in the head and a shallow grave.'

'Wow.' Grace clasped her hands together, glancing around at the others. 'Months on the run and Marc-y boy here has toughened up, am I right?' She leered at him, miming the shape of a gun. 'You gonna do the deed, tough guy?'

'Oh no, honey. That's *my* prize,' Lucy insisted, rocking on the balls of her feet.

Solomon held up a hand to silence Grace before she said something she might regret.

'Let us have no illusions here. Grace is a mercenary. But not a zealot. The Combine made her a target, like us. Our interests coincide, and she has been of great use getting us to this point.'

'Common enemy, you know how it goes,' said the woman. 'As long as Glovkonin's breathing, I have a target on my back. Like it or not, you idiots are my best shot at putting him in one of those shallow graves. Get it?'

'We don't need her,' muttered Malte.

'Or maybe we do,' said Benjamin. Marc shot the big man a surprised look, and he carried on. 'Let us not sugar-coat it. We are . . . how do you say . . . running on fumes? We failed in our mission tonight. We need help if we are going to succeed.'

Marc's gaze drifted to Kara, who had barely spoken during the conversation. He remembered something she had said back in France.

If we want to get back at the Combine, we may have to give up the luxury of the moral high ground.

Marc scowled. As much as he wanted to deny it, there was truth in Benjamin's assertion. And if he divorced himself from the visceral, emotional content of his reaction to Grace, Marc had to admit that the woman was a superlative undercover agent. She'd fooled him and MI6 when she assumed the identity of Marc's ex-lover and former team-mate. He made a dispassionate calculation, considering how they could turn those skills towards destroying the Combine.

Of course, they would never be able to trust her.

But then this is what a leader does, isn't it? Manage risk versus reward?

He had to concentrate on what served the mission best, not sentiment.

Marc took a deep breath, and glanced at Solomon once again, considering the weight the other man had carried through their ordeals in the Special Conditions Division. That burden now belonged to him.

'All right. Grace gets a stay of execution.' Marc nodded, and for a second Lucy was lost for words.

Is he actually going along with this shit?

'Oh, lucky me,' said the pale woman, fanning herself with her hand. 'Is there a team cheer I have to learn, or something?'

Lucy wanted to yell at the Brit, to criticise his decision, but she bit down on the impulse. She forced herself to see the bigger picture, the tactical advantages.

Still, Lucy couldn't quite keep silent about it, and leaned close to Grace.

'You know how it is, right? I mean, I don't actually have to make the threat out loud.' She held up the loaded Sig Sauer. 'It's implicit.'

Leaning against the classroom's peeling wallpaper, Grace spread her hands and her expression became the picture of innocence.

'If I double-cross you, I'm dead. Yeah, I hear that a lot.' She folded her arms across her chest. 'And when it's over—'

'You help us finish this,' Marc interrupted, 'and at the end you walk away and never show your face – *any face* – again.'

'I can live with that.' Grace looked back to Lucy. 'How 'bout you, *honey*?'

Lucy turned away, and found Delancort watching her.

'Did you bring anything with you when you left Rubicon?' she asked.

'Some material from the company database,' he admitted. 'Some resources.'

Kara perked up. 'Such as?'

Off a nod from Solomon, Delancort searched his pockets, finding a flash drive. He handed it across to Kara.

'You may find that of use. I uploaded files pertaining to transfers of cash and equipment that Glovkonin had ordered.' Lucy shared a look with Marc at the mention of the word 'equipment'. 'He has been using Rubicon subsidiaries for something,' continued Delancort. 'I do not know what. But it was being done with an eye towards concealment, and that alone is reason enough to look into it.'

'Agreed,' said Kara, turning the flash drive over in her fingers. She actually licked her lips at the prospect of what might be on it.

'Mr Harun.' Solomon indicated the man with the motion of his cane. 'You said your mission failed. Perhaps you would enlighten us as to your current circumstances.'

Lucy noticed how Benjamin looked to Marc for permission before he continued, and that subtle signal made her realise how much things had changed over the past few months.

The Frenchman outlined the situation that had brought the Rubicon survivors to Sochi – their intelligence gathering, the blown surveillance operation in Paris and the data from Malte's contact in Hong Kong.

Marc picked up the thread from there, leading right back to the moment at hand and the failure to recover the data from Da Silvio's encrypted book.

Throughout their explanations, Solomon remained silent, taking it in.

'This complicates matters,' he said, when Marc was done. 'Glovkonin and the Combine will have been alerted by your presence in Paris. Even if you were able to prevent yourselves from being identified tonight, they may suspect the two events are connected. I know Giovanni Da Silvio – he is egotistical, but he is not a fool. He will have security doubled throughout the hotel. You will not be able to make a covert approach to the device a second time.'

'Yeah.' Lucy frowned. 'That's for damn sure. We need another option.'

'It's staring you in the face.' Grace lit another cigarette and took a long draw on it. 'I always thought that *black turtleneck* and *swinging on wires* bullshit is trying too hard. You want access to that device? You need to *social engineer* it.'

'You mean *con* our way to it?' Benjamin gave her a sideways look.

'That's exactly what I mean.' Grace nodded in Marc's direction. 'He thinks too much like a techie. He looks for a hardware solution to every problem.' She chuckled. 'People are always the weakest link – if you know what buttons to push.'

'If we can't get to the book while it is charging . . .' Kara stared at the decrepit ceiling, thinking out loud. 'And we can't get to it while it's out and about . . . Then we have to access it while it is in transition between those modes.'

'In the middle of crowded rooms and parties, and wherever the Italian likes hanging out.' Lucy's reply was withering. 'All while not being made by the Combine's thugs. How's that gonna work?'

'You've done undercover.' Grace shot her a look. 'Hell, I heard that you don't even suck at it. So you know how it works – you walk in through the front door and play the role.'

'Blending with those well-heeled types in the motorsport crowd isn't just a matter of attitude,' countered Marc. 'We need an "in", we don't have one, and we don't have the money to buy one at short notice.'

Delancort cleared his throat. 'That is not strictly true.'

'Oh?' Lucy turned towards him. 'Just how much cash did you embezzle from Rubicon before you split?'

'Not as much as you would think,' he replied. 'But that is not what I meant. The "in" Mr Dane requires is present. One of the groups sponsoring a powerboat in Da Silvio's race is the Horizon Integral Corporation, and you will recall Rubicon has . . . I mean, it *had* a pre-existing relationship with that company.'

Delancort's words were a polite way of saying that Rubicon and the SCD had briefly brought Horizon Integral to the brink of ruin. While tracking the renegade hackers known as Ghost5, the team's investigations had uncovered industrial sabotage inside HI. Had that been revealed, it would have cratered the billion-dollar software company's share price overnight.

Deals were made to cover up those facts – something that, years later, still left a bad taste in Lucy's mouth – and the leads they had uncovered ultimately allowed the Rubicon operatives to stop Ghost5 from provoking a war in Korea.

Kara's hands clattered over her laptop keyboard as she checked into Delancort's comments.

'He's right. Horizon Integral have a boat and driver in the Veloce Cup Championship, a woman named Shayla McGrath . . .' She made a face. 'She's dreamy.'

The hacker turned her computer around so they could see the screenshot of a sleek, forest-green speedboat emblazoned with the HI logo. In the foreground, a striking young woman in her twenties with a fighter pilot attitude sat astride the racer's prow. Next to McGrath, holding a flute of champagne and taking a selfie with a gold-plated iPhone, was someone whom Lucy immediately recognised.

'I know her. That's Sunny Wehmeyer. Daughter of Martin Wehmeyer, Horizon's CEO. Met her at a party in Sydney. We bonded.'

'Yes . . .' Solomon gave a nod. 'A rather capricious young lady, if I recall correctly.'

Kara returned to her data-mining. 'Well, according to this, she's actually working with the HI racing team in a management capacity. She's here, in Sochi.'

'Huh.' A slow smile crossed Lucy's face. 'Sister's trying to make something of herself.'

'There's your angle,' said Grace, exhaling a thin wisp of cigarette smoke. 'You just need to exploit her.'

Despite her antipathy towards the other woman, Lucy had to admit Grace was correct. She could already see the beginnings of an approach, a way to charm Sunny into getting them access to the racing circus of parties and social gatherings.

'Let's be clear about the stakes,' said Marc, shifting off his chair. He stretched, stiff and fatigued like they all were after the night's work. 'We need to spin up an alternative plan to get close enough to the book while the thing is in transition. Connect to it, download the contents and get out unscathed. All that in plain sight.' He let out a breath. 'It's not going to be like picking some joker's pocket.'

'Get some rest first.' Lucy's words were directed at Marc, but they counted for everyone. 'We need to be sharp for this. No more screw-ups.'

The group broke up, finding their way to the bivouacs, but Marc was wound too tight to drop onto a camp bed and fall asleep.

His body wanted to spark out and crash, but his brain was gunning like a V8 engine, still trying to assimilate the revelation that Ekko Solomon was alive.

In the dawn light, he walked the perimeter of the derelict school's playground, failing to bleed off the nervous energy. If he stopped moving, he was afraid the tension would smother him.

'You cannot sleep.' The rich timbre of Solomon's voice drifted over the ruined yard.

'Something like that,' Marc admitted, turning towards him.

Solomon came closer, leaning on the cane, studying Marc closely. Then he smiled widely, a rare thing to see from a man so usually reserved.

'I always knew you had it in you.'

'What?'

'Leadership.'

Marc's lip quirked up in a crooked smirk. 'The only thing in me right now is a tankful of bloody tired.'

'That is how it works,' said Solomon, with wry amusement. 'You can feel it, yes? A giant has his hand around your chest, and he squeezes. Each time you take a risk, or send the people you trust into danger, his grip tightens a little more.' He shook his head. 'And after a while, you forget what it is to live without that pressure.'

'You want the job back?'

Solomon chuckled. 'You cannot trade it. The burden can only be accepted.' He winced as he moved awkwardly.

'You all right?'

Marc moved to offer him a hand, but Solomon waved him away. Accustomed to seeing the other man as vital and imposing, it was hard to admit that the urbane African was as human as the rest of them.

'It will be a long time before I consider myself whole again. If I ever can.' Solomon shifted his weight on the cane. 'I am alive. And if we are alive, we can fight, and if we can fight—'

'We can win,' Marc finished for him. He paused, turning thoughts over in his mind. 'Don't get me wrong, I'm glad you're okay. I'm even glad to see Delancort, sort of. But bringing Grace, that's a lot of trouble right there.'

'Forgive me,' Solomon admitted, 'but what other choice was there? Left to her own devices, she would gravitate back to Glovkonin. If he did not kill her, he would use her against us. So, we must keep our friends close but our enemies closer.'

'I'm already regretting it.'

'As am I,' said Solomon. 'But we play the hand we are dealt, Mr Dane.'

'Yeah. Well, we're all in now.' Marc rubbed his chin. 'Between you and me? I'm amazed we've lasted this long on the run. On the off chance we actually take down the Combine, I don't know what comes next.'

'I have some ideas.'

Marc didn't doubt that for one moment. Even after Lau Fa Weng – the former Chinese State Security agent who had been Solomon's partner in the formation of Rubicon – had suborned the corporation from within and set this whole sorry situation running, Solomon had refused to go quietly. For now, Rubicon and the Special Conditions Division might be in ruins, but if anyone could conjure something anew from the wreckage, it was him.

But there was a lot of work to be done before that could happen.

With that in mind, Marc pushed away the fatigue crowding the edges of his thoughts and concentrated on the other man.

'Tell me about the deal you made with Saito.'

'He has been the Combine's attack dog for years. More than any-one, Saito knows what they are capable of. He has done many dark deeds in their name.'

'That doesn't answer my question,' said Marc, pulling his shirt tight against the cool air. 'If anything, it underlines why he's dangerous.'

'True,' Solomon agreed. 'I am alive because of his reluctance to serve the Combine's whims. Saito has, I believe, reached the limits of the leash they have about his neck.' Solomon touched a hand to his own throat.

'He wants out?'

'In a way.' Solomon glanced up at the lightening sky. 'His price is not his freedom, but that of his daughter. The Combine hold her life over him – if he believes she is safe, he will give us everything.'

Marc folded his arms. He remembered Saito's face when the man told him how he had stabbed Lucy in the belly and left her to die, all so he could minimise the potential threat she represented. The assassin had said it so calmly, as if making a mathematical calculation of life against life. By Saito's reasoning, a trained Tier One operative like Lucy Keyes was capable and likely to survive such a wound, but the injury would keep her out of action while he completed his mission.

Lucy *had* survived, of course. Saito had turned out to be right. And in fact, his underestimation of the sniper's tenacity had earned the assassin a stabbing of his own.

'I know you have your code,' Marc began. 'I've always admired your principles, tried my best to emulate them. But Saito is our enemy. We owe him nothing.'

'Perhaps,' said Solomon. 'But his daughter is innocent. She is exactly what I created Rubicon for – to be the strength for those who are weak. The shield for those who go unprotected.' He leaned forward and placed a hand on Marc's arm. 'If we ignore our princi-ples, how are we any better than Glovkonin and his venal friends?'

Marc pulled back, Solomon's words warring with other, more vehement instincts.

'Our enemies use our code against us.'

'Yes.' Solomon nodded again. 'But that is not a reason to abandon it, not even for a moment! With the first compromise, we become lost. So we hold true, no matter what we face.' He smiled, and then set off back towards the derelict building. 'I know you understand that, Mr Dane, even if it is difficult. That is why I trust you with my people.'

And when he was alone, Marc stood there in the chilly morning air, weighing up the consequences.

The elevator doors opened at the Marine Luxe's penthouse level, and Glovkonin stepped out, his swift pace a function of his annoyance. He was barely out into the sky lobby when a pair of black-jacketed ALEPH security men moved to intercept him.

'Step back.' One of them held up a hand. 'No admittance. They should not have let you up here.'

Glovkonin's own personal security detail moved to take on the ALEPH men, and he had to shake his head in order to stop Misha and Gregor from doing anything violent.

'Do you know who I am?' the oligarch snapped. 'No. Don't answer that. Clearly you do not. It doesn't matter. Get out of my way.'

The two ALEPH guards exchanged looks, and then glanced at Glovkonin's men. The Moscow-based PMC that employed the security operatives wasn't known for hiring fools, and they silently made the smarter choice to back down.

Across the room, a pair of locals in the dark blue windcheaters of Sochi's regional police department shared a whispered comment and a snigger at the expense of the ALEPH men. Glovkonin heard the sneers and turned his ire on them as well.

'These two idiots,' he went on, giving orders in sharp, hard snarls. 'I want you and them out of here. Do it now!'

One of the police officers, a junior sergeant, started to complain, but then Gregor swaggered his way, opening his jacket to reveal the gun holstered at his hip. Like the ALEPH operatives, the two cops swiftly decided that discretion was the better part of valour, and retreated.

Glovkonin stormed into the penthouse apartments and found the object of his ire – the Italian in conversation with his assistant Willa, while the hotel manager hovered nervously around other officers from the Sochi force, as they surveyed the rooms for clues.

'We need to talk,' he said briskly.

'This is a crime scene,' said Da Silvio's assistant, her Germanic tones clipped and hectoring. 'You cannot simply barge in here.'

'I will not repeat myself,' Glovkonin told her.

At length, the Italian rolled his eyes and waved the woman away.

'Willa, perhaps you can take these gentlemen outside for a moment?'

The woman obeyed, sparing Glovkonin a sour look, and she ushered out the policemen and the manager while ignoring their complaints.

The Russian ordered his men to wait at the door, and when they were alone, the Italian sighed at the theatre of it all.

'Must you be so dramatic?'

A nerve jumped in Glovkonin's jaw and he stamped down on the impulse to slap Da Silvio across his perfectly tanned face.

'Must you be so cavalier?'

He stepped closer, narrowing the distance between them. He saw that the Italian lacked some of his usual polish, doubtless having been awakened by the screech of the hotel's alarms and unable to spend time primping himself like a woman, as he usually did.

For his part, Glovkonin was as presentable as one could be after being dragged from his bed by a panicked Andre. He had rejected Da Silvio's offer of a suite at the Marine Luxe in favour of taking one nearby at the Zhemchuzhina, but now he regretted the decision. Had he been here, his men could have reacted to the intrusion as it happened, perhaps even captured the malefactors before they could escape.

The Italian raised his hands. 'I know what you are going to say, Pytor. But trust me, you worry too much.' He gave a shrug. 'This isn't the first time this sort of thing has happened. The staff here have experience dealing with issues better kept quiet. Sochi can be a crazy town.'

Da Silvio's studied, dismissive tone made Glovkonin's blood boil. 'Do you not understand the seriousness of this . . . this *invasion*?'

'Of course I do.' He actually chuckled. 'I was asleep in the room next door while these criminals robbed me!'

Glovkonin glared at him. 'Are you so foolish to believe that is actually what took place here? A robbery?'

Downstairs, Glovkonin had left Andre working his way through the hotel's security records, but he had already determined the basic details of what had happened. Da Silvio's penthouse had been broken into, the Marine Luxe's security compromised, and gunplay had unfolded. There were no signs of bodies, of course – the hotel staff were hard at work minimising any disruption. Like Da Silvio, they wanted nothing to interfere with the frictionless idyll manufactured for their indolent clientele.

'They only took money!' the Italian said mockingly. 'Ah, Russia! I do so love your country, Pytor. Sometimes it is like the Wild West!' He made finger-guns and chuckled at his own joke. 'Don't worry. The police will find the responsible parties . . . Or perhaps I will talk to our mutual friend the Salt Seller, yes? Chumak's thugs can bring me the fools who dared to do this. We could have some sport with them.' He nodded to himself. 'I like that idea.'

Glovkonin knew that Da Silvio had a reckless tendency to leave bodies behind when his parties got out of control. He found the man's appetites to be unseemly, but right now that was of lesser importance than the matter at hand.

'Have you already forgotten what happened in Paris? Our security, violated? Those Rubicon wretches were able to get close to us!'

'And whose fault is that?' The Italian's false good humour faded. 'You promised that your complex little plan would eradicate them once and for all. But still there are survivors out there, and you keep failing to dispose of them.' He waved a hand in the air. 'Personally, I think you obsess about them too much. Who are these people? What can they do to hurt me?'

'Do not underestimate them,' warned Glovkonin.

'Don't speak to me like I am a fool.' The Italian's eyes narrowed at his tone. 'You like to think you are the clever one, Pytor, with your games and your scheming. But has it ever occurred to you that the rest of us see your ambitions all too clearly, that we indulge you out of amusement?' He looked towards the penthouse's office, where the floor safe hung open. 'Something as trivial as this matters little to me . . . Is it your doing, I wonder? A ploy of some sort . . . Did you have your pet thugs do this to test my resolve? Or perhaps you had Chumak do it. I should ask him!'

Glovkonin could hardly believe the other man's wild accusations.

'Why would I draw unwanted attention to us, two days before the next phase of the operation?'

'I can think of a reason.' The Italian dropped into a chair, with a sigh. 'You've been desperate to make me appear ineffectual since you became a vested member of the committee. You're not content with the power and status you have been granted. You want more.' He leaned back. 'You want mine.'

Not just yours.

Glovkonin almost spoke the retort out loud. Instead, he took a breath and reframed his next statement.

'Nothing could be further from the truth. Our colleagues from Switzerland and the United States will be gravely concerned when they learn of what happened here. What are we going to tell them? "You worry too much"?'

The Italian's gaze hardened. 'It's pointless to bring this up with the others. What purpose would it serve, aside than distracting them from their work? No, we won't speak of this.' He made it an order, expecting to be obeyed, and Glovkonin seethed at his conceit. 'I have already increased security at all locations. If there is more than petty theft at hand here, that will put an end to it.'

'You are so confident you are right,' said Glovkonin.

'There is a phrase the American racers use, which is appropriate now . . .' Da Silvio tapped a button on the electronic bracelet around his wrist, signifying that their conversation had ended by summoning Willa. '*Stay in your lane*, Pytor.'

Glovkonin did not deign to give him a reply, and he stalked from the penthouse and back across the sky lobby, with Misha and Gregor falling into step beside him. Outwardly, the granite-hard lines of the Russian's face were rigid and emotionless, but inwardly he nursed his fury.

The plan had always been for the other men in the Combine to be removed when the opportunity presented itself, but now he was certain that the Italian had to be excised at the earliest opportunity.

He made a call to Andre on his encrypted Blackphone as the elevator descended to the ground floor.

'I have some additional work for you,' he explained. 'I am moving up the timetable on certain contingencies.'

'*Understood.*'

The French hacker knew exactly what that meant.

'There is more,' he said. 'Set up a private meeting with Pavlo Chumak. Tell him I have a business proposition.'

TEN

Down on the seafront, the steady breeze off the Black Sea cut the heat of the late afternoon sun. Racing fans and tourists crowded the public viewing spaces to catch a glimpse of the powerboats, as the vessels roared around the course markers. The video screens erected along the walkways and in front of the temporary bleachers showed images from camera drones following the boats that were beyond line-of-sight of the spectators, as they bobbed and weaved around shallows and rocky outcrops.

It was only the second day of qualifying, and already a racer had been badly injured in a bone-crushing collision out at the far end of the course. Here in the Russian Federation, the safety regulations were a little slacker, the speeds a little faster, the danger a little closer. The spectators and the sponsors alike loved it, the crowd shouting in a single awestruck voice each time a racer dared to cut a line too close, or blast a rival with their frothing wake.

'They ought to strap guns to those boats and go for it.' From beneath the peak of a neon-green baseball cap, Grace side-eyed one of the video screens with a cynical sneer. 'That's what these chumps really want.' She adjusted the mirrored sunglasses on her nose and indicated the crowd.

'You're a real student of human nature, ain't you?'

Walking alongside the other woman, Lucy kept her pace easy even though she was wound tight.

'I am,' Grace replied. 'You ever watch Russians play soccer? It's like *Fight Club* out there. They love that macho shit.'

'Uh-huh.'

Lucy left it at that, adjusting the dark-coloured floral wrap dress that billowed around her arms and legs, conveniently concealing the holstered Beretta Nano semi-automatic at the top of her thigh.

Lucy wore mirrored glasses, too, but hers were vintage tea-shades that set off the Breton-style sun hat perched on her head. Beside Grace in her designer cut-offs and blouse, they looked every inch the pair of wealthy tourists taking in the excitement.

It was a good cover, and it had already got them inside the race enclosure with no questions asked. But Lucy couldn't dial back her tension, not for a moment. It wasn't enough for her to be on guard around the ALEPH security operatives roaming the area; she also had to keep one eye on Grace at all times. She wasn't about to let the rogue ex-CIA agent leave her sight, not for a second.

'*Mobile, checking in.*' Marc's voice hummed in her radio ear-bead.

'Active is okay,' she replied.

'*Mobile on station. Standing by.*'

That meant that the Brit and the Finn were parked out front of the Marine Luxe, ready to get them away from here if something went badly wrong. Lucy didn't foresee that kind of trouble, but this mission had been nothing but unpredictable from the get-go.

'Active copies. Going silent.'

'*Mobile confirms.*'

'Boyfriend checking up on you?' Grace studied her. 'When do I get a radio?'

'Same time you get a gun. Which is never.'

Grace looked away, disappointed.

'More cops,' she said, from the side of her mouth. She ran her finger over the peak of her cap, indicating the direction.

Lucy looked without making it obvious. A pair of uniformed officers from the Regional Police were questioning a young guy in a race crew jumpsuit, taking notes as he made shapes in the air, talking with his hands. He pointed out different parts of the boat docks, and one of the cops snapped photos with a digital camera.

The talk of the race was the 'sabotage' that had apparently taken place in the hours before dawn. That was the story that the Veloce Cup organisers and the Marine Luxe management were going with, explaining away the penthouse break-in and subsequent mayhem as a failed attempt to disrupt the race and damage one or more of the powerboats.

Tersely worded press releases had already gone out, and there was a new tension in the air among the racing teams as they cast long-eyed looks at their rivals and wondered.

All bullshit, of course, Lucy reflected, *but you gotta admire Da Silvio's ability to make things work for him.*

If anything, word of the 'sabotage' had doubled audience interest in the coming race.

'You need to relax, sister,' offered Grace. 'You're gonna blow this. Seriously, you're so stiff I'm afraid you'll break something.'

Lucy didn't dignify her with a look. 'Fuck off.'

'So chic,' she retorted. 'You have to move like you're on the catwalk in Milan. Effortless, casual. You're walking around like you have a gun strapped to your dick.'

'Keep running that mouth,' warned Lucy. 'See where it takes you.'

'Just trying to be a team player.'

A wide deck shaded by pergolas extended out over the water from the sunward side of the Marine Luxe, and the elite of the race clique were watching the action from the long, sculpted ice-bar.

The targets Lucy and Grace were looking for were up there, but it was the most 'very' of VIP areas, and neither of them had the access pass that would get them past the velvet rope.

Lucy looked for a spot where they could watch unobtrusively from outside, but Grace walked past her, right up to the rope, as if destined to be let in.

A good-looking older guy with a deep tan and a serious expression moved seamlessly to block Grace's path and said something in Russian. His body language was polite but firm. *Sorry, madam, members only.*

Lucy's grasp of the language was from her time in Delta Force – mostly phrases to get people to drop their weapons and surrender, that kind of thing – so she couldn't follow everything Grace said.

But it was slightly unnerving to watch the other woman *change* right before her eyes. Grace's posture and tone of voice shifted, going seamlessly from poised and arch towards that false-child, little-girl coy thing that some men went for. She obviously pushed the right buttons, because the guy's face grew a wide grin and Grace patted him on the arm. She actually giggled, and Lucy did her best not to react, putting on her own mask of blank vapidity.

Grace pouted, theatrically sad as she made a half-hearted attempt to enter the VIP area. It did the trick, and the man laughed, his eyes dropping to linger over the curves of Grace's body, and then Lucy's.

Lucy pretended not to notice, mentally showering it off.

His grin going wider still, the man unclipped the rope and let them in, and he cupped one cheek of Grace's backside when she passed.

Lucy sniffed. 'Should I be impressed or disgusted?'

'Like I give a damn,' said the other woman, as they moved across the sun deck. 'Just respect the skills.'

The girlish persona disappeared, and Grace's manner turned shark-eyed and purposeful once more. There was something remarkable about the woman's ability to alter personalities, but it was only one half of her talents.

'How d'you do that?' Lucy studied her. 'I mean, it's one thing to play a role—'

'But knowing *what* face to put on, and *when*?' Grace smirked, and it was chilling. 'That's the real trick. I'm good at reading people, sis.' She indicated the group around them. 'If you know how to look at them, everybody's made out of glass.'

Note to self, Lucy thought. *Never ever let this ice-cold witch know anything personal about me.*

'The spooks in Langley must have loved you.'

Lucy grabbed a long drink and sipped it through a straw, leaning up against the bar where she could see the whole of the sun deck.

'They did. At first.' Grace took the same drink and mimicked Lucy's pose down to the last detail. 'But I make people uncomfortable.'

'Can't imagine why.'

Grace licked her lips and surveyed the people on the deck.

'Guy in the green silk shirt and too-tight shorts, table two. Bratva, by the tatts on his hands and neck.' Lucy looked and found the man in question. He fiddled with a wedding band around his finger. 'He's cheating on his wife,' continued Grace. 'The way he keeps looking in your direction, I'm guessing he likes the dark meat.'

Lucy raised an eyebrow, but said nothing, letting her continue.

'The chubby one in the bad suit, table ten, with the entourage? Vitali Borodin, the Russian minister for sport. Trying to stay one step ahead of an embezzlement scandal.' She jutted her chin. 'Next table over, wise guys from the 'Ndrangheta . . .'

'Calabrian Mafiosi, yeah,' said Lucy. 'Heard of them. You're well informed.'

As much as she instinctively disliked the woman, Lucy was impressed – not that she would admit it.

'I pay attention.' Grace nodded at another knot of hard-faced men, congregating around an unsmiling thug in a sports jacket. 'Now, this charmer? Pavlo Chumak, Ukraine's answer to El Chapo. That guy's a horror show, believe it. Steer well clear.'

Lucy filed that away and continued to scan the sun deck, until she spotted a familiar face out by the guard rail.

'I have eyes on Sunny Wehmeyer. Eleven o'clock. Blue dress.'

The young woman had a vacant smile, looking out across the water with a glass of champagne in one hand.

'Oh, I see her.' Grace nodded. 'Well, she isn't happy to be here.'

Lucy frowned at that. Sunny was surrounded by her entourage from the Horizon Integral team, all of them poised, bronzed and perfect.

'You could have fooled me.'

'I know, that's no challenge,' Grace said, as an aside. 'The girl, though. Look at her. She's sitting up there like she's posing for an Instagram shot, but she's faking it. The smile doesn't reach her eyes, sis. She wants very badly to be somewhere else.'

Lucy said nothing, mentally adjusting her perception of the scene, and after a moment, she saw it, too. She had been so hyper-focused on being aware of anything and everything, the more subtle cues had slipped past her.

Reframe the target. Lucy studied Sunny's face and posture, imagining it through the cross hairs of her sniper rifle. *Which way is she going to jump?* And slowly, she started to see what Grace had picked up on in an instant.

Sunny's attention kept straying to the waves, and then back to something on the shoreline, and each time it did, her eyes became distant.

'She's looking at the crew,' Lucy realised.

In front of the viewing platform were the boat docks, and Sunny Wehmeyer couldn't stop herself from staring at the figures swarming around number 7, Horizon Integral's sleek racer.

'She has a thing for someone down there,' said Grace. 'You reckon the boss's daughter is banging one of the staff? Shocking.'

'What happens in Sochi, stays in Sochi,' Lucy noted.

'No,' Grace countered. 'What happens in Sochi, we can use to blackmail her. Isn't that the whole point of this little exercise? To get a win?'

'Waste of time.' A new voice, a Chelyabinsk accent laced with vodka and overconfidence, inserted itself into their conversation. The man with the silk shirt had installed himself at the bar, and now he leaned closer, nodding in the direction of Sunny and the

HI team. 'Betting on the Australians is no better than setting your money on fire!'

'Oh, really?' Grace did the switch again, becoming perky and wide-eyed. 'Did you hear that?'

Lucy nodded, and Mr Silk took that as encouragement.

'*Da*. They have performed badly in other races. No podium places! Everyone knows they do not have the . . . the *guts*!' He clenched his fist and bared his teeth. 'They are not serious. Just the toy of a silly little girl playing with Daddy's money. They are like . . . *makeweight*. You know that word?'

Grace toyed with her cap. 'But let me guess – I bet *your* team is nothing like that, right?'

'*Da!*' He nodded eagerly, his attention still wholly on Lucy. 'Akula-X! Fast like lightning. I am sponsor.' The man grew smug. 'We will get podium here at Sochi. You will see.' Then his voice dropped to a conspiratorial whisper. 'This is not like Europe or America races. With too many rules and politics. Here . . . anything goes!'

He finished off with a leer, making it abundantly clear his words had more than one meaning.

Lucy hesitated for a moment. They weren't going to get any traction out here, not while this idiot was getting in their faces, and given Grace's reading of the situation, she figured they needed to back off and approach this in a different way.

She sighed, and gave Silk a lingering look.

'Is your boat . . . a big one?' Lucy let her question hang.

He rubbed his shirt. 'The biggest.'

Lucy dropped her gaze to his tight shorts and shook her head.

'Doesn't look like that from where I'm sitting.' She stood and beckoned Grace to follow. 'C'mon, let's jet. I don't like the company.'

Malte put the Hunter in a parking space a few vehicles down from the front entrance of the Marine Luxe Hotel, leaving the bulky

Russian 4 × 4 nose-out so they could make a swift getaway if required. In the passenger seat, Marc shifted position and pretended to be toying with his phone.

He tapped the microphone hidden under the collar of his polo shirt.

'Mobile, checking in.'

Lucy's voice whispered in his ear. '*Active is okay.*' She sounded close.

Malte gave him a nod of affirmation.

'Mobile on station,' Marc continued. 'Standing by.'

'*Active copies. Going silent.*'

'Mobile confirms.'

The comm channel went quiet and Marc took a breath. He didn't like waiting around.

It was the worst part of the tradecraft for him – the stakeouts and the standbys. That felt like something out of Marc's past, something he had left behind, and when time came for him to slow down, he found it hard.

Beside him in the driver's seat, Malte was the picture of calm. The Finn had a way of being alert without showing it, a talent Marc would dearly have loved to learn.

He looked around, scanning the area. The hotel stood on an artificial spit of land that extended out into the water, and across the way there were berths for the biggest superyachts on the Black Sea coast.

A line of hydrodynamic shapes in gleaming pearl white and brushed silver showed their sterns, many of them populated by beautiful people enjoying the sunshine. The boats had names that largely fell into one of two categories. Either they were money-related – *Greenmail*, *Bougie Enough*, *Pay-Out*, *Net Worth* and the like – or muscular and forceful titles like *Sea Hammer*, *Thunderbird*, *Cold Deck* and *Scimitar*.

Marc's eye was particularly drawn, as doubtless the owner wanted it to be, towards a hulking, obsidian-black and gold-trimmed yacht called *Goliath*, which stuck out a mile. He remembered the *Themis*, Ekko Solomon's sleek vessel named after the mythical personification of justice, which by contrast to this monster was a refined and minimalist design.

'Look at that thing.' Marc nodded at the boat. Aboard it, hefty men in trunks and skinny girls wearing skimpy swimsuits drank and partied. 'It should have a flag flying off the back that says "my owner is overcompensating."'

'Crude men cannot buy good taste,' agreed the Finn, as someone aboard sounded the yacht's siren at random.

Marc saw a burly guy on the yacht shout at one of the women and she shrank away from him, as if bracing to be slapped.

'I get the impression that those blokes think they can buy whatever they want.'

'Money doesn't improve a man's character,' said Malte. 'It reveals it.'

Marc was about to note that the driver was rarely this talkative, but then his phone rang, startling him. He peered at the device's screen and his breath caught, the mood in the vehicle changing in an instant.

A short string of text denoted the caller's identity: 5-4-1-T-0.

Saito.

'Oh shit.' Slowly, he tabbed the answer key and raised the smartphone to his ear. 'Yeah?'

'*Mr Dane. There are matters we should discuss.*'

It was undoubtedly him, the Combine's Japanese assassin opening the conversation with exactly the same words he had used the last time they had spoken. Then, Saito had been reaching out to Marc and Lucy as they searched the city of Brussels for a far-right terrorist with a biological weapon, and despite expectations to the contrary, he had helped the Rubicon team to track down their target.

Marc switched the phone to speaker mode and watched Malte's eyes widen as the conversation carried on.

'I'd ask how you got this number, but that seems pointless.'

'*I asked Mr Solomon to provide it. It appears you have a moment to speak.*'

Marc's skin crawled with the instinctive sense that he was being observed. It made sense. He knew that Pytor Glovkonin was here in Sochi, so it wasn't a stretch to assume the assassin was as well.

He decided to press his suspicion. 'You want to talk to me, we do it face to face or not at all.'

'*A sensible precaution,*' said the other man. '*The end of the dock.*'

The call ended and Marc frowned.

Malte looked out towards the jetty, finding the area Saito had mentioned. No one was up there, and it was ill lit, falling in a pool of shadow away from the hotel proper.

'Take a weapon,' said the Finn.

'Way ahead of you.' Marc drew the Glock G19 from the paddle holster in the back of his shirt, quickly checking the semi-automatic pistol before concealing it again. 'Of course, if I need it, we're screwed. So let's hope it won't come to that.'

He climbed out of the 4 × 4 and made his way up the line of moored boats. As Marc drew near, he saw a spare, compact figure move into view. The last time Marc had seen this man, it had ended with him stabbing the guy.

Saito inclined his head as he approached.

'Good evening, Mr. Dane. I trust you are well?'

The man's cool politeness and his cut-to-length diction grated on Marc's nerves.

'What the hell is your game?' He didn't waste time on any false civility. 'What do you want from us?'

'Is that unclear?' Saito's tone remained reasonable – understandable, considering that to all intents and purposes, he had the upper hand. 'I want my daughter to live freely. I want your group to make that happen.'

'And in return, we get . . .?'

'Revenge. That is what you seek, is it not?'

Marc scowled and glanced around. He didn't like being out in the open like this.

'It's a little more complicated than that,' he retorted.

'Is it?' Saito raised an eyebrow. 'I do not concur. Forgive me for saying so, but you have always been quite predictable, Mr Dane. I understand you better than you would like.'

Marc let that go without comment.

'I have no reason to trust you.'

'I have never lied to you,' Saito countered. 'Not in Somalia, during that business with the pirates.' He touched his shoulder in the spot where Marc had driven in a dagger. 'Despite the terms on which we parted, I maintained that honesty when we spoke again in Belgium. I have always been what I appear to be.'

'What's that? A rich man's attack dog?'

'Indeed, yes.' He answered without hesitation. 'It was not always so. But I am too far along my path to recover what I once was.' Saito's gaze softened. 'You know that feeling, I think. So I must do what I can to preserve the only thing that is important to me.'

Marc chewed on that for a moment. The possibility that he might share some characteristics with the Combine assassin did not sit well with him.

'Why are we talking?'

'Because I want to be sure you understand me. I want you to know that I am serious. This is not a game, as you call it.' Saito's brittle tone fractured, and he turned away to look out over the water. For the first time, Marc heard something like fear in his voice. 'I am risking everything I hold dear,' he added.

Marc's mind returned to that fateful day nearly two years ago in Brussels, when the city had been only moments away from a terrifying biological attack.

'Before ... Why did you help us find the Shadow virus? You gave up intelligence that led me straight to the poor sod being

forced to transport it. We stopped that attack because of you –
but I don't believe for one second that you did it out of any sense
of decency.'

Saito nodded curtly. 'You are correct. Glovkonin wanted the
Combine's plan to fail, to manipulate them for his own ends. He
used you against them.'

'Bastard.' Marc bit out the word.

He heard Saito take a breath, and the assassin turned back to
meet his gaze.

'You must be convinced. So I will tell you the full details of that
incident, but you will wish I had not.'

Marc gave a wary nod, letting his hand fall within reach of
his gun.

'Keep talking.'

Saito brought his hands together in front of him.

'Rubicon's prevention of the Shadow virus release in Europe
is exactly what drove the Combine's committee to reclassify your
organisation as a primary threat. Glovkonin allowed you that
victory because he knew it would force the Combine's hand. The
Russian excels at playing the long game.'

Marc's breath curdled in his throat. Saito's explanation had the
horrible ring of truth. Exactly the kind of ploy he would expect
from the Russian oligarch, carefully manoeuvring both sides
towards the conclusion he wanted – resulting in the Combine
turning the full force of their power towards the destruction of the
Rubicon Group, and the Special Conditions Division. The ruin and
death that followed flowed from one deadly moment on a Belgian
backstreet.

'You are asking yourself if this is your fault,' said Saito, as Marc
struggled to process this new truth. 'It is not. Glovkonin is the
master of the gambit where all outcomes benefit him. He used my
own weaknesses against me, played me against you, and he has
used you in the same way. He must be stopped.'

Marc wanted to believe that Saito represented the chance to take on the Combine at their own game, but bitter experience had taught him to trust nothing on surface value. His expression hardened.

'How can I be sure you're not setting us up, like you have in the past?'

'In a way, I am,' admitted Saito, 'but this time you are aware of it. Of course I will consider all options open to me. Suspicion works both ways.' He paused. 'That was your people in the Italian's penthouse last night, yes?'

Marc looked back at the glassy facade of the Marine Luxe, wondering if his target was up there behind one of those mirrored windows. He didn't answer the question, but he didn't have to.

'The agreement is clear,' Saito continued. 'Have your friends get my daughter to safety and away from the Combine's influence. If you fail to do this or if you attempt to betray me, know that I will give you up to Glovkonin without a moment of hesitation. Only the girl's life has meaning for me. I will trade mine and all of yours for my daughter's if I must. Do we understand one another, Mr Dane?'

Marc nodded again. 'Perfectly.'

Saito turned to leave. 'Then this conversation is over—'

'Not yet,' Marc interrupted, holding up a hand. 'One more question,' he insisted. 'Why the sudden change of heart? You must have had a million opportunities to turn on Glovkonin and the rest of them. Why do this now?'

Saito took a long moment before replying, and in that brief silence, Marc watched emotions war across the other man's face.

'There is nothing sudden about this choice. I have merely . . . passed a point of no return.'

He strode away, and Marc took that as his cue to head back to the parked Hunter.

Malte gave him a questioning look as he climbed back into the 4 × 4.

'So we're doing it?' asked the Finn.

'We're doing it,' said Marc.

After sunset, when the post-qualification press conference was over and the pre-race celebrations really began, the yachts moored in clusters along the shoreline became a riot of noise and colour, every vessel transformed into a party boat for whatever team owner, oligarch or minor celebrity decided to hold court there.

Of course, the biggest bash wouldn't kick off until the following evening, on the night before the race itself, when Giovanni Da Silvio would turn the Marine Luxe into a glittering utopia of drinking, dancing and debauchery. Tonight's affairs were, by comparison, easy-going gatherings. These were the warm-ups, the parties *before* the party.

Sunny Wehmeyer sat back on the solar deck of the *Silver Horizon*, her old man's second-string two-hundred-foot superyacht, and listened to the slap of water on the hull and the whoops of the revellers. She released a long sigh.

Normally, Sunny would have been all over this action. At similar bashes in Cannes, Turquoise Bay or Cancún, she bopped from boat to boat with her entourage, never staying long enough for the vibe to go stale, swimming through the glitz and the glamour. That was how she liked to have fun, cruising the scene and leaving a trail of sweet pics for her social media followers to upvote.

She put on a good front and she made the right noises, but Sunny was, as her dad would have put it, pig-sick of the whole bloody enterprise. The needle on her fun meter sat at E for Empty.

A couple of years ago, faced with such a situation, she might have cut and run, making a big deal about how lame the powerboat racing scene was here in Sochi, and sod the bad press that might have got her.

But not these days. All appearances to the contrary, Sunny was maturing. Her dad had made it clear that the money tap which watered her expensive lifestyle would be turned off unless she showed some *growth*.

What did that look like for a young woman who was the scion of a Fortune 500 technology company? Horizon Integral's directors wanted to know that if Martin Wehmeyer did retire, his daughter wouldn't squander her hereditary position in the conglomerate on 'boys and make-up', as one of them had so snottily put it.

So to prove she had some brains and some backbone, and also to shut up the haters, Sunny had taken on what she considered a proper job: the management of one of HI's racing teams. At first it had been great. The overlapping circles of *exclusive parties*, *jet-set travel* and *exotic locations* that were part and parcel of the motor racing world dovetailed perfectly with Sunny's globetrotting It Girl lifestyle.

More than that, she'd found not only that she liked the job – she wasn't half bad at it. Her media savvy and her innate gift for reading people were assets that had real value for the team. When they kicked off with the Veloce Cup, it looked as if everything would be smooth sailing.

But soon, Sunny had seen into the murky depths below the glittering surface. It turned out that the championship was more about trading kickbacks and serving up a playground for all kinds of shady chancers. Never mind that HI's relatively new team were talented and enthusiastic; all the fun was sucked out of the races by humourless mob guys from a dozen countries. When they weren't trying to sabotage each other's crews or pawing at her arse each time she walked past, they were colluding to make sure Sunny's team would never get within sniffing distance of a podium spot.

She shifted on her couch, adjusting the massive sun hat atop her head, peering over her outsize Onassis shades, and played with the silk shift over her designer swimsuit. The race crew were down on the *Silver Horizon*'s jetty, clustered around a barbie, swigging beers and joking around. She knew they felt the same way she did – that the HI team were doing little more than making up the numbers at this point. They were making the best of it, and she loved them for that, but she wondered if keeping them in the championship did more harm than good. So long as Da Silvio kept on indulging his thug mates, HI were doomed to be at the back of the pack.

She frowned behind the big shades. A year ago, a more selfish, shallow Sunny Wehmeyer might not have registered that, but the management gig had changed her in ways she hadn't expected.

Down by the barbecue set-up, Shayla McGrath looked up and caught her eye. The team's talented driver from Canberra was a year older than Sunny, her polar opposite, all rough-cut, shaggy hair and jumpsuits. Shayla gave her a wave. Then, unseen by anyone else, she blew Sunny a conspiratorial kiss.

A sense of responsibility wasn't the only thing Sunny had learned about herself in the last few months. Impulses and yearnings that she'd never quite got to grips with had come into sharp focus after meeting Shayla. Not for the first time, Sunny wondered about what it might be like to have some time and space to figure that out.

'Sun-*nee!*' She became aware of Hector standing nearby. 'What's going on?'

Her Brazilian photographer was dressed for a night out, and he couldn't stand still. She saw the others from her entourage milling around on the deck, and clearly they'd bullied Hector into speaking for them.

'Are we out tonight?' He gestured hopefully towards the other yachts.

Hector was treading carefully. Mindful of Sunny's mood swings, he knew when she put up her barriers that the best course of action was to keep his distance.

Sunny peeled off her sun hat and removed the shades, remembering Dad's advice about always making eye contact with subordinates.

'Nah. I'm not up for it.'

'We have an *invite* to the Da Silvio team party tonight and it would be a *shame* to miss out.' Hector stressed his words dramatically.

Her expression soured. Sunny didn't like Da Silvio or his people. The man had mocked her Aussie accent and belittled her on their first meeting, and his lead driver, some oily Spaniard whose name she had forgotten, cracked jokes about dingoes like he thought he was hilarious, guffawing like a bloody bogan the whole time.

'You go,' she told Hector, waving him away. 'Have fun. I'm gonna chill.'

'Okay! Later!'

The photographer was gone so fast he practically left a vapour trail.

Sunny watched her clique wander off and felt glum as she realised they had little use for their queen. As she drowned that morose thought in another glass of champagne, a shadow fell across her.

'You'd think someone on a tub as nice as this would be happy about it.'

Sunny looked up and there was a face she hadn't seen in quite a while.

'Lucy? Holy shit! What are you doin' out here?'

'I'd ask permission to come aboard, but we already have, so . . .' The athletic, poised black woman indicated her companion, a white girl with an unpretentious look and a bright green baseball cap on her head. 'This is Grace. Grace, Sunny. Sunny, Grace.'

'Charmed,' said the other woman, with an accent that was impossible to place.

Sunny's mood lifted a little. She was genuinely pleased to see Lucy Keyes, and gave her a hug. It didn't matter to her that the woman had been part of some spy thing that had kicked off at HI's corporate offices a few years back. Sunny liked Lucy's take-no-shit attitude and innate fashion sense, and she thought it was cool that she knew someone who was, like, a secret agent or something.

'You look good,' she told her.

'You, too.' Lucy indicated Sunny's designer swimwear. 'What's that, Solid & Striped? Love that print.'

'Cheers!' said Sunny, then she lowered her voice. 'So are you here doing . . . your thing?'

'Actually, yeah.' Lucy and her friend accepted drinks and took up spots on opposite ends of the couch. 'We're chasing down some bad dudes.'

'You picked the right spot, there's a lot of them here,' Sunny noted. 'Handsy fuckers, one and all.' Then she grinned. 'But I remember that trick you taught me.' She picked up a cocktail umbrella from a spent glass on the table and twirled it around her fingers. 'Stick the pointy end under a bloke's fingernail, he sods right off!'

Grace smirked but said nothing. Sunny had the impression the other woman scrutinised everything she did.

Lucy was short on details about her reasons for being in Sochi, but Sunny found she didn't want to press too hard. She'd become bored seeing the same faces at the race circuit, and the chance to dish to someone new was ideal. Lucy and Grace let Sunny talk as the sun dipped below the horizon and the stars came out.

By the time they were on the second – or maybe third – bottle of champagne, Sunny had come around to unloading all the gripes she had about the whole damned thing.

'Honestly, babe, I'm starting to hate it here,' she said. 'Wish I could take a break, but we're in for this race and then two more events, New York and the final in San Diego.' Sunny shook her head. 'No one takes me seriously 'cause I'm a woman. These mob guys treat the gig like a combo meat-market and booze-up. And don't get me started on the bloody paparazzi! I can't even piss without some dickhead trying to jam a camera in the dunny.' She took a breath. 'I'd rather be on a beach in the Maldives, but I can't even kite off for the weekend.'

Lucy and Grace exchanged looks.

'How'd you like us to make that happen for you?' Lucy put down her glass and smiled. 'If you're serious.'

'I'd love it!' But then Sunny made a face as she caught up to the reality of what that would mean. 'I can't. The manager can't leave the team.'

'Grace can cover that.'

The other woman picked up Sunny's discarded hat and glasses. She put them on, and then arranged herself on the couch in exactly the same pose that Sunny had been in all afternoon.

'Have fun,' said Grace, and her voice became fluid, shifting into a near-perfect impersonation of Sunny's. 'I'm gonna chill.'

'Holy shit.'

It was like looking in a mirror. The woman's mimicry was amazing, and if Sunny was honest, quite unsettling.

'Holy shit,' imitated Grace. 'You ever read that story, babe? *The Prince and the Pauper*? We can do that.' Then she leaned in, and Sunny blinked. 'You find a little getaway . . . Just you and Shayla, spend some quality time together, yeah?'

'How did you . . .?' Sunny stopped the question halfway, and once again she looked down and found Shayla on the dockside. Thinking about her made Sunny smile. After a moment, she gave Lucy a level look. 'Say I agree – what do you get out of it?'

'We need a cover for a little while,' Lucy told her. 'We're gonna mess with Giovanni Da Silvio. He's up to some shady shit, and we can't get to him without being inside the circus. Will you help us?'

Sunny thought about how small Da Silvio had made her feel, and her smile widened.

'Tell me what you need.'

*

Marc stared into the middle distance, out through the 4 × 4's tinted windscreen and across the lights of the city, brooding on what Glovkonin's assassin had given him.

As much as he knew he should be keeping an eye on Lucy and Grace, he couldn't stop himself from drifting back to that day in Belgium. It had been Marc's choice to follow up on Saito's information, Marc's choice to force Lucy into helping him chase down the virus weapon and the men who had created it. Lucy had almost died because of the decisions he had made, exposed to a dose of weaponised Marburg that could have proven fatal.

But that had been the stone hitting the water, the first of the ripples. The effects didn't stop there. Assim Kader, the bright Saudi hacker whom Marc had treated like a little brother, was dead. So was Ari Silber, the team's imperturbable veteran pilot. Rubicon itself was in ruins, and Ekko Solomon himself had almost died into the bargain.

None of that might be true if Marc had made a different choice in Brussels. He had only seen the short game, the most immediate outcome. He saw two moves ahead, but Glovkonin's game was five . . . no, *ten* moves past that.

I'm out of my depth. He felt cold, sickly dread coiling in his belly. *I have* always *been out of my depth. If I get it wrong again, it's the end of everything.*

Marc's breath came fast, and his heart pounded. He had sat still too long, and allowed the fear to catch up to him.

The trill of his smartphone broke through the dark reverie and vibrated against him. He pulled the device, slipping out of the vehicle. From the driver's seat, Malte shot him an odd look, but he ignored it and walked away to the edge of the dock.

'Yeah?' Marc pressed the phone to his ear.

'*We are ready to depart.*' Ekko Solomon's level tones rumbled across the distance. '*Henri and Benjamin have prepared legends and equipment for us. We will pick up our flight in Stavropol.*'

'Right.' Marc took that in. 'What do you need from us?'

'*I hope we require no aid from you,*' Solomon went on. '*But I would ask that you have Kara remain on standby, should we need some technical assistance.*'

'I'll make sure she's available.'

Solomon was perceptive, and he picked up on the tension in Marc's tone despite his best attempts to mask it.

'*You are troubled.*'

'Is it that obvious?' Marc sighed.

It didn't take much for Solomon to intuit the root cause.

'*You spoke with Saito.*'

'He has plenty to say,' admitted Marc. 'He told me about what Glovkonin did. Manipulating us.'

'*Yes.*' He could almost hear the change in Solomon's expression. '*We have all been prey to our better natures.*'

'We can't afford to be wrong this time,' Marc told him. 'We're burning through our luck faster than our money ... and I'm responsible.'

In the background of the call, he heard the soft mutter of Benjamin Harun's voice, as the Frenchman said something to Solomon, summoning him away.

'*If we had the time, I would tell you of all I am responsible for,*' said Solomon, with the weight of the world in his reply. '*The decisions I have made that I regret. But we cannot change who we are, my friend, not at the core of our selves. We can only strive to make the just choice, when the moment is upon us.*'

'Easier said than done,' Marc noted, with feeling.

'*Oh yes,*' agreed Solomon. '*But if it was easy, it would not be worth it.*' He let that lie for a moment, then he was back on mission. '*We will be in Austria tomorrow. The girl is there.*'

Marc considered that for a moment, wondering what kind of person Saito's daughter would be. Did she even know what her father was?

'You have a plan for extraction?'

'*We have options,*' replied Solomon. '*Calling it a plan would be . . . overly generous.*'

Despite the seriousness of the moment, Solomon's words cut the tension and Marc couldn't help but give a wry smile.

'Yeah. I'm familiar with that.'

'*We will talk again when it is done,*' said the other man. '*Trust in yourself, Mr Dane. Because I do.*'

ELEVEN

It had rained earlier in the day, while Miki Kadohawa had been in her classes, but by the afternoon the clouds had parted and bright sunshine came to Vienna's elegant streets. The honeyed light gilded the baroque buildings, and the view never failed to delight her. On days like this one, parts of the city resembled something from a dream, a perfect fairy-tale Europe conjured from the pages of the romance manga she loved to read as a child.

She sat at the terrace of a cafe on the banks of the Donaukanal, soaking in the moment for a while, before turning back to the notebook before her. Wide glasses accented her oval face and expressive brown eyes, her short dark hair pulled back behind a polka-dotted Alice band. In her sensible skirt and blouse, she completed the picture of the bookish international student.

The black iron clock across the way from the cafe told her she had a few minutes before her boyfriend arrived – in fact, she knew she would have more than that, because he was always late.

She had made her peace with such behaviour, after all this time together, and decided to consider his behaviour as *endearing* rather than *careless*. Daichi always blamed it on his training schedule at the fencing academy, and she had learned to accept that.

She liked the way Daichi made her feel like the centre of the universe. He could be mercurial and moody, but then that was part of his appeal. And she loved the idealistic notion that destiny had brought the two of them together – a pair of students who might have passed on the streets of their native Japan and never known it, finding each other half a world away in the heart of Europe.

Smiling to herself, the young woman flipped through her notes, running a slender finger over a page of dense text. She had taken down much of the day's lecture, assimilating the examples from contemporary maritime law and their cross-connection to trans-national regulations. She was passionate about becoming a lawyer, and she envisioned a future for herself where she would be able to give back to the world. International law was a complex subject, but she excelled in understanding the minutiae of it, the lines of association and the possibilities they represented. She hoped to one day start a legal practice of her own, and help those who were lost in the gaps between nation states.

That made her smile broaden all the more.

Not a bad dream for an ordinary girl from Osaka, she told herself.

'*Sumimasen,*' said a low, rich voice.

She looked up to find a black gentleman in a smart suit, his patrician face marred by the dark disc of an eyepatch. He propped himself up on a cane, and he appeared very fatigued. He gestured to one of the two empty chairs at her table and continued, asking if she would allow him to sit for a moment and take a breath. He had been walking for some time and he was tired.

It would have been the height of rudeness to ignore him, and as all the other chairs nearby were taken, it would also have been cruel. The man's impairment was clearly wearing on him.

'Please do.' She inclined her head and gestured at the chair.

He bowed slightly and sat. The man spoke excellent Japanese and she felt compelled to compliment him.

'Thank you,' he said. 'It is not often I have the opportunity to use it.' Her attention wandered back to her notes, but before she could read any more, he carried on. 'You are kind to take pity on me. I'm sure you want your solitude, I won't take up too much of your time.'

'Actually, I'm meeting someone for an early dinner.'

'How nice.' He nodded at the textbooks and papers spilling out across the table from her tote bag. 'Pardon me for asking, you are a student at the Universität Wien? A law student?'

'That's right.' She showed him one of the books. 'I am learning the finer points of international law.'

'You have an area of specialisation? I understand that is the usual thing.'

She nodded, warming to her subject. 'Immigration legality and displaced persons. So many unlucky people are failed by the system and they need help.'

He returned the nod. 'A noble pursuit. That was my fate once, when I was a boy. I found my way out of it. I could have used someone like you to help me back then.' He signalled a server, who brought him an espresso. 'I am being rude. I should introduce myself. My name is Ekko Solomon.'

'And what brings you to Vienna, Mr Solomon?'

Something in the back of her mind rang a wrong note – something about the way the man observed her – but she paid it no mind.

'I am performing a service for a colleague. A task he cannot do himself.'

'Oh.' She patted her chest. 'My friends call me Miki, by the way. Miki Kadohawa.'

'Your mother's name.'

'Pardon me?'

Solomon sipped his coffee thoughtfully. 'You go by your mother's maiden name, not by your father's.' He glanced away briefly, towards an unmarked van parked on the other side of the street. 'And Miki . . . Short for Rumiko, yes?'

Her skin prickled, and suddenly the delightful, dream-world Vienna melted away, replaced by something threatening and foreign. She drew her hands close to herself, tensing.

'How do you know that?'

'Forgive me. I have not been entirely honest with you, Rumiko.' Solomon put down his cup. 'I am here because your father sent me.'

Her pleasant features tightened into a glower. 'My father is dead.'

'You know that is not so.'

'I wish he was!'

The retort came out in a hot shock. A little girl's undimmed anger and a woman's buried pain flashed through her, dredged up from the deep place where she had hidden them. Tears misted her vision and she wiped them away with the heel of her hand, determined not to give her father even that much of herself.

With a shuddering breath, she regained her composure.

'I want you to go. My boyfriend will be here soon. I will call for the police if I have to.'

'I cannot leave, Rumiko. Not yet.'

All those years ago, when her father had ruined her life, she had discovered a strength in herself she never knew she had, a steel beneath the willow. In that, she'd gained the courage to carry on and find a way forward, away from his disgrace. She had left the worst of her life behind, but now here sat this erudite stranger, and he was trying to drag her back to it.

She leaned across the table, her voice dropping to a whisper.

'Has he paid you to come here? What lies did he tell you?' She didn't wait for him to reply. 'Let me explain what kind of man my father is!'

She told the sad story, the words falling from her in a rush. The story of Rumiko Saito, not Miki Kadohawa. The story that she had never told to her friends at the university, not to Daichi, not to anyone.

'My father was a policeman in Osaka. Highly placed, respected. Part of a special unit that investigated only the very worst criminals. *The yakuza*. The clans who trafficked in people and drugs.' She bit out each word, blinking back the tears. 'But he was corrupt. He angered someone powerful, and to pay him back, my mother was murdered.' She forced herself to speak with robotic detachment, as if discussing some theoretical case for her classes. She knew if she allowed herself to go back to those memories, it would wreck her. 'He fled to save himself.'

She muffled a sigh into a napkin, her cheeks colouring, afraid that everyone around her would suddenly see what she really was – the daughter of a liar and a criminal.

'I am so sorry, Rumiko,' said Solomon, and she believed he meant it, for all that mattered.

'Now you know who Hiroshi Saito is, you can leave and never come back.' She jutted her chin. 'I have a life here.'

'But you do not have the truth,' Solomon said gently. 'Only pieces of it.'

She wanted to shout at the man to go away, but now the wound from her past had been reopened, she couldn't look away from it.

'He was police,' said Solomon. 'He was part of a task force working against organised crime across the Pacific Rim. And your mother did perish because his investigations threatened certain criminal enterprises. But what you do not know is this – your father killed the people who murdered her. He was aided in this by a consortium of rich men, for whom the deaths of those yakuza was highly profitable. He agreed to do it – to be their weapon from then onwards. The price was your safety.'

She shook her head. 'I don't believe you.'

'Your father cares for you. That is the reason he stayed away. So you could have a life untouched by his mistakes. But you *are* touched by it, even if you do not know it.' Solomon nodded to himself. 'He told me this. I sit here before you today because of a choice he made to save my life.' He sighed. 'He is a flawed man who has done many questionable things. But he does love you, Rumiko. And he wants you to be free.'

'I am free!' she snapped, her strident tone drawing the attention of one of the servers. 'And you are lying to me!'

'Hello,' said the server, in concisely polite German. 'Is there a problem?' He smiled without warmth, scanning the tables.

'When you were a little girl,' said Solomon, 'in the summer months your father would take you to the Ferris wheel at Tempozan Harbour, and you would have ice cream.'

It was as if he had reached into her mind and plucked the memory from the locked box of her past. Only her parents would have

JAMES SWALLOW | 201

known of those outings. Shaken, she drifted in the recollection for a moment, evoking the emotion of it. The endless, unconditional love. How had she forgotten that?

'Miss?' The server's tone grew terse. 'Are you all right?'

'I . . . I am fine,' she replied in German.

The server scowled and retreated.

Solomon leaned closer. 'Rumiko, please listen to me. We do not have much time. You are in danger. You must come with me. I am duty-bound to get you to a safe place.'

'I . . . I can't.'

Her mind was in turmoil. She could barely make sense of any of it. And now this stranger wanted her to walk away from her life?

She was still trying to sort through her conflicted thoughts when she saw a familiar face approaching.

'Miki-chan?' Daichi came to her as she rose and accepted her hug. 'Darling, what's the matter?'

Daichi Ito was briskly handsome, with the sort of sporty flair that only a career athlete could exude, and he switched instantly into a territorial mode as he took in both the stranger and his girl-friend's flushed complexion.

'It's all right,' she told him, but Daichi wasn't listening.

He gave Solomon a wary look. 'And who are you?' He spoke in clipped, accented German, moving to position himself between the woman and the other man.

'No one of consequence,' said Solomon, as he rose to his feet, tucking a fold of euros under the base of his espresso cup. 'Pardon my intrusion.'

'I want to leave,' she insisted, as the tears threatened again. 'Now.'

She stepped away, letting Daichi guide her.

'Ah, miss? Your books?'

Behind them, Solomon held out her tote. In her distress, she had almost left without it.

Daichi snatched the bag from the man's hand and he directed her away, pulling her close to him.

Grace leaned in to give exaggerated air kisses to the maître d' at the entrance, and she laughed loudly at something he told her.

Granted approval, Lucy trailed after Grace across the cavernous lobby of the Marine Luxe hotel, her shoes clacking off the white marble floor as her dress swished around her bare legs. The ground floor of the entire complex had been turned over to the race night party, and it heaved with the rich and the well-heeled. Men and women in blisteringly fashionable outfits tried to outdo each other in volume and performative enjoyment, the owners of the race teams and their entourages orbiting huge ice sculptures and vodka luges carved to resemble sleek speedboats or ocean waves. There were drivers in among them, too, the racers being shown off like prize gladiators before taking their turn in the arena.

Grace strode through the gathering, catwalk-confident and unstoppable. She was so much Sunny Wehmeyer's doppelgänger that it was eerie, and Lucy couldn't help but be a little creeped out at the woman's ability to inhabit someone else's skin. Grace smiled and exchanged pleasantries with people as she passed, acting as if she knew every one of them intimately.

'She's a witch, I swear,' Lucy muttered, subvocalising the comment so it could be picked up by the throat mike hidden in the choker she wore.

'*Come again?*' Marc's voice crackled through the radio bead in her earrings.

'Just thinking out loud, is all,' she replied.

'*Do you have eyes on the objective?*' Kara Wei broke in over the channel.

'Not yet.' She helped herself to a peach Bellini from a passing server and kept on Grace's six as they skirted around the dance floor and wandered out to the moonlit patio. 'Stand by.'

Grace turned to her, beaming from ear to ear.

'So far, so good, mate.' She even had the accent down to a T. With the haircut and the make-up and the jewellery, Lucy had to wonder if Sunny's own father would have been able to tell the difference. 'C'mon, cheer up. This'll be a walk in the park, no worries.' She nodded towards a more secluded area, off by the outdoor pool. 'Our bloke must be over yonder. Let's go take a look-see . . .'

But a cluster of other partygoers were approaching them, blocking their path, and at the head of the group stood the handsome Brazilian guy Lucy had seen on Wehmeyer's yacht the day before.

'Hector,' said Grace, with a boozy wink. 'Having fun?'

Lucy held her breath. If Grace's performance didn't pass muster with the members of Sunny's entourage, this whole operation would be blown.

Hector eyed her. 'Did you see the stylist today? You look different.'

'New haircut. You like?' Grace flipped her darkened tresses, but she didn't wait for Hector to reply and her tone turned acid. ''Course, I don't give a toss if you don't. I'm doing my own thing.' She shot Lucy a look. 'Ain't that right, Lana?'

'*Lana*' was Lucy's current cover identity. She nodded, covering her silence with a sip from her glass.

'We didn't think you'd be along,' Hector pressed. 'Yesterday, you said—'

'What?' Grace cut him off with a sniff. 'You reckon I need to hang with you lot all the time to have some fun?' She gave a high-pitched giggle. 'Bugger off and do what you like. You were harshing my mood anyway.'

Hector blinked, and like an obedient courtier, he knew to back down when his queen was of a spiteful disposition.

'Sure, okay.' He tried to laugh it off. 'It's just that . . . Well, you remember Richie, the crew chief?'

'I know who the fuck Richie is.' Grace glared at him, as if insulted by the implication that she didn't.

Hector coloured, and Lucy couldn't help but notice how the other members of Sunny's little circle were drifting away from the conversation, physically distancing themselves so that they didn't take any of the flak. As the new arrival, Lucy was side-eyed by the group with poorly masked disdain, and for a moment she felt as if she was back in high school, being judged by the girls in the cool clique.

'Well . . . uh . . . Richie is very upset,' continued Hector. 'He said that Shayla just upped and left. He can't find her anywhere.'

She's halfway to the Maldives with the real *Sunny Wehmeyer*, thought Lucy.

'I fired her,' snapped Grace, and Hector's eyes widened in surprise. 'She wasn't putting her foot down in the qualifiers. Why d'you think we're losing? I threw her out. Lana's gonna replace her.'

Lucy took her cue and gave a nod. 'Looking forward to it.'

'You can't fire the driver the day before a race!' Hector's hand went to his mouth. 'Oh my God, Richie is going to be *so* pissed!'

Grace prodded Hector in the chest. 'Don't tell me what I can and can't do, I'm the team manager! And Richie can eat a dick for all I care! Shayla's out, Lana's in. Deal with it.' She waved him away. 'And didn't I tell you to bugger off?'

Hector threw up his hands and walked away, regrouping with the rest of the entourage as they eagerly devoured this latest nugget of drama.

'What the hell was that?' Lucy said quietly.

'Social engineering,' Grace replied. 'I give Handsome Hector a roasting, he's not gonna be in a hurry to talk to me again any time soon. Sunny's little gang will keep their distance, so there's less chance one of them will catch me out, get it?'

'Risky play.'

Grace led her towards the secluded area. 'You let me work, sis. I know what I'm doin' . . .'

'I hope so.'

Among the partygoers, Lucy caught sight of Giovanni Da Silvio for the first time, the Italian lounging in an artfully rumpled cotton jacket as he puffed on a cigar and grinned.

Off to one side, his assistant stood patient and still, holding the digital book in her long-fingered hands.

'Objective sighted,' whispered Lucy.

They returned to Daichi's apartment at the edge of the Rossau district, and it wasn't until they were inside that Rumiko let go of her stoic silence and started to cry.

Daichi opened the shuttered windows to let in the light, and made tea. They sat on the worn leather sofa in the lounge and he held her as she sobbed it out. Rumiko buried her face in Daichi's chest, unable to bring herself to look him in the eye as she wailed about the secrets she had kept.

He didn't let on how much of it he was already aware of. He knew exactly what to say to soften the moment for her. Daichi took her chin in his hand and tilted her face up, tenderly kissed the tears from her cheeks and promised her that he would always forgive her.

'Nothing you can say or do will break the bond we have,' he told her.

So she told him everything. Her real surname. The shame of her father's legacy. The circumstances that had brought her here, and the generous scholarship grant that had allowed her to study abroad. Her second chance at a new life.

He listened, keeping his expression neutral. It was vital for Rumiko not to believe he was judging her for any of this. Now and then he made small sounds or gestures to encourage her to continue.

Between sips of the tea, she finally came to the conversation with the foreigner at the cafe. This Solomon, with his tale about Rumiko's criminal father and terrifying allusions about the danger surrounding her.

'That man must be a confidence trickster,' Daichi told Rumiko, stating it like a fact. 'Dear heart, somehow this person found out about your private life and now he's trying to prey on you. This is how they work! They put pressure on you! They don't give you time to think straight! Then before you know it, you're giving them everything you own!'

'But I don't have any money!' said Rumiko. 'I'm not rich!' She swallowed hard.

'No,' Daichi dismissed that possibility with an offhand gesture. 'It is something else . . . Perhaps information about your father?'

His thoughts raced. What if Rumiko's parent had left behind something valuable in Osaka – something that only his daughter might know about?

'I should go to the police,' Rumiko said, with a firm nod. 'Yes. They'll know what to do.'

Daichi gave her a wary glance. 'Are you sure that's a good idea? If we were in Japan, I would agree, but here? Don't forget we're in a foreign country, Rumiko. Can we really trust them? What if the police are in league with this Solomon person?'

Colour drained from her face. 'Oh no.'

He straightened, and looked her in the eye. 'I will help you. I have a friend who works at the Japanese embassy over on Hess-gasse. I can talk to him.'

'We should go there, now . . .'

'You are in no state to do that.' Daichi shook his head. 'It's better if we stay here. Safer.'

She quietened. 'I suppose you are right.'

'You know I am.' Daichi took both her hands in his. 'You're a mess, you poor thing. Why don't you take a shower, and I will call my friend? We'll stay in tonight, I'll make dinner. It will be okay. Do you trust me?'

'I . . . I do,' she said, after a moment. He drew her into another embrace, and then let go. Rumiko stood and managed a shaky smile. 'Sometimes I wonder what I would do without you, Daichi.'

'I'm here to keep you safe,' he told her, and he made a show of checking the locks on his door. 'Always remember that.'

Daichi sat on the sofa and waited until he heard the sound of the water running. Rumiko liked to take a long time in the shower – he'd timed it – so he knew he would be free of her for at least fifteen minutes.

He ran through everything she'd told him, putting it in order, weighing up the possibilities of this new situation. It was a lot to process.

Her tote bag lay on the floor where she had dropped it as they entered, the contents half out on the threadbare tatami mat in the middle of the room. He stuffed the books and notes back inside, and through force of habit, opened up Rumiko's purse and looked through it, finding nothing of interest.

He dropped it back in the tote and beneath some papers he found a black smartphone, a slick new model he didn't recognise, with an anodised case and matte glass touchscreen. Daichi frowned. Rumiko hadn't said anything to him about upgrading her phone, but that was like her; she overlooked such details. He gave the device an experimental tap, but nothing happened. Perhaps it was out of power? He constantly had to remind her to recharge her devices.

Putting the bag aside, Daichi sought out his phone. Not the one he carried for everyday use, but the cheap, disposable burner he kept hidden in the bottom of a stubby vase. He flicked it on, straining to listen. The shower was still on full blast, and he could hear Rumiko humming tunelessly.

He dialled the only number listed in the burner's memory and waited for the line to connect. Daichi wasn't calling the Japanese embassy. What he had said about his 'friend' was a quick lie that got him the reaction he needed, like almost everything that came out of his mouth.

Daichi stared at the burner and his knee began to twitch, his leg juddering as the nervousness he'd been hiding finally surfaced.

Without Rumiko around to see it, he let his mask slip, let the panic show through.

This is it, he thought. *This man Solomon. He's what they warned me about.*

'He's making a call,' said Benjamin, his low tones echoing in the back of the van. The big man was hunched over a digital tablet, his thick fingers hunting and pecking at the virtual keyboard. 'The number appears to be connected to an automated answering service.'

'Intercept it.' Solomon leaned over and indicated an option on the screen.

'Will that work?' Benjamin tapped the button, frowning. 'This isn't my area of expertise.'

Solomon nodded, shifting so he could see out through the van's windscreen and up to the apartments across the street.

'It should. Before his passing, I had Mr Kader set up several automated programs for field use. Plug and play, he called them.'

As Rumiko walked away from him at the cafe, Solomon had used sleight of hand to activate his spyPhone and slip it into her bag. The handset acted as a remote listening device, frequency monitor – and now as a jammer.

'Is it working?'

In the front seat of the vehicle, Delancort had another tablet computer open on his lap, half concealed by the folds of his coat. He looked uncomfortable in the deliberately untidy outfit, and fidgeted constantly.

Benjamin nodded. 'I believe so.'

'Where is Dane when we need him?' muttered Delancort.

An indicator turned green on Benjamin's display, and up in the apartment, an interception subroutine convinced Daichi's burner phone that it was connected to its destination number, when in fact its signal was being diverted down to the parked van.

'Hello? It's me,' said a man's voice, in heavily accented English. 'Daichi Ito. We have a problem. You told me to call this number if anyone ever came looking for the woman.'

'Is that the boyfriend?' said Delancort.

Solomon nodded. The three of them listened in silence as Daichi gave them a description of the African and a quick account of his conversation with Rumiko.

Daichi was worried. 'Look, I know we had an agreement, but I don't want to be part of anything that puts me in danger. You're not paying me enough for that. I've been doing this for nearly a year and I think that's long enough. Maybe we should wrap this up?' He sounded as if he was psyching himself up to make a decision. 'Yes. I think that's best. Let's talk exit strategy, right? I'm so tired of listening to her whine about her boring life. I . . .' He paused. 'I don't really like her.' Daichi sighed. 'Just call me back straight away. We need to talk about this!' The line went dead.

'What a charming young man,' Delancort said coldly. 'This is he?'

He held up his tablet to show the others, and on it was a spread of photos from Rumiko's social media page. Most of the snapshots showed her with Daichi out and about at restaurants or local sights in the city. Solomon nodded again, and Delancort gave a sniff.

'It is not my intention to be impolite, but he does appear a little too handsome to be dating a woman of her, shall we say, conventional looks.'

'It's a trick,' said Benjamin, echoing the words that Daichi had used earlier. 'I have seen this sort of thing before. A good-looking man or woman targets someone less attractive, sweeps them off their feet, and makes them feel special.' He shook his head. 'I imagine he used their common background to his advantage.'

'The honeytrap,' agreed Solomon. 'A ploy as old as civilisation itself.'

'He has an uncommonly small social media footprint for someone of his age,' said Delancort, following links from Rumiko's page. 'Daichi Ito, twenty-three, from Toyko, Japan,' he read aloud, 'studying professional-level fencing at a school here in Vienna. And of course, he wears a mask in all the pictures of him in action. Convenient.' He glanced at the apartment, then back at Solomon. 'I know a cover legend when I see one, sir. Too clean to be true.'

'Forward the information to Kara,' said Solomon. 'But we cannot afford to wait for her to get back to us. We must act now.'

Benjamin frowned and put down his tablet. 'I'm not comfortable with the prospect of a forced extraction.'

He nodded at a black zip-case on the seat. Inside it was an injector gun with a powerful phenobarbital load, enough to drop an average person in under twenty seconds, and certainly enough to knock out the slight Rumiko for several hours. But drugs could have unpredictable effects, and a mistake in the dosage or an unknown complication could prove fatal to the woman they were here to rescue.

'We must be realistic,' noted Solomon. 'The Combine will be monitoring Rumiko, but only as a secondary concern. This man Ito, he is clearly working for them. Most likely, he is an opportunist criminal they recruited to watch her. We have a small window in which to recover Saito's daughter before the Combine become aware of our presence here. If that happens . . .' He trailed off.

They knew the consequences. If Saito believed Rumiko was in danger, he would sacrifice their deal, and that would mean the deaths of their colleagues back in Sochi.

Benjamin cleared his throat. 'I have a suggestion.'

Staying in the basement's shadows, Marc rolled the kitchen staff smock into a tight tube and pressed it down into his backpack. The disguise had got him into the hotel grounds, and now the all-black outfit he wore beneath was revealed. He secured his gloves and pulled a lightweight mask over his mouth and nose, completing the stealthy ensemble.

He picked his way past the same circuitry cabinet they had hot-wired during the failed attempt on the penthouse a few nights ago. The metal box was discoloured and the reek of burned plastic still lingered in the air from where Malte's spyPhone had self-destructed. The Sochi police had dusted for prints and sealed off the unit, but Marc gave it a wide berth all the same.

He made his way to a service hatch in the wall and negated the alarm circuit before snapping open the latches. The smell of heavy grease and hot metal wafted out.

'Active is on site,' he whispered, his voice hissing over the secured communications net. 'Going in.'

Marc climbed in through the hatch and pulled it closed behind him. The main lift shaft for the Marine Luxe extended away over his head, the grimy darkness lit by razors of light from the edges of the elevator doors on each floor. As he watched, the closest of the lift cars came down to ground level, halting within arm's reach. He heard the muffled sounds of conversation inside, before the car set off again, rising back into the gloom.

'*Mobile in position.*'

That was Malte, signalling that the 4 × 4 was waiting outside, in the event that a fast getaway was required. It was a sensible precaution, given the outcome of their last try at this.

'*Operations here, I'm on station.*' Kara was out on the water again, this time handling things alone. The rigid inflatable boat floated out of sight around the end of the wharf, where the hacker could work unseen. '*I want to remind everyone that my access has been severely curtailed since last time.*' She couldn't keep a note of annoyance out of her voice. '*I no longer have access to the hotel's internal security network. They patched the loophole we used before.*'

'We'll work around it,' Marc replied. 'Anything from the drone?'

'*Not much.*' Kara had a replacement UAV with a camera in the area, but even that couldn't get too close. The rich and famous had caught on to the gossip magazine paparazzi using the same tech, so the hotel's security team were alert. The Rubicon team had an edge, however; Kara's drones were military-grade, with long-range optics to match. '*I see our team, I see the Italian. But there's no sign of Glovkonin or his men anywhere in the hotel grounds.*'

'Good,' said Marc. 'We don't want him identifying Lucy.'

But the Russian's absence troubled her. Everyone who was anyone was at the Marine Luxe tonight. If Glovkonin had business elsewhere, Marc couldn't help but wonder what it might be.

He pushed the concern away and concentrated on the moment. 'All units green for go.'

Daichi smiled his warmest smile when Rumiko emerged from the shower, lost in the white towelling of his oversized dressing gown.

'You feel better now, don't you?' he told her. Daichi found it best to tell Rumiko what she should be feeling in order to get the responses he wanted from her. She nodded, forcing a smile, and he brushed stray hair from her eyes. 'Good. Go get dressed. Then we'll talk about food!'

Barefoot, she padded away across the room and down the corridor to the bedroom. He'd allowed her to leave some clothes here, but consistently rebuffed her overtures about moving in together. Daichi needed time away from Rumiko to maintain his illusion of being the attentive boyfriend. If they were constantly in each other's pockets, he would not be able to keep it up.

A low buzz summoned him back to the burner phone hidden in the vase. A text message appeared: *Open the door.*

Tentatively, Daichi walked back to the front door and peered through the spy hole. A large, muscular man with a bald head and a carefully curated moustache waited on the landing.

Daichi released the locks and the man pushed open the door before he could react. With a fluidity that belied his bulk, the big man slipped inside and closed it behind him.

JAMES SWALLOW | 213

'Where's the woman?' His hushed English had a soft French accent.

'In the bedroom.' Daichi's hands knitted together. 'You got here quickly! The call I made—'

'We were close by,' he said, cutting him off. 'We know about the African. Solomon. He's dangerous.' Then the man leaned in and put a hand around Daichi's wrist. He applied only light pressure, but even that was enough to know he had fingers like iron rods. 'What did you say to him?'

'Nothing!' Daichi's colour rose in his cheeks. He tried to pull away, but the other man held him firmly in place. 'I took her from him as soon as I could! I'm not at fault here, I've been doing what you people have asked for months!'

'You like your nice life?' The man released him. 'You like living here?'

'I pay for it myself,' Daichi said hotly.

'With money *we* pay *you*,' said the man, and Daichi did not correct him, because he was right. 'You see how that works? All you have to do is keep the girl happy and keep her occupied. Is that so hard?'

Daichi rubbed his wrist and scowled.

'Try it. When she's not going on and on about her boring studies, she's whining about how sad the world is. She's even made me go fucking vegan!'

'Sounds like a great burden,' came the reply, and annoyance flashed in the other man's gaze.

The man wandered over to the window and glanced out, and for the first time Daichi noticed he was wearing a wireless earpiece. The man nudged one of Daichi's sports bags with the toe of his boot. Inside it was fencing gear, dusty with disuse.

Daichi heard a noise from the bedrooms, the thud of closet doors closing, and turned towards the intruder.

'Look, she can't see you here. Just tell me what I have to do and then get out. But let your bosses know I want to be done with this!'

'Then maybe you should leave.'

'What?' Of all the possible replies, Daichi hadn't expected that one. 'I can't do that.' He floundered. 'I mean . . . uh . . . what will you do with Rumiko?'

'Why do you care?' The man narrowed the distance between them. 'You just said you wanted to get away from her.'

'I don't want her to get hurt!' he hissed.

'You're scared you would take the blame.'

Daichi fumbled a reply, unable to dredge up a denial for the truth of the matter. The bedroom door creaked open and he heard Rumiko's careful footfalls approaching.

'She's coming, you need to go!'

The man shoved him into a bookshelf and pinned him there with barely any effort.

'I'm not going anywhere.'

Rumiko was halfway into the living room before she caught up to the presence of the intruder. Her face turned pale with shock, but the big Frenchman gave her a warm smile and held up a hand.

'It's all right, Rumiko. I'm not going to hurt you.'

'Rumiko, run—!'

Daichi tried to call out, but the man shoved him into the shelf again, hard enough to dislodge a dozen books and choke the air out of his lungs. He wheezed, unable to speak.

'I'm a friend of Mr Solomon's,' said the big man, and Daichi's heart sank as he realised he had been played. 'I'm sorry to tell you that your boyfriend has been lying to you for some time about who he is.'

'Wh-what do you mean?'

'Look in your bag. There's a phone in it. Take it out.' The Frenchman's tone was gentle, and in other circumstances, it would have been soothing.

Daichi could do nothing as Rumiko pulled out the black smartphone he had found earlier and turned it over in her hands.

He could tell from the look on her face she had never seen it before.

'Whose is this?'

'It belongs to Solomon. We used it to track you. I apologise for that, but we had no other choice.' The man sighed. 'I'm afraid that this man's name is not Daichi Ito. He's being paid to watch you, by the same men who control your father.'

Rumiko shook her head. 'No. That's ridiculous!'

'Is it?' Daichi flinched as another figure entered the apartment, resolving into the man who had been at the cafe, the one called Solomon. 'Of course it is difficult to accept. So you should hear it from him yourself.'

'Play it back,' said the Frenchman, speaking to whomever was on the opposite end of his earpiece.

Daichi felt his neat little scam coming apart around him as the phone in Rumiko's hand obediently repeated everything he had said only a few moments earlier. He watched her expression shift from distrust to confusion, and then slowly towards anger, as his monologue went on.

'*I'm so tired of listening to her whine about her boring life,*' said the recording of his voice. '*I don't really like her.*'

With tears streaming down her face, Rumiko marched over to Daichi, and mercifully, the big man removed his hand.

'I kept telling myself that I was being foolish,' she said, 'thinking you were looking down on me. Always wondering why you were with me.' Rumiko took a shuddering breath. 'But I wasn't a fool. I knew something was wrong!' She stabbed a finger at Solomon. 'Is what he says true?'

'Miki-chan . . .' Daichi poured his skill into his voice, in order to convince her. 'I know we argue sometimes, but you know I care about you. You know I . . . *love* you.'

In the past, that would have been enough, but now he looked her in the eyes and saw that the old tricks were not working. Something had changed in Rumiko, as if the veil of naivety Daichi had always used to his advantage was suddenly gone. He glared at Solomon. It was his fault. The African had messed everything up.

The hit came out of nowhere. Rumiko slapped Daichi so hard that he tasted copper in his mouth.

'You are a liar,' she spat. 'And so was I! Lying to myself about you!'

'His real name is Daichi Kyun. His father is Korean, his mother Japanese.' Solomon spilled out his secrets, giving the woman his full attention. 'One of my people uncovered his criminal record. He is wanted by the Kanagawa Prefecture police for a number of offences, mostly fraud. He fled to Europe last year.'

'Was *any* of what you told me true?' Rumiko couldn't look Daichi in the eye anymore.

None of it.

Suddenly, Daichi wanted to shout that in her vapid, plain face. Every tiny little indignity he had suffered in her presence, every joke he had to pretend to laugh at, every tedious comment she made – they came rushing back at once. He was so sick of her, so bored with her dreary little life.

But he wasn't about to let her ruin his.

'Rumiko . . .' He held out a hand to her, the other moving along the bookshelf, searching for something hidden behind the books. 'Let me explain,' he said, as he found what he needed.

He knew if the big man landed a blow on him, that would be the end of it, so Daichi moved like lightning. He grabbed Rumiko and pulled her to him, in the same motion bringing up the little Browning pocket pistol from where he had concealed it. She cried out, but he ignored her, using Rumiko as a human shield as he waved the tiny gun in the direction of the two men.

'I needed the money and a nice place to live,' he told them, as if that was enough of an explanation. 'It's not like I killed someone!'

'*Konoyaro*!' Rumiko shrieked at him, and before he could react, she drove her fist back and down, punching Daichi in the crotch with all the power she could muster.

The blow connected with enough force that it took his breath away for the second time that night. He staggered back, doubled over in agony, barely able to keep from throwing up.

'I'll take that.' The man came to him, wrenching the Browning from his grip and handing it to the African. Then he gave Daichi a shove for good measure that put him down on the tatami mat. 'Don't get up again,' he warned.

Rumiko stepped up, drawing back her foot to give him a follow-up kick, but Solomon intervened.

'Our friend here already has enough problems,' he said.

She gave Daichi one last withering look, and then stalked away to the bedroom to pack her clothes into a bag.

'Now you have a decision to make,' continued Solomon, while the big man came over and crouched next to Daichi. 'If you stay here, you will have to face the men who pay you when they realise we have rescued Rumiko.'

At Daichi's side, the Frenchman busied himself with a small zip-case.

Solomon snapped his fingers in front of Daichi's face.

'Pay attention, Mr Kyun. Your employers will blame you for Rumiko's absence. They will not be so easy to charm as she was.'

'They . . . They'll kill me.'

The horrible reality of the situation settled in on Daichi and the sick sensation in his gut worsened.

'That's possible,' the Frenchman said conversationally. 'So, the smart thing for you to do when you wake up is get out of Austria as quickly as you can, eh?'

'Wake up?' Daichi shook his head. 'I don't—'

'*Shh.*'

Producing a silver, gun-shaped device from the zip-case, the big man pressed it to Daichi's neck and pulled the trigger.

Daichi felt a flood of warmth explode across his flesh and into his bloodstream. He managed to blink twice before the drug load caught him and dragged him away into darkness.

'He'll be out for around fifteen hours,' said Benjamin.

He carefully arranged Daichi upright in a chair, so that the young man would not choke or suffocate while he was unconscious.

Solomon frowned. In the space of a day, he had come to this city and destroyed a blameless woman's pleasant illusion of a good life – and for what? For a man he did not trust, an assassin who had tried more than once to destroy those closest to him.

The mendacity of it tired Solomon out, as if he had been exhausted by an ocean swim far off shore. He wanted to believe he was doing *right* – that was all he'd ever hoped for – but it was getting harder and harder for him to see through the fog of half-truths and deceptions.

Then Rumiko Saito walked back into the room and he had clarity again. She was the victim in this, the innocent caught between the spinning gears of intrigue and conspiracy. She deserved better.

Rumiko had a bag over one shoulder, and she never once glanced in Daichi's direction as she spoke.

'I can't stay here anymore, can I?'

'No.' Solomon shook his head. 'I am sorry. You will have to leave the country.'

'Yes. I suppose . . . It's like waking up from a dream. This was never real, was it?' It took a moment before she asked the next question. 'Do you really know my father?'

Solomon picked up his smartphone and tapped out a few keystrokes.

'Would you like to speak to him?'

She rubbed at the corner of her eye. 'I . . . I think I would.'

He handed her the device, and gestured towards the door.

'Come. You can talk on the way.'

When they were safely out of the area, they found a secluded courtyard to give her some privacy, and Solomon respectfully remained out of earshot of Rumiko's whispered, tearful reunion.

When it was over, she walked back to him and returned his phone.

'My father wants to speak to you.' Her voice was thick with emotion.

'You will come with us, then?'

'I will. He told me I can trust you.'

'Do you?'

Rumiko considered him for a moment. 'I don't know. But I think you are the only person who has been truthful with me for a very long time. So that will have to do for now.'

She placed the phone in his hand and walked away to where Benjamin and Delancort were waiting. Solomon raised the handset to his ear.

'Your daughter is a very resilient young woman.'

'*That is her mother's legacy,*' said Saito. '*Take Rumiko somewhere she will be safe, where they will not find her. Do this and our bargain will be complete.*' He took a breath, and Solomon could sense the man making a silent vow. '*I will give you everything I know. I will help you end the Combine.*'

TWELVE

The Zhemchuzhina had been Sochi's iconic hotel since the days of the Soviet Union, the so-called 'Pearl' of the coastal resort built for favoured apparatchiks and Party faithful who didn't warrant their own dachas. A white block of concrete and glass, the modern facelift it underwent in the run-up to the Winter Olympics had brought the building into line with contemporary hotels, but it could not conceal the Soviet brutalist exterior of the complex.

Glovkonin couldn't help but consider the place as frozen in the eternal 1970s of some sunny, propaganda reel USSR. It was a Russia very different from the hard, pitiless nation the young Pytor had grown up in, he reflected, but quickly he killed that line of thinking before it took hold. Living in the past was a waste of time.

Across the table, taking up one half of the Presidential Suite's lounge like the advance guard of an occupying army, Pavlo Chumak and his men were making themselves at home. The Salt Seller indulged himself with a glass of Glovkonin's vodka, while his bulky guardians attacked a trolley stacked with cheeses and caviar, loading up blinis and disappearing them in one gulp.

'You like to live well,' said Chumak, taking in the room's decor. It wasn't a compliment. He made the statement into an accusation, denouncing Glovkonin for his softness.

'I have earned it,' Glovkonin told the other man, looking him in the eye. 'Life is too short not to wring the juice from it.'

'If a man is not hungry, he is not willing to fight.' Chumak grunted. He wore a perpetual scowl on a round, unattractive face that resembled a sandblasted cue ball, turning it on his thugs. 'Look at these dogs. You would think I never feed them.'

Glovkonin let the comment go. If Chumak wanted to pretend he was better than him, he would allow it. This gangster could crow all he wanted about how tough he was, and make it sound as if he was more honest than Glovkonin, but they both knew that was a front. He had finished his third glass of vodka already. Pavlo Chumak liked his pleasures the same as anyone else.

'Why am I here?' The heavyset criminal poured a fourth shot and adjusted his bulk in the chair. 'You summon me up to your rooms like some errand boy to suck your cock?'

Glovkonin's expression hardened. The man's crude, quarrelsome manner was swiftly wearing on him. He had little interest in this kind of adolescent posturing.

'I respectfully *asked* you to come here because it is in both our interests to speak privately.'

'Away from the Italian,' said Chumak, with a rough snort. 'That's what you mean.'

'Very perceptive.'

'Don't patronise me,' snapped the other man, and his thugs stiffened at the tone of his voice.

Glovkonin was aware of his own bodyguards reacting in a similar fashion, but he raised a hand to them, indicating they should do nothing. Misha and Gregor maintained their positions, and he knew that if matters went awry, the two ex-Spetznaz operators would have their weapons drawn in an instant.

But the last thing Glovkonin wanted was to turn this meeting into a pointless pissing contest. He got straight to the point.

'I have learned that Da Silvio has been in communication with investigators from Interpol.'

'Bullshit.' The creases of Chumak's glower deepened. 'Why the fuck would he do something like that? He has more to lose than anyone.'

'Exactly.' Glovkonin wanted to smile. The criminal had made his point for him. 'That is why he is working with them – to preserve his status. To stay out of prison.'

'Who tells you this?' Chumak demanded.

OUTLAW | 222

'I have evidence,' he replied smoothly. 'And more importantly, an eyewitness.'

'I want to see this evidence, this witness.' The other man's ire continued to build.

So the story went, at the start of his criminal career as an armed robber, Chumak had been betrayed by a member of his own gang and spent years in a Ukrainian prison. The eventual death of the traitor had been something out of a nightmare, and ever since, the Salt Seller had nothing but loathing for anyone who would willingly give aid to the police.

Glovkonin pushed a folder across the table and Chumak snatched it up. Inside were printouts of surveillance images from a long-lens camera, each one expertly altered by Andre to show what appeared to be Giovanni Da Silvio in conversation with a prominent Interpol officer. For the latter, Andre had specifically picked someone Chumak would recognise – a Dutchman who had been trying to dismantle one of the Salt Seller's smuggling pipelines for years.

'What are they talking about?' Chumak grew more irate by the minute. He stabbed a finger at Glovkonin. 'This is about your thing, eh? What do you call it? Combines.'

Glovkonin shook his head, like a patient teacher with a dim child.

'I'm sorry to say, he places your friendship far lower in his interests than the Combine. Da Silvio is informing on you.' Seeing that he now had the man's full attention, he pressed on. 'You lost a cargo recently, I believe? Some trucks crossing the border from Azerbaijan?'

'Yes.' Chumak bit out the word. 'Fucking cops took it. What of it?'

Glovkonin had no idea what the cargo had been, nor how it had been discovered, but it was a useful fact to anchor his story.

'Da Silvio knew about it. He gave that up to them.'

Chumak sat back in his chair, sucking in a long breath through his nicotine-stained teeth.

'Show me proof.'

'Saito!' Glovkonin pitched up his voice, so he would be heard in the suite's other rooms. 'Bring him in.'

The Japanese assassin appeared at the door to the anteroom and gave a solemn nod, returning a moment later with a slight, sweating man in a cheap suit at his side.

'This is Olezka Turgenev,' Saito explained, escorting his charge to stand before Chumak. 'An investigator with Sledkom.'

Saito offered the criminal the man's identity wallet, which the gangster gave a cursory once-over and then tossed on the table.

Chumak spat on the carpet. 'You brought a piece of shit cop in here?'

'Mr Olezka has assisted me on occasion,' said Glovkonin.

'Hello.' Turgenev managed a weak smile.

A wiry figure, animated with a nervous energy that the man could not quite be rid of, he visibly recoiled from Chumak's seething glare and bumped into Saito standing behind him.

Glovkonin never dealt with Turgenev this closely, preferring to allow Saito or someone else to handle him at a remove – but the needs of this deception meant it had been necessary to bring him in. Turgenev operated at a mid-level in Sledkom, the Investigative Committee of the Russian Federation, a federal law enforcement department roughly equivalent to the American FBI or the British National Crime Agency; he was also a Combine asset. His role today was to back up what Glovkonin said, beginning with a rapid-fire description of how Giovanni Da Silvio had actively sold out Pavlo Chumak.

He produced a digital recorder and played an audio file Glovkonin had provided, adapted from the conversation between the Russian and the Italian in the restaurant a few days earlier. The prearranged narrative Turgenev presented continued for a few minutes, and Chumak listened sourly, gesturing at one of his men to bring him the caviar while he waited.

The Salt Seller's cheeks darkened. He clearly believed what he was hearing.

'You swear this is truth?' Chumak growled, ladling a heap of black roe on to a cracker. He gripped the slender mother-of-pearl spoon tightly in his heavy, calloused fingers as he swallowed the wafer whole.

'Every word,' said Turgenev, straightening his jacket, aiming for some composure.

'You do this?' Spittle and flecks of food flew from Chumak's lips. 'You take information from the Italian, you use it to fuck me?'

'Well, yes, but—' Turgenev never finished the sentence.

Chumak grabbed the man, one hand grasping the back of his head, and pulled him close. With a bullish snarl, the criminal rammed the caviar spoon in his hand into Turgenev's eye, forcing it through the socket and into the man's brain. Bone crackled wetly as Chumak's big wrestler's hands ended his life.

Saito reacted in shock, one hand dropping to where Glovkonin knew he had a holstered pistol, but the Russian warned off the assassin with a shake of the head, silently telling him to let it play out.

Turgenev's twitching body collapsed to the carpet, and the corrupt policeman gasped out his last breath.

Glovkonin suppressed a sigh. He suspected that Chumak's notorious temper might get the better of him, but he had hoped it would not be so. Now they would have the additional chore of disposing of a body.

'Was that necessary?' he asked.

'I will tell you what is necessary!' Chumak snarled his reply. 'I'm going to gut that shit-eating rat Da Silvio and hang him from the bridge! No one crosses me and lives, no matter how much fucking money he has!'

'I thought you would feel that way.' Glovkonin raised both his hands in a gesture of conciliation. 'But if I could ask you to just . . . take a moment? Storming into the middle of a party and murdering one of Italy's most prominent industrialists is a rash act, don't you think?'

'An example has to be made!' Chumak retorted. 'Every second a traitor breathes is an insult to me!'

'I brought this information to you so we can deal with him.' Glovkonin rose to his feet, and the criminal's ire ebbed. 'Together, yes? But not tonight. *Tomorrow*. At the exchange. Then we can conclude our business in Sochi and remove this problem at the same time.'

'When he least expects it,' said Chumak.

For the first time, the thug's ugly features split in an even uglier smile.

'Will you let me tell you what excites me the most?'

Da Silvio raised his voice to be heard over the hubbub of the party. He exhaled rich tobacco smoke through his perfect white teeth, making lazy loops with the lit tip of his cigar.

'Oh, I'll let you do anything, mate.' Grace finessed her reply with a sultry giggle, her imitation of Sunny Wehmeyer pitched somewhere between seductive and daring.

The Italian spared Lucy a glance, where she perched on the arm of Grace's chair. Lucy remembered to look interested. Satisfied his audience hung on his words, Da Silvio made a clutching gesture with both hands.

'The *power*.' He made the word into a tiger's growl. 'You strap yourself into one of those boats, open up the throttles and let. It. Go.' To underline the point, the man kited one hand up into the air, like a rising wing. 'Incredible!' Da Silvio chuckled. 'But that's why my own team won't let me race our boats, I am too . . . What is the phrase? Heavy in the shoe?'

'You're a lead-foot,' offered Lucy. 'Can't stay off the gas.'

'*Sì, sì . . .*' He frowned briefly, unsure if Lucy was mocking him. The Italian looked out, across to the waterline. Now the evening had drawn in, the boats bobbing along the shore were motes of light floating around the grand illuminated form of the Marine Luxe Hotel. 'Ah. You could almost believe we were in Sicily, am I right? If you didn't look at the food, of course!' He laughed, his amusement echoed by his entourage.

'Booze is great, though,' said Grace, winking and saluting him with her oversized cocktail. 'Russkis get that right, don't they?'

'I am surprised we've never spent any time together.' Lucy could almost hear an audible thud as Da Silvio switched gears, going in for the kill. 'You've been keeping your distance from me!'

Grace gave a shrug. 'To be honest, at first I thought you were a bit of a cock, mate. But I prejudged, didn't I?'

That pleased him, and he flagged down another server.

'I apologise profusely if I gave you that impression, Ms Wehmeyer.'

Lucy watched him smile to himself.

This asshole thinks he's winning here. Negging the Aussie chick, then she comes crawling back to him.

She wanted to upend her drink over the guy, but resisted the temptation. Undercover work always had its unique challenges.

She monitored the space around them, careful not to be obvious about it, looking at the faces of the partygoers who came and went. Many of them Lucy recognised from her walk-through of the hotel a few days earlier – the racer groups, the hangers-on and the criminal cliques mingling as they necked expensive champagne and overpriced vodka.

But the one man she had expected to see here wasn't around. Pytor Glovkonin was conspicuous by his absence, and that was a mixed blessing. The Russian oligarch knew the faces of the Rubicon survivors, if not from first-hand experience then at least from their surveillance files, so if he wasn't here, he couldn't burn them.

But what's worse, seeing the shark's fin in the water or not seeing it?

Lucy's attention snapped back to the moment as the Italian noticed a group from the British Hawkeshead team walking by. He switched his attention away from the women without even the slightest consideration, undoubtedly expecting them to sit and wait patiently while he engaged with someone else. Da Silvio's voice rose, becoming macho and boisterous to match the other men.

Lucy briefly caught the eye of the Italian's assistant and received a chilly glare in return. The Germanic ice princess stood a few paces away from her boss, stiff like a statue, dressed in a drab trouser suit with asymmetric sleeves and a mandarin collar. The outfit, the stillness of her, and the fact that she didn't appear to blink made the woman resemble some kind of sci-fi show android.

Cradled in the crook of the woman's arm was the target package, the digital 'book' containing the intel they needed to access to complete their mission. Lucy kept it in sight from the corner of her eye, wondering how much longer they were going to have to wait.

Not long, as it turned out. Lucy heard the soft chime from the smartwatch on the assistant's wrist. The woman's severe expression tightened as she read something off the watch's screen.

Lucy touched the jewelled choker around her neck in a bored, distracted fashion, activating the skin-contact throat mike hidden inside it.

'Active, wake up.' She subvocalised the words, so softly that only the mike would register them.

'*Just resting my eyes,*' said Marc, his voice resonating from the radio bead in her right earring. '*Are we on? Please say yes, my legs are going numb crouching down here.*'

She pictured him in the Marine Luxe's sub-basement, hiding out in the oily crawlspaces beneath the main elevator shaft.

'Think so,' she replied.

Grace touched her lightly on the arm and nodded towards the hotel. Another of Da Silvio's assistants approached, carrying an identical tablet computer to the one in the woman's hand.

'*Signor?*' said the woman in the grey suit, catching sight of her subordinate. 'A moment?'

'What? Oh. Drake is here, already?' Da Silvio allowed himself to be drawn out of his conversation for a moment to press his thumb to a sensor on the tablet she carried. He noticed Lucy's attention and showed his teeth again in a wide smile. 'Technology. As much a benefit as a bane, don't you think?' He didn't wait for an answer and waved the woman away, returning to his over-loud discussion. '*Grazie*, Willa. Carry on.'

Lucy raised her glass to cover her mouth as she spoke. 'All units, the book is in play. We're on.'

'*Copy,*' said Marc.

'*Copy.*' Kara's voice echoed the Brit's a moment later. '*Good news, I have partial access to the elevator control subsystems. Looks like someone forgot to patch that after last night.*'

The man Da Silvio had called Drake handed the woman Willa the new tablet and took the old one into his custody, with the solemnity of someone handing over nuclear launch codes. Without a word, Drake took his burden in both hands and threaded his way back into the hotel, towards the elevator bank.

'What's shakin', babe?' Grace glanced at Lucy, but her smile didn't reach her eyes.

Lucy spoke again, but her words were for the others. 'The book is on the move. Active, the courier is coming to you.'

'Active copies,' said Marc.

He stood with his head below the level of the ground floor, where the doors to the lift shaft met the metal frame. In the basement, the grease-covered machinery filled the space, and in the semi-darkness he had to move carefully or risk snagging his gear on something.

Pale light from his smartphone illuminated Marc's face, where the screen showed a mouse's-eye view of the crowded lobby floor. A thin, flexible cable led up from the device to a tiny camera wedged in the gap at the bottom of the lift doors, sending him a live video feed. As he watched, he saw Drake moving through the crowd of partygoers, escorted by one of the hotel's uniformed security men.

Da Silvio's assistant came up to the lift doors and Marc heard the click as he pressed the call button. Marc reeled in the wire-camera, and the lift car up on the fourth floor began to descend.

He skirted back around the safety cradle at the base of the shaft, moving to his ready position. The car dropped into place and halted. As the doors opened to allow the hotel residents inside to exit, Marc stepped up and wedged himself into the corners of the lift's exterior frame. Magnetic strips in the kneepads he wore thudded quietly against the outer shell of the car, holding him in place.

There was barely a half-metre gap between the back of the lift car's exterior and the inside wall of the shaft, but Marc's narrow, wiry build was just about thin enough to fit in there. He had a couple of centimetres of clearance once the thing started to rise, and the prospect of being scraped along eight storeys of wall was more than enough to keep him hugging the lift.

With care, Marc placed a metallic pad the size of a sheet of paper against the shell of the lift and connected it to his smartphone.

Indicators blinked on, showing that the reader pad had good contact and was ready for capture. Marc kept his attention fully on the phone as he thumb-typed in a key string that activated a scanning program. The lift bounced on its shock absorbers as the last of the hotel guests disembarked, and then the weight shifted again as Drake and the security guard boarded.

The failure of the original plan to siphon off the data from the digital book meant that Marc was now forced to turn that operation inside out to get what they needed. The tablet computer used a near-field system, a wireless means of transmission that would operate when two sources were close enough to swap data. Normally, that was the book and its charging cradle, but the pad Marc had placed on the wall of the lift duplicated the same signals. Once Drake moved into range for the near-field to connect, the book would think it was in download mode and drop its guard. From there, it would only take a few seconds to copy every last byte of Giovanni Da Silvio's private and personal emails stored on the device.

Simple in theory, but complex in reality. The operating range was limited, and with a steel wall in the way, that distance reduced even more. Drake would have to be close.

The smartphone's screen flickered green as the word DOWN-LOADING blinked on, and Marc felt a surge of elation as the data capture began.

'*Elevator is ready to move,*' said Kara.

'Eighth floor, please.'

Marc heard Drake's voice from inside the lift car, heard the man moving around. With a click, an automated announcement in Russian warned to stand clear of the closing doors.

The green screen suddenly switched to an accusing crimson, the text NO SIGNAL flaring brightly. Marc swallowed a curse. The reader pad had lost its data capture as its target moved outside its range.

Drake wasn't standing still inside the lift. Da Silvio's assistant moved around, nervously shifting as he waited for the doors to close.

'Come on, come on,' said the man, as he pressed the floor button once more.

Maybe Drake had a thing about lifts, maybe he was wound too tight, but whatever the reason, he moved in and out of the near-field radius, continually making and then severing the connection between the book and Marc's spyPhone.

DOWNLOADING. NO SIGNAL. DOWNLOADING. NO SIGNAL.
For fuck's sake, stand still!

Marc willed his thoughts into Drake's skull, but it made no difference. Unless the man stayed close, they would not get what they needed.

'Problem?' said Grace, leaning in to speak into Lucy's ear as Da Silvio brayed with laughter at some locker-room joke cracked by one of the racers.

'No connection,' she hissed.

Through the windows of the hotel atrium, Lucy could see the elevator bank, and Drake moving back and forth by the open doors.

'Can your girly hold the lift?'

Grace stood up quickly, reaching for Lucy's arm as she parsed the situation.

'Uh, yeah . . . Maybe.'

'Tell her to do it.'

Grace pulled Lucy off her perch.

Lucy pressed her throat mike. 'Kara, hold the elevator.'

'*I can give you ten seconds.*'

'That'll have to do.'

'You're leaving?' the Italian called after them as the pair moved off.

'We're going to take a leak, no worries,' Grace shot back, then turned to Lucy. 'Follow my lead.'

Lucy said nothing, but she didn't stop Grace, letting the other woman guide her across the lobby.

Without slowing the pace, Grace snatched an open bottle of champagne from a nearby ice bucket and glugged down a mouthful, then thrust it into Lucy's hand. The woman's expression turned slack.

'Have some fizzy pop,' she grinned, slurring her words like a drunk and giving a boozy wink. 'And play along.'

Grace let go of Lucy's hand and released a sound somewhere between a whoop and a giggle, as if she had said something hilarious to her. Without looking where she was going, Grace pitched straight into the elevator doors as they started to close, catching them in mid-motion.

The doors hissed open again and Lucy saw Drake inside, his expression a mixture of surprise and dismay. Grace staggered drunkenly into the elevator car and Lucy followed, allowing the champagne bottle to dangle from her right hand.

This is what we're doing? Okay then.

She'd had her fair share of overindulgences in the past, and Lucy knew how to fake it convincingly.

'Sorry sorry sorry,' said Grace, and she bumped into Drake, forcing Da Silvio's assistant to back up against the rear of the car.

'It's okay . . .'

The man hadn't noticed either of the women outside at his boss's table, taking them at face value as tipsy party girls who'd had a little too much.

Lucy gave the security guard a dopey smile and chewed on her bottom lip. While the guy didn't return it, his gaze dropped to stare at her chest. A distraction was a distraction, she decided, keeping up the blank look.

The elevator was rising now, and Grace flailed at the buttons, hitting one at random.

'Where we going? Where's the party, handsome?'

'I . . . uh . . . I'm working,' said Drake, his cheeks colouring.

He clearly wasn't familiar with this much attention, and Grace poured it on, pressing a hand on his chest, holding him in place.

'*Good capture,*' whispered Marc, over the radio link. '*Keep it there a few more seconds.*'

Lucy looked at the wall at the back of the elevator car. On the other side of that thin barrier of steel, the Brit clung to the moving platform as if his life depended on it, because it did.

'How you doin' back there?'

'Bloody swell, mate,' replied Grace, her fake down-under accent rising into a chuckle.

The security guard eyed her.

'Miss, please step away.'

He moved, raising a hand to compel Grace to back off.

'Oh, look but don't touch, I gotcha.' She flashed Lucy a warning look.

Lucy shifted her grip on the neck of the champagne bottle, ready to use it as a bludgeon if needed.

Something clanked loudly against the back of the elevator, drawing everyone's attention.

'What was that?' said Drake, clutching the digital tablet protectively.

'Rats?'

Grace made a rodent-like chattering sound and then burst out laughing at her own joke.

The elevator stopped with a soft chime at the eighth floor, the doors opening to allow the two women to exit. Lucy ambled out, but Grace dithered on the threshold, smirking at Drake.

'Hey, working boy. What time you get off, eh?'

'Well, uh . . .' He straightened, trying to find some poise. 'Actually, in a couple of hours . . .'

'*Capture complete*,' said Marc, into Lucy's ear.

Lucy tapped Grace on the arm, and the other woman got the message.

'Never mind,' Grace snapped, cutting off Da Silvio's assistant before he could finish. 'Changed my mind!'

She stepped all the way out of the elevator, and the doors closed, allowing it to continue on its way up to the penthouse level.

Lucy pressed a hand to her choker.

'Active? What's your status?'

It was a long few seconds before the Brit answered.

'*Sweaty. Greasy. But we have it.*' He took a breath. '*All call signs, fall back to the classroom.*'

'So, did your limey boyfriend get the goods?'

At Lucy's side, Grace had shrugged off her fake drunk act and equally fake accent, watching her with arms folded over her chest.

'We have what we came for,' Lucy replied.

'Yay team.' Grace gave a sarcastic salute, taking the bottle for another swig. 'Don't everybody thank me at once.'

On the opposite side of the lift shaft, a dust-caked metal ladder led from the penthouse level all the way down to the sub-basement, and with care, Marc stepped off the exterior of the car and on to the rungs.

He let himself hang up there for a minute or so as the lift moved away, allowing his breathing to normalise. His wrists and ankles ached from the tension of hanging on the back of the car.

The Rubicon-issue spyPhone he'd used to gather the data from the digital book sat in the pocket of his gear vest, and he was over-aware of it, as if the thing was heavy as lead.

A win, he told himself. *Forgotten what that feels like.*

The reader device had successfully fooled Da Silvio's digital tablet into divulging its contents, the 'take' now securely stored in the phone's memory. Under other circumstances, Marc would have streamed the stolen data straight to Kara's laptop off-site as the capture took place, but here, stuck inside the reinforced concrete chimney of the lift shaft, there was no way for a wireless signal to get out. He needed to walk these stolen virtual goods out of the front door, and there were still a dozen security guards between here and clear air.

Marc descended the ladder to the basement, doing his best to ignore the rush of warm, slick air that pulled on him as the lifts and their counter-weights rumbled up and down, a few centimetres from his face. In the dimness, the descent took forever, but at last his trainers touched concrete. The rest of Marc's kit lay where he had left it, inside the maintenance hatch leading back to the basement proper. He cleaned off his face with an antiseptic wipe and stepped through, blinking into the bright light of the other room.

A stocky man in a Marine Luxe security uniform stood on the other side of the hatch, an expression of shock and surprise on his face. Before Marc could fully extract himself, the guard had pulled a Grach semi-automatic from his belt holster and aimed the pistol at his chest.

'*Ruki vverkh*!' The guard snarled the words, and then to be sure, he repeated the command in English. 'Hands up!'

Marc said nothing, but did as he was told. He studied the man. Muscular but a little overweight, the guard had the sharp-eyed manner of someone competent, and that was a problem. If Marc kicked off a fight with this guy, he knew he would have to end it quickly, decisively – or else the night would turn into a replay of his previous departure from the hotel, a mess of gunfire and *run like fuck*.

He thought of the smartphone in his pocket. He could not afford to lose the intel.

'Who are you?' demanded the guard.

'Lift inspector,' Marc said innocently.

Never taking his eyes off Marc, the guard reached up to a radio handset clipped to his pocket. Marc adjusted his stance, waiting for the right moment, the instant when the guard's attention would be split between him and the radio.

But before any of that could happen, the door to the basement opened and a sturdy Japanese man in a sharp suit stepped inside.

Hiroshi Saito gave Marc a dismissive look, and then glared at the guard. He said something in rapid-fire Russian that Marc couldn't follow, but the tone and metre of the words made the meaning clear. He was tearing a strip off the poor bloke.

The guard's arm dropped, the gun going back into the holster. The man's entire body language changed, the tension vanishing to be replaced by a submissive manner. He nodded glumly as Saito continued, offering a confused reply which was quickly shot down.

The conversation concluded with Saito making some kind of statement that was clearly a veiled threat. The guard gave Marc a sheepish glance, and then left the room.

It took Marc a few moments to process what had happened. At length, he ventured a question.

'Am I supposed to thank you for that?'

'I expect nothing from you, Mr Dane,' replied the other man.

Marc scowled at that. 'What are you doing, Saito?'

'I arrived with Glovkonin a short while ago. He is at the hotel to meet with Da Silvio for drinks. It is important for both of them to keep up the pretence of a cordial alliance.'

'Cordial alliance?' echoed Marc. 'Is that what we have?' He went on before Saito could reply. 'How did you know I was in here?'

'I confess, I did not,' said the assassin. 'I decided to check the hotel's security for myself.' He paused, considering that. 'Lucky for you. I would suggest that in future, you do not rely on good fortune to keep yourself out of danger.'

Marc shrugged as he picked up his gear.

'I make my own luck.'

'All fools believe that, until the moment it runs out.' Saito inclined his head in the direction of the man who had left. 'I told the guard you were one of my people. The staff here know well enough not to interfere with any Combine operatives they encounter.'

'You'd better hope that bloke doesn't decide to double-check.'

Saito looked back at Marc with those piercing, unblinking eyes of his.

'You need to leave immediately. I cannot protect you if Glovkonin becomes aware of your presence.'

'Way ahead of you there, pal.' Marc pushed past him, shrugging off his tactical vest to reveal an ordinary shirt beneath. He paused by the door. 'Y'know, I appreciate the assist, but to be honest, I don't like having you around.'

'I have put our personal differences aside,' noted Saito. 'This is not about our past conflicts.'

'Good for you. You're obviously the better man. It doesn't come that easy to me, sorry.'

Marc tucked his gear into a drawstring bag.

'You think we are not alike,' said Saito, after a moment. 'That comforts you, I imagine. It allows you to believe that your actions are justified.'

'And you tell yourself you're irredeemable, don't you? That way, anything you do is permitted, because you don't have to put in the effort to be anything more.'

Saito's cheek twitched in an involuntary tic, and Marc knew he had touched a raw nerve.

'You are perceptive. Too much for your own good.'

'So I'm told.'

'We have both crossed too many lines, Mr Dane, to argue over who has more blood on their hands. The . . . The weight feels the same, no matter who carries it.'

Now it was Marc's turn to tamp down his ire.

'You don't know me. Don't talk to me like you do.'

Saito fell silent again, framing his next words.

'If Solomon keeps his promise, I will keep mine.' He fixed Marc with that steady, unwavering gaze. 'See my daughter to safety and I will betray Glovkonin to you.'

'And then what?'

Saito blinked. The question had wrong-footed him. He had to reach to find an answer.

'And then . . . *nothing*. Nothing else matters to me.'

It was long past midnight when the team regrouped at the derelict school. Malte headed up to the roof to take first watch, while Kara attacked the capture from the digital tablet like a starving child at an all-you-can-eat buffet.

They were tired, but the hacker palmed a handful of stay-awake capsules into her mouth and washed them down with a tall can of some Russian off-brand energy drink. She rode the caffeine jitters like a surfer finding a curl and her hands blurred over her keyboard.

Lucy watched Kara lose herself in the panes of digital code, then drifted away, working her shoulders to ease out the tension. She scanned the room for Marc and found his shadow through the broken window, spotting him out in the yard in the middle of the classroom blocks. He sat on an overgrown concrete bench, staring into nothing.

She resisted the temptation to go talk to him. It was rare, but when Marc was deep in his own head, she'd learned to let him brood. On the way back, the Brit had told them about his encounter with Saito, but he was light on the specifics. She wondered what Glovkonin's pet killer had said that would affect Marc this way. Past experience told her he'd come around when he was good and ready, but the pull to reach out was hard to silence.

Nearby, Grace sat on a gear case, with a light jacket over her party dress and a pungent cigarette in her hand. Stripped of make-up, jewels and feigned mannerisms, she had slipped back into the changeable, caustic attitude that Lucy had come to realise was her default setting.

The other woman noticed her attention.

'What?'

'Quick thinking back there, in the elevator.'

'And?' Grace made a winding motion with her hand. When Lucy didn't expand on the comment, she sniffed. 'Well, I guess that's as close to a compliment as I'm ever going to get from you, huh?'

'Don't let it go to your head,' Lucy said coldly. 'Nobody denies that you have skills. That's why you're here. But one smart play for us don't balance out the bodies you got on you.'

Grace took a long drag on the cigarette.

'Girl tries to be a team player, still gets shit for it. Or is it that you don't like competition?'

'Listen to me.' Lucy's eyes narrowed. 'You are not on the team. You are not one of us. You're a killer with a talent we need to complete our mission, you read me? That's all.'

'You realise that description fits everyone in this building, right?' An odd expression crossed Grace's face. Sadness, annoyance, conceit – it could have been any one of them. 'Don't talk to me like you're a fucking angel. How many people have you killed, long shot?' She mimed sighting down a rifle. 'More than me, I bet. But you reckon your way is more honest? I mean, I lie, cheat and stick a knife in people's backs, but you, the sniper queen? They never even know you're out there, until *pow*.'

'Remember that,' Lucy warned, 'when you think of double-crossing us.'

'Quit while you're ahead, Grace.' Kara offered the advice from across the room. 'Lucy Keyes holds grudges like other people nurse their children.'

'No one asked you.' Lucy stalked back across to where the hacker was working. 'Anything?'

'Plenty.' Kara kept on tapping away at her laptop as she spoke. 'Like most rich, conceited idiots with something to hide, Signor Da Silvio assumes that buying an expensive digital security system is all he needs to do to keep his data airtight. *Wrong*.' She waved at the screen in front of her. 'I started with his emails and there's a lot of actionable intel here.'

'Give me a taste.'

Lucy folded her arms, willing it to be true. After all the problems they had suffered up to this point, they were due for a win.

'For starters, the unidentified hardware we've heard about in the chatter, this so-called "equipment" . . . The term is plural, not singular. It's actually *two* devices, not one.'

'Two rogue WMDs under Combine control.' Grace let out a low whistle. 'I don't really wanna be anywhere near *one*, if it's the same to you.'

'There's nothing to indicate the devices are weapons,' Kara corrected. 'Granted, nothing indicates that they *aren't*, either, but . . .' She broke off and sighed. 'It's frustrating. It's unclear.'

'Then give us what *is* clear.' Marc stood in the doorway, arms folded. Lucy hadn't heard him re-enter the building. 'You can keep digging after the fact.'

'All right.' Kara sat up straighter, leaning away from her keyboard. 'According to messages in the encoded email train between Da Silvio and his contacts in Europe, one of the whatevers has already been completed and deployed. They're calling it Unit One. From the way they talk about it, I get the impression it's something small, maybe briefcase-sized.'

'Deployed where?' said Lucy.

'Don't know,' admitted the hacker. 'I'm going through the emails in reverse order, newest first, so it's possible that information is in one I haven't got to yet. But there is a definite lead here. Remember the information Delancort brought us from the Monaco server, about the cash transfers?'

Marc nodded. 'Yeah. The Combine were channelling money from the last of Rubicon's accounts to some company in . . . where?'

'Turkey,' noted Kara. 'Specifically, Istanbul. A technology concern the Rubicon Group were part-owners of, called Altin Elma.'

'*Golden Apple*,' Grace translated, getting an arch look from Lucy.

'According to Da Silvio's emails, Altin Elma built Unit One.'

'Using Rubicon cash and know-how . . .' Grace snorted with delight. 'Shit, you gotta admire the brass balls on Glovkonin and his buddies.'

No one else in the room found it amusing.

'Okay, that's actionable,' Marc went on. 'What about the second device – anything on that?'

'Unit Two,' announced Kara, 'whatever it may be, arrives tomorrow, in time for race day.'

'Here? In Sochi?' Lucy blinked. 'Do we know how?'

'Again, unclear,' said the hacker. 'I'll keep looking.'

Grace paled visibly. 'He's not gonna . . . let it off here, is he?'

Marc shook his head. 'Da Silvio has poured millions into building a hotel on the Black Sea. He doesn't strike me as the type who'd waste that investment.' He paused, thinking it through. 'The Italian is the Combine's transport and logistics guy, remember. He's going to move it, whatever *it* is. I mean, there's a load of cargo going out of the city as part of the race circus, right? If you wanted to smuggle something dodgy across international borders, that's perfect cover.'

Lucy's skin prickled and a sickly sensation rose in her gut.

'The next race venue is New York. Around Manhattan.'

Marc came to her, reaching out to put a hand on her shoulder.

'That doesn't automatically mean New York is a target. With that gear moving around, if the device makes it to the continental US, it could go anywhere . . .' He trailed off, realising that his words were not making her feel any better.

Lucy had not been back to the city of her birth in nearly seven years, and this wasn't the first time she'd seen her home town threatened by a potential terrorist attack. But now it felt immediate, close to the bone.

She saw Giovanni Da Silvio's laughing face in her mind's eye, and in that instant, Lucy wanted to jam a gun in the face of that cocky son of a bitch and make him spill his guts.

Her mother still lived across the East River in Queens, but she worked in Manhattan as a charity volunteer. The life that Lucy had grown up with was bound up with the city. She felt afraid for it in a way that had never touched her before.

'We'll figure this out.' Marc held her gaze, speaking quietly. 'We will. We'll stop them.'

'You have a plan for that?' Grace stubbed out her cigarette and eyed him.

Marc didn't answer her. He stepped away from Lucy.

'Everyone rest up. Tomorrow's gonna be a busy day.'

THIRTEEN

They left the rented car a few blocks away across the Lower Town, and made their way in pairs through Zagreb's rain-dulled back-streets. Heavy skies pressed down on the city, suffocating the light of the day.

Delancort and Benjamin, who shared the driving duties, trailed behind Solomon and Rumiko. The two French-speaking men looked ready to drop. On false passports sourced from one of Kara Wei's numerous dark web contacts, the group had driven through the night from Vienna, on the southbound autobahn to the Slovenian border. From there, they followed the River Drava until the rented Audi crossed into Croatia after dawn.

Solomon felt the same fatigue – worse, in fact. Only the slight Japanese girl had managed to get any sleep during the journey, dozing fitfully in the back seat next to the African as they chased a front of bad weather across eastern Europe. Solomon's joints ached, the legacy of the injuries he had suffered in the explosion that had buried him alive.

He tried to keep himself fit, exercising as best he could during his subsequent captivity, but it was a poor substitute for proper physical therapy. He wondered if he would ever be the man he once was, then frowned at the thought.

Don't indulge such notions, he told himself. *Look to your duty first, your own needs second.*

He glanced at Rumiko, who kept close to his side so as to remain under the umbrella he held. She was tired, too, but at the same time the young woman took in the buildings around them. Her gaze traced up the street, catching sight of lines of blue trams carrying early morning workers to their jobs. Even after everything she had gone through in the last twenty-four hours, she still had a bound-less curiosity.

This part of Zagreb wasn't the picture-book core, however, with its elaborate Austro-Hungarian architecture, cathedrals and museums. The grey and unforgiving clouds merged with equally drab housing projects, supermarkets and petrol stations.

'Is it far?' said the girl.

Solomon shook his head as they rounded a corner.

'We are here,' he explained, gesturing to an apartment block made up of dozens of units.

Clumps of men in threadbare clothes smoked under concrete awnings, out of the chill and the rain, and they shot wary looks at the group as they approached. Close by, through a set of doors that opened into some kind of community hall, Solomon saw children and mothers moving to and fro, perhaps as part of an impromptu classroom.

He knew people like this. He saw the echoes of the hardships they had suffered in their eyes. More than once in his life, Ekko Solomon had *been* them.

And in a way, I am like them once again, he reflected. *All of us, outlaws, outcasts, finding our way forward.*

A sign over the entrance bore the words 'Emigrant Aid' and below that in smaller letters, a sentence in Serbo-Croatian that Solomon couldn't read.

'These people are refugees,' said Rumiko, glancing around. 'There's a lot of them.'

'They have much to flee from,' noted Solomon. 'Many of these people have made the crossing from Serbia and Bosnia, escaping persecution because of their beliefs or their ethnicity. Others have come from North Africa and the Ukraine.'

She nodded along with his words. 'Yes, I've heard about them. They believe Croatia is a safe path into Europe. But it's as risky as any other illegal route.' She paused. 'I've spent a long time studying the legalities of these situations . . . It becomes abstract. After a while, you can forget that these laws affect real people.'

A group of children ran out of the hall, laughing and giggling as they splashed through puddles, and Rumiko gave them an animated wave.

A young Turkish man in his mid-twenties, with a mop of curly black hair framing his handsome features, came out into the rain after the children, and gave a start as he spotted Solomon and the others.

'Mr Solomon? You're here! I can't believe it!' His face split in a beaming, infectious grin and he strode over, drawing the African into a firm handshake. 'I'm so pleased to see you again!' His smile faltered briefly. 'When we heard about what happened to your company . . . Well, we feared the worst.'

Solomon disengaged from the greeting and indicated the young woman.

'Halil, I want you to meet someone very special. This is Rumiko Kadohawa—'

'Rumiko Saito,' she corrected gently.

'Of course,' continued Solomon. 'She has agreed to work with us in our mutual project.' He indicated the building and the occupants. 'She is a legal expert. Very gifted.'

Rumiko blushed. 'Well, I don't know about that . . .'

Halil's face lit up again. 'That's fantastic! Oh, Miss Saito, we desperately need someone who understands that sort of thing. We have many people here, from many different places. They need help navigating the complexities of their lawful status – it's a bit beyond me, I must admit.'

'Halil is one of the most dedicated young people I have ever known,' said Solomon. 'He helps run this outpost of Emigrant Aid's charity.'

'I'm just giving something back.' Halil smiled sheepishly, one hand coming up to rub at the back of his neck. 'Some good people saved my life once. I'm trying to pay that forward—'

He broke off as Delancort and Benjamin approached. Halil gave Delancort a nod, but the Frenchman took the younger man into a crushing bear hug that lifted him off his feet.

'Benjamin makes frequent visits to this facility, and others,' explained Solomon. 'He is a counsellor, and there are many within these walls who have trauma in their past. His skills have great use here.'

Halil ushered them into the building, where the rich smell of food cooking hung in the air.

'We'll put some more places out for breakfast,' he said, 'and there's hot showers and beds, too, I think some of you could do with them.'

'*Oui, s'il vous plaît,*' said Delancort, with feeling.

'I have great respect for Emigrant Aid,' said Rumiko. 'One of my tutors worked at their camp in Spain. Your efforts assisting displaced persons are very commendable.'

'We do what we can,' Halil said cheerily.

When the Rubicon Group was at its best, Solomon had ensured that the corporation donated money and supplies to the charity to keep it up and running. Now that the company no longer existed, he feared for the future of the people it had helped over the past years – people like Halil. The Special Conditions Division had stopped him from dying in a terrorist atrocity, when he and several other youths had been coerced into becoming suicide bombers.

In the years that followed, Halil had taken the strength of character he gained from that life-changing experience to bring more light into the world. Solomon took pride in the fact that there was still a part of Rubicon's legacy that was doing good.

Solomon gave Rumiko a level look.

'I made your father a promise. I told him I would bring you to a safe place, where you would be out of the Combine's reach.' He gestured at the building. 'No one knows you here. These people can be trusted, you have my promise. I grant you, it is not the

Universität Wien, but it is a place where your skills will make a real difference.'

Rumiko took in the sights and sounds around her.

'I always knew that I would have to make two significant choices in my life. The first was what I would do with the knowledge I have gained from my studies. The second is how I would deal with my past. But I never expected both to be so closely intertwined.'

'Fate does have a way of defeating our expectations,' Solomon noted.

'Indeed,' said the young woman. 'I would like to speak to my father, please.'

'Of course.' Solomon handed over his smartphone to her once again. 'Take as long as you need.'

But as she walked away, Benjamin approached him, holding one of the cheap burner handsets they had picked up at the border.

'Sir?'

'Problem?' He put his weight on his walking stick, eyeing the disposable phone.

'It's Marc,' said the other man. 'You need to hear what he has to say.'

Solomon took the phone and held it to his ear, walking back out to the comparative isolation of the rain-drenched veranda.

'Mr Dane. What is the situation?'

'*We have some strong leads.*'

Marc quickly outlined the broad strokes of the intelligence take from the data they had captured in Sochi. Solomon's eyes widened as he heard mention of a familiar name.

'Altin Elma,' he said, breaking into the other man's flow. 'I am familiar with this place. A technology start-up concern which Rubicon acquired a few years ago from the Turkish government. Their speciality is developing cutting-edge communications systems – but they are a research centre, not a production facility. They build prototypes.'

'*That's all the Combine need,*' said Marc. '*We have to find out what this Unit One thing is, and what it does.*'

'Agreed.' Solomon pulled back the sleeve of his jacket to study his watch, making a quick calculation. Istanbul was only a couple of hours away by air. 'Leave it to us. We'll look into it.'

Marc hesitated. '*You sure? We have no idea what you'd be walking into.*'

'I believe you have enough to occupy you.' Solomon smiled thinly. 'Benjamin, Henri and I will be able to handle it. And I confess, I am quite enjoying being in the field. It's been a while.'

'*All right. Good luck. And be careful, sir. We don't want to lose you again.*'

The line fell silent, and Solomon walked back into the building, where the Frenchman was waiting for him.

'I know that look,' said Benjamin. 'We're not finished, are we?'

'No.' Solomon handed back the burner phone. 'You and Henri should eat, clean up, and then get a couple of hours' rest. We're going to Istanbul.'

Race day exploded across the Sochi coastline in a riot of crowds, noise and colour. It seemed to Lucy that the entire city had come to watch the Veloce Cup powerboats carve through the water, and as she walked down to the jetty, she could hear the chatter of the commentators, their rapid-fire Russian crackling from speakers up and down the promenade.

The gaudy racing suit she wore was a little tight on her – it had been tailored for the more defined Shayla McGrath – but Lucy made it work. Checking the tabs around her wrists, she smoothed down the front of the outfit, running her hand over the logo patches for the team's secondary sponsors. Horizon Integral's bright sunburst symbol cut across her chest, repeating on her back and across the crown of the helmet that dangled from her right hand.

'I feel like a walking billboard,' she muttered, and her words were picked up by the covert throat mike concealed in her collar.

'*That means you look the part,*' said Kara. Once more, the hacker was in 'overwatch' mode, observing from a vantage point near the Marine Luxe hotel. '*Don't forget the swagger.*'

'I do make it look good.'

That brought a grin to Lucy's face, and she added a little showboating to her walk as she approached the dock for vessel number 7, where Horizon's racer bobbed on the sapphire-blue water.

She heard the team's name amid the crush of Russian vowels over the PA speakers, and Lucy gave a brash salute to the crowds as a passing camera drone took in the dock. The crowd applauded and her smile widened.

'I could get used to this.'

'*You gettin' a big head, sis?*' Grace's imitation of Sunny Wehmeyer crackled into Lucy's radio ear-bead, the Australian accent back in place and nigh-on identical to the real article. '*You ain't won nothing yet.*'

Lucy looked towards the solar deck of the Marine Luxe Hotel, and found Grace there, a diaphanous white shape in a designer beach dress watching the event unfold.

'You do your thing, I'll do mine,' she told her.

'*Your thing is not to win the race.*' Marc entered the conversation, his tone curt. '*Play the part and maintain your cover. Glovkonin and Da Silvio are our targets, not the trophy.*'

The Brit was somewhere on the far side of the hotel, watching the exit routes from the building with Malte.

'Sure, fine.' Lucy tossed off the comment with a sniff. 'Just sayin', I can do both.'

She heard Grace snort in derision. '*You driven one of those before, love?*'

'I cross-trained on Zodiacs and assault boats with the SEALs,' she noted. 'How hard can it be?'

'*Well, as long you don't beach it on the sandbanks, we'll call it good, eh?*'

Grace snickered, and the sound of that made Lucy want a podium spot just to spite her.

Even at rest, powerboat 7 looked like the head of a spear, a sleek hydrodynamic shape waiting to cut loose out over the wave-tops. A giant outboard motor chugged and spat as the dock crew made last-minute adjustments to the props and the fuel mixture.

A sturdy guy with a Viking beard and straggly red hair down to his shoulders marched out to meet her. He did not look happy to see this interloper, and before a word left his mouth, Lucy had a pretty good idea that this was Richie, the grumpy HI crew chief.

'Hold it right there.' He had a gruff British accent, and he put up a hand like a cop directing traffic at an intersection. 'You Lana?'

'I guess so.'

He made a face at that. 'Look, I don't have time to express the level of pissed-off I am right now,' he retorted. 'But the boss gave this rig to his spoiled brat daughter and I've gotta live with her bullshit. Shayla was a fair hand on the wheel, but you, I know nothing about. Who'd you drive for?'

She ducked the question. 'I'm just here for the sea air and a nice ride.' Lucy remembered what Grace had told her at the party, and deliberately played into what Richie already expected – some egotistical racer who thought she had all the answers. 'Should've brought my waterskis.'

Richie's cheeks coloured. 'You can tell Sunny, my fucking boat gets even a paint chip because of you, and I quit!'

He turned around and stormed away.

'Didn't you just say it was Sunny's boat?'

The crew chief didn't reply, other than to raise his middle finger.

'That guy has no chill,' Lucy murmured, as she donned her helmet and stepped off the jetty and on to the racer.

'Got that right.'

Grace observed the sharp words between crew chief and driver through a pair of compact binoculars, then pretended to scan the rest of the boats. In reality, she held the binoculars away from her face and kept her eyes on a reflection in the glass barrier around the edge of the hotel's solar deck. In the smoked glass, she saw the other team owners and managers, mingling and enjoying the last few moments before battle commenced.

A recognisable figure appeared in the reflection – a man in a breezy, lightweight cotton jacket-trousers combo moving through the group with easy confidence.

'*Eyes on Da Silvio,*' said the hacker, confirming it for her.

'Yeah, right.'

Grace tapped the earring containing her radio-bead and returned her attention to the binoculars. She waited until she sensed the Italian standing right next to her.

'You know, I've had beautiful women walk out on me before, but not when I was being so charming.'

Da Silvio toyed with a flute of champagne, giving her an indulgent look.

'Is that what you were doin'?' Grace hid her real smile behind a fake one. 'Could've fooled me.'

This was too easy. She knew men like him inside and out. He had money and power and the run of as many sexual partners as he could want, but that wasn't enough. Da Silvio was only interested in the ones who played a little hard to get, who were married or otherwise denied to him. He liked the chase more than the win, and once she let him catch her, he'd get bored and move on to the next girl who caught his eye.

Grace knew how to make that work to her advantage.

'Aw, did I leave you feelin' sad?' She made a mock-pouting face. 'Sorry 'bout that. I was side-tracked.'

'I'm insulted. Well-mannered people don't leave a party without thanking the host first.' He gestured around, taking in the hotel. 'And this is my party. All of it.'

Grace guffawed. 'What the fuck made you think I'm well-mannered, mate?'

Da Silvio blinked, glancing at his ice queen assistant as if looking for support.

'Have I told you how refreshing it is to be around someone so . . . direct?' He recovered, grinning. 'Everyone else here is so fake.'

'You're more right than you know.'

A loud siren sounded from the waterline, and a wall of noise from the crowd came up and washed over the sun deck. The powerboats were moving into position at the starting line, and Grace caught sight of the crimson and black dart that belonged to Da Silvio's team, close to the neon-green of the Horizon Integral boat.

She turned back to the Italian, but his assistant was leaning close to him, one hand pressed to a Bluetooth headset, whispering into his ear as she relayed a message. Da Silvio's manner changed immediately, and he discarded his untouched champagne on a nearby table.

When he looked back at Grace, his playful expression had gone.

'*Scusa*. I'm afraid some pressing business requires my attention. We can continue this later.'

'Seriously?' She nodded towards the water. 'The race is about to start, and you're leaving?'

Irritation flashed in Da Silvio's eyes; another thing about his kind, they didn't like it when women questioned them.

'Some things are more important than trophies,' he replied, and he followed his assistant away, back towards the hotel proper.

Grace saw another face she recognised in there, waiting for Da Silvio to join him – a cold-eyed man with a neatly trimmed beard and granite features.

'Listen up. The Russian's here,' she whispered, tapping her earring. 'Both our boys are on the move.'

'There.'

Malte pointed over the steering wheel with his index finger, and Marc looked out across the Hunter's bonnet.

'Targets acquired,' Marc reported, pressing his mike pickup. 'Glovkonin and Da Silvio entering vehicles at the front entrance of the Marine Luxe. Two cars, black BMWs, one in each.'

'Low on the shocks,' noted the Finn, pointing out the stance of both vehicles close to the road. An obvious sign that the BMWs had internal armour plating and bulletproof windows.

'We're going to tail them, not intercept them,' Marc noted. 'Well, hopefully not,' he added.

In the Hunter's boot sat a bag of gear and weapons, but nothing that would have much impact on vehicles rated for combat zones.

'*Overwatch copies,*' said Kara. '*Marc, be advised, I have minimal tracking beyond this immediate area.*'

'We'll manage,' he replied, as Malte started up the 4 × 4. Marc threw a glance back at the race line on the far side of the marina. 'Lucy? Be careful out there.'

'*Just a walk in the park,*' she replied, her voice pitched up over the rumble of the powerboat's engines. '*Don't go picking any fights without me to cover your ass.*'

'I'll bear that in mind . . .'

The first BMW, carrying Da Silvio and his assistant, pulled away from the kerb. Marc saw someone open the door of the second car so Glovkonin could climb inside.

Saito.

'Well now,' said Marc, thinking aloud. 'How's this going to shake out?'

Malte gave him a quizzical look.

'You know the drill,' he told the other man. 'Drive casual.'

The Finn grunted and they set off, easing into the sparse traffic.

A spidery quadrotor drone floated over the water, ahead of the prows of the powerboats on the starting line. A trio of bright indicator lights beneath it illuminated one by one.

One red.

Two reds.

Lucy kept her eyes on the horizon, the drone at the edge of her vision. She tightened her hand around the throttle bar and pressed herself into the racer's acceleration chair, feeling the four-point harness around her body cinched in good and tight. Her pulse rumbled in her ears and, despite the situation, her lip twisted in a crooked smirk. She wasn't supposed to be enjoying this, but she was.

Three reds.

Three greens.

Go!

She resisted the urge to red-line the throttle off the mark, and instead applied steady forward pressure, accelerating evenly.

But the boat had other ideas. Number 7 rocketed off the line like a top fuel dragster, much faster than she'd expected, and Lucy's gut clenched as she felt the bow lift off the water.

'Whoa, easy, boy,' she told it, drawing back on the power before she went too far. Too fast, too soon, and the boat's leading edge would rise away from the wave tops and catch air.

The sleek hull was the love child of a jet fighter and a speedboat, and given enough freedom it would make a bid to get airborne. If that happened, Lucy's ride would flip up and stall, coming back down inverted. If the impact didn't crack it open like an egg and kill her with the shock trauma, it would hold her upside down as the cockpit filled with seawater.

'How hard can it be?' she said aloud, mocking her earlier statement.

'*Say again?*'

She could barely register Kara's voice over the growl of the outboard.

'Disregard,' Lucy replied.

From the corner of her eye, she saw a crimson mass moving past out to starboard and she chanced a glance in its direction. The Da Silvio Ingegneria boat took the lead, and from Lucy's perspective, less than half the vessel's hull actually touched the water, the rest of it skimming just centimetres over the waves.

The red and black boat hummed past, a shimmering vertical fin of white spray trailing behind it as the racers settled into a rough cluster. Up ahead, Lucy spotted the orange inflatable cylinder that marked the location of the first turn. In her rear-view, she could see the other boats positioning themselves, and she pictured the course in her mind's eye. Lucy and number 7 were already well outside the optimum point for the perfect race line, but that was okay. She aimed to stay in the middle of the pack, not to get the gold.

The first turn was deceptively smooth, but still Lucy lost speed as she took it too wide, allowing the Akula-X and Riverine Tech boats to thunder by. Easing the steering yoke over, she felt number 7 shudder as it skipped across their wakes. Out through the water-streaked canopy, the Da Silvio boat became a blurry dot, busy jockeying for position with Koastwell's vessel for the race lead.

The next turn was a hard 4 g hook, and it shoved Lucy back and forth against the restraints as they shot by the crowd-line beneath the Olympic stadium. She found herself among the trailing boats – a second in Da Silvio crimson and three more that jostled each other, deliberately cutting back and forth as the straightaways took them out of sight of the spectators.

Two of the other powerboats scraped hulls as they tried to pass one another, trading paint and chips of fibreglass, and Lucy gave them a wide berth. She'd been expecting something like the Indy 500 out here, but the aggressive way the drivers pushed their vessels made her wonder if it was more of an endurance race, with a little demolition derby thrown in for good measure.

She thought back to the rumours about the Veloce Cup's slack attitude towards driver safety, chewing it over.

'*How are you doing out there?*' said Kara over the radio, a note of genuine concern in her voice. '*We'll lose line of sight in a few seconds.*'

'Walk in the park,' Lucy repeated, as much for herself as for the other woman.

The airport was close to the race site, so the journey was a short one.

Saito sat in the back of the BMW at Glovkonin's side, while his bodyguards sat up front. The Russian's attention remained on the Italian's car ahead of them, and he had not picked up on the 4 × 4 tailing them from three vehicles back.

He couldn't see who was in the vehicle, but he didn't need to. Solomon's people were good, but they didn't have the resources to mount the sort of multi-car team required to run a seamless, undetectable follow.

Saito should have raised the alarm the moment he spotted any such possibility, but these were different days. He dwelled on the calls he had received from Rumiko, the most recent one coming just before the convoy left the hotel.

She was safe. She was free of the Combine.

A gargantuan, invisible weight slipped gently from Saito's shoulders. He had been carrying it for so long – the dread and the guilt – that he had internalised it, until he no longer noticed the burden. Now it was gone, everything seemed strange and new.

He tamped down the mix of emotions rising in him. It would be foolish to pretend that his fear had completely gone, now that his daughter was beyond Glovkonin's reach. Saito did not doubt that Ekko Solomon would do his best to keep his word – the man had honour – but there were other factors at play, other variables to contend with.

Until Glovkonin, Da Silvio and the other men who ran the Combine were neutralised, no one was truly safe.

The two cars left the highway and crossed into the airport grounds through a secondary entrance, away from the public terminal building and any prying eyes. Saito saw the 4 × 4 whip by, as if it were heading into the airport. It slowed, and he knew the men inside would be formulating a way to keep the convoy in sight.

'At last,' muttered Glovkonin, as the cars followed a service road across the main runway. The driver made for a series of low, wide hangars on the far side from the terminals, where commercial airliners lined up for flights to Moscow, Dubai and as far north as Murmansk. 'Be ready,' continued the Russian. 'I want you prepared.'

Off that, the bodyguard called Gregor gave a quick nod and made a show of checking the CZ 75 pistol in his holster.

Saito did the same with his weapon, not because he needed to, but because the Russian expected it of him.

He studied the terrain as the cars angled towards the largest of the hangars. Close to the coastline, Sochi International Airport was constructed around two runways that crossed at their northern ends, forming a V shape. The primary landing strip faced directly towards the Black Sea, while the secondary followed the path of a river inlet. Nestled in the middle of the two runways, the hangar complex provided something approaching isolation – exactly what this transaction required.

In front of the hangar, a Gulfstream G500 executive jet sat waiting. Saito recognised the aircraft as one from G-Kor's private fleet, in service to the energy conglomerate that was Pytor Glovkonin's personal fiefdom. Behind it, inside the cavernous hangar, a twin-engine Boeing 777 cargo aircraft was parked with its loading bays open. Beneath its wings, loading teams worked at flatbed trucks, guiding angular containers to be ferried up and on board. Saito noted that the 777 had no identifying livery other than a red and black stripe down its fuselage, but the tail number gave away its origins: the code started with the letter 'I', indicating an Italian registration. The bigger jet had to belong to one of Da Silvio's transportation concerns.

The BMWs drove around the loading operations to the rear of the hangar and halted beside a pair of Volga saloons, before which stood an unsmiling cohort of thuggish men in dark suits.

The cars halted and Saito was the first out, with Glovkonin's security at his heels. The men around the cars gave the assassin a collective sneer of disdain, and one of them opened the saloon's rear door.

A cloud of cigar smoke billowed out, and through it emerged the criminal known as the Salt Seller. His scowl remained unchanged.

'They tell me I cannot smoke in here,' said Chumak, addressing the grievance to anyone in earshot. 'I could fucking buy this tin shack and smoke wherever I want.'

'It is for safety.' Glovkonin stepped out, keeping his tone level. 'There is aviation fuel stored here. A single stray ember and . . .' He spread his hands.

Chumak spat on the hangar floor, and then ground out the glowing tip of the pungent cigar in his palm.

Da Silvio and his assistant approached from the other vehicle. The Italian was dismayed by Chumak's presence.

'I wasn't aware you would be here,' he began. 'I hope nothing is amiss.'

'A lot of money changed hands for this thing,' said Chumak, sniffing loudly. 'I like to keep a close eye on deals like this.'

'Of course.'

Da Silvio glanced at the Russian, and Saito saw the brief flash of irritation on his face. Rightly, he blamed Chumak's presence on Glovkonin.

The Russian's careful manipulation had brought the gangster to this exchange by making it a challenge to the other man. In Chumak's violent world, he had to react. Failing to do so would look like an act of weakness to his subordinates. The posturing was so juvenile and pointless to Saito. He had seen it before, among the yakuza in the country of his birth. Men like the Salt Seller dressed up their brutality with words like 'honour', but those were just ways to legitimise their own lack of impulse control.

One of the 777's ground crew spoke to Da Silvio's assistant, and the woman relayed the details to her patron.

'The advance gear for the race in New York has been fully loaded, signor, as per instructions. If we remain on schedule, the aircraft can depart within the next ninety minutes.'

'You in a hurry?' snapped Chumak.

The woman gave the criminal a brief, withering look.

'A severe weather front is forecast to strike the east coast of the United States in the next twenty-four hours. If we delay take-off, the flight may be caught up in it.'

'We can't have that,' Da Silvio said smoothly, and he made a show of looking around. 'Where is the equipment we purchased?'

Chumak pulled up his cuff and peered at a huge gold watch clamped around his wrist.

'Don't piss yourself. It'll be here soon, and then we can go on with our business.'

Every word he said to the Italian came out like a profanity, daring him to respond to it.

Da Silvio didn't take the bait, but Saito could sense the tension in the hangar pulling tighter, and again he scanned the men arrayed around Chumak's cars. They were armed – he could tell by the cuts of their baggy jackets – and their faces were uniformly expectant.

He knew exactly what Glovkonin intended this day's outcome to be, but bitter experience told the assassin that dealings with men like Pavlo Chumak did not always follow the script set out for them.

Saito let his hand fall close to the CZ 75 holstered in the small of his back.

They lost vital minutes finding a space for the 4 × 4 in the airport's parking structure, and Marc and Malte made it up by jogging across into the terminal, looking for all the world like two men late for their flight.

Marc had his daypack over one shoulder, the gear inside thudding against him as they ran. They slowed on the concourse, casting around for a way to bypass security and get after Glovkonin's convoy.

'Overwatch? Mobile two, you read me?' Marc touched the throat mike under his collar.

'*Overwatch has good copy,*' said Kara. '*Go ahead.*'

'Targets inside the airport perimeter.'

Through the open spaces of the terminal building, Marc could see out through the windowed facade and on to the runway. The hangar complex was visible on the far side, and he spotted the Gulfstream on the turning apron.

'Do they have transport here?'

'*Confirmed,*' she replied. '*G-Kor flew in a jet yesterday.*'

'I see it.'

Marc fell in after Malte, as the Finn indicated for him to follow, leading the other man towards a set of service doors.

'*I'll check for flight plans,*' Kara offered. '*If he is leaving today, they'll have to log the departure.*'

She didn't have to specify that *he* meant Glovkonin.

'Let me know what you find.' Marc paused, then added another question. 'How's Lucy doing?'

'*Holding her own in seventh place,*' said the hacker. '*Could be better.*'

'Right.'

Among the flat screen monitors showing departure and arrival times, there were a couple of screens set to local television channels, and on one Marc saw a helicopter's-eye view of the unfolding powerboat race. Of the green Horizon Integral boat, there was no sign.

Marc began to wonder how they were going to get airside without raising any alarms. For starters, the kit in his daypack would not get through security untouched, and both of the men were carrying firearms in their shoulder holsters. What ID documents Marc and Malte had were cursory snap covers, and they wouldn't stand up to any serious examination.

He was running through possible angles of approach when Malte stepped up to the service doors as they opened. Two older women in staff uniforms, caught in the middle of an animated conversation, bustled through and nearly ran straight into the Finn. Malte made a performance out of stepping aside, gesturing *after-you* with one hand like some courtly gentleman, smiling widely and raising a suggestive eyebrow.

Marc had never seen that expression – or indeed, hardly *any* expression – on the taciturn ex-cop's face in all the years he'd known him.

The two ladies shared a double take and then a dirty laugh, their gazes lingering on the rugged Finn as they passed on into the terminal. Neither of them noticed that Malte had caught the service door with the tip of his boot, stopping it from closing automatically.

Marc couldn't read the Cyrillic characters on the door, but it was clear they were some variation on *Authorised Staff Only*. He knew the drill, though, and wandered in after Malte in a nonchalant fashion, as if this was something he did every day.

The moment the doors clicked shut behind them, they took in the corridor ahead and the nondescript rooms leading off it. Away from the shiny, well-maintained passenger areas of the terminal, the working sections of the complex were basic and scruffy. Marc found a vacant break room and searched the lockers along one wall.

'Jackpot.' Inside them were hazard vests in eye-searing orange, and Marc tossed one of them to Malte. 'These are perfect camouflage. It's the international uniform of the working stiff.'

Malte shrugged and donned his. With the vests over their dark, lightweight jackets, they could blend with anyone busy on the tarmac.

Staying clear of other airport staff, they made their way out on to the apron, beneath the angular jet-ways waiting to connect to arriving airliners. Marc strode over to the low-slung shape of a pushback tug, a battered ingot of white-painted metal on four fat truck tyres. Vehicles like it were used to tow aircraft around the complex, and they were ubiquitous enough that no one would question one driving along the airport perimeter.

Marc called on some old skills he'd learned growing up on a south London council estate, and hot-wired the tug's simple ignition system. Soon they were rumbling along over the apron, past the helicopter pads and away from the terminal.

Malte used a pair of compact mil-spec binoculars to survey the cargo hangar across the runway.

'They're in there,' he noted.

'We can't risk crossing over.' Marc jutted his chin upwards as an outgoing Aeroflot departure shot past and left the tarmac in a howl of jet noise. 'This is an active runway, and we'd be seen from the tower. They'll be on to us in a hot second . . .'

He spotted a blockhouse close by and parked the tug alongside it, before scrambling out.

'Stopping here?'

Malte gave him a wary look from the tug's cab.

Marc didn't answer, instead pulling a flat rig like a laptop computer from inside his daypack. He strapped it on around his torso so the rig hung horizontally in front of him. A screen flickered on and he pulled a hand-held control unit from a mount on the side. The unit had rudimentary controls and a tiny thumb-stick, little different from the sort found on a video game controller.

'What is this?' said the Finn.

'Black Hornet,' said Marc. 'I love the names they think up for these things.'

From a compartment under the rig, he produced what at first glance looked like a toy helicopter. Little bigger than a sparrow, the device was a micro-drone, its tiny frame packed with a high-density battery, motors and three overlapping CCD cameras.

Malte made a face, clearly doubtful that the minuscule drone was up to the task, as Marc spun it up to speed. The device buzzed out of his hand and shot away, over the tarmac and the grass median. On the screen, the Hornet's digital eyes showed the Gulfstream and the hangar behind it growing larger.

Marc sat on the back of the tug, out of line of sight from the air traffic control tower, but facing the hangars. At his side, Malte dropped into a crouch and raised the binoculars to his face.

'Here we go . . . *Whoa*. Steady.' A gust of wind caught the tiny device and knocked it off course, forcing Marc to correct, but the little machine remained on track. 'I got a love–hate relationship with drones, y'know,' he said, lost in the images on the screen. 'All well and good when I'm flying them . . . Not so much when they try to kill me.'

'Cargo aircraft, inside,' said Malte.

'Yeah.'

Marc guided the Black Hornet up in a wide arc, around the waiting business jet and over the top of the hangar. The building had large skylights in the roof, and he brought the drone close to spy through them to the interior.

He picked out the BMWs and the Volga saloons. The positioning of the cars made it look like a meeting from the off, and he wondered if the mysterious 'equipment' was in one of the vehicles.

'They're waiting for someone else,' Malte said quietly.

A former undercover police officer, the Finn had an instinct for these kinds of situations and was rarely mistaken.

It wasn't long before the missing party in this handover made themselves known. Marc heard it first – the skirl of powerful, military-grade jet engines coming from the north. He set the Black Hornet drone down on the roof to conserve battery power and searched the sky for the source of the noise.

Malte handed him the binoculars, and through them Marc soon spotted a fast-moving arc of white coming down over the distant mountain range. Hazy rods of exhaust trailed out behind the aircraft, and as its angle shifted, he made out a large, dart-nosed fuselage, thin swing-wings and heavy engine pods. The jet came in to land, and it seemed to be descending too fast.

'Warplane?' asked Malte.

'Yeah,' said Marc.

The snow-coloured aircraft came down on the runway with a rolling roar of reversed thrust and the full size of the thing became apparent.

'Tupolev Tu-160, long-range strategic bomber.' Marc reeled off the details, his tech-geek recall the combined legacy of a lifelong fascination with all kinds of aviation hardware and a tour in the Royal Navy Fleet Air Arm. 'NATO reporting name – Blackjack . . .' He had to shout to be heard as the aircraft passed by, the tips of its outstretched wings cutting the air a few metres away. 'The Russians call it the "White Swan".'

The Blackjack deployed drag parachutes to slow it down, the stormy echo of its engines washing back past them, and Marc watched it reach the end of the airstrip and pivot slowly towards the hangars. It wasn't unusual for Russia's VKS air force to land military aircraft at civilian airports inside their borders, but a jet as big as the Tu-160 touching down somewhere as visible as Sochi was highly irregular. It could not be a coincidence.

'So now we know what they were waiting for,' Marc added, as the aircraft taxied to a halt in front of the hangars, dwarfing the parked Gulfstream.

'Strategic bomber,' repeated Malte. '*Nuclear?*'

Marc nodded grimly. 'That thing can carry six cruise missiles. Each one with a two hundred kiloton warhead.'

His blood ran cold as he flashed back to a previous encounter with a nuclear device in the catacombs beneath Naples. That six-kiloton Exile weapon was a baby compared to the apocalypse the Blackjack could deploy.

'*Voi vittu* . . .' The other man let out the curse low and slow.

FOURTEEN

The keening shriek of the military jet's engines dropped to a low moan. The sound lingered in the air, a faraway banshee wail echoing through the hangar.

Saito remained impassive as the huge Russian bomber made its showy arrival, but Da Silvio was unable to keep the colour from draining from his face. For his part, Glovkonin looked on with something like admiration, while Chumak openly enjoyed everyone else's discomfort.

'Your delivery,' sneered the criminal. 'Right on time.'

Crewmen in bright orange flight suits deplaned from the bomber and Chumak walked out to meet them at the hangar entrance. One of his thugs ferried a heavy duffel bag, which he passed to a junior officer. The commanding pilot, a smirking man with thinning black hair, embraced Chumak like a long-lost brother. They shared jokes made at the expense of the Italian and his entourage.

At the same time, ground crew from Da Silvio's cargo aircraft rushed out to erect temporary screens around the underside of the bomber, to conceal their work beneath the aircraft from anyone in the airport terminal.

'Impressive, is it not?' said Glovkonin, over the noise. 'When I was a boy, the world trembled at the sound of such aircraft. I hesitate to call those better days, but things were clearer then.'

'The Cold War was a flawed model,' Da Silvio replied, regaining some of his self-assurance. 'Inefficient and difficult to monetise. But I will grant you, the unlimited military budgets of the superpowers did produce some striking machines.'

Saito saw the Italian's assistant stiffen, then raise a hand to the headset coiled over her ear. A call had come in, one that only she could hear. She frowned, and walked away. The woman's mouth moved as she spoke urgently, but he could not follow what was being said.

Meanwhile, the bomber's ventral fuselage split as its bay doors opened, and ground crew wearing ear defenders scrambled to push a wheeled trolley into place beneath them. Slowly, men from the aircraft and Da Silvio's people worked to lower a metallic object down from the bomb bay.

Saito expected to see the winged cylindrical shape of a missile emerge, but the object was a bulky, rectangular form.

It reminded him of something from his youth. Saito's maternal uncle had run a fish market in Kobe, in a wet and reeking warehouse full of giant refrigerated ice-chests, each packed with cuts of bluefin tuna. The bomber's cargo had a similar size and dimension to one of those freezers, and it had an unfinished look to it.

This was the 'equipment' that Da Silvio and Glovkonin had worked so hard to procure, dealing with Chumak's labyrinthine web of contacts in the Russian military. Undoubtedly a weapon, the assassin decided, but its nature escaped him. Something nuclear, biological or otherwise toxic would not have been handled so openly and without greater protections. And, more to the point, the Russian and the Italian would not come this close to something that had the potential to harm them.

He sensed Glovkonin at his side, and decided to ask the question. 'What does it do?'

'It changes the world,' said the oligarch, absently stroking his manicured beard. 'I want you to accompany the second unit from here. It is not to leave your sight until it is deployed at the target.'

'And where is that?'

'To be determined. There are a number of options, but our American friend will handle the specifics.' Glovkonin paused. 'Is that an issue? Do you have concerns about working with Cassidy's people again?'

'No.'

Despite his reply, Saito frowned. He was aware that the other component of this operation – what the Combine committee referred to as 'Unit One' – had already been placed, but further details had been concealed from him. Now, once again, he was being kept in the dark.

He let his gaze wander past the parked aircraft towards the airport buildings on the other side of the runway. The Englishman was out there somewhere, he assumed, most likely observing them at this moment. Would Dane attempt to intervene in the middle of the transfer? To do so would be a mistake, and Saito hoped that the reckless ex-MI6 operative would not give in to his worst impulses.

'I want the rest of my money.' Chumak made the demand, coming closer, snapping his fingers. 'Then we can deal with the other business.'

He sent an acidic glare in Da Silvio's direction, but the Italian didn't notice.

'Already done,' Glovkonin replied, in a mollifying tone. 'Check your accounts.'

Chumak snapped his fingers again, and one of his men produced a smartphone, quickly tabbing out a number to call the Salt Seller's banker.

'It is not that I do not trust you . . .' He snorted in snide amusement. 'That's a lie. I trust nothing.'

Saito's attention was only half on the criminal. Most of his focus was directed towards Willa, Da Silvio's assistant, who came marching back to her patron with a grim cast to her pale features. Something was wrong.

She spoke to Da Silvio in terse snaps of Italian, and Saito feigned disinterest. He had been careful to pretend that he didn't speak the language. He couldn't catch it all, but the woman was apparently reporting a problem.

Willa mentioned the name 'Drake' – another of Da Silvio's assistants – and then talked about some kind of device, or book. Then

Saito heard the word '*manomettre*'; that meant something had been tampered with.

'*Chi l'ha fatto?*' The Italian's expression turned icy as he hissed the question. '*Pirata?*'

'*Sì.*'

Willa gave a nod, moving away again, leading Da Silvio into the shadow of the cargo jet where they could talk privately.

Marc manoeuvred the Black Hornet drone through the slim gap in an open skylight, and kept it up high in the rafters, where the buzz of the tiny props would be lost.

'What the hell is *that* thing?'

He had a good capture of the ground crew shifting their burden on a rolling dolly, moving the cargo from the Russian bomber to a loading platform next to the 777.

The block of machinery didn't resemble anything that Marc could identify, and the unfinished look of it made him wonder if it was some sort of prototype. A gun-type or implosion-type nuclear weapon would have a certain structure to it. This device looked more like a twenty-year-old computer server than a weapon of mass destruction.

He flicked to the drone's limited thermographic vision capacity, but the block – 'Unit Two', he assumed – was dull blue and inert, without even the slightest trace of radiation emanating from it. Bioweapons needed to be kept refrigerated, and that would have shown up as night-black on thermal imaging. The device could have been explosives, but that was unlikely. With their reach and deep pockets, the Combine did not need to go through this much clandestine dealing to get their hands on something as conventional as that. Marc remembered his own flippant comment a few days ago about the Combine's predilection for 'show-stoppers' and cursed himself.

'Overwatch, Mobile Two. Do you read?'

'*Overwatch copies*,' said Kara. '*What do you need?*'

'Eyes on this.' He tapped out a command on the drone's wireless control rig and sent frame-grabs from the Black Hornet's live feed to Kara's laptop. 'This is the equipment we've been tracking, but as far as I can tell, it looks like the guts of an industrial tumble dryer . . .'

'*I have the take.*' Kara fell silent for a long moment, and Marc had to prod her for a reply. When her voice returned, it was distant and guarded. '*That . . . is something.*'

Marc scowled. 'I need you to be *more* specific, not *less.*'

'*I'm not certain*,' she replied. '*I need to analyse the complete imagery. Dump it to my inbox.*'

'Kara—'

'*Just do it!*'

He clamped his jaw shut to avoid snapping out an irritable response, and did as she asked, uploading the footage from the Black Hornet through a high-density burst transmission.

Malte nudged him.

'Moving,' said the Finn, as the sound of the Blackjack's idling engines rose in pitch.

Marc looked up from the drone's control rig in time to see the ground crew dragging away the temporary screens from beneath the Tu-160. The figures had barely finished when the bomber began rolling, and they had to sprint away to avoid being blown aside by its jet wash.

The aircraft moved smoothly over the apron and on to the main approach. Sochi's control tower had clearly given the 'White Swan' the freedom of the flight-line. Every civilian airliner lined up along the terminal building retreated to a hold position as the jet rolled to a halt at the far end of the secondary runway. Then the engine tone became thunder once more, and the Tu-160 accelerated away, screaming into the sky, wings sweeping back. It vanished into the cloud deck as swiftly as it had arrived.

But Marc's attention was back in the hangar, watching through the Black Hornet's digital eyes as the device unloaded from the Blackjack rose up on a scissor jack platform to the waiting cargo plane.

He shifted the drone's position, and he saw a face turn to look upwards. His hands froze on the control stick; he knew that any motion might give away the presence of the tiny intruder.

He knew the face. Saito's cold, gunsight eyes searched the rafters, then finally dropped away. Marc watched the Japanese assassin approach another figure in a slate-grey suit, and his hand unconsciously tightened on the control as he recognised Pytor Glovkonin.

The Russian looked little different from how he had appeared in the lounge at the Marine Luxe. The same insouciant manner, the same impeccable suit and air of utter disdain for everything around him. He never changed. The oligarch moved through the world as if he owned it, and Marc hated the man's fathomless conceit.

The past few years of Marc Dane's life had been an ordeal of violence, danger and death, thanks to the Russian's greed.

'That bastard's lucky I'm not flying a fucking Predator,' he muttered.

'He will pay,' Malte said quietly. The Finn's gaze was flinty. He had lost as much as any of the Rubicon team. 'Soon enough.'

Da Silvio's annoyance burned but he refused to allow it to show, beyond folding his arms tightly across his chest to stop his hands from forming fists.

'I want to know how this is possible.' Conversing in his native language, each word he spoke was a dagger. 'I was assured the book was *secure*.'

'I warned you that the penthouse break-in was suspicious,' said Willa, shaking her head. 'Breaking into the safe was a cover.'

He cut her a look, silently reproving the woman for daring to venture an *I told you so* response.

Undaunted, she continued. 'That burglary was a failed attempt to access the book. I am certain of it.' She held a tablet computer in her hand, an identical model to the one that had been in his office a few nights ago. 'Drake found warning flags in the internal code. An unauthorised source initiated a brute-force attack on the memory core—'

'I do not want a technology lesson,' he retorted. 'I want an explanation!'

Willa sighed and manipulated something on the screen.

'Here.'

A video window opened on the tablet and Da Silvio saw footage from a security camera. The playback was framed through a fish-eye lens, its point of view looking down from the ceiling inside one of the Marine Luxe's elevator cars.

The replay had no sound component, but he could clearly make out Drake carrying one of the digital books, the man standing next to one of his security detail. They were waiting impatiently for the elevator doors to close, when without warning, Sunny Wehmeyer and her smirking companion came stumbling into the lift, acting like inebriated fools.

Da Silvio's irritation grew with each passing second as he watched the Wehmeyer woman attempt a clumsy pass at Drake, making brief physical contact with him as the elevator doors closed and the car rose.

'She must have done something,' Willa noted. 'Affected the book in some way.'

'You are sure?'

Willa gave a curt nod. 'There is no other explanation.'

'That common little witch . . .' He showed his teeth. 'I knew something was off about her.'

At first the Australian heiress had failed to respond to Da Silvio's usual charms, and he had written her off as a waste of effort. The girl was attractive, and her coarseness, while novel, had grown tiresome. It was only when she had thrown herself at him, acting for all intents like a new woman, that he had entertained the idea of bedding her for the sport of it. Now the reason behind her change in behaviour became abundantly clear. Visions of potential industrial espionage danced in his head.

'What did she get?'

'Unclear,' said Willa. 'Whatever device she used, we need to secure it to be certain.'

'The black woman, the driver. She is her accomplice.' Da Silvio considered that for a moment. 'She's on the water, now?' Off Willa's nod he let his arms drop to his sides. The brief moment of anger became a controlled fury as he assembled a plan of action in his thoughts. 'Contact the pit boss at our dock. We have secondary drivers in the race – tell them to deal with her. Yes, there will be an accident. Make it worth their while.'

'Understood.'

Willa did not need him to spell it out for her. The woman had a ruthless, pragmatic streak that proved useful in situations like this. She had already disposed of one troublesome body for him this week, erasing the man who had overdosed in Da Silvio's penthouse. A fatality on the racetrack would be a simple matter to arrange at short notice.

'But the Wehmeyer woman must be isolated,' he added. 'We need her alive, at least until we know what she is doing.'

'Drake is at the hotel. Wehmeyer is there.'

'Good. Dispatch some men, give him the opportunity to make up for his mistake.'

Da Silvio considered his response, gaming it out. If he acted quickly, this issue could be dealt with before the race was over, and more importantly, neither Glovkonin nor the rest of the Combine committee would ever be aware of any potential exposure.

That was the only thing that the Italian feared. To lose face, to be responsible for jeopardising the operation . . . He would never hear the end of it, especially if the Russian ever learned of it.

'Something amiss?'

As if the thought of the detestable man had summoned his presence, Glovkonin approached them across the hangar floor, smiling falsely.

'Nothing that need concern you,' Da Silvio replied, with an equally insincere grin. 'An issue at the hotel, nothing more.'

'Staff problems?'

'Something of that nature.'

Da Silvio wondered if Glovkonin might be behind this new problem. He had been expecting the Russian to attempt some subterfuge since the moment he arrived in Sochi.

'I hope you are not leaving.' Glovkonin cast a glance back at his assassin, and towards Chumak and the criminal's coterie of thugs. 'Some details still need to be addressed.'

Da Silvio chuckled. As if he would ever allow himself to be sidelined while the transfer of the equipment took place. This was far too important to be done by a subordinate. The Italian spread his hands.

'I am at your disposal.'

The race leaders jockeying for the first three places were already around the high-*g* turn and speeding out of sight, when the buzzing throng of the mid-race pack shot past the crowd line.

A whoop of excitement rose from the spectators as the knot of powerboats jostled one another around the sharp bend. Arcs of shimmering white spray knifed through the air, the sunshine lensing into temporary rainbows. The second-string racers duelled to find the tightest line around the marker floats, cutting across one another's paths with centimetres to spare. Frothing wakes turned the calm waters of Sochi's coastline into a churn of foam, and among the melee, boat number 7 fought to hold its ground.

'G'wan, sis-tah!'

Grace buried herself in her performance as Sunny Wehmeyer, yelling raucous encouragement from the top of her lungs, as Lucy's vessel rocketed past beneath the Marine Luxe's sun deck.

She snorted with laughter and drained another flute of champagne, ignoring the arch, judging looks from the trust fund kids watching the race from the VIP lounge.

Playing the part of the irresponsible corporate heiress was as easy as breathing. She inhabited the woman's persona, making Sunny her own. It was like driving a stolen Ferrari, putting her foot down too hard, cutting corners more than she should have – and who gave a damn? If she wiped out, it wasn't Grace who would suffer. For as long as she was joyriding Sunny Wehmeyer's life, she planned to enjoy it.

If one had been able to drill down into a self, cutting through the layers of a personality like geological strata, they would find only voids in Grace. Voids that needed to be filled with other people's lives, voices, mannerisms. Stripped bare and exposed, she was an empty vessel, less a person and more a collection of impulses masquerading as one.

But if she stopped moving for a moment, if she allowed herself to really think about that, Grace knew it would come to pieces. Momentum kept her alive, and monotony always lurked at the edges of her thoughts. One kept the other at bay. It wasn't a difficult equation.

She didn't subscribe to abstract moralistic bullshit like notions of good or evil. There was no *good* or *bad* in Grace's world, there was only *fun* and *boring*. And right now, even if she had temporarily shackled herself to Marc Dane and his collection of oh-so-righteous wannabe heroes, Grace was having a great time.

A shadow fell across her and she didn't look up, gesturing with her glass.

'Where you been, mate? Top me off, there's a good fella.'

'I'm not the waiter,' said Drake. 'Hello again.'

Grace didn't allow her surprise to show. She gave the man a sideways glance, feigning ignorance.

'Soz. Have we met?'

As far as she could tell, Drake was the assistant to the assistant, working under that cold-eyed German tart who did the legwork for the Italian. He wore the same kind of expensively uninspired suit he had been in the previous night in the elevator, but this time he had two sides of beef with him, not one. Drake's escorts had necks so thick their heads looked like growths out of their chests, and their presence had definitely emboldened the skinny guy.

He didn't like the way she pretended not to know who he was.

'I can understand how you might not recall. Last night, in the ... ah ... elevator.' Drake had a nasal English accent that became more annoying the longer she had to listen to it. 'But you did seem to have had a lot to drink.'

'What are you accusing me of?' She let her tone slip into a higher, more strident register, towards the *I want to see the manager* range that would immediately make a scene.

Drake hesitated. He wasn't adept at dealing with confrontations, and Grace took advantage of that.

'*Mobile Three, Overwatch.*' Dane's hacker chick friend started talking in Grace's ear. '*Is there a problem?*'

'Can you get lost?' Grace said, as much to Kara as to Drake and the men. She made a shooing gesture. 'Step back. I don't want you to breathe on me.'

'You need to come with us,' Drake insisted. 'Right now.'

'Nah, sod off.' She snorted at the demand. 'You got enough for a threesome already, pal.' Grace looked around, as if searching for the wine waiter. 'Where's that knobhead with the bubbly?'

Drake fumed. 'Signor Da Silvio would like to speak to you. Privately.' He nodded to one of the big men. 'Don't make me ask again.'

'Miss—'

The heavy on the right reached out a meaty paw of a hand and put it on Grace's bare arm, but before he could clasp around it, he was reeling away with a champagne flute jammed in his cheek.

Grace bolted from her chair, grabbing an empty, upturned Bollinger magnum from a nearby ice bucket. She swung the bottle two-handed and clubbed the second heavy across the temple with it. The magnum connected with a hollow thud and didn't break, allowing her to get in two more blows before it finally shattered and the man lost his balance.

Drake snatched at air as he tried to grab Grace and subdue her, but he wasn't as fast, and he hadn't been trained by the CIA in self-defence techniques.

In front of the open-mouthed rich kids in the lounge, Grace planted a kick squarely in Drake's crotch, landing it with enough force that she most likely ended any chance of the poor sap ever having children. She left him in a screaming mess and vaulted the glass wall of the sun deck, dropping to an awning below that let her slide to the ground, landing among the race-goers with the mid-tier tickets.

'*Mobile three, respond!*' Kara yelled in her ear through the radio bead in her earring. '*What's going on over there?*'

Grace relented, tapping the concealed device to reply.

'We've been made,' she snapped. 'Drake came gunning for me, Da Silvio must know something. I'm bugging out.'

'*Shit.*' Kara's voice crackled around the swearword. '*Wait, Lucy's still out there. We need to—*'

'She has a bloody boat, don't she?' Grace played Sunny's drawl once more, shouldering her way through the crowd as quickly as she could. 'Tell her to sail away.'

She pulled off the radio earrings and peeled the mike pickup from under her collar, and, without a look back, tossed them into the marina.

The inertia from the shallow turn pushed Lucy against the side of her seat, and she felt the vibrations from the outboard motor shiver up through the powerboat's hull.

As hard as she tried to maintain her position in the pack, the other, more experienced racers were passing her by, and it was all she could do to keep herself in a respectable middle-nowhere placing. She had thought about faking a mechanical failure to drop out of the race – but this was part of the cover, and she couldn't let that come apart, even if it did mean losing gracefully to these yahoos.

The race route extended away in front of her. This sector of the circuit was well past the sight-lines of the crowds, with sheer cliffs on the shoreline and open sea on the other. Rocky shoals peppered the littoral waters, so she did her best to stay clear of them. With no turns for the next kilometre or so, the boats were free to open up their throttles, and Lucy poured on the speed. Her vessel skipped across the tops of the waves, displaced water crashing over the enclosed canopy in bursts.

She chanced a look to the right, and in the distance she could see the leaders going the other way down the far side of the line of marker buoys. They had already made it up and around the tiny spit of headland that represented the southernmost end of the racecourse, and were heading back towards the starting line to complete their lap. Above them, the blurred form of a camera helicopter chased the leading boats, beaming back video to the billboard screens around the marina. Everyone's attention was on the top guns, while Lucy and her fellow trailers would be largely ignored, unless one of them made a break for the lead.

A crackle of interference growled through the headphones in Lucy's helmet and she winced involuntarily. A moment later, she heard Kara's voice over the roar of the outboard.

'*Mobile Four, do you copy?*' Her words were machine-gun quick and urgent.

The hacker had messed with the powerboat's radio prior to the race start, enabling Lucy to switch channels remotely and keep any communication concealed from the Horizon Integral dock crew.

'Yeah,' she responded, 'five by five, over.'

Kara started speaking before Lucy had finished, losing the first part of her sentence. She said something about Grace, and Lucy's gut twisted. Had the amoral undercover operative finally double-crossed them? Lucy had been expecting that particular shoe to drop for days.

'Say again, Overwatch, lost you there.'

'*Repeating, Mobile Three is compromised, we are code red, code red!*'

That was the last thing Lucy wanted to hear. If Grace's duplicity had been revealed, then the entire operation was in danger of coming apart – and it meant that Lucy had a target on her back.

That bleak thought lingered as a crimson shadow blotted out the view from her starboard rear-view mirror and a grinding impact shook the boat. The steering yoke juddered so violently that Lucy briefly lost her grip on it, and she had to snatch it back before number 7 skidded out of control.

She shouted out in alarm, and Kara hectored her for a reply.

'*Four, say again? What is your condition, over?*'

'Son of a bitch is shunting me!' she cried.

A second impact jerked her forward against the seat's harness and made her head snap forward and back, sending jags of pain down her spine. Lucy's helmet cracked against the inner wall of the cockpit and the radio channel turned into static.

With a snarl, Lucy jerked the yoke and sent her boat into a side-slip, veering away before she took a third direct hit. The bow of the crimson boat scraped across the aft of her hull, tearing off splinters of carbon fibre. Hidden from the sight of any spectators and race officials, Lucy's pursuer was trying to knock her out of the race, permanently.

Something was wrong with number 7. She felt it in the way the rudder turned fractionally slower than it had moments before. The steering became mushy and unresponsive as warning lights popped on across the dashboard. Engine pressure dropped like a rock and she tasted acrid oil vapour in the back of her throat.

The red shadow appeared again, this time off her port side, as the other racer came in fast. Lucy swore at him and put all she could into turning the yoke hard away. The powerboats were still cruising at high speed over the waves, and if she wiped out here, the vessel could flip and break apart as it hit the water.

That was obviously the plan; however it had happened, Grace's cover had been blown wide open, and dragged Lucy into the same mess along with it. Taking her out on the water, making it look like a racing accident – that would end the problem real quick for all concerned.

Speed kills, she thought.

The crimson boat shot towards her, coming on fast.

Lucy made a fist around the throttle bar and took a risk. She pulled the control back, hard against the stops, killing the power going to the outboard in one move.

Her boat stuttered in mid-air, skidding wildly over the wave-tops, losing forward momentum as friction with the water brought it to a shuddering halt. She'd planned it so the other vessel would rocket right past, too quick to come after her, but Lucy's gambit didn't account for the other racer's own limitations.

The driver who had been ordered to sink her didn't react as fast as she did, and his boat collided with hers before he could veer off. The crimson racer half-mounted the hull of Lucy's boat, forcing her vessel down into the water, and his flew up and away from the violent contact.

She heard the shredding, tearing sound of number 7's hull ripping open and the flat gush of water rushing in. Flashing by in an instant, the streamlined form of the other boat briefly left the surface of the sea, flipping up like the head of an enraged cobra. It came down badly, torn to bits by the impact, scattering pieces of hull.

Lucy never saw the other racer destroy itself. She could feel seawater sloshing around her ankles as the cockpit slowly filled, the powerboat canted to one side at a thirty-degree angle. Her gloved hands snatched at the central disc of the harness, the buckle where the straps converged to hold her fast against the safety seat. The release button clicked dully and did not disengage. She was trapped.

She flailed around. There had to be an emergency strap cutter in here, somewhere. An experienced racer would have known exactly where to look, but Lucy Keyes was only pretending to be that.

The boat lurched, sliding back into the depths stern-first, and more water gushed in through the torn hull, stinking of brine and spilled fuel. A sickly rush of fear charged through her as it rose past her knees.

'Mayday!' she shouted into the helmet mike, unsure if anyone could hear her. 'I'm trapped in here! I'm taking on water!'

'What are they talking about?'

At his side, Malte gave a mute shrug, continuing to observe the hangar through his binoculars.

Via the spy drone, Marc had followed Da Silvio and his assistant through their terse discussion, trying to guess through their body language at whatever was going on. The Italian turned away to engage Glovkonin in conversation, showing a false front, but the way in which the woman snarled into her smartphone made it clear something was up.

He couldn't watch all of them at once, so he made the choice to stay on the two men, tracking them back towards the middle of the hangar. Marc checked the Black Hornet's charge and frowned. The little drone's internal power pack was usually good for around twenty minutes in optimal conditions, but flying it against the wind had put a strain on the thing's motors. That – and running its wireless video transmission at full resolution – was sure to flatten the batteries.

He moved the drone to a better vantage point as Kara's voice cut through his concentration like a falling axe.

'*Marc! Do you hear me?*'

The fact that the usually precise hacker had forgotten to use their radio call signs was a bad indicator. Kara didn't exhibit panic like most people did, so this was a red flag.

'What's wrong?'

Her reply came, quick and breathless. '*Grace broke protocol. She said her cover was blown. I was watching from a distance, there was an altercation, I think . . .*'

'Where is she now?'

'*I have no idea,*' Kara shot back. '*They must know about the intrusion, the book, they've gone after Lucy—*'

Marc's skin prickled as she said the other woman's name.

'What? How?'

As far as he knew, Lucy was out on the Black Sea in the middle of a high-speed race.

'*Her radio is damaged, I couldn't reach her . . .*' Kara suddenly ran out of steam. '*She broadcast a mayday, her boat has been holed but she can't get out. Marc, there's no video being broadcast from out there but I can see smoke up along the coastline.*'

A horrible, familiar sensation engulfed him, reaching back from a dark memory. That feeling of the cold, unstoppable ocean rising up around his body. Stealing the breath from his lungs. Dragging him down. Smothering everything.

Years ago, a much younger Marc Dane serving with the Royal Navy Fleet Air Arm had survived a near-fatal helicopter crash during an exercise. He would never be able to forget being trapped in the cabin of the fallen Lynx as the storm-churned waters of the South China Sea rushed in to fill it. Death had been so close to him in that moment, he could swear he felt the Reaper's touch on his face.

He tore off the drone rig, ripping away the straps around him as he bolted to his feet.

'Get me a location! Hurry, Kara!'

'Marc!' Malte rose with him, shaking his head. 'Wait.'

The Finn's words didn't connect.

Wait? For what?

If Lucy was in danger, he had to get to her.

Malte had heard Kara's fearful words just as Marc had. Marc shoved the drone rig into his hands.

'She'll drown. I'm not going to let that happen!'

'The device . . .' Malte nodded towards the distant hangar.

'The racecourse isn't far from here! You stay, I'll go!'

Marc pulled away, looking for the parked helicopters they had passed earlier. A stubby, double-rotor Ka-226 sat on the nearest helipad, and he knew the model well enough to hot-wire it, to handle it. But it had no pontoons and no way to land on water.

'Can't go alone,' said Malte, guessing at Marc's plan of action.

And with that, the cold mathematics of the situation were instantly clear. If they left, they abandoned the mission. They would lose track of Unit Two, and whatever gains they had made to get to this moment would be forfeit. Marc would be putting the entire operation in jeopardy for the sake of one person's life. He knew what Lucy would tell him, if she was here.

But months ago, on a windblown African airstrip with the stink of smoke and blood still in his nostrils, he had made a vow to himself that he would not lose another friend to this fight.

Not one more.

'I'm going,' he said. 'Figure out the rest later.'

Malte saw the stubborn look in his eyes and didn't challenge it. 'Okay.'

FIFTEEN

The curved hatch on the side of the 777's fuselage closed slowly, and the ground crew began their last checks before buttoning up the cargo jet for departure.

Glovkonin checked the time on the Patek Philippe around his wrist. They were still on schedule. Everything was going as he had planned it.

Almost everything.

He glanced at the Italian. Da Silvio was hiding something from him – it was ridiculous how transparent the fool was. Whatever he had discussed with his assistant, the other man had chosen not to share it with the Russian.

That sent Glovkonin's paranoia into overdrive. His default was to assume that any secrets his rival kept would be a threat to him, and he looked around, wary for any sudden change in circumstances.

The wind carried a noise from the far side of the runway, the whine of a helicopter taking off, and he tensed – but the aircraft shot away southwards at high speed, vanishing over the buildings. He chided himself.

In a few minutes, this will be over.

'Sir.' Saito approached, his arms folded behind his back. 'The equipment is secure on board the aircraft. It has been concealed among the material for the race advance team, as instructed. There should be no problems with American border security.' He nodded towards the Gulfstream idling out on the apron. 'Your flight to Geneva has been cleared. Shall we proceed?'

'A moment.'

Glovkonin removed his encrypted Blackphone and dialled a preset number.

'*I'm here.*' Andre answered quickly. '*Is it done?*'

'Soon,' said the Russian, glancing towards Chumak and his men. The criminal sat half in and half out of his car, puffing on another of the noxious cigars he enjoyed. 'The other matter. You have the clean-up team ready to go?'

'*They are already in the country, waiting for the word.*'

'Then consider it given. Tidy up the loose ends and make sure the site is sanitised.'

The Frenchman clicked his teeth. '*How much . . . latitude should I give them?*'

He sniffed. 'You engaged our usual contractors, yes? They are professionals. They will respond as circumstances require it.'

He cut the call and looked back to Saito, who stood by expectantly. The other man's expression stiffened, and the Russian had the sudden sense that Da Silvio wasn't the only person keeping something from him.

'You will go with the second unit to New York,' he told Saito. 'Once you arrive, Cassidy's people will take over and you will observe. He will be close. He likes to watch the chaos he creates at first hand.' Glovkonin leaned in, his voice dropping. 'Be ready to remove him when I order it.'

'You want me to terminate the American.' Saito said it clearly, making it real and certain. 'He is a vested member of the Combine committee.'

'Does that go against your principles?' The snide comment came quickly. 'But I forget. You do not have the luxury of those. You do as you are told.'

'Yes,' Saito said tightly. 'But what you request will have repercussions.'

'I'm sure you'll be able to handle it,' Glovkonin said, with a dismissive turn of the head.

'I am sure I can,' replied Saito. 'That is not the issue. The committee exists for a reason, to centralise the organisation . . .'

His words trailed off. He'd parroted a rote statement Glovkonin had heard many times before, but the assassin had lost momentum, as if he could not find the will to recite it.

'Are you challenging me?'

Glovkonin let the question stand. Both of them knew what the penalty for disobedience would be. It was unlike Saito to push back, unheard of.

'No.' Saito took a different tack. 'Removing the American, in the middle of this . . . It will cause havoc.'

'I am aware.' He straightened his jacket. 'It is not your concern. I would ask you to consider your future, but we both understand what that is. Think about which side you want to be on, when this is over. Think on what is best for your continued survival, Saito. Yours, and that of your daughter.'

The smallest spark of defiance burned brightly in Saito's eyes, but then it was gone.

'I understand.'

Glovkonin granted him a nod of approval, and then waited until Chumak caught his eye from across the hangar. The thuggish criminal gave a crooked smile and climbed back out of the car. He was eager to get to work.

In a few hours, the Gulfstream would have Glovkonin in Switzerland, and after that, he would arrange a meeting with Rutger Bremmens at his estate in the Alps. The banker was difficult to wheedle out of his domains for anything other than a full meeting of the committee, but he would not be able to resist when Glovkonin came calling. The Swiss was as vain as the Italian, in his own manner, but with him it was his intellect he liked to parade, not his wealth. Indulging that would get Glovkonin where he needed to be.

He would allow nothing to stop him. Perhaps the pitiful remnants of Ekko Solomon's band of fools were still out there, desperately chasing the Russian's shadow on some vain quest for revenge.

They were hardly worth his consideration. A contingency plan was already in place to deal with them.

He permitted himself a smile. After years of effort, suffering and sacrificing, after applying himself with single-minded will to this task, he was finally within sight of his goal. The Combine would soon belong to him, and the final act of that long drama would commence here, on the grubby, oil-stained floor of an aircraft hangar.

A poor stage, he told himself, *but a fitting one.*

Lucy slammed her gloved hands against the powerboat's fibreglass canopy, fighting to dislodge it, but it held fast.

The seawater was at her chest, and every few seconds the waves sent a new surge into the cramped cockpit. Each time, the water smacked her face and threatened to choke her. A shiny layer of oil covered the surface and she felt it coating her bare skin. Lucy tasted the overpowering fuel-stink in her mouth each time she took a shivering breath.

She had managed to work one arm out from under the jammed harness, bending the limb almost to the point of dislocating it, but still she couldn't get the buckle to disengage. Swearing violently, she pulled as hard as she could on the straps, finally letting out her frustration in a wordless scream.

Another wave bounced off the boat and engulfed her, filling her nostrils with the brackish water. She choked it back out, fighting down the urge to vomit.

Someone has to be coming. Lucy made herself believe it. *Someone must have seen the collision, seen the smoke, anybody.*

Maybe they had, and maybe that slick asshole Da Silvio was holding them back until it was too late to save her. All the better to make this seem like some tragic accident in a risky sport where this kind of thing happened. Such a shame. So sad.

'Help me!'

She shouted the words, but they were trapped by the cockpit cowl and went nowhere.

The water came to her neck and she tilted back her head, stretching in the restraints, trying to keep her head above the waterline.

It was a losing game. Lucky number 7 would drag her under, slowly and surely, to the bottom of the Black Sea.

The unmarked Boeing cargo jet followed the same path that the sleek bomber had taken, down to the far end of the airport runway before powering away into the sky. Unlike the bomber, the 777 vectored around and continued to power upwards into the clouds, heading away to the south.

Glovkonin checked his watch once more, making a note of the time.

'You're leaving us, too?' The Italian offered the question as he strolled up to the doors of the hangar where Glovkonin stood. He jutted his chin in the direction of the waiting Gulfstream. 'Back home to Moscow?'

'Geneva,' he corrected. 'I will be paying our mutual friend a visit.'

'Oh?' Da Silvio's smooth smirk faltered. 'I wasn't aware.'

'Intentionally so,' said Glovkonin. 'If you knew ahead of time, I'm sure you would attempt to interfere.' He sighed. 'Shall we be honest with one another? You do not think highly of me.'

The Italian laughed. 'You try too hard, Pytor. You make everything a drama, a battle to the death!' He chuckled at his own words, relishing the moment of candour. 'Is it a Russian trait, I wonder, to be so solemn and intense?' The man's smile turned mocking. 'You would make a turn around the garden sound like an epic struggle. It wearies me.'

'And you take nothing seriously,' Glovkonin snapped. 'It's a grand joke to you. An amusement ride for your entertainment.'

'You know nothing about me,' sniffed Da Silvio. 'Why are you so resentful that I enjoy my privilege? What other reason for it *is* there?' He straightened the cuffs of his tailored jacket. 'Our power lets us walk the world unhindered. We bend it to our purpose. How joyless and bitter a man would have to be not to indulge himself in that.'

'I am bitter,' admitted the Russian. 'I have good reason.'

'Yes, I believe you think that is so.' The Italian leaned in. 'The only thing I don't take seriously is *you*, Pytor.'

Glovkonin gave a bark of sudden laughter, sharp enough that it startled the other man. 'And there is the heart of your mistake, Giovanni. Know this – it is your arrogance that has brought you to your end.'

He walked away, towards the open door of the waiting Gulfstream.

The Italian called after him. '*Cosa hai detto?*'

Glovkonin heard the low crack of suppressed pistols, and his smile widened.

The boxy Ka-226 howled over the top of the cliffs and out above the water, veering wildly towards the orange marker buoys indicating the race line.

The ungraceful, twin-tailed helicopter lurched as Marc kept the power on. Unlike the aircraft he had been trained on, the stubby little Kamov had no tail rotor and instead stabilised its flight through a pair of counter-rotating blade sets above the cockpit. He could handle the thing, but his lack of hours on similar airframes was telling, and Marc was constantly overcorrecting on the controls, skidding the helicopter through the air more than flying it.

The anxiety tightening around his chest didn't make it any easier, and the pilot had to make a concerted physical effort to calm himself.

Stop fighting the aircraft, he told himself, recalling the sage counsel of the instructors from his days at RAF Shawbury, where he had undertaken his original flight training. *Let it lead you.*

He loosened his grip on the controls and allowed the aircraft to settle. The 226 was nimble, but it needed a gentle hand. Carefully, Marc put the helicopter into a wide turn, scanning the wave-tops for wreckage.

'Overwatch, we're on site,' he called into the radio mike.

'*You have company coming,*' said Kara.

The hacker added more, but it was hard to hear her over the heavy drumming of the dual rotors.

'There?'

Malte was behind him, standing in the cabin behind the cockpit, leaning over the empty co-pilot's chair. The Finn stabbed a finger out at the sea, pointing towards a slick of black oil and jagged shreds of crimson hull floating on the surface.

Marc's heart leapt into his throat and for a moment he couldn't respond. If that debris had once been a powerboat, now it was nothing but tatters, and it sickened him to think of the fate of the driver. Then he remembered that the Horizon Integral boat was a vibrant green; the wreck was what remained of the other craft that had been in the collision.

His relief was short-lived, as the helicopter's nose came around and revealed a green and white triangle protruding from the waves like the fin of a shark. The front half of Lucy's boat canted up at a steep angle as the vessel sank backwards into the water.

'That's her!' Marc shouted, loud enough to be heard over the engines, but Malte was already moving.

The other man moved to the sliding door in the main cabin and rolled it back, opening the aircraft interior to the buffeting downwash from the rotors. Dust whirled around inside the 226 as Malte threw the lever to drop the winch on the starboard side. A repeater panel on Marc's display blinked as the motor unwound the cable towards the waves below.

Marc brought the helicopter down in a descending spiral, but the Finn wasn't going to wait. The aircraft lurched again as the other man's weight left the cabin, and from the corner of his eye, Marc saw a blur drop into the water.

He eased the 226 into a stable attitude a few metres from the ruined powerboat, aware that he was sweating. He risked wiping the back of his hand across his forehead, before halting the winch motor.

He was supposed to keep his attention on the separation between the Kamov's landing gear and the top of the waves, but Marc fixated on the cockpit of the wallowing boat and the ragged-edged gouge across one side of the hull. He could see water slopping around inside, but the canopy was locked shut. Lucy was still in there.

Malte burst out of the water close to the tilted hull, and Marc drew the helicopter back to lessen the rotor wash beating down on him. The Finn scrambled clumsily over the slippery fibreglass shell and pulled a flat-headed knife from his belt. He jammed it into the locking mechanism holding the canopy shut, slamming at it with the heel of his hand.

Marc leaned forward in his seat, unable to do any more than watch as the other man desperately attempted a rescue.

The lock broke and the canopy popped open, revealing a figure in a green jumpsuit, swamped by oily seawater. Malte moved to get her out, but his weight and his motion shifted something and the powerboat went under in a frothing surge of foam.

Da Silvio's bodyguards died first. They were part of his personal detail, a pair of men recruited from the Milanese police force. Suppressed gunshots chattered through the empty hangar as Chumak's men opened fire, and the ex-police officers went down, moaning and coughing.

Willa cried out in alarm and pulled her own compact pistol, but two rounds caught her in the neck and cheek, throwing a fan of wet red across the oil-stained concrete floor. Da Silvio didn't see her hit the ground, as he jerked back towards the hangar entrance.

The men from the ground crew had already left, but their equipment was still in place, so he sprinted towards it for cover. The Italian had no weapon of his own – such a thing would have ruined the cut of his suit – so he grabbed the first thing he could use to defend himself – a heavy adjustable spanner the length of his forearm.

He chanced a look over the wheeled scissor jack he had chosen to hide behind, in the direction of the cars they had arrived in. His driver lay sprawled on the ground near the open door of his vehicle, a halo of blood about the man's head.

In the middle of the hangar, one of Chumak's thugs walked over and carefully put a finishing round through each of the wounded bodyguards, kicking away their guns.

The open doors of the aircraft hangar were no more than a hundred metres from where Da Silvio hid, but between his cover and there was only open space. If he made a run for it, they would see him.

Chumak said something he couldn't understand to his men, and they snorted with laughter.

'Come out!' he yelled, his voice echoing around the metal walls. 'Be a man for once in your life!'

The high-pitched whine of jets pulled Da Silvio's attention back towards the open doors, as the shape of the Gulfstream taxied lazily by. He saw a face at one of the oval windows in the aircraft's passenger cabin. Glovkonin spotted him cowering in the shadows and gave him a farewell nod.

Cursing the Russian under his breath, Da Silvio snatched at his smartphone, keying in his emergency alert code. He had more men, many of them, close at hand. They would home in on the tracking device inside the phone. He just had to stall for time.

'Who are you calling?' said a voice.

The Italian twisted, bringing up the heavy vanadium steel spanner, but Chumak was already on him, and the criminal batted the makeshift weapon away. He followed through by breaking Da Silvio's nose with the butt of the pistol in his hand.

One of the thugs tore the phone from him and hurled it across the hangar, where it smashed on impact with the floor.

The agonising pain from his broken nose and the stink of blood in his nostrils made Da Silvio gasp. His vision blurred with tears and he struggled to breathe through his mouth.

'You . . .' He coughed thickly and tried again. 'You . . . know who I am. You know what you have done?'

Chumak loomed over him, savouring the other man's agony.

'I do.'

Da Silvio felt a bleak realisation settle on him.

'What did Glovkonin tell you?' He took a muffled breath, holding his nose as he tried to staunch the bleeding. 'You know it's a lie. He is using you.'

'He uses me, I use him,' said the criminal, toying with the gun in his hand. 'That is business. I don't like him, the arrogant fuck. But I know what he is. Where he came from.' Chumak prodded Da Silvio with the gun. 'You? The Euro whore with your fancy suits and your fast cars. Where the fuck do you come from, eh? You're not one of *us*.'

'I can double whatever he has paid you,' said the Italian.

It was the wrong thing to say. Chumak's face turned red.

'You think this is for money, you preening shit?' He planted a savage punch in Da Silvio's side. 'You think money makes everything go away?'

The Italian held up his hands to ward off any more blows, but it was a futile gesture. Chumak had two of his men drag Da Silvio to his feet and pin him to the side of the scissor jack by his arms. The criminal stalked back and forth in front of him like a caged tiger.

'You sell me out to the cops, eh?' He waved the gun around. 'You come to Sochi, you build your flashy hotel for your Eurotrash friends . . .' He spat on the ground. 'You do that *and* you try to fuck me?'

'I have no idea . . . what you are talking about,' managed Da Silvio. 'Can you not see? Glovkonin knows how to anger you. He's lied about this so you will end me for him.'

As the words spilled out, the awful reality of it bedded in.

He had always suspected the Russian as capable of great deceit, but to do something like this, so openly – to make such a naked grab for power . . . It was not how the Combine operated. It was vulgar, it was beneath men of their stature. In doing this, Glovkonin revealed himself to be what Da Silvio had always thought of him – an unrefined man with a street thug's sensibility, no better than a common criminal like Chumak.

This certainty brought no satisfaction, however.

'I saw the pictures,' growled Chumak. 'I heard what you said!'

'Fakes,' insisted Da Silvio. He had to believe, if he could keep the man talking long enough, his people would arrive and save him from this indignity. 'You are not a fool. Why do you let Glovkonin use you?'

The criminal fell silent, kneading the butt of the silenced pistol in his hand. When he spoke again, his rage had ebbed, reforming into a low, predatory mutter.

'You think I'm a dull brute. Risen to my status by violence, not by brains. You are right. But I have instinct, yes? Like animals know the scent of those from the same place. You stink of money and disrespect.' He prodded Da Silvio with the barrel of his gun. 'Look at me!'

The Italian raised his head, meeting Chumak's gaze. The criminal's deep-set, piggish eyes were dark with murder.

'Maybe the pictures tell a lie.' Chumak shrugged. 'Maybe they don't. I do nothing about it, I am seen as weak.' He pressed the pistol to Da Silvio's forehead. 'It doesn't matter. I never liked you. This gives me an excuse.'

The Italian's body jerked backwards as the gun barked, but the howl of jets swallowed the weapon's report as the Gulfstream left the runway, and sped into the sky.

Marc cried out as the boat sank from view. In that second, his sole impulse was to throw himself through the cockpit, out into the waves and after his friends.

If only the 226 had float pontoons . . . If only he could land it safely on the water . . .

Two figures rose out of the churn, back into the sunlight. Lucy moved, pulling weakly at her helmet to throw it away, while Malte held her up against the motion of the waves. The Finn waved at Marc and, with another surge of relief, he returned the gesture.

Working the controls, Marc guided the helicopter over to them and felt the craft shift as Lucy and Malte hooked up to the trailing end of the winch. He flicked the switch to reel them in, at the same time gently ascending.

A thumb-sized hole blew through the curved canopy panel near his face and tiny fragments of plastic skipped off his cheek, drawing blood. The impact made him curse loudly and he flinched, dragging the helicopter backwards as his hand jerked on the stick. A second impact struck the metal hull of the 226 with a dull clank, and this time he saw a flash of muzzle flare.

A Zodiac-type rigid inflatable boat approached the wrecks from the direction of the race complex. While the craft had the word RESCUE written down the hull in orange letters in both English and Cyrillic, the weapon in the hand of the man at the bow showed the true reason for its arrival. Marc had a pistol of his own in a paddle holster, but he was hardly in the best position to draw it and start a gunfight.

'Hang on!' he yelled, although Malte and Lucy would not be able to hear him.

Escape was the smarter choice, he reasoned, and with that Marc pulled the 226 up and away, pointing it back towards dry land.

The sluggish aircraft dragged the weight of two adult bodies through the air behind it, but no more rounds hit the 226 as it put distance between itself and the ersatz rescue boat.

The helicopter rocked as the winch brought Malte and Lucy up, and they scrambled inside, gasping and shaking with effort. Marc shot a look over his shoulder and saw the Finn tending to her. She looked shaky and her skin had a sallowness to it. He couldn't help but wonder how close she had come to drowning.

Once they were over land Marc flew low, staying just above tree-top level. He aimed the 226 away from the populated areas, taking a wide path around the edges of Sochi that would eventually lead them back towards the old school.

At length, Lucy pushed up into the empty co-pilot's seat and sat heavily. She glared at Marc, and then punched him in the bicep.

'Dumbass limey!'

'You're fucking welcome,' he shot back.

'You dumped the mission, didn't you? *Shit.*' She banged the back of her skull against the headrest in frustration. 'You came after me . . . You should have—'

'Don't tell me I was supposed to leave you out there,' he snarled. 'Do not say that to me.'

'How we gonna find that shit now?' She shook her head. 'Thanks, okay? But . . .' Lucy looked away. 'The trade wasn't worth it.'

'Bollocks to that.' Marc fixed his gaze out through the canopy. 'I do not trade life for life. *We* do not do that.' He paused, his tone softening. 'And if you think this is because of what happened . . . between us . . . you're wrong. I would have gone back for anyone on the team.'

'Even Grace?'

That was a low blow, given Marc's particular history with the amoral undercover operative, but at length, he nodded.

'Yeah. Even her.'

Lucy's lip curled. 'You'd be as pissed off as me if it was the other way around,' she countered.

'No doubt,' agreed Marc. 'Doesn't mean it was the wrong call.'

Lucy let out a long breath that turned into a racking cough. She recovered after a moment and drew her long-fingered hands down over her face.

'What do we do now?'

'We'll find another way through this,' he told her.

It was poor tradecraft for Solomon, Delancort and Benjamin to travel on the same flight from Croatia, but time pressure forced them to cut corners and take the risk. Under snap cover identities pitching them respectively as a Kenyan pastor, a French business consultant and a Belgian personal trainer, the three men arrived on the midday Turkish Airlines arrival at Istanbul Airport, and gathered quietly in a rented VW Tiguan.

A three-hour drive took them from the European side of Istanbul to the technology park where Altin Elma's facility was located, across the Bosphorus strait via the Fatih Sultan Mehmet suspension bridge. High winds buffeted the silver SUV as Benjamin guided the vehicle over the span, heading steadily southwards and into landfall in Anatolia. Dull, hazy clouds lying low over the landscape robbed the view of its grandeur, and they pushed on through a sporadic drizzle.

Benjamin could not escape the gloom that had settled on him following their departure from Zagreb, and the weather reflected the Frenchman's mood. He felt responsible for the girl they had left behind, with the shattered pieces of her old life and the prospect of an unknown future in front of her. Rumiko Saito deserved better than to be collateral damage because of her father's bad choices, but her situation was not a new one to Benjamin.

After he had left the *Légion étrangère* to find a different path, Benjamin Harun had made a promise to himself that he would do as much as he could in his remaining years to help people in pain, instead of causing it. He didn't realise at the time that the courage he had shown under fire in combat was a very different strength from the one needed by a counsellor, a healer. But he learned quickly.

Since putting down his gun, Benjamin had come to understand that there were battles going on in every person's life, most of them invisible to the eye. Many wounds and scars were deep in the spirit, and difficult to reach.

Rumiko was walking wounded, in her own way, and it troubled Benjamin that he was partly to blame for dismantling the happy, oblivious existence she had been living in Vienna; but ultimately, knowing the truth had set her free, and he took some small comfort in that.

He tried to put his thoughts aside, but he could not. For years, Benjamin had worked with the Rubicon Group as a trauma specialist and therapist, helping Solomon's people navigate the difficult and often brutal realities of their mission. He had left 'the field' behind, but when Rubicon collapsed in the wake of a hostile takeover, that life was taken away from him.

Benjamin no longer had the luxury of remaining on the sidelines. Worst of all, he knew that part of him missed the old days. The weight of a weapon in his hand, the rush of adrenaline before a parachute jump or a sortie . . . those were seductive, in their own way. It made it hard for him to keep to his vow.

His bag lay in the SUV's footwell. Hidden in a compartment within it, shielded to avoid detection by airport security scanners, were a Glock 17 semi-automatic pistol and two clips of ammunition. He knew the gun intimately, but he had sworn that he would never use one again in anger.

He could not escape the sense that some day soon, he would break that vow as well.

They left the highway for the local roads, but as the SUV approached the outskirts of the technology park, Benjamin stopped abruptly as crimson lights strobed brightly in his rear-view mirror. Sirens hooted as a pair of red and white fire engines hurtled past, quickly followed by an ambulance. The ill feeling in his chest tightened a few notches.

'Look there.'

From the back seat, Delancort leaned forward and pointed towards the cluster of low, blocky buildings forming the centre of the development. A wispy dome of black smoke rose from the far side of the complex.

'You think . . .?' Benjamin didn't want to finish his sentence.

'Get us there,' said Solomon, tapping him on the shoulder. 'Quickly.'

He nodded, accelerating after the emergency vehicles. A second ambulance powered past them as they turned around the main buildings and on to the approach to the Altin Elma facility.

The tech lab was a two-storey brick of sand-coloured concrete at the end of a cul-de-sac, the entrance dominated by a sculpture in brass and bronze, meant to suggest the shape of a golden apple. A flat metal roof had already caved in across several sections, allowing more black smoke to escape into the wet air. The western end of the Altin Elma building was the core of a raging fire, and orange flames coiled through broken windows in the concrete walls.

Benjamin parked the SUV on the far side of the street, upwind of the blaze. The fire engines had joined two more appliances, and firefighters in heavy flame-resistant gear had their hoses turned on the inferno, working to beat it down.

'We're too late,' muttered Solomon. 'The Combine are cutting away their loose ends.'

'Perhaps not,' Delancort ventured. He indicated the parked ambulances, where uniformed paramedics worked on a cluster of smoke-blackened figures shrouded in silver foil blankets. 'There are survivors.'

Benjamin studied the faces of the Altin Elma workers and technicians, some of them weeping, others elated to be alive, but most of them forlornly coming to terms with the fact that their lives had been brutally upended.

'Sir.' He looked over his shoulder. 'Stay in the vehicle. We'll check out the situation.'

Solomon's expression suggested he wanted to protest, but he chose not to.

'Very well.'

He knew as well as anyone that if recognised, his appearance here would lead to difficult questions. It had been many months since the release of the faked footage that led the world to believe Rubicon was a sponsor of terrorism, but people had long memories, and Solomon was a memorable man.

Benjamin beckoned to Delancort, and the two of them exited the vehicle. He left the gun behind, and fell in step, letting Delancort take the lead.

'Do you have a plan?' said the other man.

'I let you do the talking,' said Benjamin.

'Not helpful.' Delancort cast around, taking in the scene. 'So, do we play good cop and bad cop, like in the movies?'

Benjamin sniffed. 'Why don't we both be a good man for a change?'

There were a few more vehicles outside a perimeter of hastily deployed warning tape, and people from the other buildings in the park were gathering to watch the unfolding drama. Inside the line stood a single police cruiser and a harried-looking junior officer holding the cordon.

Delancort drew himself up, adopting an air of seriousness, and walked straight across to the policeman.

'What happened? Is the site manager still in there?'

The police officer blinked at his insistent tone, answering before he realised it.

'We are still trying to determine that. The manager ...' He caught up to himself and held out a hand, drawing the attention of some of the survivors. 'Please step back. This is an active scene!'

'Monsieur Delancort?' A portly man in a torn shirt called out from the group near the ambulances, and he crossed to them, dragging his foil blanket with him. He was in his mid-fifties and balding, with an avuncular face. 'Good grief, you are here! I don't believe it, on such a day ...'

'Yes.' Delancort rolled with it, although it was clear to Benjamin that Solomon's aide had no idea who the man in the shirt was. 'Are you all right?'

'Allah protects,' he said, with a shaky breath. 'Some were less fortunate than I.'

The portly man convinced the police officer to let them step under the tape, and he quickly pulled them aside. Benjamin noticed a pass clipped to the man's pocket that identified him as Burak Yerli, one of Altin Elma's senior technicians, and discreetly indicated it to Delancort.

'Mr Yerli, I am so glad you are safe,' said Delancort. 'But please, forgive me if I do not recall, have we met before?'

Yerli sat heavily on a low wall near the parking bays, and coughed into his hand.

'No, no, but I know you, sir. Everyone at Altin Elma does, it is your signature on the bottom of the authorisations we receive from Rubicon! Without your support, without the project, we would never have been able ...' He trailed off, his gaze drifting back to the burning building. His mood shifted and his voice thickened. 'Oh, my life. Our work. It's ruined. What will we do?'

'You are alive, my friend.' Benjamin saw a man in fear and placed a comforting hand on his shoulder. 'That is what matters.'

'Yes, yes . . .' Yerli stared down at the ground, and tears fell from his cheeks to the asphalt at his feet. He rubbed his face and composed himself. 'I had no idea you were coming . . .'

'A last-minute change of plans,' said Delancort, improvising a reply. 'We hoped to meet with your superiors to compliment your team on their diligence regarding the . . . ah . . . project.'

Yerli's head jerked up suddenly, and he waved at the building. 'The unit is not in there, do not worry.' The flames had taken hold despite the best efforts of the fire crews, and from inside the walls came the cracking sounds of heat-shattered glass and fracturing concrete. 'It shipped out two days ago . . .' He shook his head. 'Months of work . . . If we had lost that as well . . .'

'Shipped to where?' said Benjamin.

Yerli gave him a confused glance. 'To America, of course, as requested by the Monaco office.' He looked back to Delancort. 'The recipient in New York City. Is that not correct?'

'Quite correct,' agreed Delancort. 'As you say, a piece of good fortune. Rest assured, Rubicon will do all they can to support Altin Elma through this tragedy.'

That was a soothing lie, of course. The Rubicon Group per se no longer existed, but Yerli appeared unaware of that fact.

Benjamin gave his colleague a silent look. They were both thinking the same thing. It appeared that the team at this facility had been working to orders from the Combine, filtered through the gutted remnants of Rubicon's corporate structure. But what exactly had they been assembling for them?

'Mr Yerli,' Benjamin began, pitching his tone towards the conspiratorial. 'Do you know how this fire began?'

'No, no . . .' The man shook his head. 'We were finishing the close-down of production, standard protocol after the completion of a project . . .' His eyes misted again. 'There was some commotion in the server room. I heard some loud bangs . . . Then the alarms sounded and we moved to evacuate.' He took a deep breath and forced himself to remain calm. 'The fire was at our heels! I don't understand how it could have moved so swiftly . . . The sprinkler system failed to activate!'

Benjamin gave Delancort a subtle nod, directing him to pick up the thread.

'Did anything unusual happen today, before the fire began? Did you see anyone suspicious in the facility?'

'No . . .' Yerli frowned. 'Are you suggesting . . . someone did this *deliberately*?' He paled. 'Eight of our staff are still missing!'

Benjamin saw an opportunity to direct the conversation.

'What do you know about the project?'

'Everything.' Yerli gave him an odd look. 'I was systems lead on the assembly.'

'My colleague has not been fully briefed,' Delancort said smoothly. 'Perhaps you could precis the unit's functions for him? I'm sure you would do a far better job than I.'

'All right . . .' Yerli took another shaky breath. 'In basic terms, the unit is an *interrupt*, designed to isolate a large-scale computer network at a key nexus.' He made shapes in the air with his hands. 'Imagine it as a digital emergency stop. You can halt the flow of data transmission in the event of a crisis.'

'What kind of crisis?'

'If your system has been infected by malware and you want to prevent it propagating. A life-threatening security issue. A cascade failure. There are many scenarios . . .' He coughed again. 'It is a high-level safety measure, designed to protect critical infrastructure systems.'

Yerli talked about the device in positive terms, but Benjamin's soldier mindset immediately sensed the potential for havoc with such technology.

'How large a network does the interrupt affect?'

'That depends on where it is placed,' said Yerli, dabbing at his face with a dirty kerchief. His attention kept wandering back to the other survivors. 'The specifications of the design stipulated that it would be used in Rubicon's head office, yes?'

He glanced at Delancort for confirmation.

'Yes,' lied Delancort.

It was clear that no one at Altin Elma was aware that the Rubicon tower in Monaco had already been sold on to a new owner.

'If it was going to Monaco, why ship it to the United States?'

'For testing. We were told the analysis facility is in upstate New York . . .' Yerli drifted off, once more looking towards his colleagues. 'Please, would you excuse me? I need to check in on my team.'

'Of course.' Delancort waited until the man was out of earshot, then spoke again. '*Merde*. My skin crawls to think of what use the Combine could put that device to.'

The police officer from the line came towards them, his hand raised.

'I need you to move outside the perimeter.' His English was halting but his manner firm, and his other hand resting on the butt of his holstered gun made it clear he would not take no for an answer. 'This is now a criminal investigation.'

He nodded towards another police car that had arrived, and the officers gathered next to it.

'Does that mean this is arson?' Benjamin threw out the leading question.

'Witnesses saw men running from the building,' said the policeman, as he ushered them back towards the line. 'Shots were fired.'

'*Mon dieu.*'

Delancort feigned surprise, but a glance towards Benjamin told him that the other man had expected such a revelation.

Outside the warning tape perimeter, they made their way back to the SUV. Benjamin's gaze swept the faces of the onlookers, a few of whom were recording the conflagration with their cellphone cameras.

'It has to be ALEPH,' said Benjamin, quietly furious at the brutality of the act. 'This is their method. Burn and kill. It's how they cover their tracks.'

The SUV's rear passenger window dropped and Solomon leaned forward as Delancort relayed what they had learned. At length, the African gave a grave nod.

'If we had been here a few hours earlier, it might have been us in there along with these people.'

'We can't remain here,' said Delancort, with sudden impetus. 'If ALEPH did this, they'll be watching. They'll want to be sure that they succeeded. If we stay, the police will have questions . . .'

'Questions we don't have time to answer,' agreed Benjamin.

He jumped into the driver's seat and started the engine, scanning the crowd as Delancort climbed in behind him.

For an instant, he thought he saw a hard-faced woman in the black military-style jackets favoured by the operatives of the Russian PMC – but then the bystanders moved and she disappeared among them.

'Where to?' he asked.

'Into the city,' said Solomon. 'Rubicon had a safe house – we may still be able to make use of it.'

'Understood.'

Benjamin threw the SUV into gear and sped away, retracing their route back out of the area.

He didn't see the woman in the dark jacket watching them go, tracking the vehicle's departure with a tactical camera concealed in the palm of her hand.

SIXTEEN

Lucy marched to the 4 × 4 parked near the overgrown trees, and the evening air prickled on her bare arms. She carried a gear case, hauling it up to put the container into the back of the vehicle.

It took more effort than she'd expected, and she wobbled as the weight of the thing overwhelmed her. With a terse grunt, she shoved the case onto the UAZ's cargo deck and then rested against the flank of the vehicle, panting hard.

She didn't want any of the others to see her like this, showing weakness. Lucy did her best to make it appear as if her scarred lungs were fully healed, but she would always be, at best, 70 per cent of the soldier she was before – and while that was still pretty damned good, it wasn't enough for Lucy Keyes.

In the powerboat's cockpit, when the water filled her mouth and she was seconds from drowning, she had blamed herself.

I can't afford to be fragile. There's too much at stake.

She looked back at the derelict school, where the Brit helped Kara and Malte tear down the remaining kit so they could get the hell out of Dodge. They thought she was fearless, but that wasn't true. The one thing that truly terrified her was failing her team-mates.

A twig snapped and Lucy reacted with speed, pivoting to draw her sidearm. A figure moved out of the trees, picking its way carefully across the weed-choked playground.

'I know you wanna shoot me,' said Grace, as she stepped into the spill of weak light. 'Could we postpone it? I'm beat.'

Lucy put up her pistol but she didn't holster it. She scanned the area, disturbed by the fact that Grace had managed to get this close before she noticed her.

Note to self, don't get distracted.

Grace put her hands on her hips. 'I didn't bring any friends, if that's what you're thinking.'

She'd ditched her Sunny Wehmeyer disguise somewhere for threadbare joggers and a hoodie.

Lucy weighed her reply. 'After it went to shit, I figured we'd seen the last of you. I mean, self-preservation is your thing, right?'

'Yeah . . .' Grace replied, with a sniff. 'Not gonna lie, the thought did cross my mind. But I have what they call a transactional attitude to life, so . . .'

'You figured you'd have a better chance getting out of here with us, than without.'

'There it is.' She sighed. 'As long as that Russian prick is still breathing, I'm not safe. I'm in this 'til it's over.' She looked Lucy up and down. 'But enough about my day. You look like shit, sis. I miss a fight?'

'Something like that.' At length, she holstered her gun, and beckoned Grace to follow. 'C'mon.'

Inside the tumbledown school, Lucy heard a voice speaking over an open channel as they approached the gutted music room.

'*Where is the helicopter now?*' Solomon's sombre tones were unmistakable as they carried down the corridor.

Inside, Kara, Marc and Malte sat around a Rubicon-issue spyPhone and a battery lantern.

'I put it down in a clearing a few miles away,' said Marc. 'It's too risky to use it again.'

'I've been monitoring local police radio bands,' added Kara. 'They've mobilised a surprising amount of men for a stolen helicopter, so it's only a matter of time before someone finds it.'

She worked as she talked, her candy-coloured nails whispering over her laptop keyboard.

'Look what I found,' Lucy broke in, from the collapsed doorway.

Grace gave them a cheery wave. 'Miss me?'

'She didn't sell us out?' Marc raised an eyebrow. 'Huh.'

Malte held out his hand with an expectant look on his face. After a long moment, the Brit sighed and passed the other man a crumpled ten-euro note.

Lucy pitched her voice towards the smartphone on the table. 'How did it go at your end?'

'*Not well,*' rumbled Solomon. '*We will get to that in a moment. Were you able to interdict the second unit?*'

All eyes turned to Marc.

'No. We got close, but we had to disengage surveillance of the transfer. I made the call.'

'*Unfortunate.*'

'They broke off to come for me,' Lucy cut in. 'I'd be dead if they hadn't.'

'*The correct call, then.*' She could almost hear Solomon nodding. '*What were you able to learn about the device?*'

'Oh, that's my cue.' Kara's head jerked up from her screen. 'Well . . . uh . . . a lot of unpleasant things.' She spun her screen around so the rest of them could see it. 'Sir, if you check your secured email link, you'll find some images mirrored from my stack . . .'

Lucy moved closer to get a better look at the stills on Kara's monitor, shots taken from a drone's perspective. She saw an aircraft hangar interior, and a team of men moving a block of unfamiliar hardware on a wheeled dolly.

'That's the thing?'

'Recognise it?'

She gave a Kara a glance. 'Should I?'

'Yes.' The hacker's cat-like expression soured. 'As much as I hate to dredge up bad memories, if you go back to what happened in Korea . . .' She paused, trying to find the best way to carry on. 'Remember the Antonov? A device like this was installed on board.'

Lucy couldn't stop herself from scowling. The incident in Seoul was still a sore point for her – the moment when her friendship with Kara broke under the revelation that the other woman had been lying to her for years about who she really was. Kara Wei had been born Wong Fei Song, a criminal with a mile-long arrest record – and worse, she had been part of the notorious Ghost5 hacker group. In the end, Kara had chosen the right side, but too late to mend the damage between the two women.

A lot had happened since then, and maybe they were in a better place now, but part of Lucy would not forgive that betrayal.

She pushed that memory away and concentrated on what mattered in the moment.

'I remember it. Big Russki cargo plane. Ghost5 used it as their mobile op-centre. It blew up on the runway.'

Kara shook her head. 'More accurate to say, it self-destructed. It had a fail safe to destroy the servers and data on board. "Better off TED", we called it. A Transient Electromagnetic Device, powered by an explosive trigger.' She tapped the object on the screen. 'That is its bigger, uglier brother.'

'An EMP.' Marc cursed under his breath. 'Well, that is a show-stopper.'

'I estimate this at four times the size of the one from the Antonov,' continued Kara. 'It's definitely the same design. Ghost5 acquired their TED from a research facility operated by the Russian air force.'

'And this one was hand-delivered by a Blackjack bomber, so . . .' Marc let that hang. 'We have a genuine weapon of mass destruction in play.'

'What does it do?' said Grace, cocking her head as she peered at the screen.

'It kills anything with an unshielded electronic circuit,' Lucy said flatly. 'Sends you back to the Stone Age at the push of a button.'

Solomon cleared his throat. '*Can you estimate the device's effect from its size?*'

Kara sucked in a breath through her teeth. 'A hundred square city blocks, maybe more? Depending on where it is activated and what it knocks out, you could conceivably cause a domino effect. Failures across dozens of networks and power grids. In the right place, you could black out a major city, maybe even a small country.'

'And this thing is on its way to New York,' said Marc. 'I pulled the flight log from the Triple-Seven that took off from Sochi. It'll be landing in the States in a few hours.'

Heat rose in Lucy's cheeks and she sat on one of the classroom's broken desks and pictured her mother's face.

What would happen if I called her right now and told her to take off out of town? Would she listen to the daughter who disappointed her, the woman she believes is a criminal?

A sudden rush of emotion made her eyes prickle, and Lucy turned away, taking a shaky breath.

'It's not like a nuclear weapon,' said Kara. 'It won't be picked up by radiation detectors or explosive sniffers at the border. The TED's trigger is a binary fluid compound. Both chemical components are inert and harmless when separated, but highly explosive when combined.'

'*Your analysis corresponds with the information we have from Altin Elma.*' Solomon gave them a terse summary of what he and the others had learned in Istanbul. '*The other device, this so-called interrupt, is most likely already in the United States. All roads appear to lead to New York City.*'

'Now we know where we have to go.' Marc turned to Kara, but the hacker raised a hand before he could say more.

'Already working on it. Give me twenty to get some travel options in place.'

Home.

The notion of going back to the place where she had grown up buzzed in Lucy's thoughts, threatening to stir up a storm of powerful emotions. Since the incident that had seen her dishonourably discharged from the US Army, Lucy had felt like an exile from her own nation – a harsh reality affirmed by the fact that she was technically still a federal fugitive. It took work for her to put that aside and concentrate on the facts.

It's just another mission. Doesn't matter where.

She found Marc watching her, and knew he sensed her misgivings. Before he could speak, she threw out a question to forestall any inquiries about her state of mind.

'What about Glovkonin? He hopped a jet, so where's he at now?'

'G-Kor's Gulfstream filed a flight plan to Geneva, Switzerland,' noted Kara.

'Rutger Bremmens's backyard,' Lucy replied. 'So odds are, he's gone to see the Combine's banker.'

'Likely,' said Malte.

'Do we let that happen, or do we stay on him?'

'Fair point,' said Marc, with a nod. 'If the Combine are close to kicking off something big, we can't afford to lose track of the top players.'

He gave Lucy a searching look, silently offering her the choice to drop out of the New York operation.

But then Solomon closed that door. *'We can monitor Glovkonin's movements from here,'* he said. *'The resources at our current location should prove sufficient.'*

'Copy that,' said Lucy, making her choice.

'He's not coming back here, that's for damn sure,' muttered Grace. Marc eyed her. 'What makes you so certain?'

'I guess you haven't seen the local news?' She nodded at Kara. 'What nerd-girl said about the Sochi cops before – they're not just looking for a chopper, they're looking for Glovkonin's buddy, the Italian.' Grace explained that reports about the 'fatal collision' during the powerboat race had been overshadowed by an unconfirmed rumour that Giovanni Da Silvio had gone missing. 'Do I have to draw you a picture? The Italian ghosts at the same time the Russian flies off to a country with a non-extradition treaty? Da Silvio is either on that plane with Glovkonin—'

'Or he's been taken out of play,' concluded Lucy. 'Someone's making moves.'

'Either way, it changes nothing for us. We stay on task,' said Marc, getting to his feet. 'Solomon, Benjamin and Henri keep a low profile in the safe house, the rest of us go to New York under separate covers and attempt to intercept the devices before they're deployed.'

'The Big Apple's a big town,' said Grace. 'How do we find those needles in that haystack?'

'*Saito*,' said Solomon. '*I made good on our agreement. He will repay the favour.*'

The view from the suite on the upper floors of the Hotel President Wilson was magnificent, catching the reflection of the white and orange lights from the city and the boats bobbing on the choppy waters over Lake Geneva.

In the distance, the mountain peaks were fading into the coming night, and on the balcony, Glovkonin took a deep lungful of the chill air. With the sun long set, the bitter nor'easterly wind the Swiss called the *Bise* made itself known, blowing in from Siberia to drag the temperature below zero.

He savoured the burn through his chest as if it were a shot of fine vodka. He wore only a pair of silk boxer shorts beneath his dressing gown, his feet bare on the stone tiles of the suite's terrace. His breath left his lips in a cloud of vapour as he exhaled.

Cold was a familiar companion. The Russian thought of it as one might consider a trusted friend, a reliable constant in an otherwise unpredictable life. Cold kept him grounded. It reminded him of where he had come from. He closed his eyes, letting the icy breeze off the lake caress him.

In the past, he had hated it. The numbing, wintry chill that grew in his extremities. The talons of invisible ice that gripped his chest, squeezing. The cold had tried to kill him more times than any other enemy Pytor Glovkonin had faced, but he had beaten it. He had endured.

No, more than that. It tempered me. Made me stronger.

Once, a malnourished boy from an inconsequential town in the Soviet Union had struggled to survive the poverty he had been born into. That boy knew only hunger and anger, the last fuelled by the first. A warm hearth and a full belly were unknown to him. Perhaps that boy would have died there, if he had not possessed the will to survive.

When the poor boy came to understand that the corruption and greed of others were the roots of his troubles, he walked out into the cold, embracing it. On the frozen wastes, he lied about his age so he could join the Red Army to escape his fate. But the cold found him there as well, the hunger and the anger close behind. As the boy became the man, it tried to murder him, in storms on the frozen steppes and bitter nights atop mountain passes in Afghanistan. He endured and he learned.

It was not the cold that taught him to be ruthless. It revealed a quality already in him. The cold stripped away pretence and doubt. It gave him insight into himself, and it made him valuable to men who needed soldiers devoid of pity. That brought him influence, wealth, and eventually, control of his destiny.

That past was behind him, but its lessons were always close at hand. Glovkonin opened his eyes, his gaze finding the streets below, where tourists and locals alike suffered through the chill in heavy coats.

Fools, every last one. They exist, but they do not survive.

It had taken money, effort, murder and a single-minded focus to reach this point. His ultimate goal was so close he could nearly reach out and touch it.

The rich and powerful, the comfortable and the well fed, they were what he truly hated. The irony of it was that Glovkonin was one of them now, but only outwardly. He would never lose that shivering, starving child. The boy was a part of him, and he would always have the hunger and the fury.

The cold would not let him forget.

Back in the suite, a buzzer sounded, and reluctantly Glovkonin padded back into the central lounge. His bodyguard Gregor stood on guard in the suite's reception, and off his employer's nod, the man opened the door to the corridor beyond. Gregor's partner Misha was outside, running a sensor paddle over the woman who had been engaged for this evening's diversion. He nodded and stepped back, indicating she carried nothing untoward. Tomorrow, the two men would accompany him to the banker's estate in the mountains, but tonight Glovkonin was at his leisure.

He appraised the escort with a raking gaze. She appeared suitable for his needs. Tall but not overly so, with light Slavic features and short dark hair accenting a generous mouth. She wore an evening gown in teal-blue, and it clung to the curves of her body, revealing her.

He snapped his fingers at Gregor.

'Out.'

The bodyguard bobbed his head and stepped through the door, gesturing for the woman to enter. Glovkonin didn't wait to see if she followed, and he strode back into the lounge. The doors leading to the terrace were still open, and the biting wind made itself known by riffling through papers on the table in the centre of the room.

The woman trailed after him, maintaining a demure expression, but he could tell she was uncomfortable. The temperature in the suite was low enough to turn her bare skin to gooseflesh.

'Good evening. I'm Karine,' she began, in adequate Russian.

Glovkonin sneered at that. The name meant 'pure', and given her profession, he doubted it.

'Do not speak,' he told her. 'Take off the dress.'

With a sigh, she undid the clasps and the gown fell into a pool at her feet, revealing beneath it delicate underwear in pale purple.

'Now the brassiere.' He snapped his fingers and when she removed it, he stepped in and cupped one of her generous breasts. There was no sexual charge to his action, only clinical interest, and she flinched at his icy touch. 'Good,' he added, with the same tone he would have taken when purchasing a new car. 'Not fake.'

He scorned anyone who mutilated themselves to attain shallow models of false perfection.

There had been a girl like this one – some young boy's fantasy of her – in his past, whose affections were unattainable for a poor wretch. Now he could have that whenever he wanted. He dismissed the thought and nodded towards the bedroom.

'In there.'

She hugged herself as she stepped away into the master suite, and he moved to the wet bar to prepare himself a drink. As Glovkonin took up a narrow *stopka* glass, the low vibration of his encrypted satellite phone pressed against his hip through the pocket of his robe.

He considered tossing the device aside, but hesitated. Earlier, he had received a message from Pavlo Chumak, the single word *sdelano* – '*done*' – accompanied by gory photos of Giovanni Da Silvio's corpse in the plastic-lined boot of a car. Did the Salt Seller have more to say, he wondered. It could wait until after.

But the caller ID was Andre's. Annoyance flickered over the Russian's expression. Andre was too afraid of Glovkonin to test his patience over trivia.

He answered the call.

'I know you are not foolish enough to waste my time,' he warned.

'*We have a situation,*' said the Frenchman, without preamble. '*Kyun, the thief? He's missing.*'

The name rang a vague bell, but he couldn't place it.

'Remind me why I should care?'

'*The boy in Vienna. The one I hired to play house with Saito's daughter. She's disappeared as well. At least two days ago.*'

His fingers tightened around the handset.

'Find him and have someone beat an explanation out of him.'

'*I already have that,*' said Andre. '*You're not going to like it.*' The phone buzzed again. '*I've sent you a photo I pulled from a traffic camera.*'

Glovkonin held up the phone and flicked to the message tab. The image showed a Viennese square by a river, on one side was a cafe with open-air seating. At a table in the corner of the photo, a young East Asian woman sat across from a tall, stiff-backed black man in a good suit.

The cold shot through Glovkonin's veins like an electric shock. The picture was grainy and the man's face was blurred. But he knew.

'*It's him,*' said Andre, anticipating the question. '*Ekko Solomon is alive.*'

It took a monumental effort for the Russian to hold the sat-phone in his grip and not hurl it across the room in rage. A thousand furious retorts boiled in his throat, but he smothered them, reaching for the cold and the control it gave him.

When he spoke again, each word was carved out of ice.

'Are you certain?'

'*I wasn't. Until today, when the ALEPH team we sent to Istanbul uploaded some video to me.*' The phone vibrated again as another message arrived. '*See for yourself.*'

This time, the attachment was a four-second loop of shaky hand-held footage, filmed by someone among a crowd of people. The video panned from the burning shell of what Glovkonin recognised as the Altin Elma facility, to track two men walking towards a parked SUV.

He knew one of them – Henri Delancort, the defeated Rubicon aide-de-camp whose life he had ruined for sport – but the other was unfamiliar. Then the vehicle's passenger window dropped and a dark face became visible inside. Glovkonin felt a perverse jolt of

triumph as he saw the damage written across Solomon's aspect –
the scarification and the missing eye – but it soured with the revelation that his nemesis still lived.

'*I don't know how,*' Andre continued, once again anticipating
the most pressing question. '*I ran a facial recognition profile. The
match is 86 per cent.*'

'I know how,' Glovkonin growled, pushing against the tide of
his anger. 'Saito lied to me.'

The Russian saw the scope of the deception in a sharp moment
of clarity. The instances over the past few months where the assassin had appeared distracted, when he had been off the grid or out
of contact – those had been his concealment of this truth.

Saito had covered up Solomon's survival, maintaining that the
African had died in a firefight in the wilds of Mozambique – and
for what cause? It was obvious. He believed he could buy his
daughter's rescue with Solomon's life.

But was that all Saito had surrendered for his child? There was
much more he could give up. Nothing could be allowed to jeopard-
ise the operation in New York.

'*I ordered the ALEPH team to hold in Istanbul. They have
tracked Solomon to a location elsewhere in the city. What do you
want done?*'

Again, it took a monumental effort for Glovkonin to resist the
reflexive urge to demand bloody murder. But he wanted that for
himself. More than anything, he wanted to end the African's life
with his own hands. He had been gravely disappointed when
Saito informed him Solomon had perished. Fate now offered him
a second chance to commit the act.

'Take him alive.' He bit out the reply. 'Kill the others.'

'*Understood.*' Andre paused, gathering himself. '*Will this delay
the primary operation?*'

'No. But the timetable will need to be moved up.' He chewed
on that, scowling at the thought of having to deal directly with the

tiresome American. Then another consideration occurred to him. 'The contingency we discussed. Have you made contact?'

'*Yes. They're agreeable to the terms we presented.*'

'Proceed.' He stalked back across the lounge, towards the master bedroom. 'There can be no margin for error.'

'*Understood,*' said the other man. '*I'll contact you when we have acquired the objective.*'

Glovkonin cut the call, and tossed the sat-phone irritably to one side as he entered the bedroom. The woman lay in a provocative pose, but her nudity did nothing to stir him. Her presence was suddenly sordid and intolerable.

'Leave,' he snapped. When she hesitated in surprise, his voice rose into a shout and he raised his hand to strike her. 'Get out, *shlyukha!*'

She bolted from the bed, scrambling to grab her clothing along the way. He realised he still had the empty glass clutched in his other hand, and he hurled it at the fleeing woman's back.

He heard the door slam and sat heavily on the edge of the bed, cursing himself for his oversights, seething over the mendacity of the assassin, fighting to find his cold and calculating centre once more.

Finally, when Glovkonin's anger stilled and he had thought through his next move, he took up the sat-phone once again and dialled a number that would connect him to the American.

Saito climbed out of the truck cab as the vehicle rolled to a stop on the narrow backstreet, and sucked in a deep breath. He had slept poorly on the flight from Russia, crammed into a small bunk in the cargo plane's chilly interior. The recycled air had left him with a headache and a rasping, arid cough.

Heavy clouds loomed overhead, and he felt a faint drop of rain kiss his cheek. Saito watched the driver reverse the truck into a warehouse on one corner of the intersection, the building's roller door drawing up to allow it access.

He didn't like this location. There were too many approaches, too much civilian traffic passing close by, heading on to the Queensboro Bridge across to the island of Manhattan. The noise of the passing vehicles was a constant rumble, like far-off thunder.

On the way in from the airport, the aging, talkative driver had told him that this district was called 'Hunters Point', but the man hadn't been able to provide any context for the name. Saito expected no better. In his experience, few ordinary Americans seemed able to grasp any of their own history beyond what their media parcelled out for them. By contrast, he knew everything about the area of Osaka where he had lived before his self-enforced exile, the Tennoji district with the park he walked as a boy and patrolled as a beat cop, and the scruffy zoo where he had often taken Rumiko.

He frowned, disappointed for allowing his daughter's face to push into his mind. Once he had been able to wall her off from his work for the Combine, but now she was a constant ghost in his thoughts. He thought about her, far away on the other side of the world, full of life and so excited to be doing something significant.

Would she be happy? He wanted very badly to hear Rumiko's voice again. The last time they had spoken, his heart filled with hope. Saito dared to believe that they might bridge the divide between them.

'Look who it is.' A sour voice broke through his reverie, and he glanced up to see one of the American's men approaching. It was the one named Creel, the thick-browed gunman from the Harlow sanction. 'You bring some guts this time, pal?' He snorted in brisk amusement at his own joke.

Saito ignored him and walked into the warehouse. He was too fatigued to engage with the man, but Creel trailed after him, a sneer playing on his lips.

A smaller vehicle waited inside, the rear of it mated up to an elevated loading platform. The truck continued to back up, sounding a warning tone every few seconds. The second vehicle was a box van in a white and blue livery, with a metal rack bolted to its roof. Saito saw a logo on the door and the name 'ConEdison' – the van was decorated to resemble one of the fleet of maintenance vehicles operated by the power company. It would be commonplace on the streets of New York, blending unnoticed into the flow of traffic. The ConEd van's rear doors were wide open, the interior gutted to accommodate the device ferried in from Sochi.

A team of men in grubby boiler suits set to work, first sliding out the cargo crate from the back of the truck, then stripping it down to reveal the weapon inside.

'What the fuck is that?' said Creel, refusing to keep his distance.

'Eh, his boss sent us a water heater, ain't that right?' The other two from that night in Cape Cod stood near the van – the ex-cop, Bragg, and Weldon, the one with the scar. Bragg lit a cigarette and continued. 'So we get an instruction manual for this thing?'

'Cassidy has a guy to work it,' said Weldon. 'We gotta get it where it needs to go, then get the hell out.'

'Go through Brooklyn, be there in thirty,' said Creel, watching the men work. 'Park it in front of that big brass bull.'

'More like *never*.' Bragg snorted with derision. 'Like you know anything about driving in the city. Midtown Tunnel, then the FDR. Straight shot.'

'To Wall Street,' Saito said quietly.

On the long flight from Sochi, he had killed time studying a map of the city, and the destinations the men were discussing centred on the heart of New York's financial district. A target with all the hallmarks of a Combine objective.

'*Greed is good*,' quoted Creel, and he laughed again. 'Get it? Like in the movie?'

'Yeah, we get it,' Bragg said wearily.

He looked up as the rain made itself known, rattling off the roof above their heads.

Creel prodded Saito in the shoulder. 'You ever see that movie, huh? They get that in China?'

'I am from Japan,' Saito corrected.

The man opened his mouth to continue, but the strident tone of a sat-phone cut him off. The assassin reached into a pocket, clipping a Bluetooth earpiece into place as he stepped away to respond. 'Yes?'

Creel shrugged and wandered over to the others. For a moment, the open line was quiet, and Saito wondered if had used the earpiece incorrectly; then he heard a slow intake of breath.

'*Report*,' Glovkonin said tightly.

'The equipment is being transferred.' Saito removed the smart-phone handset from inside his jacket and took a snapshot of the van and the men loading it. 'I have sent you visual confirmation.'

'*I see.*'

A thought occurred to Saito as he studied the image, and he tapped out a string of letters and numbers.

'What more do you require from me?'

A low, predatory chuckle sounded from the other end of the line. It had no humour in it, only threat, and Saito tensed.

'*The answer to a question*,' said Glovkonin. '*Did you think I would not find out?*'

A wave of nausea came over Saito as his worst fear became real. *He knows.*

The assassin swallowed it down and kept his voice level.

'I am uncertain as to—'

'*Don't insult me*,' snarled the Russian. '*You are a traitor!*'

As Saito listened, a strange sense of freedom came to him.

'How can a man betray something he never believed in?'

'*I am gravely disappointed.*' As Glovkonin spoke, from the corner of his eye, Saito saw Weldon talking into a phone of his own. '*The Combine kept its promise about the girl. She was shielded from your mistakes. But now you are responsible for her death.*'

Saito drew himself up. 'You cannot reach her. You no longer hold my daughter's fate hostage.' The resentment that he had buried deep down for so long came to the fore. 'You are weak, Glovkonin. You believe you are strong, but that is a delusion. Immorality and wealth have protected you, but that will not last forever. You will never know true strength, you or your arrogant friends.'

The Russian sniffed, as if he smelled something foul.

'I know this. When I have completed my plans, I will pay as much as it will cost to find your little orphan bitch and have her ruined. Go to your grave with that.'

The line closed, and from behind him, Saito heard the clicks of weapons being readied. Weldon aimed the wide maw of a Kimber Custom semi-automatic towards him.

'My boss says your boss says you're out of a job.'

In his other hand he held his phone, and he gestured with it.

The men on the loading dock retreated, scrambling away to safety. They were well aware of what would happen next.

'What the hell?' Creel belatedly pulled his own gun. His sneer faltered, then shifted into a wide grin as he caught up to what Weldon was suggesting. 'Bad news for you, pal—'

Saito moved on the other man, jerking his right arm forward in a downwards punching motion. The sudden movement sent a spasm of pain through his gut, collecting around the old bullet-shrapnel wound in his torso, but he pushed through it and continued towards Creel before he could react.

The sharp flick of Saito's limb brought out the dagger he had concealed in a forearm sheath beneath the sleeve of his shirt, sliding it into his fingers.

The weapon was unconventional, something he had first seen in a history book about the mounted knights of medieval Europe. The blade was called a *misericorde*, more a thick needle than a knife. In ancient wars, soldiers on foot would use it to kill knights by stabbing the narrow tip through the gaps in their armour.

The ideal of the weapon appealed to Saito's instincts. A blade wielded by a common man, capable of ending a king if correctly applied.

The misericorde went into Creel's chest between his ribs in three quick stabs, puncturing his lungs before he could bring up his gun to bear. Saito pulled the man on to the weapon, drew him close as if to embrace him, turning Creel into a human shield.

Bragg's cigarette fell from his mouth, and the ex-cop grabbed his pistol, but he was late off the mark and he represented the lesser of the threats in the room. Saito snatched away Creel's weapon – a heavy Smith & Wesson revolver – and fired twice.

The revolver's loud report bellowed inside the building, and Saito's poor grip on the unfamiliar gun made him miss. Both rounds ricocheted off the concrete floor, singing harmlessly away into the shadows.

Weldon exhibited a calm that Saito had not expected, ignoring the shots sent his way. The scarred man made a split-second decision and fired at Creel, the other gunman already trembling in Saito's arms from shock. Weldon hit Creel in the right knee and the other man screamed, pitching forward and away as his leg blew out under him.

Saito lost his protection, clinging to the blood-soaked misericorde as it tore out of the falling man's torso.

'Fucker!' shouted Bragg as he came into the engagement, and the ex-cop pumped five rounds across the warehouse. Three of them hit Saito, the first a glancing kiss across the top of his right shoulder, the second and third into his belly.

He fell on his back with a grunt of pain, his head striking the ground with a thud. Wreathed in agony, he could only stare upwards at the rusting metal roof overhead. Raindrops made circles on the soot-stained skylights up there, and he heard thunder.

'Shit! You shot Creel!' Bragg's voice seemed to come from far away.

'See that knife? Dead already,' Weldon grunted, coming closer. 'Did him a favour. Quick finish.'

Saito had lost the gun, but he still clutched the bloody dagger. He tried to move, but agony made that impossible. He remembered the shot that had nearly killed him in Mogadishu; this was worse. He was torn up inside, he could feel it. With a hiss of exertion, he managed to lift his head.

'The fuck we do with this asshole?'

Bragg hovered at the edge of Saito's vision, glaring at him.

'Boss said to put him in the van,' noted Weldon. The sound of his words grew indistinct and hazy. 'Give the Feds something to waste their time on after.'

'Oh, right.' Bragg came closer, sighting down the barrel of his pistol. 'Okay.'

Rumiko.

Saito made himself think of his daughter. Her beautiful face and the melody of her voice.

He blotted out everything but the sound of thunder.

SEVENTEEN

The rain rattled constantly against the diner's window, pushed by the wind until it was coming in vertically against the glass. Marc leaned against it, the cold leaching the heat from his face. The chill helped him to shake off the last of his travel fatigue – that, and the bottomless cups of strong black coffee which the waitress kept topping up from a steaming glass jug.

He had no idea what setting his body clock was on. Moscow time, European time, Middle of the Bloody Ocean time, it blurred into one.

He peered out at the traffic on Atlantic Avenue, searching the street for some kind of sense of the hour. The densely overcast sky made it difficult to tell. Here on the US east coast it was morning, but exactly what part he didn't know.

Earlier than I care for, he told himself, and dumped another sachet of sugar into his mug before taking a mouthful.

The diner was two thirds empty, with a handful of truck drivers and early birds tanking up on carbs and breakfast specials. It had a faux-80s vibe with lots of brushed aluminium detailing and hot-pink neon, rejecting the more usual post-war Americana typical of such places for something closer to the present day. There were booths that could comfortably seat four people, and no security camera coverage, both of which suited the needs of the Rubicon team.

Across from him, Lucy was lost in her machine-like consumption of a plate of waffles. She forked the food into her mouth, but her gaze was distant, unseeing. Marc's expression shifted into a concerned frown.

It couldn't be easy for her to be here. The diner sat on the edge of the borough where she had been born and raised. She hadn't come back here in years, as far as Marc knew. There was too much baggage. Too many awkward questions she wasn't ready to face.

In a way, she wasn't here now, either. Lucy was barely present, deep into her spec ops preparation, being what Marc's old MI6 instructors had called the 'grey man'. The unremarkable and unmemorable person that no one paid attention to.

Lucy wore a New York Mets snapback pulled down low over her eyes, the rest of her hidden in a shapeless hoodie a size too large for her. She blended into the rest of the locals so well she vanished, and that thousand-yard stare in her eyes set off *leave me alone* vibes that even a blind person could sense.

For his part, Marc had tried his best to stay nondescript in a denim jacket and weathered work jeans. Together, they were both utterly ordinary, and that was exactly how they wanted it.

Arrival in the USA had been the usual scrum of queues through passport control, each of the team coming in through different routes to JFK International. For Marc and Lucy, that had meant flying out from Sochi via the same airport he had illegally entered with Malte earlier the same day. He spent the entire time waiting to get his collar felt by a Russian border patrol officer, fearful that someone might have caught his face, and it was only when his flight was somewhere over Greenland that Marc relaxed enough to fall asleep.

He gripped the heavy coffee mug, staring into its depths. He wanted to be moving, to be on the job, but the nature of this last-second deployment forced the team to tread carefully. By Kara's best estimates, the Combine's operation had at least half a day's lead, and there was a lot that could get done in that time.

Marc and his team were operating on intelligence gathered that New York City was the location for whatever the Combine were planning, but secretly he worried that their target might be further afield. Ten hours' head start could put the EMP device he'd seen in Sochi anywhere within the continental United States, even up into

Canada or down to the Mexican border. He dreaded the idea of waking up to find himself looking the wrong way when the critical moment came.

But we can't be everywhere at once. Losing the backing and the organisation of the Rubicon Corporation had changed Marc's team from a private intelligence service to something that more closely resembled a guerrilla cell. Smaller, more agile, but with next to no infrastructure. *We have to follow the intel and hope for the best.*

His gaze drifted back towards the restaurant counter, where a television mounted on the wall showed a weather forecast. He couldn't hear the weatherman's voice, but the animated image of a huge cyclone churning its way out of the Atlantic towards Staten Island and Brooklyn did all the talking. One of the early morning diners, an older lady with a dog dozing at her feet, finished up her food as she conversed with the waitress. The two women talked briskly about their provisions for the coming storm.

'They're saying this sum'bitch could be worse than Sandy,' said the dog owner, referring back to the devastating hurricane of 2012. 'Me an' Rex here don't want that crap again.'

'It's global warmin', honey,' said the waitress, with a wry smile. 'My advice to you? Get Rex a doghouse on stilts.'

'Better yet, we'll move to the Catskills.'

They both laughed. It was survivors' humour, grim in the face of the inevitable.

Outside, Marc had already noted the presence of plywood boards stacked in a pile near the restaurant's entrance, ready to be nailed up over the windows. Other businesses along the avenue were making similar arrangements.

He looked back and found Lucy staring blankly in his direction. 'Hey,' he said.

She blinked, coming back to earth. 'Hey.'

'You all right?'

'Sure.' He started to speak, but she talked over him. 'Got my game face on. We're green for go.'

'Right.' Marc lowered his voice. 'I have your back. Whatever you need, okay?'

She eyed him, looking right through to his core. 'You're not sure what to say, are you? I love that you're trying to find the best way to ask me if being here is messing with my head. It is. But I can deal.'

'Of course you can,' he replied. 'If you want to talk about it, or do anything *other* than talk about it . . . I'm here.'

She smiled for the first time in a while, and her fingers extended to brush against his around the coffee mug.

'I know.'

'Am I interrupting a moment?' A woman in a bright rain jacket and a woollen hat stood at the end of the booth, and gave them both a patronising smirk. 'You make such a cute couple.'

It took Marc a full second to realise that he was looking at Grace. Once more, the undercover operative had transformed herself from one persona to another, shifting selves as easily as Marc or Lucy could change a shirt. Grace had followed them into the diner less than ten minutes ago, dressed in a dark businesswoman's trouser suit with her hair up in a severe bun. She'd vanished into the ladies' room, and as far as anyone else knew, the woman who'd walked in there hadn't come back out. The person who did leave had different hair, a different gait, and a dowdy outfit topped off with a pair of horn-rimmed spectacles parked on her nose.

Lucy evaluated her new look.

'You remind me of my third grade home room teacher.'

'That a fact, Lucille?' Grace played into the role. 'Make sure you finish up that breakfast!'

'Bite me,' she replied.

Grace dropped into the booth next to Lucy and made a performance out of ordering some French toast.

'How much longer do we have to sit around here?' The food arrived swiftly and her tone changed as she ate, as she momentarily lost interest in play-acting. 'Is Glovkonin going to be on site for this? I want him on ice, but this hunt-the-WMD game you're into isn't my speed. I should have stayed behind—'

'If you believe for one second we're letting you out of our sight before this is over, you're sorely mistaken.' Marc gave her a level stare. 'No one has forgotten who you are or what you have done.'

She huffed. 'What does it take to earn a little trust around here?'

'Said the scorpion to the frog,' muttered Lucy.

'I'm a product of my environment,' Grace continued. She pointed her fork at Marc. 'You read my file. You know what I did, before I turned freelance. Believe me, when you're trained by the CIA to be a human chameleon, it messes with your sense of right and wrong.'

'I might accept that, if I ever thought you had one to begin with,' Marc said coldly. 'It didn't trouble you when you were imitating my dead friend and murdering MI6 agents.'

'And trying to kill us,' added Lucy. 'Let's not forget that.'

'That was forever ago. Don't take it personally.' Grace snorted with derision and returned to her food as the door opened.

Marc gave the new arrival a nod. Malte Riis returned it and walked down to join them, unzipping his crumpled rain slicker and peeling off the trucker cap on his head.

'Blue plate special for my friend here,' called Lucy, and from the counter the waitress gave her a thumbs up.

Malte slid in beside Marc and took in their expressions.

'Okay?' said the Finn.

'Okay,' confirmed Marc. 'Got the paper?'

'No problems,' said the other man, revealing a satchel he had concealed under the slicker.

Malte waited until the server had dropped off his food, then produced four resealable plastic bags. Inside each one was a forged driver's licence, a roll of cash and a few random items of pocket lit-ter – enough to simulate a basic cover identity should it be needed. In turn, the Finn took the passports that they had used to enter the country, to destroy as soon as possible.

There was also a generic burner phone for emergencies, which Marc pocketed. He still preferred to use his Rubicon-issue spyPhone, favouring the suite of custom apps and the clandestine software he had personally installed on it. With the shuttering of Rubicon and its Special Conditions Division, the custom-made smartphone was the last one they had between them, as the devices had an unpleasant tendency to get chewed up in the course of covert operations.

'Where'd this come from?' said Grace, dabbing her mouth with a napkin. She squinted at her fake ID. 'This is a bad match. I'll have to change my hair again.'

'Allow it,' Marc retorted. 'Kara sourced this on zero notice, it's the best we can manage.'

'Let me guess – from her dark web playmates?' Grace snorted. 'Don't ask, don't tell. We're gonna need other gear, I assume? Weapons and hardware?'

'Later,' said Malte, attacking his meal with gusto.

'Speaking of Kara,' added Lucy, jutting her chin at the street. 'Is she coming?'

Marc checked the careworn Cabot dive watch around his wrist.

'She'll be here. She's already up to speed.'

Grace folded her arms across her chest and studied him expect-antly.

'Well?' Her tone turned sickly-sweet again. 'You gonna keep us in the dark, sweetie, or tell us what the fuck we're doing here?'

Marc pulled his spyPhone and rested it against a napkin dis-penser, allowing him to position it on the table so they could see the screen.

'Solomon had an encrypted message for me when I touched down.' He swiped across the phone, bringing up a grainy image.

'This is from Saito. He set up a dead man's switch to drop a download if he didn't reset the timer every ten hours.'

'Which means ...' Malte made a throat-cutting motion, then went back to his bacon and eggs. 'Problem.'

'Yeah,' said Marc. 'Saito's been taken out. That could have serious blowback for us.'

'If they killed him, they gotta know we're on to them.' Grace peered at the image. 'What is that?'

'It's a ConEd van,' said Lucy. 'I'm guessing that piece of junk they're loading is our star attraction.'

'Saito left the geotags enabled on this photo,' Marc continued. 'It's a warehouse a few miles from here. And there's more.'

He flicked away the picture, revealing the two lines of text that had been attached to the email.

wall street

tonight

'Now we know when and where,' Marc concluded.

Lucy laid her hands on the table. 'So let's box this up. Setting off a tactical electromagnetic pulse weapon in the middle of the financial district. What does that look like?'

'A device of that magnitude, right on the doorstep ...' Marc thought it through. 'The pulse would be so strong, even shielded systems will take a hit. Everything with a chip in it for miles around goes dead. Banks, the stock exchange, the Federal Reserve, all blacked out. Then there's the effect to the city infrastructure itself. Traffic control, the Subway, emergency services ... they go down, too. And New York doesn't have the most efficient power grid, either. The wrong substation dies and it's like pulling the wrong block in that tower game. It all falls. Cascade failure.'

Marc recalled the summer of 2019, when a fire in a generator substation had killed power to thirty square blocks of Manhattan. That had been a random occurrence. A targeted strike had the capability to darken New York for days.

'Say it happens like that,' said Grace. 'What do the Combine win?'

Marc made a downward motion with the flat of his hand.

'New York's financial network goes dark and the US economy drops off a cliff. That meltdown sends shock waves around the planet. If they position themselves to take advantage, and you know these arseholes, they already have . . .'

'They'll make bank,' Lucy said grimly. 'And fuck over every little guy's life savings and 401-Ks.'

Marc looked around at the other people in the diner – the cook and the waitress, the dog-walker and the truckers. Big, mono-lithic megacorporations might be able to weather such a crisis, but tomorrow these ordinary working people could be waking up to a world where they would have nothing to their names.

Malte's lips thinned into a hard line, pushing away his empty plate.

'Fail safes?'

'There are,' noted Marc, 'but the Combine know that, too.'

'It's not just the EMP,' said Lucy. 'That other tech is out there – the interrupt. Any leads on that?'

'Nothing.'

'Shit.'

Grace shrugged. 'If you pull the plug on this thing, it won't matter.'

On the avenue, an NYPD police cruiser shot past, lights flashing as it raced towards an incident.

'Call them,' said Malte, nodding after the vehicle.

Marc considered that for a moment, and glanced at Lucy.

'Maybe not the cops. But there's your mate Gonzalez in the FBI. You trust him?'

'I do,' she admitted, 'but I don't trust anyone else.' She scowled. 'Dropping the dime is our last-ditch option. We know the Com-bine's American partner has his fingers in law enforcement and government at high levels. If I reach out to Special Agent Gonzalez, we're sending up a flare that anyone can see.'

'We alert the Combine, they can shift targets, hit somewhere else.' Marc nodded to himself. 'Hit somewhere we *don't* know about.'

'So we go it alone.' Lucy managed a rueful smile. 'Usual song. Different lyrics. Same dance.'

Grace covered a snide chuckle with her hand. 'This is how you people operate? Stumbling through everything? It's a wonder you're not dead and buried.'

'It's been said,' admitted Marc.

The phone on the table trilled, and he snatched it up. A text message from Kara's burner spelled out a single word – *Taxi!*

Lucy sensed the change in his mood.

'We're going?'

'We're going,' he confirmed, peeling off a few twenty-dollar bills to tuck under a salt shaker.

The group rose and trooped out into the damp, drizzly morning. Lucy pulled her cap down tight, folding her hood up around it. She was in the moment now, shifting states from *safe* to *armed*, like a missile on a launch rail, ready to fire. Marc's hands vanished into his pockets, hiding the twitches in them. The old nerves, the same gut-twist he always felt before the kick-off, reached out and grabbed hold of him.

Still not used to this. He decided that was a good thing. *The moment it becomes commonplace, that's when you start making mistakes.*

With a gruff rumble, a rust-marked 80s-era Ford Econoline van in primer grey came to a halt at the kerb, and Kara leaned out of the driver-side window.

'Get in, losers,' she called. 'We're going shopping.'

Walter Novick made the turn at the corner of Broome and Broadway, threading his Honda Accord into the flow of traffic behind an MTA bus and a gaggle of yellow cabs. He glanced at the clock on the dash. He was running behind, but the traffic across the

Williamsburg Bridge had been sluggish, compounding the fact that he'd left home late.

The fault was his. He'd gone out for drinks, stayed too long, and now he was going to pay for it. It would not look good if the interim systems supervisor came in after everyone else, not good at all. The golden opportunity he had would slip away, if he couldn't prove himself a worthy successor to that stuck-up prick Harlow.

Of course, the supervisor gig should have been Novick's from the start. *He* was the one who had put in the hours, *he* was the one who knew the hardware better than anyone else in the building. But because he didn't play the game like the other office mandarins, Novick had been passed over again and again.

They were jealous, obviously. Those day-players couldn't code their way out of a wet paper bag, while he had skills that could outshine them, if only he had the chance to do things *his* way.

Adjusting his glasses, he drummed his fingers on the steering wheel in sync with the swish-swish of the Honda's windscreen wipers, glaring at the avenue before him as he chewed on the same old affronts for the millionth time.

I mean, what the hell does sustained passive-aggressive tendencies *even mean?*

He wasn't supposed to have seen those words in his evaluation report, but one day it turned up in his email queue.

Some idiot in human resources screwed up and copied me in on it by mistake. More fool them!

He pulled around the bus and continued south, passing Canal Street Station as he raced the traffic signals. He'd hoped that Manhattan's regular crush of traffic would be lessened because of the storm warnings, forcing people to stay home, but the city was spiting him. Everyone on the road was getting in his way.

Novick leaned on his horn as a cabbie cut across at the mid-block, and the bored driver barely bothered to give him the finger as he passed. Novick thought about snapshotting the taxi driver's licence plate.

I could find you, he said silently, *tank your credit rating for shits and giggles, dickweed. Would you like that?*

There was a strict moratorium on using the facility's hardware for personal use, but the thought of the petty revenge made him feel a little better. He approached the following intersection, changing lanes for the next turn.

Up ahead, a truck halted and suddenly nobody was going anywhere.

A tinkling electronic tone, like music from a cheap toy, came from out of nowhere. It made Novick jump. He knew exactly what the sound signified.

Now? he thought. *You're calling me right now?*

He snatched up the bag on the passenger seat next to him and fumbled for the scruffy first-gen Nokia cellphone hidden in a rolled-up copy of yesterday's *USA Today.* Ancient tech by his standards, decades out of step with his Government-issue encrypted smart-phone, but that was exactly why it had been chosen.

Stuck there with no chance of escape, Novick could only answer it. *They'll know if I don't.*

He steeled himself and pushed the call accept button.

'Yes?'

'*Good morning, Walter.*' It was the guy with the French accent, the one he always spoke to. '*Are you ready?*'

'Ready for what?'

Novick wasn't sure if that twang was the real deal or something the man put on. He'd never been further afield than Cleveland, so he couldn't tell – it all sounded foreign to him. He looked around, scanning the faces of people on the street through the car's rain-streaked windows. Were they watching him?

'*Don't be coy, Walter, it's insulting.*' French Guy's tone turned flinty. '*Time to pay what you owe.*'

'Yeah.' He swallowed hard. 'About that. If we could hold off for a while—'

'*It's happening today,*' the other man said firmly. '*I hope you're not going to let us down. Because that would be very bad for you.*'

'I'm not really prepared . . .'

Ahead of him, the roller door on the back of the stalled truck rose halfway, and Novick's voice died as he took a good look at a man in black fatigues crouching inside.

The man wore a balaclava that hid most of his face, but his eyes found Novick's and locked with them. In one hand, half-hidden so only the two of them could see it, the masked man held an Uzi sub-machine gun with a long silencer.

'*Take a second if you want to reconsider your position. You have until the lights change.*'

The back of the truck was so close to the hood of Novick's Honda that the masked man would be able to spray a burst of fire across the windshield before anyone could react. He kept staring into Novick's eyes, unblinking.

'Okay, sure,' Novick heard himself say. 'I'll do it.'

'*Better.*'

The man in the mask nodded a moment later, hiding away the gun as he reached up to pull down the roller door.

'*Try not to worry, Walter,*' said French Guy, his tone becoming amiable. '*By the time this is over, you'll be a hero. You want that, don't you?*'

He did, he had to admit. Sean Harlow had been an impediment that Novick wanted gone for a long time, and these people had made it happen. There was an open path in front of him, and if he played it right, he could follow it straight into a permanent senior role. *Assistant director.* Maybe even *director* one day.

The lights changed and the truck drove on, allowing him to make the turning on to Thomas Street. His destination came into view as he rounded the corner.

The featureless tower of weathered concrete rose up towards the grey sky, its bleak aspect broken only by the maws of black ventilation grilles. Some people thought the blind, windowless building was sinister, but to Novick it was like a fortress out of ancient myth. And every dark tower needed its arch-wizard.

'*This is an essential task*,' said the voice on the phone. '*You and I and the other contingencies, working together. We cannot succeed otherwise.*'

'I get it.' Novick came up to the entrance to the underground car park, and he knew that once inside, he would lose the signal. 'I'm ready.'

French Guy seemed to sense that, too, his tone becoming urgent.

'*Leave the phone, you won't need it. The equipment is in a case in the trunk of your vehicle, along with instructions as to where to place it. Don't worry about passing through security, the contents are camouflaged.*'

Novick blinked. 'In my car? How did you get it in there?'

'*Does that matter?*' said the voice. '*Do as instructed. We will handle the rest.*' He paused. '*You know the consequences of failure. Harlow is not the only person who can be removed.*'

'I know,' insisted Novick, but the line cut as his car descended the ramp, into the shadows beneath the tower.

The helicopter dropped from the clear blue sky, reflected sunshine blazing off the silver fuselage and the spinning rotor blades. As it settled on its skids, the downwash blew powdery snow off the landing pad, catching it in sparking vortices.

Misha disembarked and opened the passenger door for Glovkonin to exit the leather-lined interior, and the Russian ducked his head as he strode away to where a suited aide waited for him.

'Welcome to the Bremmens estate,' said the aide. 'May I offer you a hot beverage? A glass of brandy or glühwein?'

He had a colourless mid-European accent and a young, bland face. At his side, a plain woman in a long maid's dress held a tray with steaming glasses in metal holders.

Glovkonin labelled the aide as forgettable and ignored the offer, sweeping his gaze around the buildings before them. He had seen the estate from the air as they flew up over the Alps, most of it covered with a thick forest of snow-dusted trees, but the main cluster of buildings was set in a large clearing. They were modern forms that mimicked the traditional design of Swiss byre-dwelling houses, with steeply sloped triangular roofs of heavy wood and walls of blank concrete or smoked glass.

The aide moved on past Glovkonin's lack of response with a practised smile.

'If you would like to follow me? Herr Bremmens is able to accommodate your early arrival.'

'How good of him,' said the Russian.

Gregor remained by the helicopter while Misha fell into step behind Glovkonin, as he trailed the aide along a decking walkway kept clear by heating elements beneath the planks. They crossed beneath a towering pine groaning with snow and into a reception area.

The building's interior was open-plan, divided by a few low walls and raised sub-floors connected by wide, suspended skeletal staircases. On one side, a huge fireplace burned radiantly, ferociously devouring firewood that crackled and spat tracer across the polished floor; on the other, doors led out to a great patio looking down into the valley below.

There were paintings crowding the walls – mountain landscapes of various kinds in heavy oils – and the silver nubs of electronic devices embedded in tables, armchairs and the like.

Glovkonin didn't understand the prevalence of the paintings. If one wanted to see mountains in this house, one needed only look out of a window.

'Pytor.' A voice floated down from one of the upper floors.

Glovkonin looked up and saw the Swiss at a carved balustrade, holding a tablet computer in one hand. The banker was, for once, wearing something different from the same suit he usually affected. He had on a shirt beneath a green woollen jumper and dark slacks. For such a precisely unimaginative man, the choice of clothing was almost radical.

'Rutger,' he replied. 'You look positively relaxed.'

'I am at home,' said the banker, without weight. 'You were not expected until this evening. That was made quite clear.'

'Regrettably, circumstances have forced me to move up our timetable.'

'For what reason?'

Glovkonin glanced at the aide, then away.

'It is best that we discuss that privately. Perhaps you can come down from there? If I continue to crane my neck I will develop an ache.'

Bremmens made a hollow noise that might have been approval and adjusted the thick glasses on his nose.

'Join me.'

'Wait here,' said the Russian, drawing a nod from his bodyguard.

Glovkonin climbed the zigzag stairs, and as he approached the upper level, he realised that the topmost platform was walled in on three sides by long rectangular panes of glass.

When he drew level with the Swiss, he saw that the panes were actually screens. Digital displays of graphs and numbers were projected on to them, the images visible only to someone viewing them at the correct angle. He recognised live feeds of data from Standard & Poor's Global, the London Stock Exchange, the NASDAQ, Nikkei 225 and dozens of other worldwide financial indicators. Mountains and valleys of green profit and crimson loss rolled past like the scenery from a primitive computer game, alongside virtual stock tickers charting the rise and fall of corporate fortunes in real time.

Bremmens absorbed everything, the large, watery eyes behind his glasses in constant motion as his gaze flicked from place to place. Absently, he ran a hand over his balding head, smoothing the tufts of grey hair at his temples. He was, the Russian estimated, perhaps fifteen to twenty years his senior, but the Swiss carried himself with the upright bearing of a man half that age. As rigid in posture as he was in personality.

'The Indonesian venture,' Bremmens noted, pointing out a particular pane of data as Glovkonin approached. 'I made some minor adjustments this morning, over breakfast. The correction is bedding in as we speak.'

'Ah.'

The Russian was vaguely aware of the operation in question – the organised defrauding of an offshore oil firm whose holdings would be beneficial to the Combine's greater portfolio. The company would soon collapse, leaving its assets open to be stripped by one of the group's many proxies. A similar process had been used to dismantle Rubicon's corporate holdings.

'You will explain why you are here early.' Bremmens stared into the see-through screens, occasionally typing something on the tablet in his hand. 'I do not enjoy unexpected alterations to our arrangements.'

'Quite,' offered the Russian. 'It was necessary.' He left a pause to build the drama of his next words. 'I bring bad news. Our Italian colleague has been murdered.'

Bremmens halted in mid-type. 'You know this how?'

'I have sources within the criminal sphere,' he admitted. 'You are aware he associated with several volatile felons?'

'Yes. He convinced me it was a requirement. I remained dubious.'

'Rightly so . . .' Glovkonin schooled his expression, reflecting deep concern. 'The details are not clear at this time, but it appears he fell foul of a Ukrainian Bratva faction.'

'Those people are animals.' Bremmens showed the first sign of something like emotion – a tic that drew up the corner of his lip into a brief sneer. 'I warned him.'

'Giovanni enjoyed the thrill of the illicit,' offered Glovkonin. 'It was a character flaw.'

'I will have my people look into it. I will require additional confirmation.'

'By all means,' said Glovkonin, knowing full well that it wouldn't matter.

'We must consider how this affects our work.' As the Russian had expected, the cold-blooded financier concentrated on how the death of the Italian would impact his bottom line. He worked the tablet, bringing up the current status of Da Silvio's personal holdings. 'This information has yet to be released?'

'Correct. As far as the general public and Giovanni's shareholders know, this absence is nothing of note. He has done it before.' Glovkonin cleared his throat. 'You are the first person I have told. In addition, I chose to keep this from our American colleague, for the moment.'

'Sensible,' said Bremmens. 'Cassidy is likely to react . . . expressively . . . to such an event.'

'I agree. Would it be callous of me to say he would squander the opportunity it presents?'

The Swiss gave him a brief, measuring look. 'No. Quite right. Cooler heads must prevail.' He made some quick calculations. 'When news of the Italian's death breaks, share value in Da Silvio Ingegneria will fall precipitously. This prior knowledge can benefit us if correctly manipulated.'

Glovkonin hid a half-smile. 'I thought you might see it that way.'

Bremmens continued to tap away at the tablet screen. After a moment, he spoke again.

'Did you have a hand in this?'

'I didn't kill him, if that is what you mean.'

'I find it difficult to determine if you are being deceptive,' said the banker. 'I will discover the truth if you are concealing it.'

'I have never insulted your intelligence by asking you to do something as naive as trust me.' Glovkonin nodded at the screens, and invoked the only thing he knew Bremmens never doubted. 'Follow the numbers. They do not lie.'

'They cannot,' murmured the Swiss. 'If the timeline for New York must be altered, I will need to recalculate some variables. When do we begin?'

'Soon,' said the Russian. 'I think I will have that drink after all.'

The dingy safe house in Istanbul's Nakkaştepe district was built into a sheer ravine, next to a winding road barely wide enough for cars to pass side by side. The two-storey building was wedged into the gulley, the uneven floors clinging to the steep side, and it sat so low that the roof of dusty orange slates was level with the feet of anyone walking downhill in the direction of the coast. A metal door set into what would have been the attic of any other domicile was the main entrance, but there were other routes of egress hidden along the gulley floor.

Stepped terraces of greenery and poured slabs of aging, crumbling concrete formed a misshapen chequerboard that went down and away, and hidden among them a tumbledown garage contained a Lada jeep for escape, if it came to that.

Delancort sat glumly on a stool in the kitchen, waiting for an electric kettle to boil. He stared out of a barred window towards the minaret of a local mosque, the thin tower lit up against the sunset.

'You look uncomfortable.' The big man, Benjamin, stood in a nearby doorway. 'You are accustomed to better things.' He gestured around at their shabby accommodations.

'It would be terribly conceited of me to say yes to that, but *yes*.' Delancort sighed as the steaming kettle clicked off, and he poured hot water into a mug filled with instant soup powder. The aroma of something vegetable-like filled the air. 'I'm not a field operative. Never was, never wanted to be.'

'Ah, don't sell yourself cheaply,' said the other man. 'You're doing all right.'

Delancort eyed him. 'You do not have to counsel me, counsellor. My mood may be bleak but I'm hardly traumatised.'

The reply came out too glib, more insulting than he meant, but Benjamin didn't appear to notice.

'Occupational hazard,' he said. 'I look to other people's well-being before anything else.'

'Odd career choice for an elite soldier.'

He shrugged. 'I woke up one day and decided I wanted to mend things instead of destroying them. Is that odd to you?'

Delancort noted that Benjamin had a burner phone in his hand and changed the subject.

'You have some new information?'

He had heard the other man talking on the line earlier, in low, murmuring tones.

'*Oui.*' Benjamin stepped past him, going to the barred window to peer out through grimy net curtains. 'We have confirmation that G-Kor's Gulfstream landed in Zurich, and hangar fees have been paid to house it there for a minimum of seventy-two hours.'

'Was Da Silvio with Glovkonin?'

'Unclear.'

'What is he up to . . .?' Delancort grimaced, clasping the mug of hot soup in his hands.

The Russian's wolfish, predatory expression came back to him in a moment of stark recollection. He had been in the room when Glovkonin ordered a murder, right then and there in front of him. A slight nod of the head – that was all it had taken for the Russian's bodyguard to execute someone whose existence his master no longer required. Glovkonin had given the command without a second's hesitation, even though Delancort had not been the only witness. The supreme lack of concern in the man's eyes had been stark. The Russian felt the rules of lesser men did not apply to him. And he clearly believed that *everybody* was lesser than him.

A man like that was capable of anything. Delancort suppressed a shiver at the thought.

'We need to consider our next move,' Benjamin said distantly, distracted by something outside.

'Should I wake . . .?' Delancort nodded towards the adjoining room, where Solomon slept on a makeshift camp bed.

'Did you hear that?' Benjamin's voice dropped to a whisper, and he stiffened. He was instantly on alert, although to Delancort's mind there was nothing to note.

'Hear what?' he said, but the man was already moving.

'Stay here,' hissed Benjamin, as he vanished into the other room. 'Keep low.'

Delancort slipped off the stool, glancing around the kitchen. There was nowhere to hide among the chipboard cupboards and the melamine table, and the only other door led out on to a staircase that descended into the gulley. He had nothing to defend himself, so he pulled open a drawer with the vague idea of locating a weapon, but found nothing more formidable than a blunt steak knife.

An egg-cracking sound issued out above directly him, up on the attic level, and his heart leapt into his chest.

Should I call out to the others or stay silent? He didn't know what was right. *Hide? Run?*

He couldn't fight. It wasn't something he had ever had to do.

Boots scraped on concrete, and Delancort's heart sank as he realised his hesitation would cost him dearly.

A shadow moved past the window in the kitchen door, then in the next second the door itself crashed into the room, propelled off its flimsy hinges by bursts of fire. Other blasts sounded in different parts of the house, and the lights flickered out.

He flinched away, dimly aware of a metallic cylinder clattering into the room through the gaping doorway. With a sound like caged thunder, the stun grenade went off, deafening him. The pain and overpressure rattled the window and hit Delancort with a physical blow that sent him down to his knees.

He could hear nothing but the whining scream of damage done to his eardrums. Hands shaking, he scrambled to pull himself to his feet.

Delancort was no longer alone in the cramped, smoky kitchen. A figure dressed from head to foot in black fatigues stood there, a compact sub-machine gun in both hands. A thread of bright emerald-green laser light from beneath the gun barrel connected it to a spot in the middle of Delancort's sternum.

He raised his hands, blinking furiously. The figure in black had no face, its aspect concealed behind a mask and low-light goggles that gave the intruder an insect-like appearance. There was a single dash of colour on their black tactical gear, a red insignia flash on one shoulder.

Delancort knew that sigil. It denoted a hired gun with the private military contractor called ALEPH.

The green laser flicked up to Delancort's face and dazzled him, blinding him to whatever would come next.

EIGHTEEN

They had no choice but to split up, with too much ground to cover and not enough people to do it. Malte vaulted out of the van at One Wall Street as they paused at a crosswalk, then Marc was next at the corner of New Street and Exchange. Grace followed a block after that, and Lucy left Kara in the van at Hanover Street, where the hacker could run overwatch.

She stepped out into the heavy, dense air of the evening at the foot of the Twenty Exchange building, and a familiar prickle ran up her spine. Lucy tilted her head upwards, past the blank, golem-like faces carved into the art deco structure, to the threatening skies. The towers of glass and granite on all sides vanished into the menacing clouds, as if trying to hold the coming storm at bay. The first drops of rain were finding their way down to ground level, advance scouts for the downpour that would inevitably follow.

Lucy had been away from home for a long time, but that sixth sense, that unerring knowledge of place gifted to her from growing up in New York, had not faded. She could taste it in the atmosphere. When the storm hit, it would hit hard.

'*All mobile call signs, sound off.*'

Kara's voice buzzed in her ear, and Lucy replied in the affirmative. Malte, Marc and Grace did the same, each giving their location with the same report – *no sighting*. If the suspect ConEd van was out here, so far it was undiscovered.

It stuck in Lucy's craw letting Grace off her leash, but they had no alternative. She tried to convince herself it would be okay. Grace *had* come back in Sochi when she could have fled.

But that only deepened Lucy's distrust of the other woman. Grace never did what Lucy expected her to do, and it bothered her greatly.

Frowning, Lucy looked at her phone as she proceeded towards the far end of the financial district's sprawl, turning on to Wall Street proper. She rechecked the photo of the van from Saito's final message as she walked, scanning the avenue for any sign of the vehicle.

If the Combine assassin was dead, if this was on the level, it was a chilling prospect. Lucy had a whole boatload of issues with Hiroshi Saito, starting with the fact that he had once stabbed her in the belly and left her for dead in Mogadishu. But the man had a code, for all the twisted logic of it, and with his daughter's rescue, the assassin owed the Rubicon team. If preventing a terrorist attack in NYC was how he repaid it, she was good with that.

Lucy paused on a street corner, closing her eyes to listen. The chorus of the city moved over her – the rumble of a subway train beneath her boots, the growl of passing traffic and the murmur of voices – and it was stark how much had she missed it. A lonely thread of melancholy pulled on her and she had to cut it dead.

Not the time to get nostalgic.

Lucy kept up the pace, moving west, intent on the mission. After the horror of the 9/11 attacks a few miles from where she now stood, New York had hardened itself to resist any repeat performances. Security barriers, cameras and monitoring systems kept a day and night vigil, with chemical and radiological sensors discreetly retrofitted to street lights sniffing the air for potential dirty bombs or biological weapons. But those technologies would not detect the presence of the EMP weapon. Even a terahertz-wave scanner at full power would see only a block of inert hardware, a meaningless jumble of mechanical components.

The insistent rain ticked off the roof of a greasy little trailer selling Turkish coffee and baklava. Lucy threaded around, past the bulk of a high-sided truck wreathed in steam flowing from a grille in the sidewalk. She stopped and stared in the direction of

Broadway, a few blocks distant. Groups of men in suits who had stayed in the office until the last moment were urgently finding cabs or ride-shares to whisk them away before the bad weather started to bite. Other, less moneyed types and the odd determined tourist were trooping towards subway entrances. Wall Street was emptying, even though the operation of the banks and finance hubs never stopped.

In every building around her, trillions of dollars in currency, stocks, shares, futures, bonds and whatever the hell else churned and flowed like the storm clouds overhead. Invisible lines of monetary force radiated out of this place, up through the grey towers, reaching out across the country and to the world beyond. For a moment, Lucy tried to hold that image in her head. It was hard to connect a crumpled fold of cash in her pocket to that other, rarefied reality, to the place where the mega-rich existed. That was the realm of people like Solomon and Glovkonin, where they played their chess games, and soldiers like Lucy were the pieces on the board.

The idea of that made her shudder. Even as someone who had given her life to the system, who had served in its wars and fought its battles, she still detested it on some level.

But Lucy Keyes was a realist. She knew the first step towards something better was to keep those without morals as far from the levers of power as possible – and that meant opposing Glovkonin and his scheming Combine drinking buddies wherever they raised their heads.

'You don't get to come to my town and fuck shit up,' she said to herself.

'*Say again?*'

Kara had caught some of Lucy's words through her concealed throat mike.

'Disregard my last,' Lucy said, more firmly, walking on to avoid the gaze of a beat cop looking in her direction.

Then, as the downpour began to hiss across the asphalt in earnest, Grace said the words Lucy had been dreading.

'*I found it.*'

They regrouped on Grace's position, past the intersection of Nassau and Pine in the shadow of the museum at Federal Hall. Usually Nassau Street was closed off to vehicular traffic by pop-up barriers, but one of them was down, with the white ConEd van parked on the sidewalk halfway along, nestled up to the Grecian columns of the venerable old building.

Lucy had a dim memory of her Aunt Dani taking her and her brother to visit the landmark when they were kids, showing off the place where George Washington had been sworn in as the first president. In the rain, it remained an imposing structure, even hemmed in by the corporate towers overshadowing it.

'Plates match,' said Malte. 'No one in the cab.'

Marc grimaced. 'I don't see any obvious hostiles outside.'

Lucy nodded in agreement. Aside from a trickle of foot traffic passing down the street, the only other people in the immediate area were some construction workers in the process of locking down a closed site at the foot of a nearby building.

'They'll be monitoring,' she noted. 'Maybe by remote, but somebody will have eyes.'

'Could be anywhere,' noted Grace, gesturing at the towers around them.

There were hundreds of windows looking down on Nassau Street, and an observer – in person or otherwise – could be behind any one of them.

'I don't like this.' Marc's frown deepened. 'Kara, you got anything?'

'*Negative,*' said the hacker. '*No spikes in radio transmissions. But they could be operating via the cellular network, and finding something out of place in phone traffic in this part of the city would be like plucking a whisper out of a cheering crowd.*'

'Fine.' The Brit steeled himself. 'Direct approach, then.'

'Yeah.' Lucy resigned herself to the unavoidable. 'Watch my back.'

'Understood,' said Malte.

He moved away, with Grace trailing him to a position where they could see the whole of the street and the parked van. Lucy shook out her hands as she walked purposefully towards the vehicle.

'Could be rigged,' offered Marc, falling in step with her. 'Ready for that?'

'Sure,' she said, with more confidence than she felt. 'You thinking what I'm thinking?'

'We set the van on fire and hope that does the trick?'

'No. The fact that no one's around means this thing is ready to pop.'

'Oh. Yeah. There's that.'

'Here we go.'

She stepped up, and grasped the handle on the van's rear door.

The expected resistance wasn't there. The door was unlocked, and it opened easily. No cables or wiring were connected to the handle on the inside; there was no booby trap in place to trigger the EMP device, no improvised deterrent.

There was nothing. *Nothing at all.* The entire cargo compartment of the van was bare, down to the white-painted metal floor.

'What the hell . . .?' Lucy let go of the door handle as if it had been electrified, and pressed a hand to her throat mike. 'Target vehicle is empty, repeat, *empty.*'

At her side, Marc stared into the vacant interior and the colour drained from his face.

'We've got to—'

'Hey!' An angry shout cut over his words. A broad-built white guy in a hard hat and orange high-visibility vest stood behind them, getting in their faces. 'What are you doin'?'

Lucy automatically retreated a step, taking the measure of him. He had a scarred, slender chin and hard eyes. Something about the guy rang a wrong note.

'I'm talkin' to you,' he barked. 'Why you touching that van, huh?'

'Just a mistake,' Marc said, keeping his tone even.

'That right?'

A second man, with the same hat-and-vest get-up, came out from around the front of the parked vehicle. He'd used his loud companion as a distraction so he could flank them. The new arrival had a brisk and equally aggressive manner.

She wondered why Malte hadn't warned them that this pair were coming across from the construction site, but when she glanced towards the street corner where the Finn and Grace had been watching, they were gone.

The caution that had escaped her moments earlier suddenly registered. The two men in the hard hats both wore heavy boots, but they were barely scuffed. Hardly the footwear belonging to workers on a construction site.

The man with the scar saw the change in Lucy's expression and he knew she'd made him. He snatched at something under the vest and she saw the barrel of a sound suppressor peek out from beneath the orange material.

'All right,' he said, his tone turning businesslike. 'Don't do anything dumb. You two are gonna come with us or else this turns messy.' He aimed his gun towards the oblivious people walking past them, clustered together under umbrellas or sticking close to the cover of the buildings. 'Get me?'

'Move,' said the second man.

He opened his vest enough for Marc and Lucy to see a Micro Uzi SMG hanging beneath it on a single-point sling.

'Set-up,' whispered Marc, as the men escorted them towards the construction site.

'Set-up,' agreed Lucy.

'Quiet,' said the man with the Uzi, as his companion opened a gate. 'Get in there.'

The work site was a partial excavation at one corner of an office block, where a section of the ground had been cut away for old supports to be replaced. To Lucy, it looked as if some giant rat had gnawed a hole in the foundations, exposing a section of the underground parking lot in the basement. Shielded from view of the public by tarps, the area was lit by hissing electric lamps that cast orange light into the workspaces, and scaffolding covered the building's lower floor.

Grace and Malte were waiting for them, both with their hands on their heads and guns at their backs. Another four men in hard hats surrounded them, each with a weapon at the ready. They moved in and disarmed Marc and Lucy, as they had the others.

Lucy stepped into the gloomy space, and then turned sharply on her heel to face the scarred man.

'You guys know what's going on here, right?' Making it look like a casual gesture, she reached up to rub her neck, making certain the microphone pad concealed at her throat would pick up her words. 'They tell you what it is? The bomb, I mean?'

'What part of *quiet* don't you get?'

The man with the Uzi pulled the gun forward on its sling and aimed it at her.

She sneered. 'It's a goddamn nuke. Eight kilotons.' Lucy made it up as she went, hoping to find a way to turn the tables on the gunmen. 'Trust me, you better have some Factor Four Million sunblock when that goes off.' She let out a low whistle.

'Is she right?' said one of the other men, paling considerably.

'It's not a nuke, for cryin' out loud.' The scarred man gave the other gunman a withering look. 'Would I be standing here with you if it was a fuckin' nuke? She don't know shit.'

'Feds are gonna be here any second,' she continued, and waited. Lucy's performance was as much for the radio as it was for the thugs, and she kept waiting to hear something from Kara via the comms bead in her ear. 'They're up on Hanover,' she added, 'watching everything.'

But Kara remained resolutely silent, and finally Lucy had to accept that the hacker had heard the capture and abandoned them to save herself. She glanced at Marc and he read that thought in her eyes. He shook his head.

'Enough. Move.'

Scar-face jabbed her with his pistol and nodded towards a slope.

The armed men forced them down over dust-caked platforms, below the level of the street and into a blocked-off section of the basement. The wide space had a low ceiling supported by thick cylindrical pillars, the floor marked up into dozens of empty parking spaces. More work lights illuminated the area around them, and Lucy saw other excavations where wide holes had been cut into neighbouring tunnels. The air stank of sewers.

To one side, folding tables had been set up – it was obviously a staging area, piled high with nylon gear bags, one for each man. Another fake worker in an orange vest was busy with a portable monitor, the screen flickering with an image of a city street.

Lucy let herself drift in that direction as she walked, turning her head to get a better look. The guy with the monitor had tapped into the city's CCTV grid, getting a view down on to Wall Street from a camera cluster atop a street sign.

'Stand there,' said Scar-face, addressing the four of them. 'Don't talk and don't move.'

The other men with guns stood in a loose circle around the Rubicon team, weapons at their sides. Lucy had half-expected to be lined up against one concrete wall for a makeshift firing squad, but apparently that wasn't the plan. They were captives, not targets – at least for the moment. Which meant there was still a chance to turn this around.

After a minute or so of silence, the man with the Uzi called out to his companion.

'What's the hold-up?'

Scar-face looked at his watch. 'Almost time.'

Lucy rocked on her feet, shifting a step closer to the guy with the monitor. He moved slightly, and she took a better look at the image on the screen. She recognised the little Turkish coffee stall she had passed by earlier. The unmarked truck parked next to it was in the middle of the frame.

Her breath caught in her throat. The truck was easily the same dimensions as the ConEd van, and whatever fitted in one could easily have fitted in the other.

'They changed vehicles,' she muttered. 'Ah, hell.'

If they'd known about Saito's last-gasp warning message, they had used it to their own advantage.

'Here we go,' said the scarred man, pitching up his voice. 'Get ready. Remember your route. We don't want anyone wandering off.'

The other gunmen produced slim plastic tubes – chem-lights – and cracked them in the middle, shaking up the contents until they began to glow.

Lucy looked back at the monitor in time to see the truck vanish in a ball of white fire.

The hairs on her arms stood up and she tasted ozone. A split second later, the monitor died and so did the electric lights. The comms bead in her ear let out a nasty buzz and she flinched, reflexively jerking her head. She barely registered anything else before the rumble of the explosion rolled down into the basement.

A pallid green glow lit the faces of the gunmen, as each put their chemical lights on lanyards around their neck. Scar-face had sticks for the four captives, and clipped the tubes to their jackets before securing their wrists in front of them with cable ties.

'You try anything smart, and we'll smoke you right here.' He made the threat to all of them, but he stared into Lucy's eyes as he said it. 'Start walking.'

They marched them past another curtain of heavy tarps, and the last shafts of daylight filtering down through the construction site vanished. Lucy felt the ground beneath her feet change from concrete slab to broken rubble to aging brick. The damp reek of the sewer system engulfed her and she swallowed a retch.

As they passed into the full, cloying blackness beneath the city streets, she thought she heard something from up on ground level – the faint echo of people shouting and screaming.

Marc could only make a rough estimate as to how far they walked – half a dozen blocks at least. The tunnels had few markers, and with the weak glow of the chem-light on his collar, he could not see far. Sluggish water shimmered at the edge of his vision, and glimpsed movements along the brick courses had to be the biggest rats he'd ever seen.

Walking in silence, he concentrated on putting one foot in front of another, dimly aware of Lucy walking ahead of him and Malte a few paces behind. The gunmen were either vague shadows or bobbing blobs of pale green light, but they moved surely through the underground tunnel, finding turnings and changing direction without recourse to maps. That meant that they had committed this path to memory, which also discouraged Marc from the idea of ducking away at the first convenient opportunity. It wasn't the first time he'd been stuck in underground tunnels – there'd been those incidents in Paris and Naples – but he had no illusions of the dangers lurking in such places for the unprepared.

Breathing through his mouth, he tasted more than he smelled the change in atmosphere as they progressed. It grew colder and a dank, oily breeze forced its way along the tunnel and into their path.

The narrow walkway alongside the river of effluent became steeper, and Marc leaned forward, planting his feet carefully to avoid slipping on the wet bricks.

'Look sharp,' came a whisper from ahead of him, and Lucy's chem-light bobbed as she briefly turned her head towards Marc.

He passed it on, whispering in Malte's direction but unable to know if the Finn had even heard him.

The walkway continued to take them up towards ground level, and then ahead Marc saw the twinkle of distant stars, framed inside a ragged circle of grey light. He had the sudden mental image of being inside a black hole and staring out into space, trapped in a place from which light could not escape.

He blinked and reframed the sight. They were approaching the mouth of a wide tunnel, the cast-iron security grid across it already cut down and removed for easy egress. Out beyond the tunnel entrance, a wall of grey haze hung over dark, rain-lashed water. The stars that pierced the grey were the lights of buildings on a distant shore, the silhouettes of towers and apartment blocks lost in the downpour.

The gunmen led them back into the open air, and Marc's sense of direction reorientated itself, snapping into focus. The tunnels had taken the group away from Wall Street, down to the shore of the East River, bringing them to the surface beneath an industrial pier close to the ferry terminal.

The rain leading the storm up the coast beat hard across the pier's wooden planks, and it soaked through Marc's jacket in moments. He raised a hand to wipe water off his face as the wind pulled at them, and something instinctive made him turn back to look at the city. What he saw stopped him dead.

New York was lightless and silent.

Black slabs of obsidian had replaced every towering block as far as he could see, to Battery Park at the southern tip of Manhattan. A fire burned on the upper floors of a nearby building, flames spewing from the middle of an impact crater punched through the glass facade some twelve storeys off the ground. Marc remembered that the building was close to the Downtown heliport, and he pictured some luckless pilot racing to put down their aircraft before the bad weather hit, only to suffer systems failure from the EMP and go spiralling into the side of the tower.

To the north, the Brooklyn Bridge was a skeletal thing vanishing into the rain, the spans lit by sporadic points of light, likely from the few vehicles trapped there that had wiring old enough to have survived the invisible shock of the electromagnetic pulse. Any vehicle with a microchip in its ignition system would be nothing but dead metal.

Beyond that, Marc saw the darkness had smothered the Lower East Side. As far as he could make out, everything south of the Empire State Building was without power.

He heard Lucy curse under her breath and found her with her hand to her mouth, her eyes wide.

'This is *bad*,' she murmured.

There were more fires visible down along the canyons between the towers. Backlit pillars of thick smoke filled the width of Wall Street, spreading from the point where the device had detonated.

The weapon – the so-called 'equipment' they had tracked from Russia – had performed its role perfectly. The undetectable binary chemicals in its explosive trigger had combined into a lethal mix, which in turn detonated through a complex framework known as a flux compression generator. Essentially a large aluminium tube shrouded in a helix of copper wire, with a charge at one end and a power source at the other, the device transformed the explosive force into electromagnetic energy several orders of magnitude greater. Destroying itself in the process, it produced terawatts of EM radiation to fry anything electronic while leaving nearby structures relatively undamaged.

As Marc had predicted, the pulse had not only crashed through the computer systems of the financial district, but also brought down the power grid. One or two generator failures might have been enough for the city's infrastructure to manage, but a series of them in a single great cluster had overwhelmed it.

Keystone systems would collapse. Thousands of people would be trapped in stalled subway trains and darkened buildings. Hospitals, firefighters and police would struggle to cope – and with the storm bearing down, chaos was coming.

Discarding his disguise, the man with the Uzi threw his hard hat and vest aside and jabbed with his weapon.

'You ain't here to sightsee, move your asses!'

'All right,' said Marc, pulling Lucy away from the grim sight of the darkened skyline.

She took a shaky breath and met his eyes.

'Just like you said,' she whispered. 'What the hell do we do now?'

'Play it out,' he told her, conscious of the man with the gun listening to every word they said. 'We can still survive this.'

'Yeah, that's the ticket,' mocked the gunman. 'Think positive.'

With his free hand, he gave Marc a shove towards the end of the pier.

A rigid inflatable boat awaited them, outboard motor chugging as they scrambled aboard. A few of the armed men remained on the dock as the securing line was set loose and the boat cut away into the heavy swell.

Aware of the weapons trained on them, Marc and the others crouched in the bow, shivering as waves slopped over the sides and the heavy rain bore down.

'Where are you taking us?'

He looked around as they sped away from Manhattan and into the throat of the river. None of the gunmen ventured a reply.

'Not to Brooklyn, that's for damn sure,' Lucy noted.

The RIB turned from the far shore, where the EMP's effect had not reached, and turned towards the seething mass of slate-coloured cloud advancing from the south.

Marc tried to pick out Governor's Island or Liberty Island, but both were lost behind the curtains of rain that raced out of the storm and over the boat. Then, after an eternity of buffeting, juddering motion, he caught sight of a shape out on the water. A vessel, ghost-white against the grey.

The larger craft took on definition as the boat turned towards it. A billionaire's megayacht, its knife-like bow rose out of the water, shining like glazed porcelain. The running lights were doused and the only illumination came from subsurface glows along the vessel's underside.

Marc estimated it was sixty metres long, with shrouded decks stacked four high above the waterline, and the shape of a slim helicopter lashed to a landing pad over the midline. He had the impression of figures moving on the deck in shiny rain slickers, but in the gloom it was hard to tell how many.

The RIB pulled close to the starboard side beneath a retractable rig hanging over the water, and the gunmen connected it to dangling cables. Motors whined, hauling the boat off the river, before swinging it into a docking frame.

The men on the yacht were armed with the same weapons as Marc's captors, and they were equally curt with their commands. He followed Malte, Grace and Lucy down to the wet deck, but refused to be cowed by the count of the guns.

The yacht rose and fell evenly despite the choppy waters. He sensed a low vibration coming up through the soles of his trainers. The vessel held station, keeping steady through the use of side-thrusters beneath the waterline.

Scar-face and his gruff friend marched them down to the stern, past smoked-glass windows looking in on a gaudy drinkers' lounge and an on-board swimming pool lined with faux-Grecian statuary.

Marc's lip curled. Money clearly couldn't buy good taste.

'How come this tub has power?' Lucy moved close by, glancing at him.

'Waited out of range of the pulse,' guessed Marc. 'Either that or it's seriously hardened. Which would mean the owner is rich or paranoid.'

'Perhaps both,' added Malte, a few steps behind.

Marc shot Grace a look, but the woman said nothing. She'd been uncharacteristically quiet since the ambush at the van.

The group came around the rear of the vessel to what would have been the sun deck on a fine day, a sunken space looking over the stern in the direction of the stricken city. Before them, a hooded veranda led into the main deck and a dining room beyond. Sheltering there from the rain was an older man in a navy-style pea coat. He sat in an ornate chair that had clearly been brought out for his use, a thick cigar between his teeth.

Connaught Cassidy III was no less unattractive in real life than he had been in the surveillance files the Rubicon team had assembled on the American. His face was florid and his piggish eyes were narrowed. Adjusting the coat's collar, he gave a nod and the gunmen forced the four captives down on to their knees, separating the men and women into pairs. Marc resisted, and received a kick in the belly for his troubles.

'What in the name of all the saints is that smell?' The American's nose wrinkled. 'Something stinks.'

'We ... uh ... had to go through the sewers on our way out—' began the scarred man, but Cassidy spoke over him.

'I've always said, this city smells like stale piss. First time I came here, back when I was a boy, came off the bus at the Port Authority and the reek of it hit me. All the fancy tall buildings in the world don't stop city folk from being garbage.' He snorted at his own words, and sucked wetly on the cigar, blowing out grey-blue smoke. 'And lookit, see what trash I got here.'

Lucy faked a yawn. 'You gonna shoot us, get it over with, boomer.'

'Your woman don't know her place, that's the problem with her kind.' Cassidy addressed his reply towards Marc and Malte. 'I ain't ever been rushed into anything my whole life.'

He shifted in the chair, leaning forward as if he was waiting for a reply. Marc blinked away the rain soaking his hair and down his beard, giving the man nothing.

'You don't talk but you're telling me something I already know.' Cassidy drew on the cigar again. 'That Russki heathen pissed away how much money trying to rub out you and yours, and for what? Shit, he shoulda let me do it.' The American chuckled, the sound like cracking eggshells. 'I'll show him. That'll be a fine day, yes sir. The look on his face, I can't wait to see it. It'll stick in his craw, knowing I grabbed you and he didn't. And all it took was the right bait in the trap.'

A low thud carried to them from over the water – perhaps an explosion, it was hard to be sure. Back in Manhattan, the fallout from the power outage was worsening.

Cassidy raised an eyebrow. 'I gotta know. Which one of you killed the I-talian? You?' He pointed the red ember at the tip of the cigar at Marc. 'You?' Then towards Malte.

'Guess that answers *that* question,' said Lucy, from the side of her mouth.

'First we've heard of it, mate,' said Marc, not entirely truthfully. 'But good riddance to bad rubbish.'

'Marc Dane.' Cassidy sounded out his name, centring his attention on the Englishman. 'I know about you. You reckon you're a smart guy. Don't look so smart on your knees, you limey pussy.'

'I'm clever enough to know who topped Da Silvio.' Marc played out a shrug. 'I mean, you can't be so thick that you don't see Glovkonin's fingerprints all over it, yeah? Or am I giving you too much credit?'

The American's expression hardened. 'I can handle him.'

'I'm sure you believe that. I bet Da Silvio did, too.'

Cassidy let out another crackling chuckle, then spat on the deck. 'I never liked that wop punk anyhow. A damned degenerate and a liability. If the Ivan did him in, all the better. Saved my boys a bullet.' The American glanced at the man with the scar. 'Speaking of which . . . Mr Weldon, you *did* take out Glovkonin's trash, did you not?'

The gunman nodded. 'Yes, sir. We lost Creel in the exchange, he took a bad hit. But the Jap bought it. When this is over, the Feds are gonna find what's left of Saito in that smoking crater on Wall Street.'

'Ah, Mr Creel talked too much, anyhow.' Cassidy indicated the man with the sub-machine gun. 'You and Mr Bragg can find a replacement who can keep his mouth shut when we're done here.' The American puffed on the cigar again and glanced at Marc. 'Y'see, that's how I deal with rats in the house. You people don't got the hang of that yet.'

Lucy stared at the deck, and she said what they were all thinking. 'Someone gave us up.' She looked into Marc's eyes. 'Kara cut us loose back there. She could have—'

Cassidy started talking again. 'You play this game long enough, you figure out that there's two kinds of spies, darlin'. There's the ones whose throats you slit first chance you get, and the ones you keep on a leash.' He nodded towards another of his men, the one standing behind Lucy and Grace. 'Speaking of which . . .'

The man pulled a black anodised combat knife and stepped forward. For one horrible second, Marc thought he was going to put it to Lucy's throat, but he moved to Grace instead. The man with the blade bent down, and cut away the plastic ties holding the pale woman's hands together.

'About goddamn time,' she snapped, getting to her feet and rubbing her wrists.

'You . . .' Malte glared up at Grace with open loathing. 'You betrayed us.'

'Of course I did, idiot.' She shook her head incredulously, and grinned at Lucy. 'I'm the scorpion, remember? And you're the frogs, stung to death and drowning.' She rubbed the rain out of her hair and moved to the cover of the veranda, ignoring the American's annoyance at her presumption. Grace turned that icy, sociopathic smile of hers on Cassidy. 'Honestly, what took Glovkonin so damn long to reach out to me? I was starting to think I'd have to send a valentine!'

'You nasty little bitch.' Lucy's face twisted into an angry grimace. 'You don't know anything else, do you? You sold us out because that's all you're good at.'

Grace tossed off a glib shrug that made Marc want to throw her in the river.

'When you're under pressure, you go with what you know best, right? This way, I walk and you don't. It's all upside for me, sis.'

'Fuck off and die,' retorted Lucy.

But Grace wasn't done. She wanted to twist the knife.

'I can't believe you actually blamed that hacker chick – I mean, how dumb are you? Kitty-cat Kara has too many regrets to turn on her little gang here.'

'On that point, where *is* the other one?' said Cassidy.

'The girl in the van escaped,' said the man with the scar. 'I left a team back there to hunt her down. Won't take long.'

'She'll have gone to the police by now,' Marc broke in. 'Talked to our contact in the FBI. If I were you, I'd be more concerned about your situation than ours.'

'Cops and Feds?' Cassidy snorted in derision. 'With no power and no phones? How's that gonna happen? Face it, you're the losers here.' He looked Grace up and down, his expression becoming predatory. 'This one, she's everything her file says she is.' He ran a thick thumb over his neck. 'Shoulda done her in. That'd be the smart play.'

Lucy pulled at the ties securing her hands, flexing her fingers to keep the blood pumping.

'You read my dossier, Mr Cassidy?' Grace was saying, and she made a cooing noise. 'I'm flattered, I do declare.'

'I'm about to puke,' countered Lucy. Grace had done her shape-shifter thing again, changing her manner to fit the situation, becoming a woman that Cassidy would want to keep alive as opposed to the dangerous, unpredictable opportunist she really was. 'She'll gut you in your sleep, you can count on it.'

'I'm aware of her quirks.' Cassidy smiled. 'My long-standing contacts within the Central Intelligence Agency were happy to turn over the details of asset REGAL, as your friend here was formerly known. I pride myself on knowing good material when I see it . . . Grace understands the realities at play in this situation. The Russki's boy Andre went looking for her when he figured out that Jap assassin grew a conscience. But this young lady is delightfully unburdened by that kinda thing.'

Lucy shifted, moving to make sure her legs wouldn't go numb resting too long in a stress position. Watching for a moment to make a move, she kept up the conversation.

'She's messed up in the head.' For as long as Cassidy ran his mouth, they were still breathing, and men like him loved to hear the sound of their own voices. 'Shit. Maybe you *all* are. The cruelty is the point, right?'

Cassidy scowled at the accusation. Grace wasn't the only one who knew how to push someone's buttons. The older man didn't like the inference that he was involved in the Combine's scheme for less than noble reasons. He had a personal narrative that cast him as a hero, doing what must be done in order to save a wounded nation, and suggesting otherwise raised his ire.

'Why is it your kind think you're on the right side of history? You're wrong. You're a drag on the rest of us, with your bleeding heart bullshit!' Cassidy spat again, angrily this time. 'You and that

African, getting in the way . . . Well, let me tell you, he's gonna be dead for real this time, you can take that to the bank.'

'Solomon's a ghost,' said Marc, steel beneath the words. 'You're not going to get him.'

'I beg to differ.' Cassidy made an exaggerated show of looking at the big, expensive watch on his wrist. 'Right now he's either dead in some Istanbul shithole or wishin' he was.' He chuckled once more. 'The Russki, he's got himself a serious hate on for that fella, yes sir. Sent ALEPH's shooters in there to get him.'

Against the cold and the rain, a new heat burned across Lucy's face as Cassidy's words hit home. It was possible that Grace's betrayal had not just ensnared Lucy, Marc and Malte, but she could also have given up Solomon and the others in Turkey. The brutal possibility of losing the man who had been a surrogate father to her was hard to take.

As they always did, Lucy's fears crystallised into fury and she glared at the man in the chair.

'This whole damn game of yours is a piece of shit, you dumb redneck.' Cassidy reacted in disgust at her snarled retort, and she carried on before he could respond, jerking her head in the direction of the darkened island. 'You know what that is? That's N-Y-*fucking*-C. World's biggest collection of people who take no shit and give no fucks. You reckon a power cut will knock it down? We've had worse.' She sucked her teeth in mockery. 'New York don't play. Hicks like you never get that.'

Cassidy's face darkened, turning as thunderous as the skies overhead.

'You think so?' He growled the words. 'Let me tell you what you don't *get*, girl. While you and everyone infesting that cesspool you call home strut around and make noise, the adults are running the show!' He snapped his fingers and one of his men brought him a silver tablet computer, which Cassidy flicked around contemptuously. 'Understand what this is?' He held it up so they could see the screen.

Lucy recognised a stock market track, stark lines against the black backdrop like the ones that would turn up in stern financial reports on cable news. She wasn't an expert in that kind of thing by any stretch, but anyone could see that the graph's leading point was in free fall, plummeting endlessly downwards.

'That, girl, is the dollar bill dropping off a cliff.' Cassidy snorted and toyed with his cigar. 'Like a good soldier fallin' on his sword, Ol' Bill is gonna take one for the team.' He waved in the direction of the blacked-out city. 'This is the last part of something we've been planning for years. Thousands of operations, big and small. A push here, a pull there, makin' ready for a catastrophic financial collapse.' He sat back and sucked on the cigar. 'I'm already richer than shit, but when the smoke clears, I'm gonna make trillions from currency buys – me and my associates. Why, God himself will be a pauper before the Combine, when all is said and done. We will own the debt of the world.'

'You're greedy *and* deluded,' said Marc, with a sneer. 'There are backups. Fail safes. You can't tank the whole US economy with one power cut, no matter how many banks or stock exchanges you knock out.'

'You people never see the big picture,' countered Cassidy. 'What is it your boss was always sayin'? *Small actions with large consequences*, right? Let me tell you, my organisation took a leaf outta that book. The plan you know about isn't the only one in play. You have no idea.' He glanced at the stub of his cigar, and regretfully flicked it over the side of the boat. 'You're right on the money about those emergency backups, son. But *oh no ...*' He made a mock-scared face. 'They don't appear to be kickin' in! Almost as if we dealt with that already.'

'The interrupt ...' Marc stared at the deck, thinking it through. 'The other part of the equipment – that's what it was for ...'

'Keep goin', son, let's see if you can get there on your own.'

Cassidy signalled and one of his men brought him a tumbler of bourbon.

'Titanpointe,' said Marc, with a sudden flash of understanding.

The name ran a vague bell with Lucy – something to do with a National Security Agency operation – but she couldn't place it. Marc was clearly right, because the moment he said it, Cassidy gave him an indulgent nod.

'You're sharper than you look,' he smirked.

'How did you get it in there?' Marc challenged Cassidy for the answer.

'Well, I could tell you my boys here did some clandestine black helicopter raid, but honestly?' His smirk widened into the shit-eating grin of a man who believed he was the winner. 'That'd be a lie. Human weakness is the best key for any lock. You know how hard it is to get promoted in the NSA? My organisation helped facilitate a vacancy in exchange for some unrestricted access.'

'Shit.' Marc looked grim. He stared out towards the dark water.

'Indeed.' Cassidy finished his drink and handed off the empty glass, before rising to his feet. He pulled his pea coat closed. 'You'll forgive me, but I'm a mite cold now, so I'm goin' to retire for the evening and discuss Miss Grace's future here with our group.'

'What do we do with these three?' said the man with the Uzi.

'Why, Mr Bragg, I would imagine that is obvious.' Cassidy nodded towards the man with the scar. 'You and Mr Weldon are gonna take our guests below decks.' All his false bonhomie vanished in a flash. 'Kill them and put 'em in the chiller. We'll mail their corpses to Glovkonin when we're done here.'

Lucy stiffened as the gunmen came in to grab them, and she caught sight of Grace leaning in to speak to Cassidy.

'Can I do it? I gotta admit, I've been thinking about offing them since forever.'

Malte glanced in Marc's direction.

'Will you tell her? Or should I?'

Lucy frowned, sensing a joke she wasn't getting. She remembered Marc and Malte talking to Kara before they left Queens, and now she wondered, *did they set something up without me knowing?*

When Marc looked back at Cassidy, there was a cold glitter in his eyes, as icy as the driving rain.

'Thing about scorpions,' he began, 'you know they're going to sting you sooner or later. It's in their nature, yeah?' He turned his attention to Grace. 'We knew you were going to double-cross us. And knowing what's coming, that's what keeps you alive. That's how you survive.'

From the corner of her vision, Lucy saw a shadow moving on the water, and the flicker of dim lights. She kept her eyes straight ahead, betraying nothing.

Grace laughed out loud. 'You're not going to survive this, Dane.'

'I'll take that bet,' he said.

From out of the storm haze, a shift in the wind brought the rumble of approaching engines to the rain-lashed sun deck, and without warning the stern of the yacht was flooded with the brilliant white glow of a searchlight.

'*This is the United States Coast Guard,*' bellowed a voice across an amplified PA speaker. '*Stand to and prepare to be boarded!*'

NINETEEN

The light was so powerful that it stung Lucy's eyes like acid, and she cried out in pain, bringing up her arm to shield herself.

Long ago on a live-fire exercise, she had been subjected to the effects of a flashbang grenade as part of a 'hardening' experience designed to acclimatise her to the sense-deadening properties of the weapon, and getting a million-candlepower spotlight in the face brought that flooding back.

She cursed through the pain and the temporary blindness, letting her other senses take over. Her one advantage was that everyone else on the yacht's sun deck would be in the same situation, but they wouldn't be equipped to deal with it like her.

Lucy fixed in her mind's eye where that asshole with the Uzi had been standing, and she bolted up from her crouch, throwing herself in the right direction. Her wrists were secured together in front of her, so she made fists and pushed them, double-barrelled, into the place where she thought Bragg would be.

She was off by a few degrees and the punch missed. Instead, she collided bodily with the gunman, and he panicked under the sudden, unexpected attack.

Lucy heard him yell as he floundered backwards, and then the Micro Uzi discharged in a fizzing, ripping whine of bullets as he mashed the trigger. She dived for the deck, bouncing off and behind an emergency life raft case. Bragg stumbled and went over the edge of the sun deck with a yell. She heard him hit the water with a heavy splash.

The wildfire burst from the sub-machine gun must have clipped the hull of the Coast Guard ship, because in the next second there was a shout from the direction of the other vessel.

'Taking fire!'

The response was exactly what she'd expected.

'*Weapons free!*' barked the voice over the PA, and before the echo of the command faded, sharpshooters on the ship were opening up.

Lucy shrank into her meagre cover as the firing began in earnest. Cassidy's men shot back, and the wet air was filled with shrieking rounds crossing back and forth over the water. Her vision was clearing, but blurred with purple after-images seared into her retinas. She saw one man go down with a torso hit, then a second take one in the leg and crumple.

Feeling her way down to her boot, Lucy found the length of flexible saw concealed in its heel loop and tore it out, working the cutter quickly through her wrist ties.

Chancing another look, she spotted Grace as the other woman grabbed the startled Cassidy by the folds of his bulky coat. The man was slow and out of shape, and he couldn't stop her from pivoting him right into the line of fire, giving her cover as she moved away from the yacht's open stern. Lucy saw the sudden flush of abject terror as he realised the woman was using him as her meat-shield.

Cassidy had reflexively drawn a weapon of his own in the chaos of the Coast Guard's arrival – some shiny nickel-plated replica of a Wild West-era Colt Peacemaker. A smarter man, someone in the habit of following rules other than his own, might have left the gun in its holster in this situation. Cassidy wasn't that man, waving the weapon around impotently, dazzled by the searchlight beam.

One of the Coast Guard shooters saw the gun, and Cassidy gave a sudden, twitching jerk, falling against Grace as a bloom of wet crimson appeared on his belly. She pushed him away before they could get entangled, and fled through the open glass doors into the main deck.

Lucy knew that the smart play was to stay exactly where she was, keep her head down until the shooting stopped, then surrender to the Coasties when they boarded and take it from there. But the thought of letting Grace bury the knife in their backs again, and then get free and clear, was like fire in her veins.

Her instinct about the woman had been right from the start, and if she allowed Grace to escape now, Lucy would not be able to forgive herself.

The ties around her wrists gave way and as she threw them aside, the spotlight from the Coast Guard boat shifted as the other vessel moved closer. Lucy used the moment and burst out from behind the cover of the lifeboat container. She sprinted past Cassidy, where the man's cooling corpse lay in an ugly heap on the rain-slick deck, following Grace deeper into the yacht's interior.

Marc ducked away from the glare of blinding white, into the sharp-edged shadows cast by a dinghy mounted off the deck. Still, it felt like being at ground zero for a nuclear detonation, as the wash of searing light hit him as a physical blow. It was day and night compared to moments earlier in the dimness of the rainstorm, and his dark-adapted eyes ached in their sockets.

Blinking away the after-images, he cast around, searching for Lucy or Malte, but saw only vague, undefined shapes. Then there was a sudden movement, resolving into one of Cassidy's thugs coming after him. Weldon, the one with the scar that made everything he said come out in a jeer.

The gunman had a pained expression on his face and a heavy Kimber pistol in his hand, the weapon extended out at the end of his arm as he followed Marc into the shadows.

Mistake, thought Marc.

Weldon's advance showed he was someone who relied more on the weapon than his ability with it to get what he wanted. Holding the gun out at arm's length was a street thug's move, not the mark of someone properly skilled in wielding a firearm.

Back in Fort Monckton during his MI6 training, Marc had had small arms lessons barked at him by SAS instructors who were deeply aggrieved at having to teach novice spooks like him – but what they taught had stuck, including the warning to always keep your gun close, where only you could control it.

Half-dazzled by the searchlight, Weldon let his weapon lead him, and Marc took advantage of his error. He rocked forward, slipping inside the man's guard, and threw a punch that landed in Weldon's chest.

The gunman swore and fired, the loud bang of the Kimber's discharge sounding over Marc's shoulder, the round tearing a hole in the dinghy. Marc swung again and Weldon ducked, but the gunman overcompensated and slipped on the wet deck.

Marc seized the opportunity and shot a kick at Weldon's ankle to send him down, but he didn't account for the motion of the yacht as the vessel sank into a trough between waves. The blow connected, but Marc's balance was gone. He felt his right leg bend underneath him and he crashed backwards into the side of the dinghy, striking his head on the gunwale.

'Fucker,' snarled Weldon, and he came up again, aiming the pistol at a point right between Marc's eyes.

'Quit running, Grace!' Lucy shouted the words down the corridor before her. 'You'll only die tired!'

The main deck dining area of Cassidy's yacht led into a central walkway with doors leading off to staterooms. The corridor floors – not just the one beneath her feet, but those below that – were made from some kind of turquoise tempered glass that let you look straight down to the levels below.

Shimmering light glowed from the lowest deck, and Lucy guessed there might be a moon pool there – an opening in the bottom of the yacht below the waterline where divers could go straight out into the water. Maybe that was where Grace was headed, but the thought of it gave Lucy pause. Even in a wetsuit and scuba gear, even if it had been a calm summer's day, she didn't relish the idea of swimming in the heavy murk of the East River.

Up ahead where this floor ended, twin marble-effect staircases coiled away in an open space that led down to the keel deck, and Lucy tried to catch a glimpse of what might be waiting for her, searching for some ghost of Grace's presence. She could see some gaudy art thing made of gold ropes and porcelain sea shells, an impressionistic idea of a fisherman's net filled with ocean bounty.

As if she read her mind, Grace's voice came echoing back along the corridor.

'This tub, huh? Cassidy ought to get a refund from his interior decorator. I've been in greasy clam bars with more class.' She was putting on a Long Island accent, dialling it up to mock Lucy. 'Hey, but he's dead – too bad. And so are you.'

A shadow moved near the edge of the stairwell and Grace leaned out of cover with Cassidy's gun in her hand. She fired three rounds in quick succession, both shots hitting close, blasting divots out of the panelling near Lucy's head but not tagging her.

Instinct told Lucy to draw back and seek cover, as she had out on the sun deck, but training overruled the innate reaction and she ran towards the danger, kicking off the wall of the narrow corridor so the other woman couldn't draw a bead on her.

Lucy gambled that Grace was unfamiliar with the Peacemaker, a gun she doubted Connaught Cassidy III had ever fired in anger. Another shot cut past her, the buzz of the heavy round loud in her ear.

She wanted to force Grace to *react* instead of *act*. The other woman wasn't a soldier and she didn't possess the warrior mindset that US Army Special Forces had drilled into Lucy Keyes until it became second nature.

Grace was an infiltrator, a runner not a fighter, and Lucy remembered what she had said back on the deck. *When you're under pressure, you go with what you know best, right?* Lucy cranked up the stress to make Grace revert to type.

The other woman saw Lucy coming, eyes alight with controlled rage, and true to form, she broke cover. Grace fired blind as she ran, abandoning her position to seek safety elsewhere. She dashed towards the staircase, taking the steps two at a time.

With a yell of effort, Lucy leapt off the upper deck banister, out over the open space, coming down on her target like a tiger pouncing on its prey.

Marc had nowhere to go.

The Kimber's muzzle yawned before him, rain sluicing down the pistol's blocky frame. At close range, the bullet would cut right through his skull and over-penetrate, blowing out the contents of his head across the deck in a bloody mess. He had no intention of letting that happen.

Marc threw up his hands and slammed the heel of his palm as hard as he could into the barrel of the gun, clutching at the slide, grabbing it, pressing it back.

Weldon mashed the trigger, but the pistol would not fire. With the semi-automatic's mechanism forced out of true, there was no way for the hammer to fall and set off the round in the chamber.

The two men began a desperate push-pull as they wrestled over the weapon. Marc tried to twist it away with both hands, and Weldon flailed. He landed a tooth-rattling punch that struck Marc's jaw, then grabbed at the weapon to steady himself as he felt his grip slipping. The Kimber's muzzle dipped, aiming downwards, and Marc let go.

Weldon's thick finger had already depressed the trigger back to the stop, and when Marc's grip on the pistol's slide released, the gun discharged with an angry crash.

Weldon screamed. The shot entered his right leg down through the shin and exited into the deck through the bottom of his foot, shattering bone, tearing muscle and ligament. The gunman twisted in agony and collapsed, losing his grip on the gun.

Without thinking, Marc kicked the pistol over the side and left the man there, whimpering in agony. He fled the sun deck, to find the outboard staircase that would take him to the yacht's upper levels.

The two women collided and tangled together. Lucy and Grace rebounded off the wall of the narrow atrium and fell as one, tumbling down the curved staircase, viciously punching and grabbing at each other as they went.

Grace's momentum carried them towards the open space and they fell, crashing into the gold netting of Cassidy's gaudy art installation. The gun was gone, so the fight turned into a nasty, clumsy series of kicks and strikes. For a few seconds, the net hung suspended in the air between decks; then the bolts securing it sheared off under the weight of the two combatants and they fell the rest of the way to the keel deck, slamming into the floor.

The landing shocked the air out of Lucy's lungs and she tasted copper in her mouth. Grace was quicker to recover and pitched up, planting a downward blow with her elbow right into Lucy's stomach. She cried out, coughing blood and spittle as Grace scrambled away.

They were at the end of a short corridor that terminated in the door to the moon pool. Grace was intent on something, and she didn't see Lucy come after her, throwing her weight into a tackle that brought the other woman back to the deck.

'Get off me!'

Grace directed a sharp kick behind her, her boot connecting with her attacker's cheekbone. Lucy reeled away, momentarily stunned by the blow, and before she could recover, Grace came in with another kick that hit her in the chest.

But then Grace made the mistake of trying for a third shot, and even in her shaken state, Lucy caught it as it came. She trapped the other woman's leg, tried a scissor-break that didn't pay off, and then lurched forward, briefly taking Grace off the floor before slamming her back down on it.

'*Bitch!*'

Grace howled in pain and her fist came swinging up with something bone-white and jagged in it – a broken piece of one of the porcelain oyster shells. She jammed the tip of her makeshift dagger into Lucy's leg, above the knee, and it slashed through the tactical nylon fabric and into flesh.

Lucy let go with a low, lingering snarl of agony, pulling out the fragment before it could do more damage. Ahead of her, Grace scrambled across the debris-strewn floor towards where Cassidy's revolver had fallen. The other woman snatched up the weapon.

Ignoring the stinging burn through her thigh, Lucy grabbed Grace's ankle before she could pull herself up, and yanked her as hard as she could. On the smooth floor, Grace had no purchase, and she slipped towards Lucy, twisting around.

The gun in her hand, Grace flipped on to her back and swung the weapon in Lucy's direction, her finger tightening on the trigger. Lucy saw light glint off the barrel and threw up her arm to knock it aside. The Peacemaker boomed, the bullet missing, cracking into the glass ceiling above them.

'No,' Lucy grated, and with a savage jerking motion, she wrenched the gun from Grace's grip by the searing hot barrel, and cracked her across the face with the rosewood-inlaid butt.

Grace staggered back, blood streaming down her pale skin from a cut beneath her eye. Her hands rose in a gesture of submission as Lucy twirled the gun around to aim it towards her. She stumbled back through the doorway into the moon pool room, and her face creased into a mask of childlike fear.

'No, please stop!' Tears welled and ran down Grace's cheeks. She gave a shuddering sob. 'Don't kill me, I'm begging you! I'm just trying to survive!'

Like turning over a card, the aspect Grace showed changed from one extreme to another. A heartbeat earlier, it was feral hatred glittering in her eyes. Now she appeared broken and pathetic, exuding pitiable, wretched fragility.

Most people found it impossible to be truly callous, to inflict pain on someone begging for mercy. It was conditioned into them, some deep moral human code that prevented all but the most ruthless from taking a life without pause.

Grace knew that, playing on the instinct, manipulating Lucy with each breath she took. It was her weapon. And ultimately, it was her curse. Everything about her was a lie, and this was no different.

'Please!' Grace sobbed. 'I surrender!'

'I don't care,' said Lucy, in a voice weighed down with fatigue and antipathy.

She fired the last round in the Peacemaker's cylinder, putting the shot through Grace's heart. The other woman fell away, crashing into the dark waters of the moon pool.

Lucy watched her sink into the murk and vanish from sight. She wanted to feel something – some surge of triumph – but there was only ashes. It was still a long way from anything that could be thought of as a victory.

The cleats securing the weather cover over the helicopter came loose with quick-release switches, and Marc unfastened the first few before the wind came in and tore the cover away. It snapped in the air, still locked in on the starboard side, flapping in the rain like a torn sail.

The helicopter beneath was a dark blue R44 Raven II, a four-seater with a teardrop fuselage and spindly rotors. Marc had no time on this model, but he was willing to wing it. Crouching low, he found and disengaged the clamps that held the landing skids fixed to the yacht.

The firefight on the sun deck ended in a last, desultory salvo from Cassidy's men as they woke up to the fact that their boss was dead. None of the survivors wanted to risk going overboard into the churning river, so they dropped their weapons and knelt as the Coast Guard patrol boat held station a hundred metres off the stern. A Guard RIB was already in the water, and from up on the highest point on the yacht, Marc could see it approaching. They would send a full boarding group equipped with M4 carbines and body armour and, like the gunmen, Marc had no desire to draw their fire.

The wind buffeted the helicopter and it shifted above him, one skid lifting slightly then settling again. A powerful gust might be enough to knock the whole thing off the helipad, so his next decision had to be the right one.

The moment he started the rotors, the Coast Guard operatives would know it, and they wouldn't differentiate between him and Cassidy's mercenaries. He would have to get into the air and away as fast as possible – and that led in to another grim question. The stormy skies over the East River were most definitely *not* helicopter weather, and it was 50–50 that a lightweight bird like the Raven would make it far in this punishing deluge.

The last time Marc Dane had flown in a storm as fierce as this, it had damn near killed him. The cold and the wet soaking through his clothes made him feel leaden and afraid, the old trauma of that terrible crash in the South China Sea threatening to unfold and smother him.

'Piss off!' he growled, banishing the recollection like an errant ghost.

Boots scraped on the metal ladder behind him and he rolled over, expecting to see one of Cassidy's thugs coming up to the helipad. The face he saw was a welcome one; Malte limped into view, crouching to minimise his silhouette.

'Will it fly?' whispered the Finn, nodding at the helicopter.

Marc ducked the question with one of his own. 'Where's Lucy? I'm not going without her.'

Malte grimaced and pointed downwards. Black-clad men with rifles were swarming up boarding ladders from the RIB. He heard them shouting out commands to their captives.

Then someone on the deck below gave a low whistle.

'Marc? Malte? You up there?' Lucy's voice rose on the breeze.

He felt a flash of relief. 'Yeah. You want a lift?'

'Hell yeah.'

Malte scrambled into the back of the Raven as Marc helped Lucy up the last few steps to the helipad. Below them, the voices of the boarding team were getting closer, and he saw blobs of illumination crossing the deck from the tactical lights on their weapons.

Lucy groaned and lurched against him.

'You hurt?' He eyed her.

'I'll walk it off.'

He saw a makeshift, bloodstained bandage around her thigh, deducing the source of the injury.

'Grace?'

'The scorpion drowned,' she replied.

He knew enough not to push that any further, and guided her into the co-pilot's seat. The wind pushed at the helicopter once more as Marc removed the last tie-downs on the rotors, and the blades spun lazily of their own accord.

'I hear movement,' called someone on the deck below. 'See anything?'

'Negative,' came a reply, from directly beneath Marc's feet. 'Get a light up there!'

'Shit!'

Marc leapt into the cockpit and threw the switches that would start the Raven's engine. The motor gave a choking thud and thank-fully engaged first time, the digital displays on the instrument panel in front of him blinking on. The rotors cut through the rain, rapidly picking up speed, and from that second there wasn't anyone on the yacht who didn't know what Marc was attempting. Spinning up the blades took forever, as the engine's high-pitched whine sounded out over the water.

Someone in the boarding team radioed their patrol boat, and the searchlight on the Coast Guard vessel cranked up and around, pivoting to throw its hard illumination at the helicopter. The beam pinned the aircraft against the deep grey of the storm clouds, making it a target for everyone with a gun.

They couldn't wait any longer. Marc applied power and the Raven lifted. He wasn't experienced with its yoke-type controls, so he understeered on the take-off, and the helicopter scraped across the narrow landing pad, yawing wildly to port. He worked the yoke back the other way, again by too far a margin, and the Raven bounced into the air, right into another surge of wind.

He almost lost it right there. An invisible claw of air swatted at them, rain bursting across the curved canopy. The Raven rotated around its axis, dropping alarmingly to wave-top level before lurching into a shaky ascent.

Sparks of yellow flashed on the deck of the yacht as the boarding team bracketed them with gunfire, and Marc felt the thuds of bullets burying themselves in the fuselage. The patrol boat's searchlight turned to chase them as he aimed the Raven away from the yacht and guided it back in the direction of Manhattan.

'Anyone hit?' Lucy shouted to be heard over the lashing rain and the shrill cry of the engines.

No one responded in the affirmative, but Marc knew the helicopter was bleeding out. The controls juddered in his grip, the oil pressure dropped like a stone and the air in the cabin turned acrid with the smell of burnt plastic.

Clinging to her seat, Lucy looked out into the gloomy half-light.

'Where are you gonna land this thing?'

'Wherever I can,' said Marc.

Lucy chewed on the pain from her leg and used it to keep herself centred. The helicopter flight became a hellish roller coaster ride as the constant wind buffeted the aircraft.

She banged against the inside of the cockpit door, struggling to strap in. She was like a bug in a jar inside the helo's bubble canopy, shaken about by some bored kid. Outside, it was impossible to tell where the grey water of the East River ended and the grey clouds of the storm began. With the sunset long gone and half of Manhattan as dark as a tomb, all she could pick out were fires and a few hazy pinpricks of light on the shore.

Marc's face was drawn and pale, eyes locked to an invisible horizon as he fought the controls. The helicopter rose and fell at random intervals, and with each stomach-lurching drop, Lucy was sure they would go spinning into the turbulent waters of the bay.

She locked her straps in and shot a look at Malte behind her.

'What happened back there? Who called the cavalry?'

'Kara,' said the Finn. 'Like he said.' He nodded towards Marc. 'She called the police.'

Lucy wondered what that conversation would have sounded like. How would New York's law enforcers react to learning, in the immediate aftermath of an attack, that international fugitives were in their city chasing down a criminal conspiracy?

Of course they would send the Coast Guard, armed to the teeth, she thought. *Everyone believes Rubicon are terrorists, thanks to the Combine's propaganda.*

The helicopter dived again and Marc let out a yell of surprise as a huge, slab-sided shape reared up out of the rain-fog before them. Lucy had a brief impression of a window-studded orange wall with STATEN ISLAND FERRY along the side, before the pilot desperately kicked the pedals to veer them up and away from the darkened hulk of the boat.

The skids bounced off the ferry's central funnel in a shower of sparks, and she heard cries of fright from passengers trapped aboard the drifting, powerless vessel.

'Marc, tell me you got this!' Lucy held on with a white-knuckled death grip.

'I'm shitting myself,' he shot back, matter-of-factly. 'Other than that, bloody brilliant.'

'We need to put down,' she went on, and out through the canopy she saw a familiar expanse of trees swaying in the squall. 'There! The Battery!'

'Good enough.' Marc aimed the nose towards the clump of parkland at the tip of Manhattan. 'This'll be rough,' he warned.

Whatever weather gods were playing with the helicopter must have been listening, because they chose that moment to swat the lightweight little chopper with a hammer of air and rainwater.

The Raven fell out of the sky too fast for Marc to correct, and he wrenched back the controls, flaring the nose. The tail rotor clipped the branches of a plane tree and ripped clean off.

Striking the grass a hundred metres short of the old Castle Clinton fort, the port landing skid snapped and the helicopter rolled. The rotor blades chopped into the muddy earth and shredded as the aircraft skidded to a halt on its side.

'Out!' yelled Malte, kicking open the hatch.

Rain poured in, whipping around the cabin.

Lucy fumbled at her straps, grateful that she had taken the time to secure them. Marc took her arm and she took his, and together they climbed awkwardly from the creaking wreck.

Dropping to the ground sent a new shock of pain up Lucy's leg and she let out a sullen growl. Malte offered her support, but she waved him away and limped doggedly towards the street.

Dozens of stalled cars choked the road and shadowy figures moved in the dimness, the people caught by the effects of the EMP still struggling to grasp what had happened to them.

Driving rain moved across the asphalt in hard sheets, and the three survivors of the crash huddled together. With no shelter, they pushed forward, fighting the wind with each step.

Marc surveyed the darkened streets and lightless buildings.

'You know this town like the back of your hand, yeah?'

'Sure,' said Lucy, catching her breath.

'Hanover Square,' he added. 'Where's that?'

She paused to orientate herself, then pointed.

'That way. It's not far.'

'Show us,' said Marc.

The location Marc wanted was around the corner from a triangle of ornamental gardens dedicated to Queen Elizabeth II. A patriotic in-joke, he explained, a deliberate choice by MI6 planners in the placement of a clandestine safe house in New York City, putting it right under the noses of 'the Cousins', as the men in charge liked to call the American security services.

A skinny door led into the dark, narrow hallway of a shabby four-storey brownstone that shared the street with a gentrified cafe and craft beer bar. Those places were full of worried people afraid to go out in the storm, and they didn't notice the injured woman and her two friends enter the neighbouring building, just as they hadn't noticed the old Ford Econoline van that had parked up shortly after the power went out.

A second door at the end of the hall looked like it was made of wood, but it had a bulletproof steel core. Marc frowned at the lifeless electronic lock and considered his next move.

'How d'you know about this place?' said Lucy, leaning against the wall.

'Not my first visit,' he admitted. His tactical unit, the OpTeam codenamed Nomad, had run a covert snatch and grab mission here in the mid-2010s, basing themselves out of the safe house for the duration. 'I'm just glad it's still operational.'

'MI6 will not be happy,' noted Malte.

'Yeah, well, they can send me the bill, can't they?' He made a fist and pounded on the door, deciding that the low-tech approach was the best. 'Kara? You in there? It's us!'

At length, the door groaned as the bolts on the other side were manually released, and it creaked open. The muzzle of a shotgun peeked out into the hallway.

'What's the password?' hissed Kara.

'Reindeer flotilla,' retorted Marc.

The movie reference would be lost on most people, but he knew Kara would appreciate it.

'Nerd.'

The hacker beckoned them inside.

Malte secured the door behind them as Lucy made a beeline for a first aid kit. The place hadn't changed much in the last half-decade. The walls were stripped to bare brick, the windows sealed up, the high-ceilinged interior divided into three main sections – a kitchen area, a workspace and a set of bunk beds. The wind outside moaned through the air vents, giving the scene a grim chorus.

Lights burned around the work area, powered by battery packs stored in the basement for such an eventuality as a power outage. Kara's ruggedised laptop had centre stage, its screen alight with data.

'How is that thing still working?' Lucy nodded at the machine as she peeled off the makeshift bandage around her leg and tended to her wound.

'Please,' said Kara. 'We go looking for a military-grade transient electromagnetic device, of course I'm going to bring my most hardened gear.' She tapped the laptop lovingly. 'It's tempest-screened, ray-shielded and armour-plated. It could get struck by lightning and you'd still be able to check your emails.' She waved at the air. 'Most of the tech in this place was fried like everything else, but I managed to get some systems back up. Lucky for us no one was using it.'

'Yeah, lucky. Good job.' Marc gave her a pat on the shoulder and helped himself to a bottle of isotonic drink cooling on the counter. 'We'll patch up, re-arm and stage from here.'

He looked around, then sat heavily on a threadbare sofa in the middle of the room, blowing out a sigh.

'Someone want to bring me up to speed?' Lucy winced as she applied an anti-infective and fresh dressings to the cut in her thigh. 'Start with what you didn't tell me.'

Marc, Malte and Kara exchanged glances.

'Sorry about that,' said the Englishman. 'But I needed you to keep Grace occupied while we set it up.'

Kara threw Malte a questioning look, asking, *Where is Grace?* The Finn made a silent throat-cutting motion. The hacker pursed her lips and nodded.

'We knew she'd stab us in the back,' continued Marc. 'So I put a contingency plan in place. Kara calls the law and tells them we're here, lets them come after us.' He held up a hand before Lucy could complain. 'I know, it's a shitty plan, but as usual, our options sucked.'

'I don't like being outside the loop,' retorted Lucy.

'Won't happen again,' he promised.

'How'd the Coasties find us, anyhow?' She looked at Kara.

'Rubicon-issue smartphones have a redundant emergency tracer installed in them,' said the hacker. 'Even if the device is zapped by an EMP, the last thing it does is crack a tiny low-level radiation source inside the case. That can be located with the right gear. I tracked that, and gave the co-ordinates to the Feds.'

Marc pulled his spyPhone from his pocket and his expression turned sorrowful.

'Ah, bollocks.' He gave it a shake and heard what sounded like particles of sand shifting around inside it. 'It's buggered. And this was the last one. I feel like I've lost an old mate.'

Kara took it off him. 'Leave it with me. I'll see what I can do.'

'We could have ended up shot or in jail.' Lucy came over and snatched the drink bottle from him, draining the rest of it.

'I did say it was a shitty plan. I'm not denying that.'

She sat next to him. 'I hope you got a better one to follow.'

'I have.' He shook his head. 'You're not going to like it.'

'Do I ever?' She made a *come on* gesture. 'Back on the boat, that name you mentioned to Cassidy. *Titanpointe*. Where do I know that from?'

Kara's jaw dropped. 'Did she just say . . .?'

Marc nodded. 'Titanpointe is the designation for a classified NSA facility right here in the Big Apple. It's a monitoring and security hub that sits on top of the main digital communications lines going up and down the east coast, and beyond.'

'The NSA use it to spy on the internet,' said Kara. 'Read your emails, watch your cat videos . . .'

'But it's also a protective measure.' Marc made a turning motion with his hand. 'In the event of a catastrophic incident that could potentially affect the whole of the US digital network, it can reboot the system.' He mimed the action, as if typing on a keyboard. 'It's supposed to be the unjammable fail safe.'

'You know a lot about it,' noted Malte.

'Let's say that MI6 and GCHQ took a few passes at the thing back in the day, and leave it at that, yeah?'

'But the fail safe isn't kicking in?' Lucy said, off Marc's nod. 'So the interrupt, that tech from the lab in Turkey, how does that figure into this?'

'The Combine implanted it inside Titanpointe, inside the hub,' said Marc.

'It's preventing the network from rebooting itself,' said Kara. 'Every second the interrupt is active, stocks, shares and currency values are in a nosedive, and the Combine rake in the profit from betting against them. Eventually, it will self-correct, but that could take days. By then, trillions of dollars will have been wiped off the US economy. And then there's the knock-on effect to global markets—'

'Enough,' said Lucy, raising her hands. 'I get it.' She looked at Marc. 'So we find the interrupt, disconnect it, stop the . . . whatever. The system reboots, the Combine are shit out of luck, right? Where is this thing?'

'Thomas Street. Number 33, the Long Lines building.'

She grinned. 'Hey, no problem, that's like a mile away . . .' Then the expression slipped off her face as she realised what Marc was referring to. 'Wait. You're talking about that blind skyscraper in the middle of Tribeca. Five hundred feet high, not a single window. Like something out of *The X-Files*.'

'That's the one.'

Of course, Lucy knew the building they were referring to; anyone who knew Manhattan would – the sinister sandstone-coloured tower that lurked behind the nearby Federal Building. There were countless urban legends about the place, ranging from UFO-nut tinfoil-hat stuff to details of mass surveillance programs based there, as leaked by intelligence community whistle-blowers.

She took a second to process that.

'We have to break into an NSA secure facility, inside a hardened building designed to withstand a nuclear attack, in the middle of a city-wide power outage, during the worst storm of the year. That's your plan?'

Marc nodded. 'I said you weren't going to like it.'

TWENTY

Sunset over the Alps brought new snowfall, and with it fell the plots displayed on the screens around Rutger Bremmens. Outside the temperature plummeted, and the indicators of the global financial sphere were on a similar downward trend, fuelled by panic in the markets as the news from New York echoed around the planet.

The data feed from the NY Stock Exchange was dead, a blackened pane among the cascades of failure-red dominating the other indicators. Another glass screen showed news from several international channels, and all of them had the same images behind their talking heads – shaky hand-held video of Manhattan's stormy skyline, shrouded in darkness.

Bremmens lost himself in his work, tapping at the tablet computer with his wrinkled fingers, the glow of the screens reflecting in his unfashionably bulky glasses. Nearby, Glovkonin rested against a thick wooden balustrade and watched the banker in his element, the older man's bloodless face taking on a vacant quality as he communed with his numbers. Bremmens blinked his watery blue eyes, muttering under his breath.

'Why do you wear those?' Glovkonin asked, bored with his inactivity. He pointed at his face.

'What?' Bremmens retorted sharply, perturbed by the distraction.

'The spectacles?' Glovkonin pushed off and approached him, swirling the brandy in the glass he held. 'I've never understood that affectation. You could afford the finest ophthalmic medicine in the world.'

Bremmens blanched, losing pace for a moment.

'The thought of someone firing laser beams into my corneas sickens me.'

'If you cannot see clearly, imagine what you might miss.' It amused Glovkonin that something so mundane could unsettle the banker. But then, he was a peculiar sort, fussy and obsessive over some details, and blinkered in other matters. At length, the Russian relented and gestured at the screens. 'How goes it?'

'It goes as well as it did when you asked me that question thirty-two minutes ago,' Bremmens said irritably, and he pointed to a secondary display where the value of the Combine's monetary worth showed as a rising graph. 'We grow wealthier by the minute. Does that satisfy you?' He didn't pause for a reply. 'Please do not distract me.'

The older man's tone chafed, and Glovkonin considered a retort, but then a voice called out from the floor below.

'Sir?'

It was Misha, his bodyguard. He held a satellite phone in one hand and the ex-soldier's craggy face was sombre. Standing at Misha's side, the bland aide working for Bremmens looked equally discomfited.

'There has been a development.'

The Swiss muttered again and put his work on standby, stalking away down the wide stairs back to the atrium level. Glovkonin followed him, draining the last dregs of his brandy as they descended.

'I left strict instructions not to disturb us,' Bremmens told his aide.

'Unless certain criteria were met,' said the man, shifting nervously. 'They have been.'

'Speak up,' snapped Glovkonin, glaring at Misha.

'There is an unconfirmed report from New York,' said the bodyguard, his voice a sullen bear's growl. 'The American Coast Guard opened fire on Mr Cassidy's yacht. He may be dead.'

Bremmens stiffened, turning to his aide.

'Is this accurate?'

'It is difficult to get confirmation, given the situation in the city,' said the younger man. 'But the initial report appears to be authentic.'

Glovkonin schooled his grave expression, but inwardly he smiled. After making contact with the woman Grace, his generous offer to her hinged on the completion of two actions: first, that she betray any efforts by the remnants of Rubicon to interfere with the New York operation; and second, that she find a way to terminate Connaught Cassidy III after the fact.

Has she succeeded?

The end result was the same. The controlling cabal of the organisation known as the Combine now comprised solely the Russian oligarch and the Swiss financier.

'You are dismissed. You and the rest of the staff are to remain in quarters,' snapped Bremmens. 'I do not wish to see any of you again until you have complete information on this matter.'

'Yes, sir,' said the aide, and he backed away, bowing anxiously like some courtier chastised by his king.

Glovkonin told Misha to make himself scarce, and then it was only he and the banker in the echoing room before the roaring fireplace. The older man stared into the middle distance, recalculating, mentally sifting through the profits and losses in his head as he balanced Cassidy's death against their current situation.

The Russian strolled back to the well-stocked bar and selected a bottle of Zuger Kirsch, slow-pouring a measure of the brandy into a fresh glass.

'This is an unexpected development,' he offered.

After a moment, Bremmens came back from his contemplation.

'Unexpected,' he echoed, 'but we can adapt.' He advanced on Glovkonin, distrust glittering in his gaze. 'First Giovanni meets his end, and now Connaught. The timing is suspicious.'

Glovkonin savoured the brandy. 'We have many enemies.'

'Did you do this?' With unexpected speed, Bremmens grabbed Glovkonin's arm before he could raise the glass to his lips again. His bony fingers dug into the Russian's skin through the sleeve of his Brioni jacket. 'You cannot lie to me,' he said, 'I see your ambitions, Pytor. You wear them as plainly as these tailored suits you fetishise.'

'If Cassidy drew the attention of law enforcement, that is no one's fault but his,' the Russian grated. 'You know the man. A braggart. A bully. And sloppy with it, like most Americans. Convinced of his own infallibility.'

Bremmens never blinked, staring into Glovkonin's eyes. It was like looking at a machine, something bereft of emotions. The Russian recalled the Italian joking about the Swiss, describing the older man as 'a flesh-and-blood lie detector'. He saw that now, as Bremmens searched his face for indications of deception.

But Pytor Glovkonin had learned to lie from the best.

'I am not responsible,' he said firmly, and gestured with the brandy bottle. 'Come. We will salute Cassidy with a drink and then discuss what must happen next.'

Bremmens let go, allowing him to pour another glass.

'I know you had Celeste Toussaint murdered,' he said quietly, fishing for a response.

Glovkonin did not react. 'She wasn't good for the Combine.' It was not quite a confession, but it was close enough. The waspish French media mogul had been Glovkonin's barrier to the Combine's inner circle, and her unwillingness to allow him access to the cabal had sealed her fate. Her death had left a void that the Russian eagerly filled. 'She was self-indulgent. She lacked vision.'

'I do not disagree with that characterisation,' said Bremmens. 'But still . . .'

'But what?' Glovkonin turned and offered him the other glass. 'Be truthful. You were wholly indifferent to Toussaint's death. In fact, it benefited your portfolio.'

'Both points are correct,' he allowed, taking the brandy.

'So no more dwelling on those absent.' The Russian raised his glass. 'Let us toast present partnerships.' He took a deep draught,

savouring the taste. Bremmens did the same, a flush of colour coming to the banker's pale cheeks.

The other man blinked as the brandy warmed him, completely
unaware that Glovkonin had added something extra to his glass.

The Russian moved towards the fireplace, and Bremmens took
a sluggish step after him, his expression showing the first signs of
confusion.

'Do you know the difference between you and me, Rutger?'
Glovkonin didn't wait for him to reply. 'Your experience has
taken you very far. But it has ossified your thought processes. Your
focus is strong and extremely precise.' He nodded to himself, as
his words filled the room. 'But it is *narrow*. Outside your areas of
expertise, you are poorly equipped. Da Silvio and Cassidy – they
complemented you in their own ways. You covered one another's
shortcomings.'

'I . . .' Bremmens swayed, putting out a hand to the mantel to
steady himself. 'I feel giddy . . .?'

'I, on the other hand, make a plan for every outcome,' Glovkonin
continued, speaking as much for himself as for the other man's
benefit. 'I ensure that no matter what end state transpires, it will
be one that benefits me.' He put aside his glass and brought his
hands together, in a conciliatory gesture. 'When the smoke clears,
blame will be apportioned. The millions of people who will lose
their money over the next hours . . . they will need to find someone
responsible.'

'What did . . .?' The glass in Bremmens's hand slipped from
his fingers and shattered against the floor. He peered down at the
fragments, as if he could not connect the broken pieces of crystal
with the torpid thoughts oozing through his mind. 'Something in
the . . . brandy . . .'

'Yes.' Glovkonin put a friendly arm around the banker's shoulder, guiding him away from the fireplace and towards the doors
at the rear of the house. 'An interesting cocktail of chemicals, put

together by a comrade of mine who once served the KGB. The first blocks the enzymes in your body that break down alcohol, allowing any you imbibe to enter your bloodstream much quicker than normal. The second element renders the victim rather suggestible. The third makes the other two untraceable to any conventional post-mortem toxicology tests.'

'What . . .?' They were at the doors now, and Glovkonin pushed them open, allowing the bitter alpine wind to wash over them. Bremmens immediately began to shiver violently. 'So cold . . .'

'Let's take a walk,' insisted Glovkonin.

The icy chill was a mother's embrace to the Russian, and he directed the other man off the warmed path and into the ankle-deep snow. Fresh falls drifted down out of the sky, settling in silence around them.

Glovkonin reached up and gently plucked the thick spectacles from the banker's pinched features.

'No . . .' Bremmens said weakly, 'Without those, I cannot see. My vision is very poor . . .'

He tried to take them back, but the long fingers that had been like claws moments before had become feeble.

'You have no need of these.' Glovkonin tucked the glasses in his jacket pocket. 'We will walk. And eventually, you will fall.'

The snow deepened, coming up to their shins as they passed beneath the trees. The ground stretched away towards the valley beneath. Gravity drew their path down the steepening slope towards the darkness, away from the estate.

'I d-do not . . . uh-understand . . .' The banker's teeth chattered, making it hard for him to speak.

'Tomorrow, Federal Police officers and specialists from the financial crimes division will arrive here with a warrant for your arrest.' Glovkonin pushed Bremmens forward, so he was walking in front of him. 'I have arranged it so that you and poor Cassidy appear to be the masterminds behind what took place in New York

City.' He halted, letting the older man carry on into the snow. 'You can be certain the Swiss government will not wish to be connected to anything that would make their banking system appear untrustworthy. They will be happy to lay the blame on rogue actors.'

Bremmens muttered something, but he was too far away for Glovkonin to hear it. The older man stumbled and tottered over, crashing into a snowdrift. He tried to get to his feet, frantically shivering, peering in every direction, unable to get his bearings.

'They'll find your body out here, in a day or two. Dead from exposure, or perhaps heart failure,' said the Russian, his voice soft so it did not carry.

He pulled the spectacles from his pocket, wiped them clean of any fingerprints, and dropped them in the snow before setting off back towards the main house.

He heard Bremmens cry out once, but the man's voice grew faint, and by the time Glovkonin returned to the house, there was no sound at all.

Misha waited by the fireplace, warming his hands over the crackling flames. He stiffened, coming to attention as Glovkonin entered.

The banker's tablet computer was where he had left it, sitting on the bar, and the Russian glanced at it. The money in the Combine's coffers continued to rise, while the balances of countless others sank ever lower. Thanks to the work of Andre and others in his employ, those trillions would be laundered through countless blinds and a myriad of shell companies, eventually coming to rest in the dark corners of G-Kor's corporate empire. The Russian's company would quietly become one of the richest private interests in the world.

All the power, the wealth, and the influence those fools hoarded, I have taken, Glovkonin told himself, savouring the sweet rush of his victory. *As of this moment, I am the Combine.*

'Sir.' Misha coughed discreetly. 'While you were ... taking your stroll ... another message came.'

'From New York?'

'No, sir. From the ALEPH team in Turkey. They have captured the African. The other men with him were killed during the recovery operation.'

Glovkonin tipped back his head and laughed. Misha flinched at the sound. He had never seen such a display from his employer, and he did not know how to take it.

'If there is a fate at work in the world,' said the Russian, showing his teeth in a fierce, feral grin, 'then this is a sign that it hates the weak and righteous, and favours the strong and ruthless.'

Malte slowed to a halt on the steel landing in the echoing stairwell, and turned back as Kara climbed up after him. In the sickly green glow cast from the chem-light in his hand, she looked unwell, taking the metal steps one at a time with laboured motions, huffing and puffing.

'I hate you,' said the hacker, without heat. 'You and your fit Scandinavian dad bod. Mister *I can run up fifty flights and not break a sweat.*' She drew level with him and sucked in a shuddering breath, pulling up the daypack she dragged behind her. 'How much further?'

Malte held up four fingers.

'Carry me?' She gave him a pathetic look, which he rebuffed with his silence. 'I know this is like the tenth time I've asked . . .'

'Not far,' he said.

'Okay, okay.' She waved at him. 'Fine. Let me catch my breath. Can't show up looking out of character.'

Malte nodded, adjusting the heavy bag over his shoulder. He drew a Sig Sauer P220 pistol from his waist holster and checked the weapon's slide.

'Hey,' warned Kara. 'Let's not go waving that around unless we have to.' The hacker straightened the dark blue FBI windcheater she wore, and nodded towards Malte, who was similarly attired.

'I mean, we're already committing a felony by impersonating Federal Agents, I don't want to make it worse.'

Malte said nothing, and looked up. Above and below them, the white-painted steel stairs ranged away into the dark. Glow-in-the-dark numerals designating each floor were the only visible signs of their progress up the inside of the exclusive residential tower, but they were close to their destination.

Kara straightened up, the colour returning to her face.

'All right, let's do this.'

They marched up until the glowing numerals changed to the letters 'PH'. A security panel that proved no obstacle to Kara's skills got them into the sky lobby for the penthouse. She strode past the stalled executive elevators to a heavy door of oak and glass.

'Watch and learn,' she told him. 'This is how you knock like a Fed.'

Kara balled her hand into a fist and banged hard, *one-two-three*, left it for a breath, then repeated it.

Malte didn't bother to remind her that in another life, he had been a police officer, and concentrated on looking imposing. He didn't have to do much work in that department.

'Who's out there?' said a man's voice, pitching up to make himself heard through the door. He sounded equal parts afraid and pissed off.

'Mr Schell?' Kara yelled back. 'Mr Matthew Schell?'

'Yes?'

'Sir, this is Special Agent Parker of the FBI. My colleague Agent Banner and I need to speak with you on a matter of the utmost urgency!' She put on a commanding tone at odds with her slight frame.

Malte heard Schell moving around inside, and the indistinct burble of other voices.

'What do you want with me? Haven't you noticed, but there's a major goddamn power outage going on right now?'

'Why do you think we're here, sir?' Kara made a face at Malte, but kept up her performance. 'If you can please open the door . . .'

'Do you have a warrant?' Schell yelled back. 'Do I need to talk to my lawyer?'

'By all means, if you have a working phone, go ahead,' Kara shot back. 'But do you really think the Bureau would make us climb this many stairs if it wasn't serious?'

Schell pondered that for a moment.

'Is this about the power cut? Oh God, it's not terrorists, is it?'

'Sir. This is the last time I will ask you.' Kara squared off in front of the door. 'Don't make me force the issue.'

Mechanical locks rattled, and presently the crack opened. A worried-looking white man in his fifties appeared in the gap, holding a lit scented candle.

'Can I see some ID?'

Kara and Malte produced the facsimile Federal badges that had been in storage with the FBI windcheaters at the MI6 safe house. They were high quality fakes, enough to satisfy Schell, who opened the door wider.

Kara strode in, looking around the darkened apartment. Malte followed, wary of the dark corners.

Dotted on every surface were more scented candles, giving off a riot of floral and woody odours as they burned. A woman around the same age as Schell stood to one side, her hands knitting together, and she noted Malte's attention.

'It's the only thing we had,' she explained. 'Lights, phones . . . nothing works!'

'I understand, ma'am,' said Kara. 'Good thinking.' She looked around. 'Just you two in residence?'

'Our daughter . . .' The woman called out. 'Tiffany, come in here!'

A sullen young lady in her late teens emerged from a darkened doorway. She clutched a gold-plated smartphone in one hand, peering morosely at the device's blank screen.

'I got no bars, no nothing,' she said glumly. 'I am officially socially dead.'

'What's this about?' said Schell.

'Let's talk in the lounge, shall we?' Kara gestured to lead the way, and Schell grumbled but obeyed.

With glass floor-to-ceiling windows on all sides, the penthouse sat at the top of the apartment tower, on the corner of the streets one block down from the building where Titanpointe was situated.

On a clear day, the views from this level – as high as the Empire State Building's observation deck – would have been unparalleled. But in the grip of the storm and the blackout, all that could be seen were dots of illumination down on the streets and the occasional flicker of light from one of the neighbouring towers.

The lounge was part of a long single space that took up one third of the penthouse's footprint, including a library and what looked like a dining area. An actual log fire burned in a recessed pillar, throwing orange flame-glow over the windows, reflecting off a mirrored sky balcony that wrapped around to an open-plan kitchen. Malte wondered if they had their firewood brought in by helicopter.

'I'm not going to lie to you, Mr Schell,' Kara said briskly, dumping her pack on the floor. 'What's happening right now is an attack on New York City and the United States of America. You have been targeted.'

'I *told* you we should have stayed in Bel Air,' snapped the wife.

'Why me?' demanded the husband, ignoring his partner's jibe. 'Is this about the petrochemical deal in Indonesia? Because my attorney assures me that is legal and above board!'

'Actually,' said Kara, 'this is about geography, not history.'

'What's she talking about?' said the daughter. 'Mom, get rid of these people, they're freaking me out.'

'There.'

Malte walked to the glass and indicated the dark planes of the Long Lines building. The uppermost level of the hardened tower was a few storeys below them and to the south-east. The direct distance from the penthouse balcony to the roof was no more than two hundred metres of open air.

Schell followed Kara to the window, and he scowled.

'That thing? It's an eyesore! Some sort of government facility, we were told. You know they run security checks on everyone who lives in this building, just because we are neighbours?'

'It's creepy,' bleated the daughter. 'That's why my bedroom's not on this side! I don't want some stalker watching me with their spy cameras!'

Schell suddenly jolted back in surprise as he realised the red anti-collision lights atop the tower at 33 Thomas Street were still on.

'How come they still have power and the rest of the city doesn't?'

'That's classified,' Kara said firmly.

'Oh no.' Schell's wife raised a hand to her mouth as terrible possibilities warred with one another in her thoughts. 'This is like what happened in San Francisco a couple of years ago, with that bomb in the bay . . .'

'Worse,' said Malte, seeing the opportunity.

'I assume you have a panic room?' Kara looked Schell in the eye, and her tone became steely and uncompromising.

'Yes?'

'I think it would be best if you go lock yourself in there.'

Schell raised a hand, as if to disagree, but then he saw the hard look on Malte's face and decided otherwise.

'You know . . . That's a sensible idea. Come on! You heard the agent!'

He propelled his wife and daughter out of the lounge, leaving the others alone.

'*Go lock yourself in.*' Kara mimicked herself, dialling up the menace. Then she laughed. 'Honestly, how do you guys keep a straight face with that badass-speak?'

'Practice,' offered the Finn.

'Uh-huh.'

Kara opened her pack, and tipped the contents out onto a sofa. She unfurled spools of cable and connected it to a cluster of military-grade tactical lasers taken from the safe house armoury, the kind of add-on that soldiers would clip beneath the barrel of a rifle to paint a red dot on their targets.

Malte removed the car battery he'd been carrying in his bag. 'Will this work?'

'Sure.' Kara wired up the lasers, attaching them with duct tape to chairs, a lamp, a coffee table. She sighted down each one, so that their five-megawatt emitters were aimed at security cameras and alarm sensors on the roof of the Long Lines building. When she was done, Kara stepped back and raised her hands. 'Okay, ready up. Give them the signal.'

Malte pulled a heavy Maglite torch from the inner pocket of his windcheater. The sliding door to the balcony opened with a sucking pop of air. The wind came howling into the penthouse, raking through loose papers, dragging the rain with it and snuffing most of the candles. Acting quickly, Malte moved to the north end of the balcony, pointing the torch down towards the street.

'Do it!' he called.

Inside the penthouse, Kara completed the last connection, and a fan of thin crimson threads extended out across the darkness.

With his thumb on the torch's button, Malte sent a word in Morse code. Two dashes, one dot. A pause. Three dashes.

Go.

'That's it,' said Lucy, shielding her face from the downpour, looking up towards the Tribeca tower's penthouse. 'Maybe you should let me drive . . .'

She adjusted her grubby disposable coverall, pulling the zip up to her throat, and walked back to the heavy truck idling at the corner of Church and Duane Street, picking her way through stalled late-model SUVs and modern hybrids as the rain lashed the asphalt.

Marc leaned out of the boxy cab and gave the grubby, white-painted vehicle a friendly pat.

'What, and miss out in this? Nah.'

The three-axle Mack snorted like a mechanical rhino as he revved the engine. Lucy's brother had owned a toy trash hauler that looked just like this one when they were little. The battered old vehicle was worse for wear, coated in patches of rust and layers of dirt that had to be years thick. Her nose wrinkled at the rotting stink wafting from the rear compartment, so she breathed through her mouth as she climbed into the narrow cab.

Marc crunched the gears and they rolled away, the windscreen wipers thudding back and forth across the glass. They picked up speed as he weaved around the stalled traffic, splashing through potholes filled with rainwater.

'My maths teacher once said to me, *Marc*, she said, *if you don't buck your ideas up and do your homework, you'll end up driving a dustcart for a living.*' He grinned. 'Turns out she was on to something.'

'A dust-what?'

'Dustcart. Bin lorry.' He banged the steering wheel with his hand. 'This thing.'

'Garbage truck,' she corrected, then jabbed her hand to the left. 'There! That turn!'

'Got it . . .'

He hauled the wheel around and the truck complained, the rear wheels skidding over the wet street as he forced the tight corner. The vehicle clipped a Buick sedan and shoved it sideways out of their path.

'Sorry!' Marc called out of the window, putting his foot down.

Lucy found the makeshift detonator control at the end of the wire trailing back into the truck's trash compactor. Hitting the test switch rewarded her with a green light. She double-checked her seat belt, and grabbed the two gas masks sliding around on the dashboard.

'You know when to jump?'

'More or less.'

'Go left!' she yelled, as the next turn came up.

Lucy pulled one of the masks down over her face as the vehicle lurched up and cut the corner, across the sidewalk. The cab knocked away a scaffold pole and something crashed to the ground behind them.

She leaned across, slipping the other mask over Marc's face so he didn't have to let go of the wheel. The truck roared, the speedometer indicator twitching as it went flat out.

'Here it comes!'

Marc pushed back into his seat. Ahead of them, Thomas Street and the sheer, featureless facade of the Long Lines building rose like the wall of some alien citadel.

They burst out of the side street and Marc jerked the steering wheel to the right, shouldering another parked car into the front of a darkened restaurant as they veered the wrong way across the single-lane road.

The garbage truck thundered towards the building's main pedestrian entrance. It was a narrow entryway, closed in by walls and a thick veranda, up two flights of stairs lined with metal banisters.

They bounced off the kerb, mounting the staircase, and Marc threaded the truck through the eye of the needle, aiming into a set of revolving doors that led inside.

Lucy mashed the detonator button and vaulted out of the cab a split second before it struck with a grinding, howling shriek of tortured metal. She landed hard on the wet concrete steps and rolled into the wall.

A wall of thick grey smoke washed over her and visibility dropped to nothing. She heard alarms clanging and voices calling out in panic. Picking herself up, Lucy rushed back towards the garbage truck, feeling for the side of it.

As planned, the heavyweight vehicle had done its job. If 33 Thomas Street was a modern castle keep, then the trash hauler was the diesel-powered battering ram that blew through the outer doors and security gate behind it.

They didn't have long to get inside. The cluster of smoke bombs wired up inside the rear of the truck were burning, spewing a screen of choking grey haze that filled the building's lobby and gave them cover.

'Marc!' she called. 'Sound off!'

'Here,' said a voice, and a white man-shape with a bug-eyed gas mask reared up out of the smoke. 'Go, go!'

Finding their way, the two of them picked a path over the broken concrete panels and smashed-in doors. Lucy's boots hit marble flooring and she knew they were in the lobby proper.

She made out the faint glow of lights in the ceiling above, and the yelling she heard before was closer.

'Breach, breach!' a woman shouted, coughing as the smoke curdled in her throat. 'Entrance is compromised, repeat, compromised!'

The burble of a radio replied and a fraction of the tension Lucy felt eased off. So far, the plan was working. The lasers Kara had set up to mess with the sensors on the roof had sent most of Titanpointe's security detail rushing to the upper levels to investigate, leaving the entrance under-protected.

'Is someone there?' said another voice, a man on the verge of panic, closer than she would have liked. 'Shit, I hear movement! I can't see anything!'

The first voice, the woman with the radio, called out again.

'All right, fall back! That thing could be a truck bomb! We're sealing off this level!'

A blurry shape moved past her, and Lucy ducked low.

'I can't find you,' said the other voice. 'Where are you?'

'Here!' the woman called out again, and in the distance, a rectangle of dull, faraway light appeared as a set of elevator doors opened. 'This way!'

Lucy felt Marc's hand on her shoulder.

'That's it,' he whispered.

'Copy that.'

Lucy made for the light and the voices, shrugging off the paper coverall and discarding the mask. Marc did the same, following close behind.

People crammed into the wide, smoke-filled elevator car – a pair of uniformed security guards, one of them retching into the corner, along with a woman clutching a walkie-talkie and a man collapsed on the floor, coughing violently.

'That everyone?' said the woman.

Lucy and Marc stumbled in, taking up places on either side of the car. Beneath their coveralls, they wore regular clothes that made them look like any other office worker.

'Okay . . .'

The woman spoke into the radio and the elevator doors slid shut. There were no controls inside the car, Lucy noted, which meant it was operated from somewhere else. The car ascended and the smoke thinned.

The woman with the radio wiped her eyes, blinking as she took in the other passengers. Her vision cleared and settled on Lucy.

'Who the hell are you?'

Lucy had hoped they might actually make it to the upper lobby before anyone noticed anything amiss, but it wasn't going to go that way. She whipped out a spray bottle from her jacket pocket and shot a blast of droplets right into the other woman's face. The contents of the pretty pink bottle were not Chanel, but halothane anaesthetic.

The woman dropped the radio and sank like a stone. Marc was already on the closest security guard, pulling the guy into a sleeper hold before he could go for his sidearm.

In the tight confines of the elevator, they had nowhere to hide, so Lucy went on the offensive, kicking the man on the floor in the head, and dosing the second guard with another puff from the spray bottle.

'Whassgoinon . . .?'

The collapsed man raised his hands to cover his face as the guards hit the floor around him.

'Camera,' said Lucy.

'You ready for this?'

Marc produced one of the same lasers that Kara had used and fired it into a glassy bowl mounted on the ceiling. Anyone watching would see only smoke, and then nothing as the digital camera's flash-blinded CCD chip cycled through a reset.

'You're asking me *now*?' Lucy scowled and removed the last of their smoke grenades from her jacket as the lift slowed. 'Hold your breath,' she added, pulling the pin and letting the canister drop.

A fresh surge of grey haze gushed up into the confined space as the elevator gave off a cheery ping. The doors opened and they spilled out into the upper lobby in a cloud of smoke, dragging confusion along with them.

Lucy spotted the exits leading deeper into the building and skirted her way towards them. Meanwhile, clutching a pass card liberated from one of the unconscious guards, Marc deliberately stumbled straight into the closest member of the armed security team waiting for them in the lobby.

'What's going on down there?' said one of the security detail.

Marc feigned wheezing, as if he couldn't talk. His performance wouldn't win any Oscars, but it was enough to draw the attention of the guards and give Lucy the time to get some distance.

'Stop . . . Stop her!' Marc finally gasped, pointing in Lucy's direction as she fled. 'Intruder . . .!' He faked another attack of racking coughs and staggered back.

It did the trick. As Lucy broke into a sprint, she heard one of the guards calling out to lock down the entire building.

Now I gotta play rabbit long enough for us to pull this off, she told herself.

After a while, Walter Novick put his jacket back on, despite the warmth inside the operations centre. He had to hide the fact that he was sweating through his shirt. It was a vain attempt to project some kind of presence, to show he was in control, but he couldn't tell if it was working.

Months ago, when the Frenchman and his colleagues laid out their proposal to him in a dingy bar in Hell's Kitchen, it had sounded straightforward. Like something out of a movie, a clever script that would play out in fast bursts of action, and end with a rousing conclusion.

At first he'd thought it a test of his loyalty. Something the NSA mandarins had cooked up to make sure that Novick deserved his security clearance, dangling what he desired in front of him to see if he would betray his position for greed. But that didn't last long; in Novick's experience, that three-dimensional chess bullshit was more the CIA's style. The Langley farm boys missed the Cold War and they loved playing their byzantine games. The NSA was straight down the line. Less imaginative. That was part of the reason why he was stuck where he was.

Walter Novick had been part of Titanpointe's full take surveillance mission for five years and passed over for promotion at the end of every one. The Frenchman and his friends were shrewd judges of character. They knew what he really wanted – not money, not power, but *recognition*. Novick wanted to be appreciated for his service. He wanted to be valued.

More than that, he wanted the job that idiot Sean Harlow had been given instead of him.

The men had told him a story about how America had become slow and self-indulgent as its status on the world stage was eroded. They talked about a much-needed wake-up call to stir the country back to greatness.

Like 9/11, they said, *but smaller, with less casualties, and controlled by us. It will shake people out of their complacency.*

An event like that would need men of intelligence and skill in the right places, to guide the outcome. Men like Walter Novick.

On some level, he understood they were appealing to his vanity, but Novick didn't care. They told him they would remove Harlow from his position and facilitate Novick's promotion instead, and past that point he wasn't really listening anymore. He agreed to it, of course.

How much of what the Frenchman had said was a lie? He couldn't be certain. But now the plan was fragmenting, and Novick was losing his nerve.

It was supposed to last an hour, maybe two. They were six hours in, with no end in sight. Harlow would take the fall when the interrupt device was eventually discovered inside the building, and Novick would be the hero of the day for keeping a cool head during the crisis.

But he was terrified. Isolated and alone at the back of the ops centre, he watched system after system go offline and listened to the technicians grow frantic as they botched each attempt to reboot the grid. As long the interrupt remained in place, they would continue to fail.

Novick looked at his shoes. The interrupt sat directly below him in one of the subsections on the floor beneath, connected to a secondary signal bus, a malignant spider in the middle of the network's complex web.

He had been careful to direct the tech teams to different locations as they searched fruitlessly for the source of the problem. In many ways the Long Lines building was a self-contained micro-city, and to search every possible piece of it would take days.

But eventually Novick would run out of blind alleys to send them down. He would have to decide when he would miraculously 'find' the interrupt and save the day.

He fingered the burner phone in his pocket. Each time he'd managed to slip away to the men's room and turn it on, the Frenchman had not answered his calls. Novick's mind churned with the possibilities that silence suggested. Had his co-conspirators been arrested? Or cut their losses and left him twisting in the wind?

Now someone had deliberately driven a garbage truck into the Thomas Street entrance, and that someone was inside the perimeter.

He sat down and his stomach rolled over. Novick eyed the waste-paper basket beneath his desk, fighting the urge to vomit into it.

'Walter.' He looked up to find Margaret Mooney hovering nearby, clutching a laptop to her chest. 'Diagnostics on 47, 46 and 40 are complete. Nothing there.'

'Okay, carry on,' he said dismissively. 'You know you don't have to tell me when they're done, just tell me when they're *all* done.'

She made no move to leave.

'I don't consider this a smart use of my time—'

'I didn't ask your opinion, Margaret!' Novick snapped. 'I told you to clear the rest of the diagnostics!'

He didn't want the petite woman bothering him, with her cute Irish-American accent and her blunt manners. The feeling appeared to be mutual, especially after that ill-judged pass he had made at her during last year's Christmas party. He always felt she was quietly judging him, as if she had the right to do that. It was no secret that Mooney had liked Harlow a lot – most people did. Novick had never been able to understand how the dead man had managed that.

'When Sean was here, we—'

'He's not!' Novick broke in, bringing her up short.

Mooney blinked, taken aback at his tone. She'd sobbed at Harlow's memorial service, he recalled.

'Sir?' One of the security officers, a round-faced man named Roper, interposed himself between them before any more could be said. 'Report from the ground floor. The lobby is secure, looks like the devices inside the truck were smoke generators. No explosives, so that's something.'

Novick nodded along with that, clutching at the tiny fragment of relief.

'Where's the intruder now?'

Roper frowned. 'In sector 6 or 7. We've sealed off the stairwells. We'll get her.'

'Are there any others?'

Roper made a tutting noise. 'Unclear. Maybe.'

'*Maybe?*' Novick glared at him.

'I have people in the infirmary,' Roper shot back, matching his mordant tone. 'I'll debrief them when I can.'

'Then go ahead!'

Novick sat back in the chair, making his dismissal clear to the other man. Roper's lip curled, but he went on his way. Novick blew out an exasperated breath, only to realise that Mooney was still standing close by, clutching her computer.

'Walter, I think I should—'

It was too much for Novick to take, and he bolted to his feet.

'Can you just do your fucking job, Margaret? Is that too much to ask?'

She recoiled. 'You want me to leave the ops centre again, while there's a lockdown in place? There's a terrorist out there!'

'You were not supposed to hear that,' he told her. 'It's not your concern. We're safe here, so get it done!'

Novick rapped his finger on the side of her laptop, and then pushed past her, making for the men's room once again.

When he was certain he was alone, he locked himself in a stall and reactivated the burner phone with trembling fingers.

The text on its tiny screen read, No Messages.

TWENTY-ONE

The workstation from which Margaret Mooney had to monitor the diagnostics was one of dozens of identical rooms throughout the Long Lines Building, a part of the complex-within-the-complex that belonged to the National Security Agency. While most of the tower was still technically the domain of the telecoms provider that owned it, in reality the NSA oversaw most of the day-to-day operations within the sandstone-coloured skyscraper.

The room possessed the same bland landscape of white walls and sky-blue support pillars as the others, the only differentiation coming in the colour-coded panels on the doors to show the security levels of the various floors.

New assignees from Fort Meade or one of the agency's other stations often became lost in their first weeks working at Titanpointe, and Mooney sometimes joked that the layout of the place was an intelligence test. If you couldn't find your way around, you didn't have the smarts required for a career in the NSA. But some days, even Margaret felt like the building moved rooms around on its own just to spite her.

She stared at her screen, watching the program loop back over and over, as it marked each operational subsection as free of tampering. Green indicators popped up one by one, and Mooney grew increasingly frustrated with each new report indicating ALL CLEAR.

It was absolutely not. Something was seriously wrong. By now, the entire communications grid for the east coast should have been back up to operating status. Nothing short of a massive nuclear attack could produce such a result, but yet here it was. The problem wasn't just that the grid had been knocked offline, and it wasn't the huge power outage making it worse. There was a third factor that no one could nail down. And that pig Novick had his head so far up his own ass that he would never listen to the suggestions of a second-string tech like her, even if she hadn't been a woman.

The other ladies on the team had told her exactly what to expect from him. Novick was the kind of man who referred to women as 'females', like they were some other species, and who hung out on sleazy pickup websites when he wasn't busy taking credit for the rest of the team's work. How such a person could be elevated to running the operations centre was beyond her, but after the horrible circumstances surrounding Sean Harlow's death, the agency had been hard-pressed to find anyone else suitable to replace the affable man at short notice. Like it or not, Novick knew the systems inside and out, which made him the logical choice – on paper. The fact that most of his co-workers could barely tolerate the guy had not made its way up the chain.

When this is over, Mooney thought, *I should talk to someone in HR about a transfer.*

The workstation door opened and a man she didn't recognise entered. He gave a start as he spotted her.

'Oh. Sorry. Didn't realise this unit was in use.' In his late thirties, he had a scuff of facial hair and dirty blond hair, and the indisputable air of an alpha geek about him. His accent reminded her of a guy from Toronto she had dated. 'Can I . . .?' He indicated a vacant computer opposite her.

'Sure.' Mooney narrowed her eyes as he took a seat and tapped a security pass on the reader pad next to the screen. 'Did Novick send you to check on me?'

'Novick?' he repeated. 'No. He never . . . uh . . . said anything.' There was a pause. 'He giving you a hard time?'

'He's a prick.' The words escaped before she could stop them.

'Most bosses are.' He hesitated. 'Any luck with the . . . uh . . .' He gestured around at the air. 'Everything?'

'I'm sure the second we find something, Novick will tell everybody.'

'Right.' That gave the man pause. 'Because he's handling the checks personally?'

'Well, that's his job now.'

Mooney frowned. She couldn't put her finger on it, but something about this person was off. She knew most of the new intake from the previous month, and the bearded man's face didn't fit with them.

Mooney thought about what Roper had said, back in the ops centre. The security officer had noted that the intruder in the building was a woman. But then Novick had asked, *Are there any others?* And Roper didn't have an answer.

'I hear that a lot of people don't like Novick,' said the man, clicking his mouse and tapping at the keyboard in front of him. 'That true?'

Her skin prickled. He was fishing for an answer.

They had trained them for this kind of thing. *Social engineering,* the instructors called it. A soft kind of interrogation, where opposition agents tried to draw out information from an unsuspecting staff member in everyday conversation. Before you knew it, you would be telling them about where you grew up, the name of your first pet, and anything else that might come in useful for cracking your passwords.

Mooney decided to play her suspicions.

'Have we met before? You look real familiar.'

'I don't think so.' He glanced away, focusing on the computer screen she couldn't see. 'I'm new. I work upstairs.'

'Oh, they bring you in to help out with the lockdown?'

'Yeah.'

'Are you on Sean Harlow's team?' she said. 'The big guy, you can't miss him.'

She'd laid out her trap. Anyone who had been working at Titanpointe for more than a couple of days would have heard the tragic story about the shooting of Harlow and his sons in a home invasion gone wrong. Management had put an 'In Memoriam' poster on the main noticeboard, and it was all people talked about in the cafeteria.

'I haven't met him yet,' said the man.

Mooney knew then she was on to something. She rolled her chair to the right. Behind the guy, she could see a mirror image of the computer screen he was working at, reflected in the plastic casing of one of the servers.

The display showed the login screen, still waiting patiently for a password to be entered. Which meant blondie here was faking it, tapping away and pretending to work.

A chill rushed through Mooney and she straightened the sweater over her shoulders. The phone with the emergency call button was on the far side of the room by the water cooler, a good five metres away.

She feigned a cough. 'I swear, the air con in this place is so dry. My mouth is like Death Valley.' Mooney stood and walked towards the cooler. 'You want something to drink?' She paced out her steps, trying not to hurry.

As the cooler glugged cold water into a paper cup, she let her hand drop towards the phone.

'Please don't do that.' The Toronto-ish accent vanished and all of a sudden the guy sounded English.

Mooney looked up and froze. He aimed a pistol at her, a bulky cylindrical thing like the ones zookeepers used on runaway animals. She raised her hands.

'What gave me away?'

'Sean died two weeks ago.'

'Oh.' The English guy stood up and motioned her away from the phone, then grabbed her ID card from the reader at her station. He glanced at her photo. 'Margaret, is it? Look, I know you may not believe me, but we're both chasing the same target.'

She scowled at him. 'I'm not telling you anything.'

'Well, you've already told me most of what I want to know.' He flicked a look at her screen. 'Like, who is in charge of getting the grid back up again. This Novick bloke, yeah? And it should be sorted by now. Except it isn't. Like someone is deliberately making sure the system stays offline for as long as possible.'

'You're the one who drove a truck into the lobby,' said Mooney. 'You're the only troublemaker I see right now.'

He sighed. 'All right. Cards on the table. I'm a covert operative working against the terrorist group that attacked New York today,' he insisted, 'and for the record, my partner and me didn't hurt anyone. We're looking for something.'

The British guy described a device he called an 'interrupt', capable of keeping Titanpointe's fail safes from activating.

Mooney's blood ran cold. In the first hours after the grid had gone down, she had wondered openly if something similar might be to blame for this situation, but Novick had loudly talked over her until she gave up trying to make a point.

'Let me ask you this,' he added. 'If somebody had tech like that, where would they put it? In a subsection, right? Like the ones you're checking.'

She couldn't help herself from nodding. 'I guess.'

'Am I right in guessing Novick has full access to those areas?' She didn't reply, but she didn't have to. 'So here's the big question – is there a subsection your boss hasn't had you check yet?'

Yes.

Mooney almost answered out loud. When the checks had started, her first instinct had been to look at the secondary arrays in subsections 15 through 20, the ones most likely to malfunction under the vastly increased data load. But Novick had assigned her to subsections two levels above that. At the time, it didn't make sense, and she'd chalked it up to his constant need to give orders rather than listen to suggestions.

'For a second, entertain the possibility that I might be telling you the truth,' said the man. 'If you help me, Margaret, we might be able to put a stop to this.'

Mooney folded her arms defiantly over her chest.

'You're pointing a weapon at me. Why should I trust anything you say?'

He looked at the pistol, then flicked on the safety catch and tucked it back into his jacket.

'The interrupt is all I care about. Help me find that and I'll give you the gun. Then you can do whatever you want.'

She looked back at the phone. 'I hit that red button and a security detail will be in here in less than a minute.'

Mooney wasn't quite sure if that was true, but it sounded good.

He nodded. 'Probably. But I'm trusting you not to. So how about it, Margaret?'

Mooney thought about the look in Novick's eyes as he yelled at her back in the ops centre, and frowned.

'Follow me,' she said.

So far, Lucy's tactic of staying agile and leading Titanpointe's security team on a merry dance had worked, but she knew the net was closing on her. There were only so many places to hide inside the blank-walled skyscraper. With the elevator shafts secured, and the stairwells being monitored, the guards would soon run her down.

She was meant to be the hare to the hounds, keeping the focus away from Marc while he found a quiet spot to do his geek thing and locate the interrupt. She had a few ideas about exfiltration after the fact, but it woudn't matter if they couldn't find the device. She had a compact walkie-talkie in her jacket pocket she could use to radio Marc, but it was an *if all else fails* option. Not only would the signal be unlikely to carry far inside the heavy concrete structure of the building, but it was possible the security team might be able to track her position if she used it.

Lucy didn't like leaving the Brit to his own devices. He had a tendency to be reckless at the worst possible moment, and even though he was good at what he did, it troubled her that she wasn't there to watch his back.

She pulled a face and muttered to herself, 'Gettin' sentimental, Keyes? Knock it off. He'll manage.'

On top of everything else, it didn't help that the interior of the building was – to put it mildly – unimaginative. Lucy was pretty certain she had already sprinted past the same wall with the motivational posters and softball sign-up sheet at least twice already.

At each T-junction, she used the laser Marc had slipped her to blind the cameras in the ceiling, but even that would help them narrow down her location. She heard voices from the corridor to her right and backed up, taking the left branch down a short path and through a set of double doors into an empty cafeteria.

High School flashback, she thought, her footsteps echoing around the big lunch room. Like the one she remembered from her teens, it had rectangular tables and lightweight chairs in orderly rows, a rank of vending machines along one wall and a station for cutlery and trash on the other. The far side of the cafeteria had serving hatches where fresh food could be doled out from a kitchen behind. That was closed off behind shutters, but another door led into the preparation area.

She ran in that direction. Inside the kitchen there would be a service stairwell. The voices behind her were closing in, so she had to be quick.

Lucy shouldered into the door, expecting it to be one of those opens-both-ways things they had in restaurants. It didn't give a millimetre, and she bounced right off, slipping on the smooth linoleum floor.

'Oh, shit . . .'

She grabbed the door handle and gave it a hard twist, but the lock did not give. Lucy cast around, her gaze raking over the shutters, the tables and chairs. The only path out of here was back the way she came. Her gamble had crashed out, and she had unwittingly cornered herself.

'She went in there!' shouted a woman from out in the corridor. She sounded angry and frustrated. 'Form up!'

'Okay. New plan.'

On the wall was a power box controlling the cafeteria's lights, and she yanked down the scissor-switch, plunging the cafeteria into semi-darkness.

Enough rabbit, she told herself. *Time to be the wolf.*

Two of the security team opened the double doors while the other two advanced into the gloomy dining room. The only illumination came from the coloured glow of vending machines.

'No lights,' said the man in the lead, flicking the switches by the door.

'I can see that, Wayne,' said the woman behind him, curling her lip. 'Get your ass in there.'

'Sure, Janelle,' he replied, 'but Roper said to wait for backup?'

Janelle put her large boxer's hands on her heavy hips and gave Wayne a withering stare.

'You wanna stand there holding your dick while this terrorist gets away again?'

'Okay, when you put it like that . . .'

'Move it!' Janelle gave him a shove, then beckoned the other men by the doors. 'Dooley, you go left, Max, go right. She has no way outta here.'

'Copy that,' said Dooley, leading with the Sig Sauer semi-automatic in his hand.

Separating to spread out, the security guards pulled their torches and panned them around the darkened space.

The beam from Wayne's torch passed over a shadow beneath a long table and he turned his gun that way.

'Hey, who's—?'

Wayne never finished the sentence. A plosive chug of compressed air sent a hollow dart loaded with a synthetic phenobarbital compound his way, the needle hitting him in the belly through his shirt. The icy-cold rush of the drug-shot flooded his system, and the guard's legs stopped working. He collapsed into semi-consciousness, releasing a drawn-out groan.

Dooley heard Wayne go down and the other guard swung his torch in that direction. The beam found him in a sprawl, his mouth wide open and gaping, and his eyes glassy and unfocused.

A boot scraped on the floor, and Dooley spun in the direction of the noise, only to meet the back of a chair full in the face. The thin wooden seat-back broke across his head and shoulder, and he glimpsed the dark-skinned woman wielding the seat like a weapon. She hit him again with the bits of the chair's frame and he called out in pain.

'What's going on?' Max called out from across the cafeteria, but Dooley was too busy fighting back to reply. In the half-dark, the intruder was a blur of motion, fists and feet striking him at the weak points of his knees and the soft tissues of his throat. A particularly hard hit rattled him, making him choke.

He tried to point the gun at his assailant, but even a generous observer would have considered Dooley as way outside the physical fitness specs for his job. Regretting those missed days in the gym didn't stop the woman from cracking him hard across the legs, or help him stay on his feet. Racked with pain, he crashed into a table and felt his gun drop, heard it go skittering away into the darkness. He fell to his knees, the agony holding him down.

'Quit screwing around!' Janelle's angry shout carried across the room. 'Get them lights back!'

'Okay!'

Max knew where to find the emergency scissor-switch for the cafeteria's lights – right next to the fire extinguisher hanging near the kitchen doors. If he got the overheads back on, the intruder would have no place to hide.

He was close when something flickered at the corner of his vision and Max pivoted. He saw a figure moving fast, silhouetted against the glowing fascia of the vending machines.

'Stop!' he shouted, and then fired two rounds from his Sig.

The shots cracked the plastic panels and the ghost he was aiming for dropped down in a sliding motion, like a baseball player making a desperate run for home.

'Over here!'

Max held his torch in one hand and his gun in the other, aiming both into the gloom where the intruder had disappeared beneath a table.

'Where?' Janelle was on the other side of the room. 'Dooley, Wayne, sound off!'

The other men didn't respond.

Max ducked low, shining the torch into the space below the table. He saw a forest of aluminium chair legs, but no intruder.

She was waiting for him when he straightened up, standing atop the table. Her boot was level with Max's face, which the woman demonstrated by introducing one to the other with a whip-fast spin-kick. Fireworks burst in his skull and he staggered back.

She pounced on him, and they went into a spinning dance, crashing off a support pillar, knocking chairs aside as they fought over his gun. Max fired into the ceiling tiles and he was dimly aware of Janelle calling out in surprise.

His other wrist flared with a surge of white-hot pain as the intruder twisted it the wrong way, making him lose his grip on the big tactical torch. Too late, he realised that she hadn't been interested in getting his gun at all. That was the distraction to separate

Max from the heavy metal-shelled torch which, with its load of dense D-cells, served as a perfectly serviceable bludgeon.

Stark white light blazed in his eyes, dazzling him. She broke his nose with the first blow, fractured his forearm with the next one, and chipped his collarbone with the third. Max stumbled into the serving platform and crumpled against a stainless steel chiller. Despite the cold of the metal, his torso felt as if it was on fire.

Janelle didn't bother to go to the aid of the men in the team. They knew what they had signed up for, she reasoned, and if they couldn't hack it, that was not a Janelle Problem.

She jogged back across to the double doors leading out of the cafeteria, reasoning out the intruder's next move. With her broad, linebacker profile, Janelle blocked the doorway with ease. Before this gig, she'd been a bouncer at a high-end dance club in Midtown, but night after night of dealing with drunken trust fund kids had made her seek something different. She liked working for these spy nerds. It was easy, it paid well and her clean police record had made her a perfect candidate.

But she missed the opportunity to crack a head now and then, so she welcomed today's turn of events.

The intruder came pell-mell out of the darkness, hurling a torch at Janelle's head as she tried to get around her. Janelle batted the torch away with a grunt and caught the woman with her other hand, her fingers tightening around the intruder's bicep.

She noted the presence of good muscle density there. Whoever this was, the intruder worked out, not that it would make much difference. Janelle jerked her to a skidding stop and glared into her dark eyes.

'Where d'you think you're going, honey?'

The woman's face creased in a snarl. She fired two rocket-fast punches into Janelle's left breast, drawing a grumble from her but little else. That would bruise tomorrow, she thought, but it was nothing a little arnica wouldn't help with.

Seeing the strikes had had no effect, the intruder grabbed for a pistol in her waistband with her free hand.

'Nuh-uh,' said Janelle, and smacked the weapon from her grip with a hard backwards blow. 'Sit your ass down,' she added, giving the woman's arm a savage twist that made her cry out.

Janelle propelled her to a nearby chair, forcing the woman into the seat. In the light spilling in from the corridor, she had a good look at the intruder for the first time. Average height, good body tone, darker than Janelle's own features, with sharp eyes framed by tight, unfussy cornrows.

Unlike Wayne and the other boys, Janelle recognised another fighter when she saw one, which was probably why they hadn't been on their guard with this girl. She whipped out her steel hand-cuffs – *none of that plastic zip-tie crap for this one*, Janelle decided – and snapped one bracelet closed over the woman's right wrist.

'Ah, damn it!' the intruder cried out, and Janelle detected the twang of a local accent.

She twisted the open end of the cuffs around to control the woman's arm, bending it back so she could snap the second brace-let into place, but the intruder squirmed and blocked the move, momentarily reversing the reverse and pivoting back up out of the chair.

'Oh, you done this before,' said Janelle, gritting her teeth.

'Yeah,' came the reply, and with it, a series of fast kicks that landed the tip of a combat boot in Janelle's stomach and thigh.

The hits were no love-taps, setting her nerves on fire.

No wonder she took down those three idiots so fast, thought Janelle. *Gotta knock that out of her.*

She gritted her teeth. The intruder's eyes widened as the other woman took the blows, then Janelle hauled her around by the wrist and threw her across the floor.

She slid to a halt, face down in an ungainly sprawl. Janelle heard Dooley groaning nearby but ignored the noise, marching towards her target.

'Play time is done, girl. Give it up.'

'Not in this life.'

The other woman rolled over, and she had the pistol in her hand. Janelle had thrown her right where she wanted to go.

The gun chugged and Janelle felt a sharp pain in her leg. A dart as thick as her thumb lodged in her flesh and a sharp tingling sensation spread from the point of impact.

'What is this shit?' she demanded, and pulled the dart out, tossing it away. 'That s'posed to work on me . . .?'

Janelle advanced, even as the floor turned mushy beneath her feet.

Startled, the intruder frantically worked the slide on the pneumatic pistol, racking another shot.

The second dart went into Janelle's shoulder and she swore. Suddenly she was wading through invisible molasses, hardly able to put one foot in front of the other. Her thoughts slowed and the room swayed around her.

'Oh,' she managed, tottering forward, 'you skinny little biiii—'

Her words turned into a gasp, and Janelle was out before she hit the floor.

Novick sat behind his desk in the ops centre, keeping his hands out of sight so he could clasp them together and stop the nervous tremors from showing. He stared into his screen, not really registering the panels showing live feeds from the security cameras dotted around Titanpointe's corridors.

He thought about the burner phone. Twelve unanswered calls sent out to the unlisted number the Frenchman had given him, each one ignored. Across the months of setting up this thing, Novick had never known his contact to take longer than an hour to get back to him.

His mind filled the silence with dozens of horrible possibilities. For all he knew, it could be them behind the attack on the Long Lines building; it could be another of their operatives on the loose inside Titanpointe, here to do who-the-hell-knew-what. His gut twisted with fear.

Is the intruder here to kill me?

Novick had never dwelled on the circumstances surrounding Harlow's murder, but he knew it had to be the work of professional hit men. Someone like that could be closing in on him right now, preparing to silence him.

He fingered his access card. With it, he could unlock any of the elevators and make a run for the basement parking garage. But with the blackout still in effect, would he be able to get off the island? The bridges and tunnels out of Manhattan would be blocked by vehicles rendered useless by the EMP, and crawling with cops.

He discarded that notion. They had been able to put the interrupt in his car's trunk without him knowing. What if that wasn't the *only* thing they had left in there?

When this began, he had been arrogant enough to believe he was untouchable, here inside of one of the best-protected buildings in the country. That comfortable lie had turned to ash. It didn't matter how strong the walls were if the enemy had already breached the gates.

'Sir?'

Roper's voice made him jump, and Novick struggled to regain his composure.

'What do you want?'

Roper ignored the sharp retort. 'I sent two teams outside the perimeter,' he explained. 'One to the apartment block where those laser blinders were set up, another to the Javits building. They just reported back.'

'I didn't authorise that!'

'I don't need your authorisation,' said Roper.

One block east on Broadway, the Jacob K. Javits building was the New York field office for the Federal Bureau of Investigation. The absolute last thing Novick wanted was a bunch of G-men sticking their noses into this mess.

'And . . .?' he said warily.

The FBI and the NSA didn't play well together at the best of times, but Novick couldn't tell how that might change in a crisis.

'The Feds have their own problems dealing with the situation at Wall Street,' said Roper, with a grimace. 'We're on our own for now.'

Novick had to look away to hide the relief on his face.

'What about the lasers?'

'Found a rig in the penthouse. Residents say a man and a woman posing as Federal agents talked their way inside. They were long gone when my team arrived.'

'A distraction.' Novick wiped sweat from his brow. 'To make us look at the roof as an ingress point so the lobby would be wide open.'

'Obviously,' Roper replied.

The accusatory tone in the security officer's voice was enough to switch Novick's worry into annoyance.

'Perhaps if you had kept those teams inside the building, we would have caught this intruder by now! Can you not just *get* her? Do you have any idea the kinds of damage she could do?'

'I'm aware,' Roper said firmly. 'I've lost contact with a search team, we're isolating that floor now . . .' He halted as he realised that the other man wasn't listening to him.

Something he'd spotted on one of the camera panels had captured Novick's gaze. Two people, unlocking the door to Subsection 18 on the level beneath the ops centre, the very place he had *specifically* ordered no one to enter. One of them was Mooney, the other a total stranger. A man with a hawkish look in his eyes, glancing around to make sure they were alone.

'Novick!' snapped Roper. 'Are you paying attention?'

'Just get that intruder!' Novick bolted up from his chair and pushed past him. His hands balled into fists as he made for the door. 'I have to check on something . . .'

The bright green laser danced over the lens of the camera pod mounted on the low ceiling, and the red active light beneath it winked out as it cycled into reset mode.

'Okay, we're covered,' said Marc, casting around the room. 'How many more of these subsections are there?'

The space was filled with humming computer servers, the indicator lights on their systems blinking yellow, green and red as they ran through operational cycles.

'A dozen more on this floor,' said the woman as she moved from unit to unit, giving each one a practised, professional examination. 'Two more floors below this one.'

'Easy job, then,' he deadpanned.

Marc knew that time was not on his side. Not just with the security teams prowling the building, but also from the risk of losing whatever ground he had gained with Mooney. She was a tech geek like him, and he had correctly piqued her innate interest in solving a hardware problem. He'd been able to get her on side temporarily, but that would only last so long.

She walked around behind another set of servers and he moved across to the other side of the room, looking up and down the racks. Mechanically, the systems appeared intact, but the constant flashing of crimson alert indicators showed that on the software level, things were amiss.

'You do this a lot?' Mooney's voice carried to him. 'This whole techno-espionage thing?'

'Too often,' he noted.

'Does it pay well?'

'Not as much as you'd think . . .' He shrugged. 'Perks are good, though – when you can take the time to enjoy them.'

'You single?'

That brought Marc up short. He wasn't quite sure how to reply.

'It's . . . uh . . . complicated. Why – you asking?'

'You're not my type.' Mooney chuckled. 'I like bad boys.'

'I don't know if I should be insulted by that.' When she didn't reply, Marc halted. 'Margaret? You there?'

'This interrupt gizmo . . .' Mooney's voice filtered back to him. 'Does it look like a metal box? With a bunch of hard drives and cables inside?'

He rushed over to her. An aluminium flight case nestled between the server stacks, festooned with wired connectors feeding into the closest system. It had been carefully positioned so that anyone making a casual survey would miss it completely, and it was clearly *not* part of the standard set-up.

'Hello, ugly,' Marc said to it. He pulled the trank gun from his jacket and handed it to Mooney. 'Here you go,' he told her. 'A promise is a promise.'

'I could shoot you with this,' noted Mooney, weighing the pistol in her hand. She flicked off the safety catch, but didn't quite aim it at him.

'Can you wait until we get this disconnected?' Marc nodded at the interrupt. He fished his walkie-talkie from a pocket and squeezed the push-to-talk button. 'Lucy, do you copy? I found the equipment. Get here if you can.'

He told her their floor and location, but when he released the button, all that came back was static.

'Lucy,' echoed Mooney. 'Is she the *complicated* part?'

Marc's lip curled. 'I thought *I* was social-engineering *you*.'

'Whatever you say, James Bond.' Mooney stuffed the trank gun inside her jumper and eyed the device warily. 'So you reckon Novick put this here? I mean, I don't find it hard to believe he's a misogynistic asshole and an opportunist, but committing treason? That'd take more balls than he has.'

'Don't mince words, Margaret,' said Marc, feeling around the cables that fed into the server stack. 'Tell me what you *really* think.'

'Yes, Ms Mooney, please do,' a snide, strident voice called out from behind them. 'You don't have to hold back. This is a safe space.'

A sweaty man in a cheap suit jacket emerged from the end of the server row. He aimed a Ruger pocket pistol at Marc and the woman, and the muzzle wavered back and forth between them.

'Mr Novick, I presume?' Marc pitched the question to Mooney, who nodded stiffly.

'He has a gun. A *real* one.'

'I noticed, yeah.'

'Look at me, not at her!' Novick snarled at him. 'Where's your partner? You figure you'd get the drop on me? You are sorely mistaken!'

Marc kept his hands where they were, holding on to the bundle of cables.

'Take it easy, Walter. Don't do something you can't walk back from.'

He looked past the man with the pistol and saw, to his dismay, that the indicator light on the security camera was still dark.

'Monitoring has been temporarily suspended on this floor,' said Novick, noticing his attention. 'Which means I'm free to deal with you as I see fit.' He gestured with the gun. 'Move away.'

Mooney raised her hands, but Marc stood his ground.

'You're not going to shoot,' he said, 'because if you do, the round from that LCP will over-penetrate right through me and hit this server. Who knows what kind of damage it might cause?'

'He's right about that,' said Mooney. 'My dad taught me to shoot a pistol when I told him I was moving to New York,' she added, by way of explanation.

'No one fucking cares,' grated Novick. 'Where's the woman?'

'No idea,' Marc admitted. 'Causing havoc, I would imagine.'

'Fine.' Novick took a step closer. 'I'll deal with her later.' He drew himself up and gave Mooney a haughty glare. 'I'm disappointed, Margaret. I wonder what people will say when they find out you were in on this conspiracy with Harlow . . .'

'What?' Mooney blinked, uncertain of what he meant.

But Marc could see where this was going. Novick carried on, laying out his version of events, making it up as he went.

'I don't know – maybe you and Sean were lovers or something. He got lonely after his wife divorced him. That's how you were drawn in. He took money to put the interrupt in place and you helped him. But his co-conspirators killed him. So sad.'

'What is he talking about?' Mooney turned towards Marc, and he saw a flicker of intent in her eyes.

'Nice story,' said Marc, covering for her. 'You need to work on the details a bit, but it's almost there.' He shifted his weight on to his back foot. He would only get one chance. 'Let me see if I can figure out the rest. You're going to kill me, then Margaret, and set it up to make it look like you discovered us with the device. This Harlow bloke you're on about gets blamed and . . . what? Instant promotion for Walter, yeah?' He shook his head. 'You have absolutely no idea who you're working for, do you? You're out for yourself.'

'You did this?' Mooney said, stiffening. 'Sean and his boys are dead, you son of a bitch!'

'Do you ever stop talking, woman?' Novick growled out the words, then aimed the gun at her. 'I'm sick of the sound of your voice!'

Now.

The instant the pistol was off him, Marc gave the cables a sharp jerk, yanking them out of the server. The interrupt came away with a fizzing crackle of static, and the racks in the room shut down at once, briefly dimming the lights.

'No, stop that!' Novick twisted back in Marc's direction, the pistol coming his way again. 'What did you do?'

'He fixed it,' said Mooney, as the servers came back to life and the lights blinked on again. She had the trank pistol in her hand, and shot Novick with it. At close range with good aim, she couldn't miss.

The dart went into his neck, and Novick became still, making an odd gurgling noise. Slowly, he slid against one of the racks and sank to the floor.

'Nice shot!'

Marc gave an appreciative nod and pulled the Ruger out of Novick's limp, sweaty hands.

Mooney released a sigh. 'Is it bad that I really enjoyed that?'

'No judgement here,' Marc replied, making a quick search of the unconscious man. He found Novick's access card in one pocket, and a burner phone in the other. He palmed both before rising to use the walkie again. 'Lucy? Target neutralised, repeat, target neutralised.' This time a static-choked voice answered back, but he couldn't pick out any words. 'I'm moving to the secondary elevator shaft. Meet me there. How copy?'

'*Sol—opy.*'

The buzz of interference cut up Lucy's words, but he was sure she'd got the message.

'Hey, look at that.' Mooney indicated the server racks.

The tide of red warning lights ebbed, each turning green as the system purged the interrupt's malignant influence. In a matter of minutes, the stalled reboot commands would propagate out across the whole of the grid, and the US financial network would come back online. The Combine's gambit had been cut short.

'So, you gonna tell me who you're working for?' Mooney gave him a long look. 'British Intelligence? SHD? Interpol? Give me a clue.'

'I could say No Such Agency,' he deflected, using the old spy community nickname for the NSA. 'Let's say some threads are best not pulled on.'

Marc didn't want to risk admitting he was part of Rubicon's disavowed Special Conditions Division, a group that many still considered to be no better than criminals. He placed the interrupt device in Mooney's hands.

'What am I supposed to do with this?' she asked.

Marc nodded at the insensible Novick. 'How would you like *his* job? I'm sure a perceptive person like you could figure it out.'

The radio crackled. '*Marc, you read me?*' He was relieved to hear Lucy's voice once more. '*I'm at the elevator, where are you? I got incoming, we need to be gone.*'

'On my way,' he replied.

He made for the door and Mooney muttered a question after him. 'Who *are* you guys?'

'Thanks for trusting me, Margaret.' Marc paused on the threshold. 'In the next few days, you're going to hear from people who'll say we're killers and rogues. You can make your own mind up who you believe.'

He threw her a wave and vanished into the corridor.

TWENTY-TWO

By the middle of the following day they had finally left Manhattan, starting from a cold, wet pre-dawn in the aftermath of the storm, joining the thin trickle of vehicles that still worked, up and across the Brooklyn Bridge.

The rusty old Econoline van had nothing in it that the EMP could affect, and it formed part of a convoy of aging cars, trucks and school buses ferrying people over to the other borough.

It was touch and go when they passed through a temporary National Guard checkpoint on the far side, but the fresh-faced soldiers who had been ferried in overnight were swamped with New Yorkers making the exodus, and Marc and Lucy used that to slip through the net. Their faces were on the watch lists of the CIA and the FBI, and after last night's work, most likely the NSA as well.

The window of opportunity for them to get out of the country would not stay open forever. Kara and Malte had left by a different route, and if everything went to plan, they would meet them at John F. Kennedy International, with tickets in hand for separate flights to Europe.

Marc hoped that the chaotic fallout from the EMP blast on Wall Street would cause enough confusion that the Rubicon team would be able to slip out of the US before anyone caught up with them – but it didn't stop him from worrying that every passing car might be carrying a pursuit team. The increased numbers of military and police helicopters passing overhead only served to rack up his tension.

He changed lanes through the sluggish traffic as the lines of vehicles oozed slowly northwards. In the passenger seat, Lucy had retreated into the depths of her hoodie. She had barely spoken two words to him in as many hours.

He looked past her, through the gaps in the buildings and across the East River to the streets they had left behind. In the light of day, beneath clear blue skies blown free of the storm, New York appeared as impressive and invulnerable as ever. Only the careful observer would note the damaged windows on some of the upper levels of the skyscrapers. The city had shrugged off another attack on its citizens and lived to tell the tale. Marc wondered what narrative would emerge from the reality of those desperate hours.

Back at the checkpoint, he heard a snatch of news over a radio from a parked car, a stern recounting of what was being labelled a terrorist cyberattack like the ones that had struck San Francisco and Seoul in previous years. He imagined any survivors from Connaught Cassidy's crew would be in interrogation rooms right now, and most likely Margaret Mooney and the team from Titanpointe would be in a similar situation. Whatever they told the authorities would likely not be made public.

'What?' Lucy eyed him, thinking his attention was on her.

And now it was.

'We're almost in the clear,' said Marc. 'Couple of hours from now, we'll be in first class, sipping sundowners.'

'Not soon enough.' She stared glumly at the buildings sliding past them. 'We should've gone through Jersey.'

Marc realised what he'd been missing. In their haste to get out of the city, he had forgotten that their route would take them within a few miles of the streets where Lucy Keyes had grown up.

Idiot, he chastised himself. *Should have thought of that.*

Like him, Lucy was a virtual exile in her native country, wanted for breaking numerous laws by a government that had been happy to use her skills to their advantage when it suited them.

'We're close to being finished with this,' said Marc, his tone softening. 'When it's over, we never need to come back here. You can be free of it.'

She gave a slow shake of the head. 'That's just it, I don't *want* to be free of it, Marc. I don't want to walk away and not look back.' Lucy gave a sigh. 'You know, I thought I could, but ... Being here ... It stings more than I ever thought it would.'

Marc focused on the road ahead, contemplating his own circumstances. He had come a long way from the South London council estate where he had spent his childhood. His own sentiments for home were bittersweet and hard to categorise. Some days he missed London like a long-lost relative – the familiarity and safety of it. Back home, he had always known who he was and where he was going. But since becoming part of Rubicon, that certainty had gone away. Liberating, but daunting all the same.

They drove along in silence for a while, and then he noticed Lucy lean forward in her seat, craning her neck to see something off the highway. She looked down at her past, at sidewalks she might have wandered along as a girl.

On an impulse, Marc pulled the van across as they came upon the next off-ramp, and instead of making the turn south in the direction of the airport, he took them on to the local roads cutting through Queens.

She jerked up in her seat.

'Where are you going?'

'Last time we were in London, I didn't get the chance to look in on my old ends. Seems unfair to force that on you as well.' He pointed over the top of the steering wheel. 'Where to?'

'This is a bad idea,' she said. 'People around here think I'm a felon.'

Marc didn't need to press to know that by *people* Lucy meant *her family*.

'You want me to turn around?'

'No,' she added, after a moment. 'You're right. Keep driving.'

Lucy directed him around side streets and residential roads, gradually opening up. She pointed out the site of the old cinema where she'd had her summer job, and the mini-mall that had felt like the centre of the universe in her teens.

But then they came up on a particular bodega – a compact all-in grocery store on a street corner – and her expression darkened.

'Pull over,' she demanded.

Marc felt a chill run through him.

'Is that . . .?'

'Where my dad died. Yeah.'

In the past, lost in a freezing Icelandic wilderness, Marc and Lucy had clung together for warmth in the cold of a pitch-dark night, and to stave off the effects of hypothermia they had talked about their old lives to keep up their spirits.

Lucy's story was a heartbreaker: a young girl with a troubled older brother and a single mum, a father cruelly taken from them in a robbery gone awry. He'd been in the wrong place at the wrong time, caught in the crossfire when he tried to intervene. And it had happened here.

Marc put the van in gear, meaning to move off.

'I'm sorry, I never should have—'

But Lucy's reply was the slam of the passenger door as she jumped down from the vehicle and strode across to the store's entrance.

She was already inside by the time Marc arrived, and as he entered, an older Hispanic man in a baggy shirt gave him a distracted wave from behind the store's counter.

'Card machine's out of order,' he said, indicating a freshly written sign taped to the door. 'System's down because of the power cut, cash only.'

'Yeah, no problem . . .'

Marc made his way down the shop's narrow aisle, between piles of packets and cans. The size of the place was deceptive, and its passages went back a long way. He found Lucy near a rack of snack bags, atop which dozed an elderly tabby.

'Hey, Georgie,' she whispered, stroking its chin. She had a smile that made her face light up.

The old cat's eyes were milky and his fur was greying, but he reacted as if he knew her, nuzzling her fingers.

'I used to feed him bits of jerky,' she explained. 'Can't believe he's still here.'

'Hey, puss.' Marc gave the animal a stroke. 'What was Lucy here like when she was younger, George? A right troublemaker, I bet.'

The cat emitted a low purr, and Marc took that as agreement.

Lucy looked around, and exhaled a deep breath. 'Doesn't feel real.' Then she shook her head. 'No, that's not it. It feels . . . *smaller*.' She sounded vulnerable. It was something rare for her. At length, she pointed back down the aisle, towards the counter. 'That's where it happened. Where Dad got shot. He's buried over in Cedar Grove, but this place is more of a marker than some headstone.'

Marc looked. Nothing indicated a man had lost his life in this place. It seemed so mundane.

He thought about the loss of his mother, and her last moments in a hospital bed. Ever since that day, Marc had loathed hospitals, and the cloying atmosphere inside them that brought his worst memories to life. He did his best to avoid them whenever he could.

But Lucy walks straight back in here, looks it right in the eye.

He wondered if he would have been able to do the same thing in her place.

Of its own accord, Marc's hand found Lucy's.

'You okay?'

'Yeah.' She nodded, then gave a regretful chuckle. 'We should go. Coming home, this is bad op-sec. But I had to do it.' She gave his hand a squeeze. 'Thanks for being here.'

There was more to say, but the moment slipped away from them when a man spoke up from behind her.

'Lou? That you?'

Lucy heard the voice and froze, her hand gripping Marc's tightly.

Marc turned slowly to see a tall black guy wearing a New York Mets baseball jersey and a white kufi cap. He had a paper bag filled with groceries in one hand and a carton of milk in the other.

He had never seen this man before, but Marc noted a familiar pattern in his features. He had the exact same expression on his face that Lucy did when confronted by something unexpected.

'Hey, Johnny,' Lucy managed, letting go of his hand. 'Marc, meet my brother – Jasur.'

'Who is he?' Jasur eyed Marc coldly.

'I'm a friend of your sister's.' Marc stiffened, uncertain how to react.

Different emotions warred across Jasur's face. 'Lou, why are you here?'

'Doesn't matter.' Lucy stepped past him to make for the door. 'Marc, c'mon.'

Jasur struggled to find the right thing to say, and Marc felt a pang of sympathy for the man. His own relationship with his sister Kate was a poor one, and he knew how it hurt when you couldn't pull up the right words to tell someone how you felt about them.

'Mom's at home,' Jasur called after her. 'You know she talks about you all the time.'

Finally, Marc interposed himself between the two siblings.

'Look, mate, sorry about this. We shouldn't be here. We don't want to cause any trouble. Maybe it's best if we just leave.'

The irony of his words, based on what he had said only moments before, wasn't lost on him.

Jasur studied Marc straight-on for the first time.

'You're trying to look out for her. I appreciate that. But if you know my sister, you know the woman makes her own choices.'

'That she does.' Marc turned towards Lucy. 'Stay or go? Your call. I'll back you up either way.'

She gave Marc a sorrowful smile.

'Yeah. My call.'

The Keyes' house was a few blocks away.

Rust-red in the afternoon light, the brick-built two-storey house had white-framed windows and a sloped roof. It sat on a street lined with identical homes, behind a patch of lawn, and stairs led up to a stoop and the front door.

Marc felt like an interloper, and he hung back as they walked up. Lucy gave him a questioning look, which he answered with a shake of the head.

'You go ahead. Don't mind me, I'll wait outside.'

Jasur led her in, and Marc heard him call out as he opened the door.

'Mom? We have a visitor. Lou's come home.'

Lucy hesitated on the threshold, and for a second, the fearless soldier-sniper faded away and she was filled with doubts. Then she disappeared inside and the door closed behind her.

Marc heard a faint sound from within the house that might have been a sob or a gasp of joy, and nodded to himself. After the trials and losses the Rubicon survivors had endured, it was uplifting to find something good in the world, even if only for a moment.

He sat on the steps with his back to the house and took in the street, letting the time pass in silence. It was nothing like his child-hood home, and yet it was exactly the same. Ordinary. Conventional. The kind of place where you might grow up and never range too far.

But we're not like that, are we?

Marc considered that truth about Lucy and himself, about Ekko Solomon and the rest of the Rubicon team. As different as their diverse origin stories might have been, they shared the same instinct to push back against the darkness in the world.

He watched a silver SUV rumble past as the door behind him opened again and Jasur emerged with a glass of lemonade. He offered it to Marc, but didn't sit down next to him.

'Mom said "that skinny white boy looks thirsty", so here you go.'

'Cheers.' Marc saluted with the glass and took a sip. It was home-made and tart. He nodded at the house. 'How's it going?'

'Hard work,' admitted Jasur. 'It's worth it.' He paused before continuing, then changed tack. 'What happened in the city last night . . .? The news says terrorists.' The other man watched him carefully. 'You part of that?'

'Yeah. We couldn't prevent it from happening. But we did stop it, in the end. Would have been a lot worse if we hadn't.'

'Worse.' Jasur's manner hardened around the word. 'My sister was sent to military prison because of something she did halfway around the world in some war zone. Then she vanishes for years. A card at Christmas is the only way we know she's alive.' His gaze bored into Marc. 'Months ago, Feds come to my house and my family, and to this house and my mom, and you know what they say? *Lucy Keyes is a terrorist. She killed innocent people.*' He scowled. 'You have any idea what it's like to hear that? And I'm a black man who converted to Islam. What do you reckon those Feds did next? Questioned me for days.'

'I know she never meant to bring any of that on you.' Marc gave a slow shake of the head. Like Lucy, he, too, had been framed by the Combine, and they were still no closer to proving their innocence. 'You don't believe what they told you, though.'

'I don't know what to believe,' said Jasur. 'I don't know you. I'm not sure I know Lou anymore.'

'Yeah, you do,' countered Marc. 'You asked her to come here. Would you have done that if you didn't trust her? You and your mum still love her, that's obvious.' He put down the glass and stood up. 'I'm a big believer in instinct. Let me tell you what *I* know about Lucy Keyes. She's a hero. She's saved hundreds of lives, mine included. I'd be dead ten times over if not for her. I trust her implicitly, no question. You should be proud of her.'

'You care about my sister.' Jasur made it a statement, not a query.

'I do.'

Marc wanted to say more, but he didn't know how to frame the reply beyond that simple statement.

What he and Lucy shared was more than bonds forged under fire, more than friendship. But they had never quantified it, never had the time to decide what it truly meant. In that moment, Marc found himself hoping that when this was behind them, they might have the chance.

A flicker of silver caught his eye, drawing his attention back to the street. The same SUV he had seen pass by a few minutes ago drew up at the kerb and halted. Four doors opened at once, allowing men in dark suits to exit the vehicle with practised precision.

'Get inside,' Marc snapped. 'Lock the doors and stay away from the windows.'

Jasur nodded, sensing the same danger.

'Those aren't cops, man.'

'I know.'

Marc advanced on the men, coming forward to meet them. He let his hands fall to his sides, aware that the only weapon he had was in the van parked on the far side of the road.

Two of them waited by the vehicle while the senior agents came up to flank Marc. He scanned their faces with a flash of recognition.

The handsome man on the right carried himself with a self-assured air and a smirk playing on his lips. He clearly believed he was in control of this situation. The rough-edged man on the left had the same height and build as his colleague, but his suit wasn't so neat. He had a flinty gaze, with the prospect of violence glittering there.

'Mr Dane,' said the first man. 'It's been a few years, so I'll assume you forgot what I told you at our last meeting.'

'Something about staying off our radar,' said his partner, with a sneer. 'And staying the hell out of this country.'

He remembered their names now.

'Cahill. Durant. You blokes still working out of Langley, or did the CIA get shot of you?'

Cahill ignored the question. 'It's nice to know we made a memorable impression. That almost makes up for you impersonating me at that black site in Poland.'

'Needs must,' said Marc. At the time, temporarily adopting the CIA agent's identity had been a vital step in getting information on a rogue nuclear weapon. 'Hope it didn't sully your reputation.'

Durant made a snorting noise.

Cahill gestured at the Keyes house.

'Why don't you ask your partner there to come on out, nice and easy? We don't have to make a thing of this.'

Marc shook his head. 'I don't think so.'

'Who gives a shit *what* you think, limey?' Durant took a step forward, but Marc held his ground. 'Get Keyes out here right now, or we'll break down the door and drag her family into the street, kicking and screaming. The whole neighbourhood can watch.'

Marc gave Durant a steely look. When they had first met, he had been hard-pressed to conceal how intimidated he was by the CIA operatives – but a lot of water had passed under the bridge since then, and Marc Dane was a different man.

'Nice to see you've mellowed with age, Durant,' he replied, then shot a look at the other agent. 'Can't you keep your dog on a lead?'

Cahill's smirk didn't shift. 'You made a mistake coming here. You gave us time to track you down. We have Kara Wei and your talkative Finnish friend in custody at JFK.' He tut-tutted. 'Bad tradecraft, Dane. I expected better.'

'Yeah, well. Sometimes other things are more important.'

'Look, we know Cassidy and the Combine are behind the Wall Street attack,' he added, in a companionable tone. 'The men we pulled off his yacht have shown good judgement in their decisions to assist us. The NSA are conducting their own investigation into the incident at Titanpointe. I understand Mr Novick became very talkative once he understood he would be charged with high treason.'

'Nerds got no guts,' noted Durant, with an air of challenge.

Cahill continued. 'Along with additional intelligence from some confidential sources, we have the big picture. We're just missing the pieces involving Rubicon. So we need you to come with us.'

'For *debriefing*,' added Durant.

Marc pointed at him, as he spoke to Cahill.

'You know he's not exactly selling me on the idea? And what are these *confidential sources* you mentioned?'

'They wouldn't exactly be confidential if I revealed them.'

Cahill's mask of self-confidence slipped a little. Marc saw the fraction of doubt in the other man and seized on it.

'You know Glovkonin's pulling the strings, right? He's been angling to run the Combine from day one. Cassidy's card was marked from the moment this operation went into action. Glovkonin's already taken out at least one of the other members. I wouldn't be surprised if he's the last man standing by now.' Neither of the agents replied, and Marc carried on. 'Let's cut the bullshit and the chest-thumping, yeah? Real talk. Glovkonin is the problem, and as long as he's still out there, this isn't over. His ambitions won't stop with screwing over your stock market.'

Cahill's smile compressed into a thin line. 'We cleaned house after our last encounter,' he began, referring to a failed Combine-sponsored terrorist bombing in Washington. 'Purged as much of their influence as we could from the agency and the government.'

'Couldn't touch that slime Cassidy, though,' Durant said bitterly. 'Son of a bitch was too well connected. He's the reason why we were looking the other way when Wall Street happened. His people tied us up with false leads.'

'You don't have to thank us for dealing with it,' said Lucy, as she emerged from the front door. 'You're welcome.'

'Ms Keyes,' said Cahill. 'Nice of you to join us.'

'You've been listening?' said Marc, as she moved up to stand shoulder to shoulder with him.

'Every word.' Lucy eyed the two agents. 'Watch where you put those shoes on Mom's lawn. Don't make her get the hose.'

'The Company appreciates your efforts,' said Cahill, ignoring her comment, 'but we can't be seen to associate with wanted terrorists.'

Marc let out an incredulous snort. 'Have you ever actually read the CIA's history?'

'We're not terrorists,' insisted Lucy. 'We were framed. That video of us shooting those soldiers in Cyprus is a deepfake.'

'We know,' said Durant, with a sneer.

'But you won't go public with that information.' Marc looked to Cahill. 'Because it doesn't benefit you.'

'Well, we might,' mused the other agent. 'For the correct incentive. If we could ascertain the location of one Ekko Solomon, for example. He has a lot to answer for.'

'Pass,' said Lucy.

'Okay.' Durant folded his arms across his chest and threw a nod at the other agents waiting by their vehicle. The two men placed their hands on their holstered weapons. 'Back to where we started. You come with us or we drag you away.' He grinned. 'Please resist. I really want an excuse.'

'You won't get it.' Marc reached into the pocket of his jacket, and every gun there came out to aim in his direction. 'Calm down,' he retorted, revealing the burner phone he had taken off Walter Novick.

While they had been stuck in the stop-start traffic leaving Manhattan, Marc had dug into the simple software of the device,

JAMES SWALLOW | 443

dredging the burner's memory for any useful fragments of data. Nothing could truly be deleted without a full factory reset, and Novick had not had time to tamper with the phone before Marc secured it. He had forwarded what he found on the burner to Kara, who had already come up with some interesting information.

'Novick got his orders through this,' Marc explained. 'Tracking the calls routes them through multiple blinds in Europe and the Russian Federation, back to the offices of the G-Kor corporation in Moscow. Glovkonin's turf.'

'That's no use to us. We can't touch him there.' Cahill's expression soured as he re-holstered his sidearm. 'Directives from the current administration have limited special activities and Ground Branch operations inside Russian borders.'

'Well, you have an opportunity here,' Marc began, and he tossed the phone to Durant. 'You can wrap up this attack today. Take us in and soak us for everything we know. Declare victory. You can pretend it's all over. But we know it isn't.'

'Not as long as that arrogant Russki asshole is still vertical,' added Lucy.

'Or we can do the other thing—' Marc continued.

'No!' Durant broke in. 'Not this shit again! You're not going to talk your way out of it this time, Dane.'

'For crying out loud, Milo,' Cahill said wearily, 'learn when to shut up.'

Durant scowled. 'Screw you, Simon.'

Cahill made a *carry on* gesture. 'Keep talking.'

Marc gave Lucy a look and she returned it. She would back him every step of the way.

'I've been hunting this bloke ever since a bomb went off in Barcelona six years ago,' he said. 'We can go after Glovkonin, to the place you can't reach. And we can end this. Kill the king. Burn down the castle. You know the drill.' He opened his hands. 'For that to happen, what you need to do is . . . go away.'

'Tempting,' offered Cahill.

'What stops you from running, and leaving us holding the bag?' said Durant. 'What do you get out of it?'

'Payback,' replied Lucy.

After a few moments of silence, Cahill gestured to the other agents, sending them back to their vehicle. He glanced at Marc and Lucy, weighing up his choice, then produced a smartphone and speed-dialled a number. As Cahill walked out of earshot to conduct a conversation, Durant's glower deepened, and he spat.

Lucy spoke quietly out of the corner of her mouth. 'You think they're gonna go for it?'

'If I've learned one thing about the CIA,' said Marc, 'it's that if they can get somebody else to do their dirty work, they will.'

She nodded in agreement. 'Yeah, the Virginia farm boys do love that *plausible deniability*, right?'

Durant stared at him. 'You think you're so fuckin' smart,' he growled.

'I do,' Marc admitted. 'Because I am.'

'Yes, ma'am. Understood, ma'am.' Cahill walked back, finishing his call, then rang a different number. 'Cut the other two loose,' he told whoever was on the end of the line, before hanging up. Cahill studied Marc and Lucy, then smiled thinly. 'Have a nice flight,' he said, and walked away.

Andre shifted uncomfortably in his seat, and peered through the thick window of the armoured Audi limousine. He watched the traffic flash past across the multiple lanes of the Varshavskoye Highway as they sped southwards. Rain had come in with the nightfall over Moscow, turning the road into a ribbon of shining black. Red and white lights blurred in both directions, the other vehicles on the road rendered into indistinct, colourless shapes.

He was convinced they were being followed. The hacker's default mindset was high-functioning paranoia. The trait benefited him in his chosen profession, first with the renegade cyber-mercenaries known as Ghost5, and more recently in his service to the Combine and Pytor Glovkonin.

The Russian sat across from Andre in the back of the limo, idly toying with the illuminated pane of a digital tablet. With the hard granite-cut planes of his face lit by the cold blue glow of the device, Glovkonin resembled something inhuman.

'They say that dogs can smell a man's fear,' he said, without looking up. 'Perhaps it is the wolf in my blood, but, Andre, you reek of it.'

The Frenchman made a pinched face. 'I'm concerned, yes. We should have left hours ago. In situations like these, every moment counts.'

Glovkonin raised an eyebrow. 'Do you believe I have something to be afraid of?' He pitched it like a question, but it was really a warning.

Andre hedged his answer. 'Moscow is full of opportunists. And considering that our current situation is . . . in flux . . . I would say discretion is advisable.'

'No one in the Duma or the FSB would dare to move against me. Not now. It is not in their interests. And no one else has the courage.'

'It's still a risk!'

'Transitions of power are always destructive acts,' the Russian replied. 'But not for those who ascend.' He looked up. 'You should be content. You've done well. You chose the right side.'

'Yes.' Andre swallowed hard.

When Glovkonin's moves against the other members of the Combine's ruling cabal had become apparent, he had acted out of self-preservation more than any belief in the Russian's goals. Survival was and always would be his prime motivator.

He wanted to be far away from Moscow, safe in the compound at the foot of the Urals that G-Kor's owner had built as his private sanctuary. Little short of a full military strike could threaten them there, but here on a crowded motorway, they were vulnerable. Even behind the Audi's centimetres of armour plate and bullet-resistant glass, Andre could not settle.

'Oh, how tragic.' Glovkonin said the words with a quirk of the lip as he read something on his tablet. 'See.'

He turned the device around so Andre could read it. A page from the Russia Today news site had an article about the death of Swiss financier Rutger Bremmens, whose body had been dug out of an alpine snowdrift that morning by local authorities.

'Heart attack.' Andre picked out a few key phrases from the text. 'Accusations of financial malfeasance . . . Police suspect suicide.'

'Indeed. When the connections between Bremmens and that fool Cassidy come to light, they will suspect him of much more.' Glovkonin drew back the tablet and settled against his chair, allowing a sigh to escape. 'It is disappointing that the Wall Street gambit was cut short before it had a chance to do some serious damage. If I could have had a few more days, we might have pushed the Americans to the brink of ruin. But there will be other opportunities.'

Andre had seen the numbers from the shorted stocks and gamed currency gains that resulted from the temporary blackout of the US financial grid. He had personally ensured that the billions of dollars harvested by the illegal operation went to G-Kor's coffers, not to those of the Combine. Had everything gone to plan, that number would have been in the trillions. The figures were hard to grasp. Beyond a certain point the digits became incomprehensible, and the ruined lives connected to them became nothing more than a statistic.

'You're richer than you have ever been,' noted the hacker.

'Money does not matter,' replied the Russian, glancing out of the window. The limo crossed the MKAD ring road that marked the outer perimeter of Moscow and continued south, in the direction of Podolsk. Glovkonin studied the teeming traffic as it began to thin out around them. 'Ordinary minds put too much stock in it. But money is only a tool. Power is the only true commodity.'

'Now you have it in abundance,' offered Andre.

Glovkonin gave a dismissive grunt. 'It is not a destination. Power is not a goal, not a mountain that can be climbed. It is a marathon that never ends. Power builds upon power, and if one ceases to accrue it, one begins to fail.'

At times, the Russian would hold forth like this, and Andre had learned to let him speak. Glovkonin enjoyed lecturing others.

'So what comes next?' the hacker prompted. '*Combine 2.0*? Or something else?'

'I have been mulling a change in career,' admitted the oligarch. 'The political arena beckons. The current president has been allowed to hold on to power for far too long. Russia is overdue a change in leadership.'

Andre's eyes widened. 'He won't step down. Everyone who has tried to unseat him has failed. Not to mention the ones who are dead or in the gulag.'

'Everyone who has tried did not have the resources of the Combine behind them.' Then Glovkonin waved away the notion. 'A conversation for another time. Tonight, I have other matters to attend to.' A feral smile grew on his lips. 'A rare indulgence, if I am honest. One I have been looking forward to for some time.'

Andre felt the limousine changing lanes and looked out of the window again. They passed by a long strip of roadworks ringed with yellow warning lamps and finally a sign flashed past, indicating an upcoming turn-off towards their destination: Ostafyevo International Airport, just a few kilometres distant.

A former military airfield that had been converted for civilian use, the complex currently operated under the control of one of the corporate giants that lived in a symbiotic relationship with the Kremlin. Glovkonin often used Ostafyevo to slip in and out of Moscow unobserved, but tonight he was here for a different reason.

The limousine rolled to a stop on the apron as an Antonov cargo plane taxied in off the runway. The An-72's distinctive over-wing jet engines keened through the sound of the hissing rain, and it halted a hundred metres distant, pinned under the misty white glow from nearby spotlights. The aircraft had flown in directly from an airstrip in northern Turkey, bypassing the usual challenges from air traffic control, thanks to G-Kor's influence.

Glovkonin's ever-present bodyguard Gregor exited the front of the Audi and came to the passenger door, unfolding a large umbrella. His comrade Misha remained in the driver's seat, keeping the limo's motor running.

The Russian climbed out, pausing to straighten his jacket, and Andre followed, pulling his coat closed and turning up his collar. Glovkonin's sideways look made it clear there wasn't room under the umbrella for the hacker.

The Antonov's boarding hatch dropped open and three men disembarked, staying in the lee of the jet's wing. One of them took up a position that allowed him to scan the airfield – a thin figure with a baseball cap pulled down low over his eyes, whose motions betrayed nervousness,. The second was a large man, easily as muscular as the heavyset Gregor. Both of them wore the signature outfit of the private military contractor ALEPH: black tactical trousers and combat jacket, with red rank flashes on their arms and the sigil of a vulture on their shoulder patches. They each carried PP-2000 sub-machine guns on two-point harnesses.

The third man was marched forward by the second. He was tall, his skin as dark as teak, and he moved with a pronounced limp. In the blaze of the spotlights, the state of the clothes he wore was clearly visible. Once, his attire had been an expensive Savile Row suit, but now it was ripped and torn, a tattered version of its former elegance.

The dark-skinned man looked up, shivering in the wet, presenting a scarred face with one ruined eye as the Russian approached.

'Ah, Solomon,' said Glovkonin. 'You have been a singular pursuit.' When the African didn't respond, he stepped closer. Gregor moved with him, holding up the umbrella to keep off the downpour. 'Nothing to say? We are finally face to face, and you have no words?'

Nearby, Andre moved to find some cover from the rain and his attention shifted to the man in the cap. The ALEPH mercenary turned his back on the hacker, but the action rang a wrong note with Andre. Something about the man was familiar to him, but he couldn't place it.

'Very well,' said Glovkonin, frowning. 'One does wish for some crowning, cathartic moment of triumph after a victory, but I will settle for this. An ending, in the darkness and the pouring rain. In the grip of the cold.' He turned to Gregor. 'Draw your gun.'

Gregor produced an Udav semi-automatic and displayed it, pulling back the slide to show a bullet already in the chamber. Glovkonin nodded his approval.

'I have won,' said the Russian. 'Go to your death knowing that, Solomon. Everything you have done to oppose me ultimately counted for nothing.'

'Are you sure?' Solomon said softly, his voice barely louder than the sound of the rain.

'Your people are dead,' Glovkonin answered. He had seen the post-operation message from the hit team that captured the African in Istanbul, noting the killings of Solomon's comrades. 'Those remaining are scattered and powerless. They won't survive.'

Dane, the woman Keyes and the others were a spent force. They might have disrupted the Wall Street attack, but that was the best they could manage. They were not a real threat. In the end, despite all they had done, Pytor Glovkonin had what he wanted.

'You are mistaken,' said Solomon. 'You think you have broken us. But instead, you have ensured that we have nothing to lose.'

He bowed his head forward, as if he were about to pray.

Glovkonin frowned. Something about the motion seemed off.

Sheltering beneath the wing, Andre half-listened to the conversation, bracing himself for the gunshot that would bring this bit of theatre to an end. The ALEPH mercenary with the cap actively avoided his gaze, turning away whenever he tried to get a good look at him.

'Show me your face,' demanded the hacker.

'Go away,' said the mercenary.

His voice was gruff, but the tone was forced. Andre detected a familiar, nasal register beneath the words, and his eyes widened with surprise.

I know this man.

'Delancort . . .?'

'Ah, *Tabernak*.' The man in the cap swore, his native Québecois accent emerging.

Andre made to call out a warning, but the chance was stolen from him.

A low whistling hum droned past the hacker, causing him to flinch, and in the same instant as the sound of a rifle shot reached him, a web of cracks appeared on the limo's windscreen, splintering the bulletproof glass directly in front of the driver.

Misha reacted with a jolt, jamming the Audi into gear, but a second shot came a split second after the first. The next bullet hit the same spot as the first and penetrated. Bright crimson spattered against the inside of the glass, and the limo lurched forward and stopped.

Andre's sense of self-preservation kicked in, and he spun away. The heavy stock of a sub-machine gun struck him in the belly before he could run, and he crumpled to the tarmac. Incongruous in his military attire, Henri Delancort stood over him, brandishing the SMG.

'Stay down, *salaud*!'

Near the cargo plane, Gregor reacted as he was trained to, bodily shoving Glovkonin behind him, as the other false ALEPH merc brought up his gun. The bodyguard opened fire with his pistol, shooting at Solomon and the second man.

Benjamin Harun mirrored Gregor's last act by putting himself in front of Solomon as two shots from the Udav pistol slammed into his chest. The infernal heat from the bullets knocked him back into Solomon, and together they collapsed against the fuselage of the Antonov.

Gregor kept firing, switching targets towards Delancort. He bellowed at his principal to get back to the car, his full focus on making sure that Glovkonin escaped alive.

Delancort was no soldier, and he did not stand his ground, diving to the wet tarmac. Gregor's shots sparked around him, and a stray shot from the wild fire clipped Andre, tearing out a divot of blood and bone as the round entered the hacker's skull.

But Gregor's act of loyalty was in vain. Before he could end Delancort's life, the next bullet screaming in from the darkness creased his throat and opened his neck to the air in a steaming arc of crimson.

In her sniper post set up on the edge of the airstrip, Lucy's view of the Antonov gave her a clear line of sight. The heavy calibre round fired from the bolt-action KSVK anti-materiel rifle was powerful enough to kill the bodyguard with one shot, almost decapitating him in the process. But saving Delancort's life had given the Russian the moment he needed to get into cover behind the limousine.

'Shit!' she cursed, as she saw movement behind the blood-spattered windshield. Glovkonin hauled the corpse of the other bodyguard out and scrambled into the driver's seat, crouching low where she couldn't see him.

Switching targets, Lucy aimed for the Audi's engine compartment, hoping that the last armour-piercing 12.7mm rounds in the magazine might strike something vital. But it was a forlorn hope. The limo was better protected than most military assault vehicles.

Glovkonin floored the accelerator and the limo vaulted forward, whipping around the Antonov in a skidding arc, aiming back towards the airport's exit road and the highway beyond.

Lucy pressed the radio headset clipped to her ear and called out a warning.

'Marc! Glovkonin's coming to you!'

'*Copy that,*' said the Brit. '*He won't get far.*'

TWENTY-THREE

The strategy was an ambush. A straight takedown to neutralise Glovkonin's bodyguards and isolate the man himself – but battle plans, as the old soldier's saying went, never survive first contact with the enemy.

What had been the second part of the trap to slam shut on the Russian was now the only thing preventing his escape. Inside the security hut at the end of the access road, Kara worked frantically at a control panel. Out in the driving rain, Marc and Malte took up hasty positions either side of the vehicle barrier that bisected the road. The heavy metal ramp remained in its lowered position as the limo's headlights washed over them.

The black stretch Audi hurtled towards them at a fast clip, the heavy engine roaring.

'Hurry it up!' shouted Marc, but Kara didn't look up, responding with a raised middle finger as she worked as fast as she could.

'Tyres?' Malte called out the question, raising the assault rifle in his hands to aim at the oncoming vehicle. He and Marc had identical AK-12s, supplied thanks to an anonymous CIA source in-country, but it was doubtful that even a salvo of fully automatic fire would be enough to stop Glovkonin's armoured beast.

'Run-flats,' said Marc, with a shake of the head. 'Aim for the driver and hope for the best.'

'Driver,' repeated the Finn. 'Firing!'

Malte's AK brayed, emitting a tongue of flame from the muzzle as he lit off bullets in three-round bursts.

Marc did the same, and the rifle bucked against him. It was hard to stop his shots climbing off the target, and each hit sparked away from the bonnet and grille of the limo as it drew closer.

So much for quick and quiet, he told himself. *They'll hear this in the Kremlin.*

The blazing glow from the headlights came up in a tide of white as Glovkonin hit them with full beams, but even as it dazzled him, Marc kept firing into the oncoming machine.

He heard Kara give a shrill cry of delight and behind him the security ramp rose, thudding into position with a crunch of hydraulics. The metal barrier was too high for the low-riding, heavyweight limo. If Glovkonin struck it at speed, the vehicle would be wrecked.

The Russian wasn't willing to concede yet. Spotting the blockade, Glovkonin wrenched the blood-slicked steering wheel to the left and the limo slipped into a wide fish-tail skid, turning to go off-road.

Marc threw himself out of the way, but the rear quarter of the long car came around like a wrecking ball and clipped Malte where he stood, the impact sending the Finn flying through the air. Marc's gut twisted as he saw Malte bounce off the outside of the security hut and crumple.

Picking himself up, Marc sprinted after the limo's crimson tail lights over churned-up grass and earth, firing into the vehicle until his magazine emptied. The limo bulldozed through a chain-link fence and across a car park, knocking aside an aging Lada and a trio of parked motorcycles. Even with bullet-riddled panels, broken windows and torn-up tyres, the thing still stormed on, getting further away with every passing moment.

We're going to lose him.

Rubicon's last roll of the dice would be wasted. The gamble they had set in motion months ago on a dusty African airstrip would fail, and Glovkonin would slip away. He would never surface again. They would never have this opportunity to be so close. It had to be now, tonight.

We have to finish this!

There were helicopters on the other side of the runway, but Marc had no way of knowing which were fuelled, and if he went for one of them, he risked losing sight of Glovkonin altogether. Replacing the AK's spent magazine with a fresh one, he ran towards the car park, shouting out to Kara as he moved.

'Check on Malte!'

'On it!' The woman sprinted out to meet him and urgently pressed something into his hand. 'Take this!'

'What . . .?'

The object was a metal saucer the size of a compact disc.

'Just get after him, I'll explain on the way!'

Marc didn't waste any more time with questions, dashing across to the unlucky motorcycles that the limo had shunted out of its way. One of them was a wreck, the front wheel badly buckled where the heavy car had ridden over it, but a well-used Suzuki scrambler was still in working order – and more importantly, Marc could hot-wire it in less than twenty seconds. With a tinny roar, the bike's motor caught and Marc gave it the revs. It got away from him with an initial surge of speed over the wet ground, but then he leaned into it and found his balance.

He followed the limo's path of destruction out through the remains of another broken fence and on to the road, closing the distance as he powered up an on-ramp leading to the main highway.

Rain streamed off his face, soaking his beard and hair. The down-pour coming right at him made it hard to see, and there hadn't been time to search around for a helmet.

But soon, across four lanes of sparse traffic, he spotted the low shape of the limousine. Glovkonin was unaccustomed to driving something as big as the armoured Audi, and the car had to steer like a boat in full sail. The twitchy motions it made told Marc that at least some of the rounds that had hit the vehicle had done real damage, but it was still a long way from being stopped.

He risked taking a hand off the steering to shift his AK on its strap, so that the assault rifle aimed forward across the handlebars. As he moved, Marc felt the weight of the metal disc in his pocket. He tapped his radio headset to voice-active mode.

'Kara?' He had to yell to be heard over the wind. 'You hear me?'

'*Marc?*' The hacker sounded faint and far away. '*What's your location?*'

He ignored the question. 'How's Malte?'

'*Says he broke something, so you know he's not happy,*' she replied breathlessly. '*Do you have the target?*'

'I see the fucker, yeah.'

'*Listen carefully!*' Kara spoke over him. '*Get that disc on the car! As close to the engine as you can, understand?*'

'What is it – a limpet mine?'

'*Close enough! Just do it quick, before you get out of range, I have to trigger it from here!*'

Glovkonin's heart hammered in his chest. A potent cocktail of adrenaline and emotion surged through him. There was rage and fear and strange elation, and he found himself cackling with laughter as he urged the Audi on into the rain.

Once more, fate and his enemies had tried to destroy him, and once again they had failed. He had to give the African his due – the ruse had almost worked.

It was obvious what had happened: the ALEPH team Andre sent to Istanbul had walked into a trap set by Solomon and his people, and once dispatched, they were impersonated to sell the lie that Glovkonin's quarry had been captured.

'You were too eager to believe it, Pytor!' Glovkonin said the words aloud, over the hiss of the rain coming in through the limo's shattered windscreen. 'You wanted it too badly!' He shook his head. This was a salient lesson. He had allowed himself to become overconfident after the dispatch of Bremmens and the others. 'A good attempt, Solomon,' he muttered, pulling his jacket tighter against the chill. 'But not good enough.'

Soaked through and stained with the blood of his luckless driver, he was still alive. He had survived far worse. He would *endure*.

Glovkonin reached for the encrypted smartphone in his pocket, already planning the next moves to get himself to safety. As he did, he caught sight of movement in the limo's wing mirror. A single headlight – a motorcycle – came up fast behind him.

'I see you.'

He knew who it would be. The Britisher, Dane. No one else was such a bane to his life.

Keeping one hand on the steering wheel, the Russian grabbed the Udav pistol he had taken from Misha's corpse and shoved the driver's-side door with his shoulder. It creaked open, letting in the foul weather and the spray from the road.

Twisting in the seat, he aimed the pistol over his shoulder and leaned out. Firing towards the motorcycle, he paced three rounds at his pursuer, rewarded by a sudden flicker as the rider tried to evade.

A split second later, yellow flame flashed and Glovkonin recoiled back into the driver's seat as a burst of return fire hammered into the open door. Bullets chewed into the frame, and a ricochet flicked around the interior, causing the Russian to cry out in surprise. But the deflected bullet missed him and he grinned wolfishly.

'It will take more than that,' he growled.

The open door struck the back of a slow-moving truck in the neighbouring lane as the limo sped past, the impact tearing off the wing mirror and slamming it closed. Glovkonin cursed and cast around, trying to catch sight of the motorcycle. Pushing the accelerator to the floor, he changed lanes, hoping to draw Dane out.

It worked. Another flash of reflected light told him that the Britisher had cut across the limo's slipstream to race up the inside, between the limo and the concrete barrier of the highway's median strip. The motorcycle came on fast, level with the driver.

Glovkonin granted him a second to believe he was in the clear, and then with a violent jerk of the wheel, he veered towards the median, intent on crushing the bike between the vehicle and the barrier. Sparks bloomed as metal kissed concrete and Dane skidded, braking hard – but not before slamming something on the flank of the limousine. The motorcycle fell away, vanishing again, but Glovkonin's attention was drawn to a line of flashing yellow lights warning of roadworks just ahead.

'Green for go!' Marc shouted, hoping that Kara would be able to hear him.

'*Fire in the hole,*' said the voice in his ear. '*Well, EMP, but you know what I mean.*'

A moment later, the silver saucer that had magnetised itself to the limo gave off a flash of actinic blue, like a jag of lightning from a distant storm. Instantly, the vehicle's crimson tail lights faded and it began to veer to the right, dragged by the damage to its steering. The electronic systems in the limousine failed at the same time, knocked out by a tiny version of the same device that the Combine had set off on Wall Street.

The limo crashed through safety barriers, one after another, bouncing over unfinished sections of roadbed as Marc kept up the chase. Up ahead, the highway ended, becoming a section of deep cutting into the earth where huge plastic water pipes waited to be buried.

The vehicle rode over a line of flashing warning lamps and fell off the edge of the road, flipping on to its side as it went down into the steep-sided ditch.

Marc applied the brakes too late and the scrambler skidded. He felt the bike folding away under him, then he hit the roadbed and tumbled away.

For a second or two, he wavered on the edge of dizziness, but the driving rain refused to let him lie there. Scowling at jolts of pain from his joints, Marc levered himself up off the ground and recovered the AK-12 from where it had fallen.

He risked a look down into the cutting, and saw the black shape of the limo. It was dark down there, and the deep shadows concealed any movement. Marc took a shaky breath and tasted the faint, acrid odour of stopped-up drains. The ditch had to lead into a watercourse or a sewer – and if Glovkonin was still alive, if he found his way to it, he could still get away.

'*Marc.*' Lucy's voice cut in over the radio network, fuzzy with static. '*Status check?*'

'Limo's out of action,' he reported, shifting his grip on the assault rifle. 'I'm going after him.'

'*Stay put, we'll be there soon!*'

'No time.'

Marc gathered up one of the flashing warning beacons and started the climb down into the cutting, using the pulses of yellow illumination to light his way.

The inside of the limousine was empty. He'd half-expected Glovkonin to come bursting out from the back seat, screaming like a horror movie slasher, but the interior of the vehicle was a mess of debris from the passenger compartment. Bottles of posh vodka and crystal glasses were scattered around, but no fugitive oligarch hid among them.

Marc adjusted the AK-12's strap to hang it at his hip, muzzle aimed forward, his finger on the trigger guard. He advanced past the beached limo and deeper into the earthworks, searching the shadows.

The regular half-second blinks of light from the beacon turned the scene into a strange, alien sight. Thick mud sucked at his shoes as he advanced, and the going underfoot was uneven. He panned the AK's barrel left and right, aiming into the gloom cast by sections of pipe and earth-moving equipment.

A voice carried out of the dark towards him.

'You are a persistent man, Mr Dane.' Glovkonin's words were dull and flattened by the rush of the rain, making it hard to pinpoint their source. 'That's a dangerous trait to possess.'

'It's been said,' admitted Marc. 'But here we are. Me coming after you, you running away into a sewer. Best place for you, I reckon.'

The Russian's harsh laughter echoed around him. 'This is not the worst I have ever known. I think we both know the cold, yes? We both come from humble roots—'

'Fuck off, mate,' Marc broke in. 'Don't give me that shit!'

'Quite.'

In the darkness between the flashes of light, a shadow detached itself and Marc heard the squelch of mud. Glovkonin dashed from his cover, brandishing the Udav, and opened fire.

Marc dropped the lamp and dodged towards a section of pipe as shots chewed lumps out of the plastic. He fired back, more to cover his move than to hit anything, squeezing off a burst in the Russian's direction.

He heard a metallic snap close by and recognised the sound. The Udav's slide had locked back and Glovkonin's gun was empty.

Marc veered back the way he had come, ready to bring his weapon to bear on the Russian – but Glovkonin was gone, and the light over the slick mud made it impossible to follow his footprints.

Marc hesitated a moment too long. The yellow light moved behind him, the shadow he cast turning of its own accord. He spun, firing another wild burst, but the warning beacon came up and around in Glovkonin's hand as the Russian flanked him. The lamp smashed across Marc's chin, the plastic casing splintering and cutting his cheek, the heavy battery pack inside acting like a cudgel.

He lost his footing and fell face-down into the mud, falling atop the AK. Marc rolled over, pulling the trigger, but the rifle refused to fire. He tried to work the slide clear of the sludge jamming the mechanism, but Glovkonin struck him again with the lamp and he fell back, losing his grip on the weapon.

Snarling like an animal, the Russian charged at him, raining down blows on Marc as he struggled to get his guard up. Glovkonin was spare and lean, but he had muscle hidden beneath his tailored shirt and expensive suit. Marc blocked a series of punches to his abdomen and head, finding the briefest of instants to hit back with a strike drilled into him a lifetime ago in a Krav Maga dojo.

Following the move, Marc swung an off-hand right and it failed to connect as Glovkonin recoiled, trying to get beyond his reach. The Russian didn't realise it was a feint until his opponent's left shot out and grabbed a handful of his grime-spattered silk tie.

Marc yanked back on the tie and pitched forward at the same moment, bringing his forehead down to crack Glovkonin's chiselled nose across its brow. Fire exploded behind his eyes, but the pain Marc felt wasn't half of the agony that coursed through the other man.

He fired two punches into the Russian's solar plexus, winding him. Marc fought the urge to keep it up, to carry on punching and punching until his hands were raw, but at the last second he shoved his wheezing opponent away.

Marching to where the mud-clogged AK-12 lay, Marc picked it up, methodically cleaning out the rifle's slide and mechanism. Carefully, he dislodged the spent cartridge that had caused the stoppage.

Glovkonin slumped down against a pile of earth, hugging himself. He had trouble catching his breath, but he could still speak.

'Enough,' he managed. 'What will you . . . achieve . . .?'

The AK's sickle magazine came away with a flick of the release, and Marc saw a single bullet remaining. He replaced it and worked the charging handle.

Even in the weak light of the broken beacon, the Russian could see the grim expression on Marc's face. He raised his hands.

'I surrender.'

Marc gave a slow shake of the head. 'We're not doing that.'

Glovkonin jerked back against the pile of muddy earth, but Marc had the rifle aimed at him before he could move.

'You fool!' The Russian snarled the words, fuelled by rage and rising panic. His eyes darted around as he searched for a way out and found nothing. 'Can't you see, Dane? What I have done? I destroyed the Combine!' His mask of stony poise fractured and disintegrated. 'I did what Ekko Solomon never could!'

'No,' said Marc. 'You took it for yourself.' A bleak understanding of the reality of his enemy settled on him. 'That's all you're capable of. All you know is one thing – how to fuck over everyone else to make yourself richer.' The words spilled out of him. 'And you don't feel it. The pain from the deaths you cause, the lives you ruin. It doesn't *matter* to you.'

His fingers tightened around the rifle's grip, whitening around the cold metal.

Glovkonin's hands dropped. 'What do you think happens if you kill me, Dane? Do you believe the Combine's network will instantly evaporate? Will the terror cells and criminals we armed give up their plans? We keep thousands of threats in line, under control! Without the Combine, without me, that is lost!'

'We'll deal with them like we dealt with you.'

Marc raised the rifle and aimed down the iron sights.

'Is this your code? Solomon crows about ethics and integrity, but now at the end, you show the truth . . . You are a common killer like him!'

'The only thing you know about my code is how to exploit it,' retorted Marc. 'You used it against us. You think it makes us weak. But what you don't understand is . . . it's flexible.'

He pulled the AK's trigger, and the last round in the rifle tore a bloody gouge through Glovkonin's thigh, shredding flesh and shattering bone.

The Russian screamed, long and low, the sound reverberating along the cutting. Glovkonin trembled as he ripped off his tie. Shuddering with aftershock, he desperately tried to fashion it into a tourniquet.

'That's for Assim Kader and Ari Silber,' said Marc, invoking the memory of his Rubicon colleagues murdered by Combine machinations. 'Gavin Rix. Rob Bell. Bill Marshall. Owen Davis. Leon Taub. Samantha Green!' He spat the last name with venom, ending the roll call of those lost from his MI6 team years earlier. 'Them, and every other soul on the butcher's bill.' He took a breath to steady himself, before tossing away the spent rifle. 'By the look of that hit, you've got no more than three minutes before you bleed out. I'd tell you to make peace with whatever you believe in . . . but I know the only thing you venerate is *this*.'

Marc dug a crumpled banknote from his pocket, and threw it into the blood-streaked mud at Glovkonin's feet.

Then he turned away and started back up the cutting.

'Dane!' The Russian bellowed his name, lurching forward. He collapsed in the muddy trench, inching forward as he tried to drag himself up. 'You can't leave me here! I have what you want . . . Help me! I can clear your names, you and Keyes!' He gasped as pain washed over him. 'The real video from Nicosia – I can give it to you!'

Marc halted, but he didn't look back. He had no doubt that the Russian would have kept the original recordings of the attack in Cyprus – the incident the Combine had used to frame the Rubicon team. Somewhere out there was the footage that would exonerate them. It was exactly the ploy he'd expected from this man. Glovkonin always had a way to turn his defeats into victories. He just needed Marc to be willing to pay the price.

'You can prove your innocence,' he shouted, 'if you help me!'

'We'll manage without it,' said Marc.

He walked on, into the rush of the rain, leaving the other man to die in the darkness and the freezing cold.

TWENTY-FOUR

An orange-red sun descended over the island of Draccios as Marc guided the speedboat towards the shore. He cut the power to the outboard and let inertia drift it up to the mooring pier.

On the wooden quay, Benjamin Harun waited for him, clad in cut-off jeans, flip-flops and a gaudy Aloha shirt. The man gave a stiff wave, the movement revealing the dressing wrapped around his chest. The shots that had hit him back in Russia hadn't penetrated his body armour, but the close-range impacts had been enough to fracture several ribs and he was still healing.

Benjamin tossed Marc a rope and they tied up the boat.

'You made it in time,' he told him. 'We're having a barbecue on the beach. You like fried fish?'

'If you're cooking, yeah.'

Marc tossed his bag on to the pier, then climbed out after it.

'You know, not all Frenchmen are expert chefs,' warned the other man. 'That's a stereotype.'

'I trust you,' said Marc, patting him on the shoulder.

He looked away and found another familiar figure waiting on the white sand. He smiled at the sight of Lucy Keyes, in a bright parrot-green shift dress. She had her hair down and she looked perfect.

'Hey,' he said, as he approached.

'Hey,' she replied, falling in step with him. 'Glad you made it. You want the ten-cent tour?'

'I do.'

They followed an overgrown path littered with palm leaves, winding through the trees into the island's interior, to emerge before the low shell of a derelict hotel complex. Marc saw a drained pool filled with dirt and a collapsed gazebo, but the building itself was in fairly good order. Inside, a generator chattered and he spotted recently installed solar cells and a high-spec satellite antenna on the roof.

'Needs some work,' he offered.

She laughed. 'This place was a big deal when they opened it, back in the Oughts. But it took a hit one hurricane season and never bounced back. The owners cut their losses and abandoned it, which is how Rubicon ended up acquiring the land.'

The rights to Draccios had fallen through the cracks, which explained how the island had been overlooked during the Combine's vicious asset-stripping of the Rubicon Group months before.

'As hideouts go, it could be worse,' added Lucy. 'White sands, clear water . . . almost a tropical paradise.'

Marc nodded. The main structure was sun-bleached and shabby, but it was definitely liveable – and, most importantly, the rest of the world didn't know about it. Some rooms had already been repurposed as a makeshift operations centre, with bubble-tents erected inside the hotel's halls, while others served as quarters, equipment stores or server space.

'C'mon, I wanna show you something.'

Lucy took his hand and led him into what had once been the main reception, a two-level atrium with a skeletal dome in the ceiling.

In the middle of the space stood a huge coco-de-mer tree, which had probably been a manicured feature when the resort was operating. Left to its own devices, it had escaped the planter it stood in to take over the reception. Small wooden panels were fixed to the trunk, and as Marc drew closer he saw they had names burned into them.

Ari.

Assim.

Sam.

'It's not exactly Arlington,' said Lucy, with a bittersweet smile. 'But it's something.'

'Yeah.'

Marc reached up with his free hand and ran a finger over the plaques.

Sleep sound, he thought. *Your bill's been paid.*

They looked at the memorial in silence, and after a while Lucy spoke up.

'You know, after Russia, when we went our separate ways . . . I thought it might be a while before we'd see you again.'

Marc gave her hand a squeeze. 'Why would you say that?'

Following the takedown of Glovkonin, the Rubicon team had split up to exfiltrate from the country, and it had taken days for them to regroup here on the island.

'You had a look about you,' she said, her brow creasing with concern. 'You were way distant. What you did back there, I know it doesn't come easy to you.'

'True,' he admitted, remembering the weight of the rifle in his hands. 'But that's not going to keep me away.' Marc lost himself in her dark eyes.

'Get a room, you two . . .' Wearing cargo shorts and a faded black T-shirt emblazoned with the letters *L33T*, Kara emerged from behind the tree, carrying a cooler box with her. 'Seriously, go for it. There's like a hundred suites in this place.'

Lucy pulled away, a little self-consciously, as the hacker paused next to them.

'Nice to see you, too, Kara,' said Marc, although he had to admit her timing was poor.

'Got something for you,' said the other woman, fishing in her pocket. She pulled out a glassy rectangle and tossed it to him.

Marc caught the device and his eyes widened.

'My spyPhone? You fixed it? I thought it was ruined.'

'Please,' said Kara, 'give me some credit. Also, not just fixed – improved. I packed more in. You can stream movies or crack military encryption – it's versatile.' She walked on. 'Coming to the beach? I have beer.'

Marc looked at Lucy, but the earlier moment had evaporated.

'I suppose we are.'

They followed Kara out, down another path towards the western edge of the island. A long, low shore spread down to a sea glowing pre-sunset gold, with a cluster of picnic tables set up around a crackling fire pit. Benjamin worked on the food, and the smell of frying red snapper made Marc's mouth water.

Delancort and Malte sat at one of the tables. Marc noted that the Finn had a brace on one leg, a reminder of the hit he had taken when Glovkonin had tried to run him down.

Malte took a Tiger Beer from Kara's cooler and uncapped it, saluting Marc with the bottle.

'Good job,' he said, which from the quiet ex-cop was the equivalent of effusive praise.

Marc took a beer of his own and passed out more to the rest of the group.

'Where's Solomon?'

'He is around,' said Delancort, accepting the drink. The man was out of place, dressed in a cotton shirt, slacks and deck shoes, resembling a resident of the derelict hotel back in its heyday. He noticed Marc's attention and straightened. 'We may be on a lost island, but that is no excuse to let standards slip.'

'Quite right,' agreed Marc, sitting on the edge of the table.

Delancort had a ruggedised laptop in front of him and he tapped the keyboard.

'I have received some new updates from our contacts. It appears the Combine's clandestine network is fracturing at an alarming rate. It will be quite a while before the dust clears.'

'We called in a few markers,' noted Lucy. 'Funny thing, a lot of people have a grudge against the Combine, and the moment they smelled blood in the water . . .'

Anonymous dumps of incriminating data culled from Combine servers had mysteriously appeared on the desks of certain people across the world – Simon Cahill at the CIA, agents Tom Rowan and Lee Gonzalez at the US Secret Service and the FBI, Nils Jakobs and Gesa Schrader at Interpol, the GRU's Rada Simonova, John Farrier at MI6 and others. The Rubicon team could rely on them to sweep up the remnants of the conspiracy Pytor Glovkonin had hoped to command.

'Is this what a win is like?' Kara offered the question to the air. 'I can't tell.'

'It's close enough,' said Marc, and took another swig of his beer.

Delancort reached into the bag beneath his laptop and produced a wad of passports from various nations and other identity paperwork.

'In the spirit of that, here are your new covers. We have your policeman friend Mr Pavic in Croatia to thank for his help in facilitating these.' He handed them out to everyone. 'You will notice that you are now employees of Rubicon Agile Solutions – a private security agency, incorporated in Panama earlier today.'

'Rubicon,' echoed Lucy. 'Didn't we kinda get that name a little dirty? Doesn't exactly have the best rep right now.'

'Exactly why we chose it,' Delancort explained. 'Hiding in plain sight, in a way.'

'Where did the money for this come from?'

Marc examined his new passport, frowning at the less than flattering picture in it.

Kara gave a cat-like stretch. 'Well, data wasn't all I took from the Combine's servers on the way out of Moscow. I figured it was fair to robin-hood a little.' She explained that while a chunk of digital currency had been diverted to the team's coffers, several needy organisations and charities around the planet had also received huge anonymous donations in the last few days, among them the people at Emigrant Aid. 'Rumiko Saito sent a message to say thank you. She seems to be settling in okay with her new life.'

'Her dad paid his dues,' Marc noted. 'Even if it took him a while to get there. His daughter deserves a shot at a decent future, out from under his shadow.'

'So, what's our deal from now on?' said Lucy, after a moment.

'The same as before.' Ekko Solomon walked out of the line of trees, and while he moved stiffly, Marc was pleased to see him managing without his walking stick. 'Our mission does not alter. Small changes in the world to effect greater ones. Defend the defenceless. Push back against injustice.' Then he smiled. 'But tomorrow. Today, we have earned our rest.' He beckoned to Marc. 'Walk with me?'

Marc nodded, leaving the beer behind, and followed Solomon to the water's edge. For a while, they stood in silence, watching the sun drop towards the horizon.

'I did not thank you, Marc,' Solomon said, at length. 'Months ago, when the world believed that I was dead, when my people had no one to guide them . . . you stepped into the breach. You kept them alive.'

'I only did what you would have. What had to be done.'

'Yes. You led them. I knew from the moment we first met that you were capable of great things. The challenges we have faced, they have tempered you.' Solomon put a hand on his shoulder. 'I am honoured to call you my friend.'

'Same to you, boss.'

Marc smiled, but inwardly he was conflicted. He was uncertain where the other man was leading him.

'The work never ceases,' said Solomon. 'We broke the Combine, and at such cost, but there will be other threats. Our names must still be cleared.' He paused. 'But I would understand if you . . . and others . . . would wish to seek another path. You have earned it.'

Marc's gaze ranged over the calm waters of the sea.

'I'm not ready to jack it in yet.' He turned and caught Lucy's eye. She picked up two beer bottles and started towards him. 'Could do with a bit of shore leave, though.'

'Then you are in the perfect place.'

Solomon patted him on the shoulder, and walked away.

Marc sat down on the pale sand and Lucy dropped into a settle next to him. She handed him a beer and they clinked the bottles together.

'Hey,' he said.

'Hey,' she replied.

The fading glow of the setting sun warmed them both, and she rested against him. Her skin felt cool on his, as if she had just come out of the water.

'It feel weird to you?' Lucy said quietly. 'For once, not having to worry about getting shot at?'

'It does, yeah,' admitted Marc. 'It's probably not going to last.'

She smiled, and he couldn't help but join her.

'Probably not.'

Marc leaned in, and in her kiss, he could taste the ocean.

Acknowledgements

These stories would not exist without the help and support of people like Robert Kirby, Kate Walsh, Zoe Ross, Jonathan Lyons, Ben Willis, Nick Stearn, Margaret Stead, Kate Parkin, Ellen Turner, Felice McKeown, Steve O'Gorman and all those at my agent and publishers.

My thanks must also go to Ben Aaronovitch, Peter J. Evans, David Mack and Kara Mack, Adam Hamdy and the Capital Crime team, Kimberly Howe and folks at Thrillerfest for their comradeship and insights; and to Brett Forrest, Yefim Gordon, 56 Tribeca, BSS Holland, Field of Vision, FLIR Systems, Knightscope, Prox-Dynamics and The Intercept for resources and research materials.

This novel was written during lockdown, and some billionaires may have been harmed during its production.

Hello!

I hope you enjoyed reading OUTLAW, the sixth novel in my Marc Dane action thriller series! This book brings together plotlines and story elements from across all five previous novels, and it's my intention that you have as much fun reading it as I did writing it!

I want to extend a special thank you to all my returning readers who continue to follow my writing – your support of this series has made it a success, and I greatly appreciate it! And if this has been your first exposure to Marc Dane, Lucy Keyes and the rest of the Rubicon team, welcome aboard, and please do check out the other books!

After the events of NOMAD, searching for vengeance and racing to stop a brutal terrorist, Marc finds himself in dire new circumstances for EXILE, chasing down a rogue nuclear device. In GHOST he faces a betrayal in his own team, while he fights to stop a bioweapon attack in the heart of Europe in SHADOW. In ROGUE, Marc and the Rubicon team finally come face to face with the forces that have been plotting their downfall, and as you've just read in OUTLAW, they risk everything on a high-stakes mission to bring down the ruthless power brokers known as the Combine, once and for all!

For me, writing these novels scratches the itch I have to write modern, tech-savvy action-adventure thrillers with the pace and detail of the high-octane fiction I loved from the 80s and 90s. Marc is my ideal everyman facing off against deadly threats, inverting that familiar trope of the "bloke in the van", always on the sidelines while others are in the thick of the action. What would happen if that guy was pulled kicking and screaming out of his comfort zone and into danger? I love the idea of a hero who *isn't* the toughest guy in the room, but instead has to rely on his wits and his resourcefulness – and over these novels, I've been able to explore that and send Marc on a journey from reluctant protagonist to determined hero.

If you would like to keep up to date about my books or find more information about all of my writing, check out my official website at *www.jswallow.com* – and while you're there, you can download a free copy of ROUGH AIR, an original Marc Dane novella. Elsewhere on the World Wide Web, you can chat to me on Twitter at *@jmswallow*.

You can also visit **bit.ly/JamesSwallow** where you can become part of the JAMES SWALLOW READERS' CLUB. It only takes a few moments to sign up, there's no catch and no cost. New members automatically receive an exclusive scene cut from the original draft of NOMAD – think of it as a novel version of a "DVD extra" with a bit of author's commentary! Bonnier Books keep your data confidential, and it will never be passed on to a third party. We won't spam you with loads of emails, just get in touch with occasional updates from me, and you're free to unsubscribe at any time.

If you would like to get involved in the larger conversation about my books, please do review OUTLAW on Amazon, GoodReads, or your favourite books website – or talk about it on your blog and social media accounts, with friends, family or reader groups! Sharing your thoughts helps other readers, and I always like hearing about what people enjoy about my writing!

Thanks again – and keep reading!

Marc Dane will return . . .

Best regards,

James